KEEPERS OF THE HIDDEN WAYS

Book Three
THE CRIMSON SKY

JOEL ROSENBERG

AVON · EOS

This is a work of fiction. Names, characters, places, and incidents either are the product of the author's imagination or are used fictitiously. Any resemblance to actual events, locales, organizations, or persons, living or dead, is entirely coincidental and beyond the intent of either the author or the publisher.

AVON BOOKS, INC.
1350 Avenue of the Americas
New York, New York 10019

Copyright © 1998 by Joel Rosenberg
Published by arrangement with the author
Library of Congress Catalog Card Number: 98-92635
ISBN: 0-380-78932-9
www.avonbooks.com/eos

First Avon Eos Printing: December 1998

AVON EOS TRADEMARK REG. U.S. PAT. OFF. AND IN OTHER COUNTRIES, MARCA REGISTRADA. HECHO EN U.S.A.

Printed in the U.S.A.

WCD 10 9 8 7 6 5 4 3

In memory of
Joshua Smotkin

Big Bang, Big Crunch, Big Headache?
by Elise Matthesen
Special to *The Gleaner*

09-MAR-98
HARDWOOD ND USA

The universe will end. Not soon—perhaps it will take another two hundred billion years or more—but the universe *will* end.

Recent findings from astronomers have left scientists with that uncomfortable conclusion. Five separate teams of scientists from Princeton, Yale, the Lawrence Berkeley National Laboratory, and Harvard have all recently announced studies that show that the universe, which began with the cosmic explosion called the "big bang" approximately fifteen billion years ago, will expand forever, until nothing remains throughout space but widely scattered hydrogen atoms and cold rocks.

Scientists investigating the possibility of a future "big crunch," where all the matter in the universe combines to form a single extremely dense package and then blasts outward in a rerun of the big bang, discovered that the universe contains only twenty percent of the mass needed. The universe is "open" and will not "close," they say.

The results of these years-long studies are provoking an uproar among those scientists wedded to the steady state hypothesis, the notion that the universe is "closed." The skull-splitting question: if the steady state hypothesis is true, at least eighty percent of the matter in the universe is undetected and undetectable. Where is, they ask, the missing eighty percent of the universe's mass necessary to bring on the next big crunch/big bang cycle?

Dr. Erwin Rice, director of the Astronomy Department at the University of North Dakota in Grand Forks, is unsurprised by the findings—or the furor. At a Macalester College debate in Minneapolis last week on the implications of the study, Rice said, "These steady staters believe in a universe that goes back and forth like a yo-yo. No grand design—it's a video game: push the big bang button and start over."

Rice calls the steady staters' theories "wishful thinking and sloppy science—like running another study if you don't like the results you got the first time." Rice says the five studies are "jointly and severally conclusive" and says, "It proves what we already know."

Assistant Professor Kim Coleman of the University of Minnesota's Astronomy Department, speaking at the same gathering, said the study doesn't answer as many questions as it raises. "Where did the matter go? Why can't our instruments detect it? If it's gone, when and how did it get converted to energy—and why haven't we picked up the traces of such a process? If the steady state theory is correct, how does the necessary mass reassemble itself?" asks Coleman. "If it isn't true, then what happened before the big bang?"

"That's a meaningless question, scientifically," Rice interjects. "But if the evidence states the big bang was a singular event that will not be repeated, how many alternative studies can we con the taxpayer into funding?"

Coleman admits that some of the hypotheses suggested to shore up the steady state model are "pretty far-out"—ranging from new types of interference that block the effects of gravity to pocket universes straight out of sci-fi novels.

"Or maybe the cat knocked it under the couch," jokes Rice. "We're talking enormous amounts of lost matter here—at least four times all the measurable matter in the universe!—not some little key chain doodad you can leave lying around someplace and forget!"

The Reverend Georges Friedmann, who holds a Ph.D. in Astronomy from Cal Tech, as well as a Master of Divinity from Pacific Lutheran Theological Seminary, and who teaches two classes in astronomy each semester at Macalester in addition to his duties as associate pastor at Christ Evangelical Lutheran Church in Minneapolis, finds the controversy both fascinating and amusing. "If the universe is open, and proceeds from a beginning, I think the religious implications are obvious," he says, smiling smugly. "If you find my smile smug, you have gotten my point."

"Well, maybe you should have your Jehovah check his pockets," answers Coleman. "The fact is, we won't know what happened to it until we look further. And, not having certain funding advantages—"

Debates may end in rancor, but the question remains: If the steady staters are right, and the universe is an uncreated, self-regulating series of big bangs and big crunches, then where's the missing mass?

Whoever borrowed that extra matter had better put it back, according to Rice, or the steady staters are going to be "very, very unhappy." Rice waggles an admonitory finger. "And very, very embarrassed, when study after study shows the same result: the universe is open."

Friedmann is more conciliatory. "It's long been a fundamental cornerstone of science that the existence of an extra-normal Creator is untestable, and as a scientist, I have to say that it still is. But as a man of God, I'm not entirely displeased that the cornerstone seems to be crumbling just a little."

Professor Coleman declined comment.

PROLOGUE

The Faerie Ring

Winter was coming.

She could smell the frost in the air, mingled with the tang of ozone. The cold, wet wind rattled the few remaining brown leaves that still clung in dead desperation to the branches of the old oak. The lightning flashed, and the thunder boomed not far away upwind, high on the eastern ridge where the road to the Dominions twisted like a silver thread through the gray and the green.

The cold didn't bother her, even though all she wore was a knee-length shift, belted tightly to accentuate her slim waist and the full breasts and hips that were only sometimes in style, but always popular with men down through the ages.

At this altitude, soon there would be snow, even this far south, but that wouldn't be more than a mild inconvenience—for her, at least—if she decided to make the climb to forage again.

Lighting flashed and thunder boomed, yet again.

The lightning and thunder didn't bother her, either; in fact, they amused her.

Boys will be boys, after all.

A human eye wouldn't have caught it, but the lightning didn't flow down from the dark clouds overhead; instead, it splattered outward and up from a single point of impact in the mountains, white-hot sparks fountaining up and out from a blacksmith's strike against his anvil.

The woman the locals called Frida the Ferryman's Wife grinned to herself as she stooped to part the soft moss at the base of the old oak tree, and reached her hand through the musty humus into the tight-packed, chalky soil, her fingers probing carefully, gently, tenderly. They emerged filthy, the dirt packed hard into the creases of her knuckles and even under her short nails, but cupping yet another truffle the size and shape of a baby's fist: brown like old wood, veined in black and white, covered in coarse polygonal warts, each with a tiny depression at its summit.

They were rarer here in the south, but they often had rings of brown mushrooms up in the Dominions. A drifting spore, too small for human eyes to see, would fall to the ground and find just the right combination of dank and dark to grow and send out shoots; and from those shoots would grow brown-capped mushrooms, in a ring perhaps two, three, four paces across.

Overnight, in a meadow, perhaps, or even on the green, green grasses of the Cities, a perfect circle of mushrooms would appear, as if by magic.

Fairy rings, the children called them, and they would shy away. There was something chilling in their sudden appearance, in their unnatural regularity.

Some fairy ring mushrooms were quite tasty; others, often similar in color and shape, were quite deadly. Perhaps an apothecary would be summoned to identify them as wholesome, taking a share as his pay and a bite as his proof. Or perhaps not.

But, as with all things, the center would die. Still, the shoots would live, each to send out its own shoots, to form rings of rings, and then rings of rings of rings until, finally, the circle was too large and subtle to be detected by ephemerals, who could no more detect the shape of an ancient fairy circle than they could watch a high, jagged mountain range slowly crumble, writhe, and wither into shrunken old age, like a snake with a broken back.

It was all a matter of perspective and patience. These were useful attributes even for an ephemeral, and it was difficult to get through even one's first few centuries without developing both.

She added the truffle to her basket and considered for a moment whether or not to follow the ring. The next truffle should be over . . . there.

Let it lie, she decided. If she sliced them paper thin, as she preferred, there were more than enough to line the skin of the goose that was, even now, hanging from the meat-hook in the cottage she shared with the Thunderer, and even a few to pop into the drip cup of fat, to sizzle and smoke for a few moments, before she would pop them in her mouth.

Again, thunder rang out. Arnie's explanation was that he had seen three Vandestish patrols out this way in recent weeks—and, quite certainly, he had: her sharper eyes had spotted seven—and that it was only reasonable to show a little force, to make the sky rumble a trifle and the land shake ever so slightly, if only to remind them who was who, and what was what.

That was the truth, and nothing but the truth, but it was not the whole truth.

She grinned.

It was the way of women in general and a fertility goddess in particular to understand that men, be they ephemerals or gods, really never stopped being boys. She had seen this sort of thing for the first time when the world was young, and more times than she cared to count since, but it still amused her.

A boy with a new toy was always the same, whether it was a toddler with a pair of round stones that he had just discovered made a delightful crack! when slammed together, or a pubescent young boy with his first real orgasm, or a man in his sixties who found that he was one who could wield Mjolnir, Murderer of Miscreants.

Boys: they had to play with their toys.

The wind picked up. Winter was coming.

She picked up her basket and hurried up the road to the cottage.

Winter was coming.

Perhaps even the Fimbulwinter?

Not yet, she thought. Not yet.

Freya shivered, but not from the cold.

Please. Not yet.

PART ONE

HARDWOOD, NORTH DAKOTA AND MINNEAPOLIS, MINNESOTA

CHAPTER ONE

~✦~

Something in the Air

Torrie Thorsen first picked up the scent just east of Lyndale, on Lake Street.

He had gotten off the Number Four bus—his car was buried in S-Lot under a bank of snow from the snowfall of two nights before, and he hadn't had the time to dig it out, not yet—at Lake and Lyn, and thrown his book bag over one shoulder, and his gear bag over the other.

He considered stopping for some takeout at the Greek place at the corner—Maggie liked their gyros, and Torrie liked the taste, if not the name, of their "Cheeseburgeropoulis"—but it was kind of cold out, and he was dressed for the city, not for the country, and Maggie and her roommate kept their apartment warm, and since she was expecting him there would be a fresh pot of coffee on, and—to be honest, and Torrie Thorsen made it a policy to at least always try to be honest with himself—the sooner he got into her apartment and out of his coat, the sooner he could get Maggie out of her clothes and into her bed and get himself into Maggie, and if that sounded awkward and crude even within the privacy of his own mind—and it did—he wasn't going to say it that way out loud.

11

Even if it was true.

Food could wait.

Dirty snow stood piled high, covering the curb, the little red flag on the fire hydrant peeking out. In the summer, it looked like an antenna, as though city fire hydrants were really radios in bad disguise, maybe planted by Boris and Natasha, broadcasting hidden messages to the Pottsylvanians.

But in the winter, it was just a piece of red plastic.

The smell of winter was in the air: diesel fumes from the buses mixed with the scent of cold, and with the mouth-watering smell of sizzling gyrobeast on the rotisserie at the Greek place that just had to be deliberately pumped out at street level . . .

. . . and with a distant foul smell that was vaguely familiar, although he couldn't place it.

He shook his head and sniffed again.

It was gone, replaced with the rich meaty scent of roasting peppers and maybe some lemongrass.

You got a good mix of tantalizing scents in the air in this neighborhood, what with a half dozen cheap little restaurants—most of them quite good—vying in different ethnic dialects for the local palate and wallet.

There was a Vietnamese place down half a block that had a remarkable way with those crisp egg rolls filled with cellophane noodles, crunchy cabbage, and spiced shrimp; a hole-in-the-wall Ethiopian restaurant that served horrid-looking but wonderfully spicy glops of indeterminate mush that you swept up with pieces of warm flatbread; and the fryolators at that Arabic café always had something tasty going.

Maybe it was just a bad day for the shashlik.

He sniffed the air again, and picked up his pace. Nothing this time.

He shrugged. Probably nothing at all.

He frowned to himself. *I'm just being silly.* It was probably just that he didn't like having to make this trip. Maggie had moved off campus and to an apartment on Bryant, just off Lake. Torrie didn't quite understand it, but he was more than sure he didn't like the way it cut into her time.

The amount of time you had to spend to keep an apartment clean, to go shopping for groceries, and to do all the other stuff that went with off-campus life, well, that time came out of your schoolwork time budget, your social life, or your time in the gym, and neither he nor Maggie was willing to cut down on their practice time, and she wasn't willing to slack off on any of her courses.

And then there were her evenings on the phone at the Rape Hotline, and her shopping expeditions with that roommate of hers and *her* circle of friends—

—all of which meant Torrie was seeing even less of Maggie than he had since well before they had taken time off from school—not to mention the months they'd spent traveling together—and he really didn't like that.

Not that what he liked necessarily made a difference, but he had sort of assumed that after spending time bouncing around Europe—and Tir Na Nog—together, the two of them would move in together after school was finished, and work out something even less formal in the interim.

And then she had taken an apartment, complete with roommate, without so much as hinting that that was what she had planned. The first inkling he had had about it was when he had checked in at her former dorm and was given her forwarding address.

Some hint.

Not so much as a word in advance—that was very, very Maggie.

He was more disappointed than angry. This was Torrie's senior year, after all, and he finally had a single room—not that Ian had ever had a problem sleeping on the couch in the dorm living room—and while she grudgingly kept a couple of changes of clothes in his bottom drawer for those rare occasions when she stayed all night, that was about the limit to which she was willing to move in.

Women, he thought. *Can't live with them—not when they won't let you.*

Fact is, he liked just being around Maggie, and with Ian on a leave of absence from school that was probably going to be permanent, she was the only person in town that he could really talk to without watching himself.

And there was more to it.

They'd been through some things together, her and Ian and him—and Mom and Dad and Uncle Hosea, for that matter. You sweat and bleed and shiver in fear enough with somebody, and they're part of you, and you're part of them, in a way that transcends any ordinary understanding.

Call it magic; Torrie Thorsen had no objection to magic.

He grinned. And that felt kind of nice, even if he had to share that special closeness with Maggie, with Ian, and his family. At least, he didn't have to share every—

There was that smell again. Bitter and acrid, but distant. Like . . .

. . . like he couldn't remember what.

You learn a lot of things on a fencing strip, and one of the first you learn is balance, although Torrie had learned that from his father a long time before he had ever set foot on a fencing strip. The three pillars of fencing were balance, timing, and space, and if you didn't have all of those down solid, there was no point in even thinking about strategy, because somebody with whatever attribute you were missing could score on you just about nine times out of nine.

He spun around, quickly, his weight on the balls of his feet, not sliding at all, despite the slipperiness of the sidewalk.

The middle-aged woman in the heavy coat, weighed down with the canvas Byerly's bags, let out a gasp, her eyes wide, and dropped one of the bags.

Paper-wrapped packages of meat fell to the sidewalk, cans rolled into the snow, and the small glass bottle of Crystal hot sauce bounced once, twice, three times on the ice before deciding not to break after all. Which was just as well. Torrie would have had to offer to pay for it, and this being the city, that would have been awkward.

"I'm sorry," he said, bending over to help her put the groceries back. "I thought I heard something, and I kind of, I don't know, I kind of twitched."

"That was different," she said, her mouth twisting into a smile.

He brushed snow and grit off the bottle of Crystal sauce and put it back in her bag.

"Can I carry one of these for you?" he asked, reflexively, then flinched. You just didn't do that in the city.

But surprisingly, she nodded. "Sure—you bet." She smiled knowingly as she handed him one of the gray canvas bags. "You can take the boy out of the country, but not the country out of the boy, eh?"

"It shows, does it?" He slung both of his bags over his left shoulder and kept step with her.

"Well, yes, it does." She smiled again. "But it's very sweet." She took the small, sort of mincing steps that old people did when they walked on a slippery surface, but at least she took them quickly enough that he didn't have to slow down too much. "Whereabouts are you from?"

"Hardwood, North Dakota."

She frowned, as though she had expected the name to be familiar.

Lady, it could have been famous, but we like things the way they are, thank you very much.

Hell, even Hatton, with half the population, had its famous native son in Carl Ben Eilsen, an early barnstormer, but nobody famous had ever come from Hardwood. Which was fine, really, and the way it should be, although there were times and ways in which that grated on Torrie's nerves.

"Hmmm . . . no, I guess I never heard of it," she said. "I've got an uncle who lives in Bismarck—is it anywhere near there?"

He shook his head. "No. Other side of the state, about forty miles out of Grand Forks."

"Ah: East Dakota." She nodded. "That's what my uncle Ralph always used to say, that the Dakotas were divided the wrong way. That they should have been East and West instead of North and South."

Torrie had never thought of that before, but it did make sense, sure—the west was badlands and mountains, the east was flat farmland. "There'd be some sense to that."

"Yup. So, do you like the city?"

"Well, it has its points."

"But you miss Hardfield."

"Hardwood. And, yes, actually I do." Minneapolis was

a nice enough city, as cities went. But it was a city—it was filled to overflowing with strangers.

"I see." She gave him a grin that told him she thought she knew what he was thinking, and she probably did. "Didn't anyone ever tell you that you can't ever go home again?"

"Well, yes, I have heard that, actually." But you didn't need to believe everything you heard, after all. Torrie would have shrugged, but that would have made his gear bag slide off his shoulder, and he didn't want that.

What he did want to do was to ask how much further she was going, and that was awkward.

Not that he wouldn't carry the bag wherever it was (and it couldn't be far enough for it to be a problem for him, or she wouldn't be carrying so much—it wasn't like she was a young woman—she was at least forty, forty-five); he just wanted to know.

But this was the city, and you didn't ask a woman where she lived, for fear she'd think you'd be lurking outside around her house all night, baying at the moon or something.

He was thinking about the right way to ask how far away her place was without asking where it was when she turned left at the camera store onto Bryant Avenue.

He wouldn't have been very surprised if she had climbed up the steps to the fourplex where Maggie lived—he didn't really know any of Maggie's neighbors; this was the city, after all—but she gestured at the next building down, and reached out her hand for the bag.

"Thank you for your help, but I think I can take it from here," she said.

He had lived in the city long enough to know that she meant *I'd rather you not walk up to my door,* and that that wasn't just a figure of speech meaning *Can you carry the bag all the way into the house?* as it would have been at home, and he was only very slightly surprised when he noticed that she had a little blue pepper-spray canister on her keyring, which was already in her hand, and probably had been in her hand all the while they were walking and talking together.

Well, good for her, he thought, as she walked up the stairs, glancing once over her shoulder to make sure he was moving away.

Which he was.

It made him feel funny. No, not funny: bad. Shit, a woman didn't need pepper spray—or a knife or a gun or a squad of cops, for that matter—to prevent Torrie Thorsen from committing robbery or God-knows-what, and it hurt to think that that didn't show on his face.

No. That wasn't fair, and Torrie tried to be fair, even in the privacy of his own mind.

Ted Bundy had looked like the clean, all-American boy, too. And the city wasn't the country. You could pretend it was, if you were foolish enough. You could leave your car or your room unlocked, or not worry about what time of night it was when you went out, or assume that any footsteps behind you were somebody you knew, and you—

And you would be burglarized, mugged, robbed, and murdered, more than likely more than once.

He grinned.

Except for the murdered part, of course.

He had keys both to the outside door and to Maggie's front door, but he rang the bell instead. Her roommate had a habit of walking around with what Torrie thought of as insufficient clothes, and that embarrassed him when he came upon it suddenly.

It wasn't like she looked all that good in just panties and bra, either.

The wind picked up, driving the cold into him, as he waited, reconsidering digging into his pockets for the keys. A quick beep could have meant *Throw on some clothes, I'm on my way up, after all.*

And then there was that smell again. Still distant, but bitter and acrid and harsh, and . . . what was it? It was familiar, and it almost had the hairs on the back of his neck sticking up, but—

He just couldn't place it. Damn.

He was still considering when he heard her feet thumping on the stairs.

Maryanne Christensen opened the inner door as he opened the outer one. Her hair was up in some sort of complicated ponytail type thing that left the back of her slim neck bare, and her face was slightly flushed at the cheekbones.

"Come in, come in," Maggie said, then turned and headed back up the stairs. He didn't blame her for hurrying. The hallway was unheated—the landlord never turned on the hall radiators, apparently—and she was dressed only in black leggings and a long, loose red silk shirt they had picked up off the Bois de Bologne.

He enjoyed the view as she moved quickly back up the stairs, taking each step with a bounce. Some would have thought her too skinny, but she was built along what his mother would have called greyhound lines, and while her muscles didn't bulge, a pleasant combination of heredity and exercise had given them a tone that made her worth watching from just about any angle.

Certainly including from behind.

If she'd caught him staring, she would have glared, the way she had at Ian that one time. Ian had just smiled and said, "Hey, I like girls. Sue me." And Maggie had decided to take that with a smile.

Hey, if she didn't want to be looked at, she could dress ugly.

"I was starting to worry," she said. "I thought you said you'd be here around one."

"Well, I did say 'around' " He glanced at his watch—2:17, it said; he was later than he'd thought—as he followed her down the open hallway to her open door. Maybe he should have some words with her about answering the door with pepper spray in hand. It was the city, after all.

"I took a little longer at the library than I thought I would," and never mind that part of the time was spent chatting with the new assistant in the reference department, who wanted to know what the fencing gear case was about, and who, underneath a remarkably long set of lashes, had a pair of very large and very brown eyes that a guy could enjoy spending a few minutes looking into, "and then I decided to take the bus instead of digging my car out."

"Well, good," she said, taking his bags and coat, then unceremoniously tossing them onto the couch in front of the spool table. "Long as you're here, you can give me a hand with this for a few minutes. It's not a rush, but I need to have it taken apart in two weeks."

The apartment was built along standard South Minneapolis railroad-car lines: one long room, cut in half by a craftsman-style built-in mirrored buffet that Torrie had identified as Stickley, the kitchen built into the hall that opened on the bedrooms, beyond where the buffet stood as the outer wall to Maggie's room.

The buffet, though, was partly disassembled, the drawers stacked to one side, its joints and innards lying exposed, as though it were some wooden creature, disembowled by somebody in a rush.

"That's new," he said.

She nodded. "My landlord offered me a break on the rent if I refinish the built-in."

Torrie raised an eyebrow.

She smiled. "And your uncle Hosea offered to come down for a week and do the stripping and refinishing and rebuilding for me, when I called him to ask for some advice, and maybe some help."

Torrie smiled. "Just don't let him go wild with abditories."

"Eh?"

"Nothing. Never mind."

It was the sort of piece Uncle Hosea would love to put hidden hiding places in. This buffet was similar enough to the one in the Guest Room at home to receive the same treatment: a silent little pressure lock hidden beneath each of the door hinges, holding a drop-down compartment in place. Put a piece of paper inside each of the hinges, press the two glass-paneled doors shut hard enough to make the hinge-plates flex just enough to set the pins correctly in the keyway, then slide open the top drawer—just soooo far, and no farther—before a quick thump on the top of the buffet, and a two-inch-thick inner drawer would drop down.

That abditory, the one in the buffet at home, contained a set of spare passports and other papers that might be useful under extraordinary circumstances. Other abditories, like the compartment under the front hall stairway, contained survival kits, or weapons, or money, or things as prosaic as the emergency roll of toilet paper.

But Uncle Hosea often built such things just as an art form, like the tiny one in Mom's bathroom for her tampons, which Torrie had only found accidentally, while clearing hair out of the sink's trap. And back when Torrie was a kid, Uncle Hosea had built him a secret compartment in the side of his closet that was just the perfect size for a stack of *Playboys*.

Giving Uncle Hosea a week to put this buffet back together was like locking a kid up in Toys "Я" Us for a night.

Well, let him have his fun.

She gestured at the tools spread out on the canvas drop cloth covering the floor. "All I have to do is take it apart without doing much damage, and I can do that."

"I did have other ideas as to how to spend the afternoon," he said, reaching for her.

"You did, did you?" She grinned as she wrapped her arms around his waist. "Hmm . . . well, it appears you did. I think we ought to do work, food, and some studying first. We've got the place to ourselves—Deb's spending the next couple of nights over at Brian's, and I'd be surprised if she even stops by to pick up her mail. So, what would you think about us doing some grunt work, then some studying, then grabbing a quick supper and see what happens after that?"

"Is that one of them there rhetorical questions?"

"Yup."

"I never liked rhetorical questions."

"Work first; then food. And then, well, maybe we'll see. You work better when you're horny." Her smile turned her maybe into a promise, and a quick kiss sealed it.

"I think my good nature is being taken advantage of," he said as she stepped back. He dropped his jacket and then opened up the toolbox, giving in with as much grace as he could muster, which wasn't much.

"Work."

He made a low rumble in his throat.

"Don't growl."

"Sorry."

He didn't like it, but he didn't have to. But still, shit, Maggie didn't need to get a break in the rent. She didn't need to have a roommate. She could have afforded the apartment all by herself. And even if she couldn't, she did have a boyfriend who could have and would have picked up the rent without worrying about it.

Torrie sighed. He'd just as soon pay the rent—no, he'd rather have paid the rent on a place closer to campus, for the two of them.

But no. No, it wasn't about money. Maggie's parents were taking care of her rent and tuition, and Torrie's mom had invested Maggie's share of their Dominion gold for her. It wouldn't make her rich, but it would take care of rent and food and such indefinitely, if needed.

It wasn't about money. Most things about money weren't really about money—Torrie had learned that from Ian Silverstein.

For Maggie, this was about doing things the right way, and it was important to her to do things the right way. Apartments near the U were undersized, and the ones that had any character at all were hideously overpriced. So she had arranged her class schedule to pack her classes close together, and had looked over in South Minneapolis, near the bus line.

Two-bedroom apartments tended to have decent-sized kitchens and living rooms, and rented for significantly less than twice as much as one-bedroom ones.

And if you had a two-bedroom apartment, not renting out the second bedroom would simply be wasteful, and renting it to your boyfriend—who could afford it even more easily than you could—would smack of him picking up your rent, and that was where this whole thought started, with Maggie not being willing to let him do that, because it wasn't about money.

Damn.

The nice thing about money was that that MacKay guy—Harry? Ralph? The guy who owned that envelope company and gave all those speeches—was right about it. If you had a problem that you could solve—not put off, but solve—by writing a check, you didn't have a problem.

All you had was an expense.

"Don't pout," she said. "You look about ten years old when you pout." She came into his arms for a quick kiss, hesitating for a moment before her lips parted and her tongue was warm in his mouth. His left hand cupped her bottom, pulling her toward him, while his right sought her breast.

But she pushed him away.

"Later," she said. "Maybe." She smiled as she stroked a finger down the front of his zipper. "Delayed gratification is the best kind."

Well, there were times when no didn't mean no, but this wasn't one of them.

Damn. *I should have stopped at the Greek place.* A Cheeseburgeropoulis would go down well, right about now. And it was looking like food would be about the only goddamn thing that would be going down in the near future.

"Coffee?" she asked.

"Fresh pot." He sniffed. Yes, that was good, rich, dark-roasted coffee, and it wiped out any trace of that strange scent in the air.

What had that been? It was familiar, and disquieting, but he couldn't place it.

He sighed, and reached for a chisel.

CHAPTER TWO

~~

The Hidden Way

Ian Silverstein shrugged into his parka and stepped into his boots, then bent to lace them up the front.

He was still enough of the city kid that it felt strange to be wearing boots that you wore instead of, rather than over, your shoes, but going around in your stocking feet wasn't an embarrassment in Hardwood anywhere that was too nice to wear snowy boots.

Hell, he had a cheap pair of Chinese slippers in one of the pockets of his parka, but he'd never found the occasion to use them, and he was thinking about taking them out and putting them in permanent storage in the closet. He couldn't wear them around the house, after all, not if anybody came over—it would make it look as though he expected everybody else to do the same.

Boots laced, he opened both the heavy wooden front door and the storm door to take a quick sniff of the frosty air, shivering at the almost arctic blast that answered him.

Hmm . . . maybe he should put up one of those outside thermometers.

But sniffing the air was the way that everybody in Hardwood seemed to decide how many layers to put on, and that was the way Arnie Selmo had always done it, and that was the way Ian would do it, too.

It was probably silly, but it was part of feeling like he belonged here.

He looked around the room to make sure he had shut off the lights. That was another small-town thing he was getting used to: you shut off the inside lights when you went out, perhaps leaving the porch light on to light your way back in, but not leaving on lights and a TV or a radio to dissuade burglars. That was wasteful.

He had made changes around the house, as a friend had suggested and as Arnie had given permission, but each change, no matter how minor, had been deliberate and calculated, something he could justify to Arnie, and something that, through some strange coincidence, just happened to remove yet another reminder of Ephie Selmo.

The wall between the kitchen and the living room had held Ephie's knickknack shelves, so he and Thorian Thorsen had knocked down the wall when they redid the kitchen, dining room, and living room all into one very homey sort of room, half carpeted, half tiled, the two sections separated by a counter that stood where the wall had been. You could cook dinner and chat at the same time, or stretch out on the battered old couch with a newspaper and a cup of coffee while keeping an eye on a simmering pot of soup.

And if doing that made this look less like Ephie's house, well, there was no harm in that, as long as he had another explanation.

In doing all the construction, he had learned more about working with joists and microlams and Sheetrock and electrical cabling and phone wires than he had ever expected to, but Hosea was always available to help out, and Thorian Thorsen was usually available to help out, and when one of them didn't know how to do something, or when there were four or more pairs of hands needed instead of two, there was always somebody available, if you had the time to wait.

Ian had time.

Besides, usually there were other neighbors to help out—

he didn't have to do a lot of waiting. If you worried more about making yourself useful and less about whether or not you were getting the better of the deal, it worked out okay, most of the time.

Ian Silverstein, he thought to himself, *you're developing patience.*

You had to, to live in Hardwood. Probably true in any small town.

And now, a counter stood where the wall that had held the shelves where Ephie Selmo's collection of little metal bells, small glass sculptures, and other knickknacks had stood for something like half a century.

Each item had been carefully cleaned, then wrapped in newspaper and put away, the boxes properly labeled and stashed in the attic. Ian wasn't sure what Arnie needed, but whatever it was, he didn't need constant reminders of his late wife. He carried enough of those inside him.

Ian yawned. It was still too damn early. Another cup of coffee was not a good idea—he'd be drinking coffee all morning.

And, besides, there was another way. Maybe. At least . . . there *should* be another way.

No harm in giving it another try.

He lifted the hem of his parka to get at his right-hand pocket, and he came out with a plain gold ring, too thick to be a wedding band but heavier than it looked.

He slipped it first over his thumb, and then his ring finger; it fit both perfectly, although his thumb was visibly thicker. It didn't seem to change size—at least he couldn't see it do that. He should be used to that now, but maybe there were some other things that he should be used to, as well.

He thought, *I am awake.* Which was true, although he was still sleepy. But the idea was not to be just awake, but wakeful, and he hadn't slept well last night, and it was too damn early in the morning . . .

No. Thinking that way wouldn't solve anything.

He yawned. "I am awake," he said. "I am awake, and alert, fresh for the morning, all traces of sleepiness banished from my mind and body."

He willed it to be so . . .

And yawned again.

He grunted. It wasn't working. But it was important that he be alert, and he would be. He leaned back against the doorpost as he closed his eyes painfully tight, until bright spots danced in the inner darkness.

Ian took a deep breath, and let half of it out. He was awake, and he was alert, and he was fresh and ready for the morning, all sleep banished . . .

. . . and the ring pulsed against his finger, painfully hard, like a boa constrictor's embrace: once, twice, three times before it stopped.

It felt warm. And he felt kind of silly. Why had he bothered to use the ring again? It wasn't like he was sleepy or anything. It would have been wasteful if the ring's virtue could be exhausted.

And if my grandfather had had tits, the old Jewish saying went, he would have been my grandmother.

"And that would have made my grandmother a lesbian."

That was Ian's own addition.

Ian slung his rucksack over one shoulder, and the over-sized pool cue bag containing Giantkiller over the other, and he stepped outside, closing the door behind him, still enough of a city boy that he had to remind himself not only not to try to lock it but also that he couldn't—in Hardwood, probably nobody knew where the key to their front door was.

Across the street, there was a light on in Ingrid Orjasae-ter's living room, and the movement of a shadow against the drapes said that she was up and around. Which was good. Old Ingrid was a notoriously early riser, and Ian would have worried if he hadn't seen any signs of life in her house. Not that it would be a problem to stick his head in the door and call out to her—it wasn't like it would be locked or something.

Lock your front door?

Why would you do that?

What would happen when a neighbor needed to get in? Your neighbors never needed to get in? What kind of person are you, a city type?

The west wind picked up, driving a fine mist of hard snow up and into the air and his face.

He shivered and then set out down the road. The snow squealed beneath his boots as he walked, and he gradually picked up his pace so that the high-pitched sounds kept pace with the dull thud of his heartbeat. Movement could keep you warm, or at least less cold, although too much movement could start you sweating, which could freeze you to the bone in a matter of minutes. The trick, which had taken him quite a while to learn, was to ratchet up your level of effort slowly and carefully. It was just like the gym; you didn't go into a full workout without a good, solid warm-up before.

Although here and now the punishment for overdoing it wasn't so drastic. You could pull a muscle or hurt a tendon in the gym, and for Ian that would have meant going without tutoring fees for several hungry weeks; here, all that would happen in town at least was that you'd get painfully cold.

It was bitter out, and it wasn't going to get any warmer, not for several hours. What was that bit from that old Crosby, Stills, and Nash song? Something about it being the darkest time just before the dawn? Well, that wasn't true, except maybe metaphorically—and the coldest time of day was usually just after dawn, during that hour or so before the air and ground had a chance to build up and hold whatever heat from the sun it could.

And anybody who didn't think there was a difference between five below, fifteen below, and thirty below probably had never set foot on squealing snow in all his life.

He pulled back his sleeve, the cold air painful against his wrist, and glanced at his watch. It was 7:33, and shit, and he wasn't even where the street ended in a T and the shortcut path through the woods to the Thorsen house began.

He picked up the pace.

Thorian Thorsen's big blue Bronco was sitting in the Thorsen driveway, the engine running at idle, sending up billows of smoke and clouds into the air. A long orange extension cord led from the grill into an outlet on the side of the house; a long thin rope just a few feet shorter than the cord was tied to both the car-side plug and a thick stainless steel O-ring bolted to the house.

Running the car was profligate, by local standards. Of course, by local standards, when you accidentally cut your arm off with a piece of farm machinery you waited in the bathtub after calling 911, so that your blood wouldn't unnecessarily stain the carpet.

Still, the engine block heater alone would have let the car warm up quickly, once started, although the main purpose of it was to make sure the damn thing would start in the cold—it was for necessity, not comfort. But that was Thorsen's way: go for the luxury of a heated car, and damn the expense.

Torrie's dad was certainly willing to suffer discomfort—Ian had been around for some of that, and knew about some more—but only if there was some real benefit to be gained from doing so. The notion of deliberately suffering to build character was foreign to him.

Ian had no argument with that philosophy. Life was full enough of pain and heartache and just plain ordinary discomfort to build more than enough character; there was no reason to go looking for it. Hell, if the only pain Ian ever again had to suffer was from doing his stretches before he worked out, that would be fine with him.

He chuckled. And this from somebody whose itchy feet were going to be taking him back through the Hidden Ways to Tir Na Nog sooner than later.

Do as I say, people, not as I do, he thought, and laughed at himself. It wasn't just that he wanted to see Marta again—although he certainly did—or Bóinn, or even *her,* although that was true, as well. And he wanted to see Arnie Selmo, for that matter. It would be good to look into Arnie's lined face again, and see if Freya's influence had lightened the dark cloud that seemed to have taken up permanent residence behind his tired eyes.

But it wasn't just the destination. It was, as Freya had suggested to him, the going.

Home wasn't just a place that you came back to; home

was a place you had to leave every now and then, if only for the coming back.

But when?

There was no rush, and the fact that there was no rush warmed him in a way that the cold couldn't even begin to touch.

After all, he was home.

Ian stashed his bag in the back of the Bronco—it was unlocked, of course; who would steal your car?—then walked up the path from the driveway (which was as free of snow as though it had been blasted with fire) and clumped up the wooden stairs to the porch, opening the storm door so that he could get at the heavy oak door.

He knocked at the door, tentatively, with his gloved hands, to no response, then shrugged and pounded once on the oblong brass knocking plate in the doorpost.

Thrummmmm.

The whole house vibrated with the deep bass note.

Ian didn't wait for an answer; he turned the knob and pushed the door open six inches or so.

"Hello the house," he said, his voice just above a low whisper.

The knob slipped from his gloves as the door opened the rest of the way to reveal Doc Sherve, dressed in a plaid shirt and jeans that, together with his beard and the small knit cap covering the top of his head in a way that reminded Ian more of a yarmulke than anything else, somehow made him look more like an ancient lumberjack than a physician.

A steaming mug of coffee was in his right hand, and he grinned as he beckoned Ian inside. "Don't just stand there. It's cold out, in case you haven't noticed. Come on in and get warm."

This didn't make much sense. Where was Doc's car?

Sherve brought the mug up toward his mouth, then his face wrinkled up and he shook his head and held the mug out to Ian, just as Ian finished stripping off his gloves and dropping them on the air vent next to the door.

Hmmm . . . the ring was still on his finger; he slipped it off and put it back in his pocket. He could feel the warmth of it even through his thermals.

Ian stomped his feet a couple of times to clear his boots of snow, then wiped them carefully on the snow runner as he followed Doc toward the kitchen, sipping at the coffee as he did. It tasted better than coffee usually did in Hardwood: it was weak but hot, and at this time of year hot was far more important than strong.

Sit around outside on a cold day drinking strong coffee whenever you needed to warm up, and you would piss brown for the rest of the day and climb the walls with your fingernails all night.

Thorian Thorsen and his wife, Karin, were sitting at the breakfast table, drinking coffee. From the remnants of egg and scraps of bacon and pancakes on his plate, it was obvious that Thorsen had just finished polishing off his usual huge breakfast, while Karin toyed with a piece of coffee cake.

Thorsen was half-dressed for the cold, the ropy muscles of his chest bulging against the smooth tightness of his satin polypropylene undershirt. His light brown, almost blond, hair was damp and combed back against his head, and despite his genuine smile his expression looked vaguely threatening, and made Ian want to avoid looking at his wife.

Ian was probably just projecting. It was probably the squareness of Thorsen's jaw, combined with the bend in a nose that should have been straight, and it was certainly in part the long white scar that ran down the right side of his face, white stitchmarks like legs on a centipede announcing that the wound had been sewn together by somebody a lot less dexterous than Doc Sherve.

"Good morning, Ian Silver Stone," Thorsen said.

"Morning, Thorian." Ian didn't correct him. He'd gotten used to it, in Tir Na Nog, and, what the fuck, eh? That's what Silverstein meant, after all.

Doc chuckled, as he always did. "That's Ian. The nonstick surface." That hadn't been funny the first time, or the fifty-first.

It still wasn't. At this point, it was about as funny as Arnie's joke about the pope and his chauffeur, which everybody in town seemed to have to tell him at least once, and which he had to smile through as though he had never heard it before.

For this, at least, he didn't have to smile. But if glares could raise boils, Doc's face would have exploded with pus some decades before.

"Good morning, Ian," Karin said, looking up, but not quite meeting his eyes.

He had avoided looking at her, afraid, as always, that he would gawk. She was quite literally old enough to be his mother, but Ian found nothing matronly about her. She smelled of some vaguely lemony perfume that should have been too young for her but wasn't. God, she was lovely, even at this hour of the morning, dressed in a thick red terry cloth robe that set off the hint of black lace where it opened at the swell of her breasts.

Her blond, almost golden, hair was tied back in a high ponytail that left the back of her neck bare and made his fingers itch.

Not that he would ever try to scratch that itch. There probably were a few better ways to screw up his life in Hardwood than making a pass at Torrie's mom, but he couldn't think of any, not offhand, unless it was, say, pissing on the Sunday smorgasbord at the Dine-a-mite.

She still had trouble meeting his eyes. "Can I get you some breakfast?" she asked, as she always did.

Ian shook his head. "No, thanks," he answered, as he always did. Breakfast might well be the most important meal of the day, but Ian had always found that it went down better after he had been up and around for an hour or two. "I've got a few Poptarts in my bag."

"Poptarts." Doc shook his head, disgusted. "Not exactly the breakfast of champions. Lousy nutrition."

"Hey, check the package. They're not as bad as you think."

"Don't confuse me with facts. I'm a doctor, and I know better than you."

There was no answering that.

Ian sat down and sipped at the coffee. "So, what are you doing here at this absurd hour of the morning, Doc? I didn't see your car." The huge white Chevy Suburban that Doc used as a portable office—and, when necessary, an ambulance—would have been distinctive for the light bars on top, even if it didn't have the word *Ambulance* backwards on the front, forward on the back, and five little deers with red x's painted through them on the driver's door.

And if there had been a problem with Hosea, surely the car would be here, and Doc Sherve wouldn't be sitting around drinking coffee with the Thorsens.

Doc might as well have read his mind. "No, he's fine. He is just sleeping in."

Ian heard the soft footsteps in the hall outside the kitchen.

"That turns out not to be the case," a low, slightly slurred voice said. "I am quite well, but I am not asleep."

Ian turned in his chair. Hosea Lincoln—well, that was what he was called here—stood in the kitchen doorway, wearing an ancient herringbone robe over yellow silk pajamas and slippers that looked to be as old as the robe. The robe was belted tightly; he seemed unhealthily skinny that way, much more so than in his usual outfit of plaid shirt and overalls, which at least gave the illusion of some bulk.

His skin was the color of coffee au lait, but there was something exotic and strange-looking about his eyes, and the way he appeared to be freshly shaved, as always. If he had any trace of beard, Ian had never seen it.

"Good morning, Hosea," Ian said.

"Ian Silverstein," Hosea said, with a slight nod. "A good morning to you, as well." He limped into the kitchen; his right hand, as usual, hung down by his side, the fingers curled into a loose and almost useless fist.

Karin started to get up, presumably to pour him a cup of coffee, but desisted at a slight gesture from his left hand. Hosea preferred doing for himself, when he could. Which was most of the time.

"And since you're not here to see to my medical needs, Doctor," he said, as he poured steaming coffee into a mug covered with big red letters that read She Who Must Be Obeyed, "may I ask why this home has been graced by your most welcome company this morning?"

Once, Ian would have found his phrasing awkward, but that was before he spoke Bersmål—and that was the exact construction he would have used in Bersmål—and before he had met Hosea or any of Torrie's family.

"My snowmobile's out back," Doc said. "I had another middle-of-the-night." He grinned. "A birth, for once." Doc liked delivering babies.

Ian searched his memory. "Leslie Gisslequist, maybe?" It was a bit early, but . . .

Doc's grin widened. "Very good. A cute little girl, and a full seven pounds despite being two, almost three weeks, early—nominal delivery, everything you could ask for, except for Ottar's stupid comments about the placenta." He raised his palm. "Don't ask, or I'll tell you."

And the snowmobile? Ian tried to remember where the Gisslequist farm was. Somewhere to the northeast, diagonally outside of town. Somebody who knew what he was doing could probably get there by snowmobile, cutting across snowed-over fields, faster than a car could by the road, what with the roads covered in spots with black ice that forced a sane driver to approach any intersection at a crawl.

Still, to hear Doc talk, you'd think that being woken in the middle of the night for some medical emergency was an unusual event, but Martha said it was a rare week that went by without him being called out at least twice, and it was one of the reasons that his talk about retirement was probably getting serious.

Doc was in fine shape for a man his age, but he was a man his age, and he wouldn't last forever.

Nothing did. Not even the universe.

Ian sighed.

Ian shook his head. Trying to take the long view had never been a workable strategy for him, and probably wouldn't ever be. It just wouldn't be the same, when the nearest physician was in an ER in Grand Forks.

"So why all the interest?" Doc asked. "Just curiosity? Or what?"

Curiosity? Sure. "Mainly, it's a bad habit," Ian said. "Do tell."

"I . . . try too hard to figure things out."

"And that's a bad habit?"

"Can you figure everything out, Doc?"

"Hey, I'm a doctor. Of course I can."

Ian shrugged. If Doc didn't want to give a serious answer, well, then Ian didn't have to, either.

Sherve bit his lip. "Okay, fine. There's a lot I can't figure out, but I don't let it bother me."

"Good for you. I do. It's more a compulsion than anything else."

You try to outgrow it, but you never can.

What you grow up with is normal; it's only later that it turns crazy on you. It was normal to have a father who would strike out at you with his words or his hand, and it was normal to try to figure out what you had done wrong that had made him do it, this time.

If only, you thought, if only you got all your ducks lined up in a row, if only you understood everything, and knew everything, then you could do everything right and this time he'd smile at you, he'd hug you, he'd like you.

But that was bullshit. Ian hadn't gotten beaten for not cleaning his room (the books were out of order and the loose papers were shoved under his bed), although he hadn't, and he didn't get shoved down the stairs for dawdling on his way home from school, although he had. Those were the triggers, the excuses, not the reasons. You couldn't stop it by figuring it all out and doing it all right, because it wasn't about you, and it didn't matter what you did.

The trouble was, he couldn't stop trying to figure it all out, and when he wasn't watching himself, that old superstition welled up, that old myth that only if he knew everything, if he understood everything, it would all be all right.

Hosea's hand griped Ian's shoulder. "Do not whip your own spirits," he said in Bersmål—for privacy perhaps, although both the Thorsens spoke Bersmål as well as Ian did. "I beg your pardon, Doctor," Hosea said, this time in English. "I told Ian to be easy on himself. There is a reason that they call it 'abuse,' you know."

"Yeah." Doc shrugged an apology. "It was a stupid question. Kathy Aarsted's the same way."

"Kathy Bjerke," Ian said, correcting. "And it wasn't Bob Aarsted who abused her."

Doc grinned. "You can put money on that, kid. If you can find somebody fool enough to bet with you."

Karin Thorsen still wouldn't meet his eyes.

You know, he wanted to say, *maybe it's about time we put all that behind us.*

The last time he had taken a Hidden Way to Tir Na Nog, it had been at her pressuring, and she had rushed him into going through in an attempt to preempt either her son's or her husband's having to walk the soil of Tir Na Nog once again.

"It's okay, Karin," he said, quietly, knowing what she was thinking about.

Thorsen's face was as impassive as carved granite.

Hosea smiled, and Sherve nodded his agreement. "It worked out well enough, in the end."

The fact that a gorgeous woman, even one in her early forties, could wrap a man just barely into his twenties around her little finger with no more than a chin quiver was hardly news.

Besides, Ian had a thing for gorgeous older women. One—particularly gorgeous—and remarkably older—woman, in particular.

How old was Freya? And how could you measure such a thing? What was the proper yardstick? Given that the Old Gods had retired to Tir Na Nog long ago, and simple years wouldn't do. Was it eons? Legends? Ages?

Never mind.

The problem was here and now.

Ian's hand dipped into his pocket, and his fingers closed around the warmth of the ring once more. He slipped it onto his thumb.

He concentrated, and thought, *Really, Karin, it's okay. I'm not mad, not any more.* She had viewed him as more expendable than her husband and son, and she had quite cleverly manipulated Ian into a dangerous situation that could easily have gotten him killed. But Ian wasn't angry at her. He was jealous of Torrie and Thorian, sure—nobody had ever been that devoted to Ian Silverstein—but he wasn't angry.

It's okay. All is forgiven, he thought, willing her to believe him. It was true. You were allowed to persuade your friends that you had forgiven them, if you had; it wasn't wrong, it wasn't an abuse of the ring.

The ring pulsed, painfully tightening and then releasing on his thumb in time with his heartbeat.

Hosea nodded in agreement.

Karin Thorsen sighed, and visibly relaxed, and cocked her head to one side. "You look far away."

Hosea chuckled. "That he's been."

He sat down next to Ian, reached for a roll of lefse from the plate on the table, and took a tentative nibble. Nice—the usual way to eat the soft potato flatbread was to spread a thin layer of butter over it, sprinkle on a little sugar, and then roll it up, but Karin had substituted a generous portion of her summer raspberry preserves—and maybe a little lemon zest?—on the lefse before rolling it up and cutting it like sushi.

Hosea was capable of putting away more food than Ian would have thought possible to fit into that skinny frame, but he didn't follow the local custom of a heavy breakfast any more than Ian did.

"That he will be again, I don't doubt," Hosea said. "The winter out on the plains here is an acquired taste."

Was Ian's restlessness that transparent?

Hosea nodded, answering the unasked question. Yes, it was that transparent. At least to him. But maybe not everybody else could see it.

"Be that as it may," Thorian Thorsen said, rising to his feet, "for now, Ian Silverstein and I have a shift to take, and little enough time to get there." He rose to his feet and took a last bite of toast, washing it down with a last swig from his coffee cup. "Come, Ian Silverstein."

"You bet."

There was an old tan-and-Bondo Ford LTD station wagon parked down the road that led to the small stand of trees surrounded on all sides by snowy fields, which was all that remained of what had been some sort of sacred place a few hundred or a few thousand years before. Off in the trees, a wisp of smoke worked its way through the gray branches, only to be caught and shattered in the light wind.

Thorian Thorsen eased the Bronco onto the hard-packed ground next to the Ford, leaving plenty of room for Ian to swing the door all the way open, which he did.

The air in the Bronco had been wonderfully warm; the outside air hit Ian with a cold slap.

You know it's cold when you take a sniff and your boogers freeze, Ian thought, adjusting the cuffs of his parka to nest over his gloves before he shouldered his bag and Giantkiller's cue case and followed Thorsen down the path of squeaking snow and into the woods.

It was a short walk, and it was good to get out of the wind, even though the naked trees only broke it up a little. At minus-God-only-knows, even the lightest breeze sucks every bit of the heat right out of you, and any relief whatsoever is always welcome.

The area around the cairn had been cleared that fall, and a warming hut, built out of an old ice fishing house, had been brought in. One wall had been cut almost completely away and left open toward the fire, which was still burning on a circle of three flat stones just behind the dark hole in the snow, itself in front of the old stone cairn that dated back to God-knows-when.

It wasn't Lakota—Jeff Bjerke's mother was a quarter Lakota, and she had talked to some tribal elders down in Pipestone and Rosebud—and the history of this part of the world before the Lakota was kind of sketchy. The various Plains Indian tribes had been too busy trying to scratch a living out of the forest and plains between making war on each other to take copious notes.

Or maybe it was just that they were considerate of future archaeologists?

Mmmm, probably not.

There was something about a fire that was even more warming than the temperature, which was just as well, given the temperature. Fire had melted down through the snow, and the snow had turned to water, trickling down into the hole. It was easy to ignore the hole in front of the fire, and in fact, it took some work to look at it for the first time.

Ian wondered, again, how much water it would take to fill up the hole.

Was it even possible?

Probably not. The properties of the Hidden Ways were built into the very structure of the universe, and it wasn't likely that men or Man could change them. It was hard enough to notice them.

Davy Larsen was already halfway out of the warming house, a Garand rifle cradled in his arms, the muzzle carefully pointed in a neutral direction, the butt of a .45 semi-auto sticking out of his open parka.

Ian didn't know much about guns, and wasn't much interested in them. They didn't have any, well, life to them, not the way a sword did.

And, besides, Hosea had said that they wouldn't work in Tir Na Nog. No, that wasn't quite it—he'd said they wouldn't work, or would work too well. Ian didn't particularly like the idea of confronting a Köld with a gun that would either blow up in his hand or only make clicking sounds. Come to think of it, he didn't particularly like the idea of confronting a Köld, not if there was another good option.

"Morning, Ian, Thorian," Davy said as he limped toward them, his words turning into a yawn.

"David." Thorsen nodded.

"Hosea and Karin well?" he asked, politely, although there was just a hint of emphasis on Hosea's name.

"He's doing just fine," Ian said. "Haven't seen a seizure all winter, and he's down to his old doses of the anticonvulsants, Doc says."

"Well, that's good." Davy grinned as he held out the rifle to Thorsen. "Wouldn't want him ad-dicted," he said. "Here. Have a rifle."

Thorian Thorsen accepted the Garand and yanked the bolt open, catching the ejected round with a surprisingly quick movement of his right hand, which Ian had never seen anybody else dare to try, much less pull off in such a casual, matter-of-fact manner.

His gloved hand thumbed it back into place, but not before Ian noted that the bullet was silver.

As well it should have been. One of the manufacturers made bullets called Silvertips, but these weren't them. These were cast from jeweler's silver—the silver carefully mixed with old typesetting lead to give the bullet more heft and make it expand better in either human or nonhuman flesh—then formed, swaged, and loaded in the Thorsens' basement with that funny-looking machine that reminded Ian of a blender with a thyroid condition.

Any bullet would hurt a Son of Fenris, at least for a few moments, but it took more than lead to put one down dead. It could be done, mind; the skeletons of six Fenrir lay buried in a field not too far from here as proof that that could be done, that they could be killed.

Giantkiller could do it, too; Hosea had tempered the edge in his own blood.

Ian set the cue case down on the crude table, opened it, and brought out Giantkiller in its scabbard. The new bell guard that Hosea had fitted to it was too shiny; maybe he should take some steel wool to it and blur the surface. His sword, like all the blades that Hosea had made for them, had been tempered in the blood of an Old One, and that gave it a certain authority. Magic? Not quite. But close enough—Giantkiller had slain a Köld and Ian himself had killed a fire giant with its hilt in his hand, and it was perfectly capable of doing in a Son, if it was necessary.

As it might be. This exit from the Hidden Ways had remained open at least since the Night of the Sons, and showed no sign of closing.

Could it be closed?

Even Hosea couldn't say.

And if it was closed, did that make them safe? Or was there another exit, another adit, perhaps a thousand yards or a thousand miles away, that would open instead? You couldn't fill it up, you couldn't close it. Not so you'd be sure it stayed closed.

But you could watch it, and the men of Hardwood took their turns on watch.

Ian shrugged. What else could they do? Announce to the whole fucking world that there was a Hidden Way in a small clearing in a stand of trees surrounded by cornfields in eastern North Dakota?

What if somebody believed them? What if word of the Night of the Sons got out? Werewolves, attacking a North Dakota town, killing two people and injuring more?

Look what one silly little story had done to Roswell, New Mexico.

And this would be far worse, because it was true.

It isn't only evil that hates the light. So does privacy. So does normality.

So does life, at least as lived in Hardwood.

Hardwood could become famous, and while the Hidden Way would conceal itself from those who didn't know what they were looking for, life here would wither and die in the light of the flashbulbs of the *National Enquirer.*

That sort of publicity would be the end of life in this little town, and this little town suited its people just fine, thank you, and if keeping yet another secret would protect that life and that town and those people, then Hardwood could watch over the Hidden Way until the end of time.

It was boring, mainly, is what it was, but of all ways you could suffer in the world, boredom was Ian's absolute favorite. You could let your mind wander when you were bored, and while he preferred to keep busy, that was better than some things.

If only it wasn't so damn cold.

If only—

He heard a distant whimper, and was on his feet even before Thorsen was.

Guns were foreign to him, but at least a gun stood a chance of stopping a Son before it came close enough that he could feel its breath on him, so as he tore off his gloves to draw Giantkiller, he grabbed the pistol out of his pocket, as well.

The sound came again, and if his ears weren't playing

tricks on him, it was coming from the direction of the fire, from the exit, from the Hidden Way.

Finger off the trigger until you have a target, he reminded himself, hoping that his hand was trembling more from the cold than from fear.

But shit, he'd been frightened before, and he'd be frightened again. It didn't matter how you felt, as long as you did the right thing.

"I'm to your right, Ian Silverstein," Thorsen's voice said in a rasp. "Careful, now."

A thick, hairy hand reached up from inside the hole and grasped the edge of it, followed immediately by another, and for just a moment, a shock of black hair, and then a heavy eye ridge over two wide eyes peeked out.

And then, with a sound that was more a groan of pain than a grunt of effort, the fingers slipped and disappeared back down the hole.

Later, he wasn't sure that his claim that he had thought it through was accurate.

It was more reflex than reason that had him drop the gun to one side and run for the hole, leaping down it without so much as a moment's hesitation.

It was probably stupid, but he did have Giantkiller in his right hand, and as he landed on the hard ground at the bottom of the hole, he broke his fall as best he could with a roll like a skydiver's.

Pain tore through his left shoulder in a horrid red wave that pulled a scream from his lips but didn't loosen his grip on his sword.

He slid on the icy ground and into—

—and into the Hidden Way, and the curious silence that had no ring of tinnitus in it, the lack of cold that had no warmth, the absence of pressure that gave no release.

—peace. And silence. And an absence not only of pain but also of feeling.

Ian stood, surrounded by the gray light that seemed centered on him, vanishing off in the distance of the tunnel.

He wasn't cold anymore. Nor tired, nor hungry, nor full,

nor much of anything. Not even in pain. His ankles, his hip, no matter how well he'd broken his fall—

But even his shoulder didn't hurt. He worked his left arm. It didn't seem to want to move easily, but there was no pain at all.

He remembered banging his head against the hard ice at some point, but that didn't hurt either, and even though his probing fingers found a bump, and came away tipped with red blood, there was no feeling of wetness of blood running down the side of his neck because there wasn't blood running down the side of his neck.

There was a timelessness, a feelinglessness that came with the Hidden Ways, and while he should have been expecting it, each time it had come as a dull surprise, and this time was no different.

It wasn't a bright shock, not reassuring or even frightening—in some ways that would have been better: that would have meant he was feeling something—but just a surprise, just different.

He was breathing—but not heavily, not panting, not gasping, just breathing in and out—but he had the strong sensation that he could just stop and it would make no difference at all.

The body lying on the floor of the tunnel wasn't breathing. It was a short, thick man, wearing rags that looked like they had once been a tunic of sorts, belted only with a length of tattered rope.

Or not a man. The forehead was too low, and sloped, and the hair was thicker on his arms and legs than Ian had ever seen on a human. He had been badly hurt. A gash on his right thigh leered wide and red, and another on his ribs revealed white bone.

He wasn't bleeding, not anymore. The dead don't bleed.

Ian nodded. It was a vestri, of course. What Ian would once have called a Neanderthal, perhaps; what the legends had called a dwarf.

Ian should have felt something about it lying there dead, but he didn't. The Hidden Way robbed him of feelings in much the same way that it robbed him of feeling. Intellectually, he knew he should look around for danger, for some sign of whatever it was that had killed the dwarf, but the thought had no emotional weight to it.

Still, he looked down the tunnel as far as he could see. Nothing. Just grayness, vanishing off into darker grayness, eventually becoming black.

No, there was no feeling of danger here, and that was only in part because feeling itself was damped.

He turned back. Beyond the body of the dwarf, the grayness led out to a snowy patch, where traces of light filtered down onto the ice that was marked with the red of fresh blood. That was reality, and home, and solidity; the other way would take him, once again, to Tir Na Nog.

He would feel again, no matter where he came out.

And that would be a good thing. There were times when he could only prefer numbness, but death was the ultimate numbness, and he didn't want to die.

In a distant, passionless way, part of him wanted to follow the Hidden Way, to Tir Na Nog, to Marta—and to *her*—and deep inside the numbness that lay over his feelings like a sodden blanket he thought that maybe that was, after all, the right thing to do: to heave the dwarf to his shoulder and carry it back to Tir Na Nog where its bones would lie with those of Vestri and his children.

Now that was a fit place for a Son of Vestri to lie in death; not deep beneath the almost impossibly black soil of a cornfield in North Dakota.

But Ian wasn't prepared for a trip to Tir Na Nog. And it wasn't just the lack of supplies and people waiting for him back in Hardwood. Those were details that could be handled, one way or another. He wasn't prepared emotionally for it.

But why not? There were no emotions here; he could just go, and who would say he was wrong?

But, no: No. The gray dullness was not the right place to be making any sort of decision at all. Important decisions shouldn't be made by a feeling-numbed mind, trapped in a gray timelessness that allowed only dry intellect. It was wrong to do such things when your mind was dulled by alcohol, or by the Hidden Ways.

It was illogical to rely solely on logic. Important decisions needed to be made with both intellect and emotion, with the heart and balls and the brain, with your mind and with your guts, not divorced from a human reality that was feeling as much as it was thought.

But he couldn't just leave the dead dwarf lying here, caught in the interstices between worlds. And if he wasn't going to take it to Tir Na Nog, then cold gray logic dictated that he would have to take it back with him.

There was no fourth choice, after all, and to not decide was a decision.

His parka was in the way, so he stripped it off and dropped it to one side, unsurprised that he was neither cold with it off nor sweating with it on.

But removing it let him slide Giantkiller through his belt, which he did, and he stooped to pick up the vestri.

It was limp in death, and that should have made it hard to lift, although not impossible; the advanced first aid class he had taken some years ago had taught him how to get a limp body up into a fireman's carry.

But it just wasn't all that hard: maybe the vestri was lighter than he looked, but it was only the matter of a few moments before he was able to get the little man's limp body up to his right shoulder, balanced properly.

And, with one last look that would have been a longing one if the Hidden Way permitted such a feeling, he walked back toward the ice and—

—groaned in pain at the blazing agony in his left shoulder. He would have dropped the dwarf's body, but he staggered up against the wall of the hole, bracing the body there, his feet finding purchase somehow or other.

"Ian!" Thorian Thorsen's broad face leaned out over the edge of the hole, impossibly high, impossibly far away.

Ian was about to let the body drop when it moved against his shoulder.

The dwarf wasn't dead; it was just unconscious, and the gray unchangingness of the Hidden Way had hidden that.

Something warm ran down Ian's leg.

Shit. Its wounds were bleeding. No, *his* wounds were bleeding.

His jaw clenched tightly to keep any groan or scream from escaping, Ian braced himself hard against the wall and ignored the way that every movement of his left shoulder made him want to scream as he pulled Giantkiller from his belt and lowered the dwarf, as gently as he could, to the ground.

He glanced up. Thorsen was gone. All his effort to avoid whimpering had been for nothing.

Well, that was reassuring, if not particularly surprising. When it all went to hell around you, Thorian Thorsen could be counted on to do something constructive, if not necessarily the best thing.

Ian took a deep breath, regretting it as the cold dry air triggered a fit of coughing.

Okay, first thing was the airway, and with the dwarf's wide mouth sagging open and the vapor from its breath in the air, he knew it could breathe.

Second thing was to stop the bleeding.

He had to stop the goddamn bleeding. Warm blood still seeped from the thigh wound, steam rising and vanishing in the cold air. He grabbed at the edges of the wound and tried to squeeze them together, but the thick, hairy skin was slippery with blood and dirt, and his frozen fingers couldn't get any purchase around the dwarf's broad thigh.

He was disgusted with himself almost to the point of nausea at how good the warm blood felt on his numbing fingers. But, shit, it did.

Ian stripped off his outer shirt, trying as hard as he could to ignore the way the movement of his left shoulder brought sparks to his brain and tears to his eyes, and he wrapped the shirt about the wound, tying the arms of the shirt together as tightly as he could.

That slowed the flow of the warm blood but didn't stop it. But maybe that was enough until they could get him to a doctor, to Doc Sherve.

Where the fuck was Thorsen, though? What was he doing? It had been . . .

. . . it had only been a few seconds since Ian had emerged with the dwarf, and whatever he was doing would take more than just a few seconds—

The roar of a powerful V-8 and the smashing of brush cut through the sound of his own ragged, painful breathing.

—although maybe not much more.

Thorsen was back at the hole, in his hands what looked at first glance like a surfboard.

He lowered it on a rope. It was a board with holes for grips around the edges, but it looked like some strange bondage device, more than anything else, what with the Velcro straps on its side.

"Strap him on tightly, Ian Silverstein, then keep the board from turning over as I pull him up."

Easier said than done, with only one arm. Ian tried to keep the board still and roll the dwarf over onto it, but it kept slipping away.

Useless piece of shit, he could practically hear his father say.

Fuck you, Dad, he thought, and redoubled his efforts, bringing up his left hand. He would roll the dwarf onto the board, dammit, he would.

Ian screamed as something tore loose in his left shoulder, and the board skittered away on the ice, out of reach, useless, like Ian.

A distant sound of whimpering came to his ears as he struggled to kick himself over to the board, and he wasn't surprised to realize it was his own voice.

Dammit, I just can't.

But excuses didn't count. Not doing what was necessary when you had a good reason was, in the final essence, just not doing what was necessary. Results count; good intentions aren't a substitute.

Shit.

"No. Wait," Thorian Thorsen said. He lowered one end of an extensible walking stick. "Wrap the loop around your wrist, and let me pull."

Ian slipped his right hand through the loop and fastened his bare fingers on the cold rubber.

"Hold tightly," Thorsen said, unnecessarily. What was Ian going to do? Hope it stuck to his goddamn hand?

He was leaning over the hole, with absolutely no leverage, but Thorsen was a strong man, even stronger than he

looked, and Ian found himself being raised up, his feet finding purchase against the wall of the hole.

He slid up to the cold snow, gasping with the pain and
the cold like a fish on the shore. Thorsen already had the
other end of the rope tied to the hitching ball on the back
of the Bronco, and at a dead run came back to Ian to carry,
more than help, Ian up, and then over to the Bronco.

He lifted Ian up to the driver's seat and helped him swing
his legs inside.

"Wait for my signal," Thorsen said, "then slowly. For
the sake of the Scion, drive forward slowly, if you please."
He shut the door, hard, and ran back to the hole and
dropped right down into it.

The Bronco was still warm, and Thorsen had turned the
heater all the way up.

Hot air from the vents pushed the cold away, and he
found that his teeth were chattering, so he just clamped his
jaw together.

Thorsen had told him to wait, but when it was time to
move he would want to start right away. So Ian stomped
on the parking brake with his left foot, but kept his right
foot firmly on the brake while he moved the car from park
into drive. It wouldn't take Thorsen—

"Now, Ian Silverstein, now!"

Ian released the brake and put his foot gently on the
accelerator. *Easy now,* he told himself as he applied the
tiniest pressure.

The Bronco rolled forward, taking up the slack in the
rope, then stopped.

It would have been easy to use too much force, but Ian
slowly, gently, added pressure . . .

. . . and the Bronco rolled forward, quickly, pulling the
dwarf strapped to the restraining board out of the hole like
a cork out of a bottle, with Thorian Thorsen clinging with
both hands to the back end of the board, his legs spreading
wide to keep from rolling, toes digging into the grass to
stop the board from sliding under the Bronco.

He leaped to his feet and busied himself untying the
board from the hitch.

Ian cursed himself for an idiot. There, sitting right under

the radio, was the cell phone. While Thorsen wrestled the
board toward the Bronco, Ian picked up the receiver,
punched a number, and hit SEND.

It rang only once before Karin Thorsen's Hello? was
sweet in his ears.

"Is Doc Sherve still there?"

"Yes, he's just on his way—is—"

"Put him on right now. Emergency." There wasn't time
to explain, and Karin, characteristically, didn't waste time
asking for an explanation.

"Yes, Ian?" Doc's voice had that note of professional
calm that made Ian not sure whether he wanted to sigh in
relief or to scream in frustration.

"We've got a patient for you. Multiple wounds, but I
got the worst one pretty much stopped. Unconscious—I
think it's from lack of blood."

Thorsen slammed the back hatch, and was in the
passenger-side door. Ian handed him the phone—he
couldn't drive and talk with one hand—and stomped on
the gas.

"No, stop the car!" Thorsen shouted, his eyes wide, his
voice ringing in Ian's ears. "Now, Ian Silver Stone."

Ian hadn't heard that note of command in Thorsen's
voice before, and he found that he had braked the car to a
sliding stop without even thinking about it.

Thorsen held up a hand for silence. "It is Thorian," he
said into the phone. Then: "Yes. The clinic, yes. Bring
Hosea with you. Say to him: 'Ilst nicht ver brehnenst vestri.' Tell him that: 'Ilst nicht ver brehnenst vestri.' "

He is not a human. He is a vestri.

Thorsen was out the door, and slammed it hard enough
to rattle something in the glove compartment. "Drive to
the clinic!" he shouted. "I will stay here, on watch, until
relief arrives."

The phone bounced to the floor as Ian stomped on the
accelerator.

You could trust Thorian Thorsen to think clearly, even
when it was all going to hell around him. He was right—
this could, just possibly, have been some sort of ruse to
draw attention away.

Not that Ian believed that for a moment. But it didn't matter what he believed; the world didn't necessarily agree with him, and what mattered was what was, not what he believed, after all.

He could hear Karin shouting into the phone, but he couldn't quite make out her words over the rumble of the car, and he couldn't retrieve the handset and drive, not at the same time.

That could wait.

CHAPTER THREE

Valin

Martha Sherve had just finished her early morning rounds and was looking forward to getting some real work done when her beeper went off.

Her rounds, such as they were, hadn't taken much time at all: only one of the four beds was occupied, and that was only with old Orphie Hansen, and all old Orphie was doing was snoring gently while he slept off about three too many beers from last night at the Dine-a-mite in the one place in town where Ole Honistead was confident that Orphie wouldn't drown in his own vomit.

Not that much of a trick to it: all you had to do was make sure he was sleeping on his stomach, with his head near the edge of the bed, but Martha had wired him to that new monitor anyway—she wondered if the electrodes would really stick to his hairy back without having to shave off a patch of hair—and then had set alarms for heart rate, sound, and breathing troubles. Bob had spent more than enough money on all these high-tech toys, and the maintenance contracts were ridiculously expensive—Martha wrote the checks that paid the bills, or, rather, had the new computer and Quicken write the checks for her—so they might as well get some use out of them while they were under warranty.

She really should be doing some paperwork in the office—Doc was always late with his paperwork, and it was just as well that both she and Donna could sign his name better than he could—but she hadn't been sleeping well lately, what with the shift change, and she was thinking seriously about a quick nap when her pager went off, again, with that horrible beeping sound that she had quickly learned to hate.

She shut the beeping off as she ran down the hall, tearing open a wipe, and wiping off her hands as she did. Putting on a pair of surgical gloves from her pocket didn't even slow her down much.

Granted, she didn't run quite as quickly as she would have thirty years before, but she did run, and that was what counted. If you took care to choose the right food, the right exercise, and the right parents, you could still manage to move quickly when you had to, and if there was an ache here and a pain there, well, either you dove into a bottle of Demerol and Vistaril and maybe never came out, or you just did what Martha did and took enough Naprosyn to take the edge off the aches and the pains, and otherwise you just learned to live with it.

A little pain wasn't the end of the world, after all. You could live with it.

Bob was only half out of his snowsuit, his cheeks red above his beard, but he and Donna and Ian Silverstein had managed to get the bloody little man off the restraint board and on to the exam table, and Donna, gloved as always, was already getting a large-bore needle into his incredibly thick right arm, two bags of Ringer's hanging on the stand, waiting.

Good veins.

"Get a BP, then get the Ringer's started in the other arm," Doc said.

"Venous bleeding at interior of left thigh, patient unconscious, pupils dilated and nonresponsive," Donna said, a trace of excitement in her voice coming through the familiar monotone litany.

Martha quickly had the cuff around his other arm. She pumped it up with a few quick squeezes, then slipped her stethoscope into her ears. The temptation was always to rush, but then you'd have to do it over again, and after all these years, Martha had never quite gotten used to the look on Bob's face when she had to do it over again.

But no. Shit.

The needle dropped to ninety, then eighty, seventy, and kept dropping all the way to forty before she got the thump-thump-thump in her ears, it dropped all the way before the sound went away.

"Systolic is forty," she announced, "and I can't get a diastolic."

"Okay," Bob said, as matter-of-factly as if she'd reported that dinner was ready. "Then let's get a second bag of Ringer's going," he said. "Then push two units of blood for a start." The clinic wasn't large enough or well-staffed enough to keep a full blood supply on hand, but Doc seemed to get a pint out of Hosea Lincoln every week. It typed as O negative, but there was something as strange about his blood as there was about the tall black man himself: it crossmatched against anything, and vice versa.

A universal donor couldn't be a universal recipient—any blood type other than O negative would make the body start developing antibodies to the foreign proteins.

Hosea's body and blood, apparently, had other ideas.

Martha tore the wrapping off a large-bore needle, and cleaned off the inside of the little man's almost impossibly thick wrist with a wipe while she looked for a vein. Not that that took long: a ropy vein that was almost the diameter of her little finger lay right under the skin.

She pushed the needle into the thick skin, but instead of sliding in, it just pressed the skin down and slid along the wrist, scratching a thin white line.

Damn, damn, damn. Two dull needles in the last ten years, and both of them had been in emergencies. Why the hell couldn't it happen when she had time?

She dropped it to the floor and unwrapped another as the dropped needle pinged away.

Again the needle slipped on the skin.

"No." Donna, across the table from her, was shaking her head. "It's not the needle. Just push hard; you've got to push hard to break the skin." She stalked off through the curtains, toward the refrigerator.

That sounded silly, but Donna wasn't crazy. Too young, too bouncy, maybe, but she knew her job.

So Martha pushed.

It was like trying to shove a fork through hard plastic, but the skin finally gave, and she attached the tube from the bag of Ringer's, and then taped the whole mess into place, sloppily but solidly.

That would do.

Donna had already put the oxygen mask over the little man's mouth and nose, and Martha had been too busy with taking his BP and then getting the second needle in to pay any attention to his face.

But he looked funny. His forehead was too low, like a slice had been taken out near the top of his head, and his heavy brows came within a finger's-breadth of his hair. His jaw was heavy—all his bones seemed to be too thick—but receding. All that looked vaguely familiar, but it was strange.

She could think about that later—right now, his pulse was fading, and his pressure was probably still dropping, and it didn't have very much further to drop.

"Damn," Doc said. "I don't like this. Let's try two, no three cc's epi, Martha, and Donna where the hell is that goddamn blood?"

"I'm goddamn warming it, dammit," her voice came back, "and it'll fucking be the hell there when the hell it fucking gets goddamn there, okay?"

Doc chuckled. "Fair enough." When things went all to pieces around him, Doc always seemed to relax, as though by pretending he had it all under control he could make the rest of the universe believe him. It didn't always work, but sometimes it did, and Martha always believed him.

She always had tended to, ever since they had been kids in school together, at a time that felt both like yesterday and a million years ago.

But it was more than that. You live with a man for so

many years, you work with him during the day and lie awake next to him, hearing his breathing enough nights, and it gets so that you don't really know where you leave off and he begins, sometimes, and while he can't lie to you, or you to him, not without the both of you feeling like a neon sign has gone off, anything he tells you that he believes, you will believe it, too, because his reality and yours have melded together in a way that's sometimes reassuring and sometimes frightening.

Doc glared at the overhead display.

"Ah . . . damn. I think we're going to lose him," Doc said, pulling the crash cart a little closer with his foot, not missing a beat as he cut away at the bloody rag wrapped around the little man's thigh. You went to the paddles if you had to, and about half the time you could get the heart started again.

For a while.

But in all her years, Martha could remember only two, three times that they'd actually ended up with a live patient after jump-starting him.

Doc had him hooked up to what he always called the MGP, and it kept pinging away regularly. The little man may have been funny looking, but his heart was strong.

Ian Silverstein stood shivering, like he was looking for something useful to do. "Ian," Doc said, "there's a sink over in the corner. Wash up—don't spare the scrub brush—then put on a gown and a set of gloves. I can use another set of hands here."

Martha was expecting some sort of protest, but Ian Silverstein just nodded as he more ran than walked toward the sink.

Doc winked at Martha, and Donna, on a dead run, dashed through the curtains, two red-black bags in her hand. She moved faster than Martha could have as she connected up the blood to the IVs, then started the flow, cutting back on the Ringer's to let the real thing snake its way down through the coils of plastic tubing and into the veins.

"Okay," Doc said. "Warm up another two units. I want to get at least six into him . . ." he grunted as he worked a hemostat into place, then reached for another ". . . and then we'll stick in the dipstick and see if he's full." He glanced up at the monitor, at the rippling green mountains and valleys that were now getting larger. "Good boy. Stay with me, just a little while longer," he said. "You just hang in there, and let ol' Doc Sherve sew you up, you hear?"

Ian Silverstein, now gowned and gloved, was by Doc's side the next time Martha looked up.

"Okay," Doc said, "you know those things you call roach clips? They're called hemostats, and I'm going to need a bunch of them. You just slap them into my palm when I call for one—shit." A small geyser of blood erupted from the wound, covering Doc from shoulder to waist before he could get it stopped. "And Martha, I need some suction here, if I'm going to have a chance to see what the hell I'm doing."

She was already on her way, the Davis in hand.

Ian had been concentrating so hard on not screwing up— even though Doc Sherve hadn't asked him to do anything really difficult, and he was half-wondering if it was just Doc's way of playing with his head—that he didn't notice that Hosea and Thorian Thorsen were in the room, until Doc, his eyes never seeming to leave his work, said, "And a good day to you, Hosea and Thorian."

Ian had gotten tired of staring at the instrument tray, although it had been minutes since Doc had asked for another hemostat. So Ian had kept his eyes on the dwarf's face, to avoid looking at where Doc was working on the gash in the thigh, and to avoid feeling guilty for wanting Doc to give him something for the pain in his shoulder.

Ian had seen blood before, although not much, thankfully; his reputation in the Eastern Hinterlands of Vandescard to the contrary, he had only fought one real duel, and his winning had been more of a fluke than due to any great skill, but there was something frightening about the calmly professional way Doc Sherve stuck his gloved hands and his shiny metal instruments right into a wound, clamping here, sewing there. It was almost inhuman.

He tried to distance himself. It wasn't a human Doc was

operating on; it was a vestri, a dwarf, a Neanderthal. Another species entirely.

You could, possibly, mistake the dwarf for a human—although an awfully strange-looking one—if you didn't have another context in which to place it. But not if you gave it more than a second glance. A ragged beard covered his chin, but the chin receded improbably, and the brows were just too thick.

It seemed strange that the vestri had such long eyelashes, although Ian didn't know why he shouldn't. Or why he should.

"The vestri," Hosea said, his voice slurred more than usual, "can you say if he will live?" He was dressed in an orange hunting parka over his overalls. It was bulky enough to hide the skinniness of his torso, although his legs stuck out like two sticks below.

"You know, there is that possibility," Doc said, as he stripped off his blood-spattered gloves and gown, and stepped back. "He just might make it." Donna was already holding out another pair of gloves and had him re-gloved and re-gowned in less time than Ian would have thought possible.

The vestri's eyelashes fluttered for a moment.

"Doc—"

The eyes opened.

"Shit. He shouldn't be—" Doc Sherve shut himself up as he reached for a syringe and a bottle of something; he quickly filled it and injected it directly into the injection port below the plastic bubble chamber beneath the IV bag, where the blood pooled as it dripped, before snaking its way down and into the needle.

One thick dwarven arm reached up for the oxygen mask; blunt fingers clutched at the mask and pulled it down and away, more ignoring than deliberately resisting the desperate, frantic way that both Martha Sherve and the much younger Donna Bjerke tried to hold it on his face.

Martha quickly gave up and pulled the IV stand closer to the table.

Ian nodded, not that anybody was asking his opinion. That made sense: deal with one problem at a time—he didn't need to pull the stand over, or yank his needles out.

The Vestri's eyes were larger than they should be, the pupils narrowed to pinpoint, the irises brown and somehow grainy-looking. He seemed to have trouble focusing, but then he looked first at Ian, then at Doc, and then his eyes swung past Hosea to fasten on where Thorian Thorsen stood.

"Thorian del Thorian," came out in a rasp. "Vernisth beldarasht Vestri del fodder del fodder vestri."

Ian hadn't known until this moment that he understood any Vestri—the gift of tongues that Hosea could bestow, sometimes, never announced itself before it was used. *Thorian del Thorian,* the dwarf had said, *friend of the father of Vestri, himself, the father of the vestri.*

Thorian Thorsen nodded. "I am that one," he responded in the same language. "But liest thou still, Son of Vestri, and let my friends treat thee. Thy wounds are grave, and we have no chirurgeon here to lick them to health."

The little man kept struggling. "No," Ian said, in Bersmål, "lie still, as he says. Please."

"This one—" The vestri gasped for air. "No, thou must listen to . . ." he trailed off into a fit of coughing that left flecks of bloody phlegm at the corners of his thick lips. "This one has come to warn thee and thine, friend of the Father: a Son of Fenris has been dispatched to seek thy blood."

This wasn't news. The attack of the Fenrir was what the Night of the Sons was—

Oh, shit. Again?

But—

Doc Sherve was swearing under his breath—something about the constitution of an ox—as he injected the contents of yet another syringe into the tubing.

"Just tell him to shut up and rest, Thorian. He's really shocky, and I've already buried my goddamn quota of patients this year. You can talk to him later if he lives, I promise."

Thorian Thorsen laid a gentle hand on the vestri's leg. "Sleep now, Son of Vestri," Thorsen said. "Thou has done thy duty, and preserved the name of thy father, and his father, Vestri.''

"Sleep? No." The eyes started to sag. "The final darkness reaches for this one." The dwarf's jaw clenched as tightly as its fists.

"It is but sleep. Do not fight it; let it take thee, Son of Vestri.''

"Please. Do thou remember the name of Valin, son of Durin, before the Folk," he rasped. "Say, I beg of thee, 'He did give me warning, as he was charged.' I charge thee: remember this one's name before the Folk."

The eyes sagged closed.

He was so still that for a moment Ian was sure that the dwarf—Valin, was it?—had died.

But no: the monitor overhead still went ping. Ping. Ping. And Doc smiled at the green waves on the oscilloscope as he gently fitted the oxygen mask back into place over the vestri's nose.

"I take it that was his death speech," he said, stripping off his gloves and stepping away from the table. He waved a finger at the dwarf. His fingertips were wrinkled, like he'd left them in water too long.

"Save it for another time, little man," Doc Sherve said, with a tremor in his voice that Ian had never heard before, not from Doc Sherve. But the grin the old man gave the monitor was familiar, if wider than usual. "Just save it. You're not going to need it today."

He turned to Ian. "Now, let's see about that shoulder of yours," he said, his gentle fingers probing carefully.

"It's not too bad."

"And when you get your medical degree, you can make these technical medical diagnoses like 'not too bad.' In the meantime, I'm the doctor, and my medical opinion is that you banged the shit out of it, and I'd better take a look at it.''

Ian unlocked his shoulder from where his muscles had it clamped to his side. The pain was so sharp that he found his stomach rebelling, and it was all that he could do to stagger away from the table so that the foul stream of sour vomit splashed on the tile.

Thorsen's strong arm came around his right side, and pulled him over to the next exam table, levering him up on his right side.

Doc already had a syringe in his hand, and Martha Sherve had his trousers loosened and his belt undone.

There was a coldness on his right buttock, and then Doc said, "Small sting coming," and he felt a burning pain that was nothing in comparison to the other pains.

"Like the man says," Doc Sherve's voice boomed, "Demerol and Vistaril: write it down, and ask for it by name." A quick pat on the hip, then, "Give him about fifteen minutes to get all warm and sleepy, and then let's get some pictures."

Ian's vision started to blur. This wasn't supposed to take effect so quickly, but a warm numbness was spreading all through his body and mind.

"Hey, didn't you hear me with Valin? Same deal for you—just go with it, boy. Don't fight it."

No. He couldn't. There was something wrong. He couldn't relax to it, not while there was some part of him missing. He struggled against the helping arms and the darkness, but he was barely able to hold his own.

"Ah. I see." Hosea's voice held a note of amusement.

Feet thudded away on the hard floor, and then in a moment returned. Firm fingers opened his fist, and then a familiar grip was placed in it.

His fingers closed around Giantkiller's hilt.

But now it was back in his hand, and he was whole again.

He let the warm darkness reach up and drag him down.

CHAPTER FOUR

~

Town Meeting

J eff Bjerke parked his patrol car on what would have
been the front lawn of the Thorsen house if it were
summer, right next to Bob Aarsted's big old GMC
van.

He slipped the shotgun into its clamp and wiggled it a
couple of times to make sure it was locked into place before
he opened the door.

No, he wasn't going to have to worry about some kid
climbing in and getting at it, not on a frozen night like
tonight, but if you do it right every time, he had long since
been taught, then you don't have to worry about whether
or not you did it right this time.

He started to slip on the ice, and would have gone down
if one flailing hand hadn't latched on to the mirror extending from the side of the big van.

Thanks, Bob, he thought, as he recovered. With his luck
he would have fallen on his gun—again—and bruised himself seriously—again—on the right hip. As it was, all he
had done was given himself a little adrenaline rush, and
knocked the mirror out of alignment. He thought for a moment about trying to straighten it, then shook his head. No,
better to let Bob do it for himself and get it right.

It wasn't just that he would have recognized his father-in-law's car anywhere—although he would have, if only because of those horrible-looking yellow fuzzy dice that Bob Aarsted had inexplicably kept hanging from his rear-view mirror for, well, forever—but a conversion van was a rare vehicle in this part of the world. There were lots of pickup trucks and a few station wagons and utility vehicles like the ubiquitous Blazers and Broncos and Chevy Suburbans, but vans seemed to be a city thing. Or at least not a Hardwood thing.

Nothing wrong with being a little different.

He stripped off his right glove as he clumped up the steps to the porch, but Karin Thorsen opened the door just as he was about to knock.

"Good evening, Jeff," she said, her smile looking a bit forced as she closed the door behind him and helped him out of his parka.

The wall of the foyer bristled with coats and hanging pegs; he hung his parka on a free peg, then stooped to unlace his boots.

Doc Sherve's laugh boomed from the direction of the kitchen, to his left, but Jeff could hear Bob Aarsted and Reverend—Dave, he was supposed to call him Dave, unnatural as that felt—and Dave Oppegaard talking over in the living room over the clicketyclicketyclick of Minnie Hansen's knitting needles, so he walked through the archway and plopped down in one of the big leather recliners in the living room, about six feet from where flames flickered in the oversized fireplace.

It was nice to be warm and off his feet, and life would be perfect if—

"Coffee?" Karin Thorsen asked as she hurried in, a serving tray in her hand, and set out another coffee cake and a plate of rolled lefse on the coffee table before she followed through by offering him the cup.

"Please," he said, accepting the terra-cotta mug with both of his hands. It warmed them delightfully, and when he sipped at the steaming black liquid it warmed his insides like a shot of cheap whiskey.

"Good evening, Jeff," Dave Oppegaard said. His usual

cable-knit sweater was conspicuous by its absence—he was wearing his minister's collar, although that had been loosened and the first two buttons of his shirt unbuttoned. His hair was white and cottony, and it was just as well he kept himself clean-shaven—with a beard he would have looked like a buffed Santa Claus, and his voice was deep enough that a "Ho ho ho" would have been clichéd enough to be scary.

"Dave," Jeff said, leaning back in the recliner and letting the footrest come up and support his feet.

But, as usual, his gun got in the way. Damn. He stood up and removed the gun from his belt, paddle holster and all, and stuck it up high on a bookshelf behind him.

In his two years on the job, his handgun had never been anything but part of his uniform and an ongoing irritation and annoyance. Same thing had been true for all the years old John Honistead had held the job. A cop really didn't need a gun in Hardwood, but you carried it anyway.

It was part of the ritual that went with things like ticketing a speeder, more like the badge than anything else. Hell, whenever he had to put a car-struck deer or dog out of its misery, he went to the lever-action carbine in the trunk of his car, just to be sure it would be over quickly.

It would have been nice to be able to do without hauling the iron around.

He snickered. And this from somebody who had spent the afternoon stalking carefully through the woods, carrying a just-barely-legal short-barreled Mossberg shotgun, looking for wolf tracks?

Bob Aarsted's broad face threatened to split with a grin that revealed a shiny new gold cap on one of his front teeth, a very strange note in such a wide, Norski face. "You'd think that you professional peace officer types would learn to handle your shooting irons," he said.

There was a serious undertone in that that Jeff didn't much care for, but he didn't say anything. Not the time or the place for that. Bob was his father-in-law, after all, and if he had a problem with him he could take it up later, privately. There were some problems that had to be dealt with by the unofficial but very much de facto town council of Hardwood, but that wasn't one of them.

"And you'd think," Jeff said, "that somebody who has been driving as long as you would know that his side view mirror should be angled so that he can see what's behind him."

Minnie Hansen looked at him over her glasses. "That means, Bob, that Jeff accidentally knocked your van's mirror out of line," she said, eyeing him levelly for just a moment, not missing a stitch as her needles clicked. She was working on something blue and generally tubular—the arm of a sweater, perhaps?

Jeff nodded. "Guilty as charged. Sorry."

"Enh." Aarsted shrugged. "No problem. How is Kathy doing?"

"Fine, she's fine," Jeff said. It wasn't like Bob Aarsted didn't see his daughter almost every day. Hell, she was on the phone with her mother and her sisters so much that he was surprised she didn't have a divot in her shoulder from where she held it.

"Good. Dinner tomorrow?"

"It's Wednesday," he said, agreeing. Jeff liked the regularity. There was Wednesday supper at the Aarsteds; Sunday dinner with his parents, right after church. The first Monday after the first Tuesday of every month was the official town council meeting, followed by the unofficial bull session over at the Dine-a-mite. Women's Club on alternate Thursdays, which gave Kathy more time with her mom and sisters, and Scouts every Friday.

You tended to count your life with ticks of regularity in Hardwood, and while that wasn't for everybody, it suited Jeff Bjerke just fine.

"Am I the last?"

Minnie didn't look up. "Michael's late, but I don't think we should wait." She glanced up at the ceiling, as though she could see through it. It wouldn't have entirely surprised Jeff if she could; back when she was his second-grade teacher, she had apparently had eyes in the back of her head.

"Let's begin," she said, her voice carrying.

Doc Sherve and Thorian Thorsen trooped in from the kitchen, Dave Oppegaard trailing. For once, Thorsen seemed uncomfortable; he stood, uneasily, next to the fireplace, as though he felt like he didn't belong.

Well, normally he didn't.

"Okay." Doc Sherve set his coffee cup down in his usual spot next to the outflow. "Unless anybody's got something I don't know about, we've got five major items on the agenda tonight."

"Five," Minnie nodded.

"Well, do we take the obvious problem first, or last?" Aarsted asked, jerking a thumb toward the ceiling.

"Last," Dave Oppegaard said. "I'd be uncomfortable deciding on that without Michael."

Aarsted nodded, and took a last long swig from his coffee mug before setting it down, empty, on the coaster. He sat back and folded his hands over his ample belly. "Okay. Let's take the Peterson boy first."

Jeff nodded in agreement. "Yeah, we're going to have to do something, although I'm not sure what."

Doc Sherve's forehead wrinkled. "Which Peterson boy, and what's been happening?"

"Well . . ." the clicking of Minnie's knitting needles slowed. ". . . it's David Peterson, Brian and Etta's son, and he—"

"I thought he was at Macalester."

"Nope. He decided to go to Hoople instead." Jeff shook his head. Idiot. Macalester had offered him Early Decision, and he went to Hoople.

Minnie's mouth set itself in a straight line. "Barbara Ericson went to Hoople, as well."

"Yeah." You could only do so much to save somebody from his own stupidity. David had followed his girlfriend, and predictably, she had dumped him for an upperclassman—or, to hear the gossip, several upperclassmen—within the first couple of weeks. What hadn't been predictable was the depth of the tailspin he'd gone into.

"Well, I got a call from an old classmate of mine," Jeff said.

"You don't have old classmates, Jeff—you only graduated two years ago—"

"—who is now working Security, while he goes for his MSW."

"Really?" Doc grinned. "A cop-turned-social worker? I like it."

"Shhh." Minnie Hansen glared him to silence. "Go on, Jeff, please."

"Well, David's pretty well screwed himself up there. Got into a few fights—and got the shit kicked out of him in each and every one—and then flunked all his midterms, and didn't say a word to Brian or Etta about it."

This was the sort of thing that should be handled by the Petersons themselves—if they had two clues to rub together.

But they didn't. Assholes—they had always been more concerned with appearances than anything else. House always immaculate, kids always clean and well-dressed, schoolwork always in on time and never talk about problems with outsiders. Much better to cover over problems, and let them hide and fester in the dark?

No.

"Well, hell," Bob Aarsted said, "I don't see what the big deal is." He shrugged. "All he has to do is drop out before final exams, and come home. No grades, good or bad. Now, he probably can't get into Macalester this year, but next fall shouldn't be a problem—not with his SATs."

"You know what his SATs are?" Minnie Hansen raised an eyebrow. "Is this a special case, or do you try to memorize them all?"

"I am on the school board, after all, but no, I don't know the SATs of every kid in town—but I do go over the scores, and we don't get a lot of 1480s."

Thorian Thorsen did his best not to look smug as he stood, silently waiting. Torrie had done even better than that, and while Thorsen probably never did quite understand what the SATs were all about—although Jeff would have bet heavily that he knew what the numbers were—Thorsen did understand competition and winning better than most.

"The problem," Doc said, patiently, "is going to be with his parents. 'Uff dah! Oh, for shame, oh for disgraceful.' " He put the back of his hand to his forehead. " 'My son and heir has dropped out of school; surely the world will now end.' " Doc spread his hands. "I wouldn't put it past Brian to kick him out of the house."

"Yeah." Jeff sighed. "Throwaway kids are supposed to be a city problem."

"They are a city problem," Minnie Hansen sniffed. "And a city problem they'll remain. We, no, *I* won't have that, not here." Her voice was level, but she had put down her knitting, and her hands were clenched, knuckles white, in her lap.

"Well, of course not." Bob Aarsted shook his head. "But easier said than done, that is." He raised a hand to forestall an objection. "Still, yes, I know, everything is easier said than done, we've fostered kids before, and we can do it again. Sandy and Sven have a bit of an empty nest right now, and Sven can use another hand on the farm."

"Over the winter?"

"Sure." Aarsted nodded. "Wouldn't cost that much more to pay David to take care of the place and let him live there than it does to board the animals over at the Quists. And Sven's pretty much back on his feet since the harvest—had a good year, for once."

"He paid up?"

"Almost." Aarsted nodded. "With any luck he'll be clear by this time next year."

And the chances of him saying no to Bob—who had bullied the Hardwood S&L board to approve the loan that had saved Sven's farm four years before—were minimal.

That would be good. Sandy's parents had given them their usual Christmas present of tickets down for a month-long Florida vacation, and Jeff liked having farmhouses occupied. In town, it wasn't a problem, but unoccupied farmhouses had a tendency to draw trouble, and it wasn't just embarrassing but downright maddening when one of his people came home to a ransacked house, and worse if he couldn't identify the culprits—that would leave everybody a suspect, on one level or another.

"But how's Brian going to take that?" Aarsted shook his head. "Not well," he said, answering his own question. A big sigh came out with a whoosh.

Dave Oppegaard nodded. "I've always thought he'd be a better father—and a better Christian, for that matter—without that broom stuck up his ass." His eyes twinkled for a moment. Dave liked shocking people every now and then with a bit of coarse language. "Sounds like we need a sermon on the family this Sunday. Prodigal son and all that."

"You think that will do it?" Doc Sherve said, his tone and eyebrows making very clear that he didn't think that could possibly do it.

"No, I don't." Oppegaard puffed his pipe back to life. "On the other hand, if the church is packed, pews to rafters, and if everybody gives me something just this side of a standing ovation when I reach the crescendo, and when somebody points out to Brian Peterson that about half his accounting business is barely restraining itself from standing and clapping—well, I think he'll accept a word to the wise."

"And if not?"

Minnie Hansen had picked up her needles again. "And, if not," she said, her voice thin and icy, "he will lose all his local business, and he will move away, and be an object lesson to anybody else who forgets that we take care of our own." Her expression was unreadable. "And that would be a great disservice to Etta and the girls, as well as David, so you men had better be sure he listens." Her eyes rested on Jeff's.

Jeff nodded. Understood, Minnie.

She eyed Dave Oppegaard steadily. "And it hasn't escaped these ancient ears that, once again, your solution to a problem involved a church packed—floorboards to rafters, is that the phrase?—to hear you speak."

Oppegaard nibbled at his coffee cake. "Guilty as charged. Let's move on."

*   *   *

From the Peterson problem, they moved to the school bond issue, and then the ongoing difficulties with the Svenson clan, and Jeff found his mind wandering until Doc Sherve jerked his thumb toward the ceiling.

"We've got two sleeping up there. One's Ian Silverstein; he's just got a wrenched shoulder, and he's sleeping off some Demerol. The other," Sherve said, with a shake of his head, "well, the other is what Thorian says is a vestri, Ian calls a dwarf, and I think looks like a Neanderthal. It—he came out of the same damn hole the Sons popped up out of."

"Who has seen this Neanderthal, this . . . vestri?" Minnie asked.

"Well, I have, if you've any doubts." Sherve's mouth twitched.

"That was not what I meant, Robert."

Sherve accepted her correction—it was as close to an apology as he would get—with a nod. "So far, not a lot of folks. Me, the Thorsens, Ian, Donna, and Martha. But—"

Minnie interrupted him with a sniff. "I don't see that as a serious problem; a closer-mouthed bunch it would be rather hard to find."

"But, as I was saying before I was interrupted, during the two minutes it took to get him from the examining room and into my car, that was the time that Orphie Hansen had to wake up and stagger out into the hall." He spread his hands. "Donna hurried him back into his room, and I don't think he noticed anything, but . . ."

Minnie cocked her head to one side. "So why bring the vestri here? Why not just call Grand Forks General, and have them send out an ambulance? It's not like he's one of our people. I'd like to be able to stand guard over the whole wide world, but we can't. We're . . . just a small town, trying to keep its business to itself."

Aarsted nodded. "I don't see the problem, not really. Maybe he got shoved out of a car on the county road. Nobody saw the license plate." He spread his hands. "You told me he doesn't even speak English."

"No," Dave Oppegaard said, shaking his head. "Bob

told you that he doesn't appear to speak English."

Thorian Thorsen shifted uneasily on his feet, but Reverend Oppegaard and Doc Sherve and Minnie Hansen were so involved in the friendly bickering that flowed around them constantly that they didn't notice.

"Excuse me. I think Thorian has something he wants to say," Jeff said.

"Well, then, speak up, Thorian," Minnie Hansen said. "Don't just stand there with your mouth open; if you have something to say, well then, say it."

"He—Valin is his name. Valin, son of Durin, he claims to be."

"That means something?"

Thorsen pursed his mouth—a thoughtful expression, fairly rare for Thorian Thorsen—and then furrowed his brow. "Perhaps. Perhaps not. Both of those are very old names; the Folk always have more than a few Valins and Dvalins and Durins in every family and clan, in each generation. But when Thorian and Maggie and I went in search of Ian and Hosea, we were helped by a vestri named Durin, who claimed a particularly ancient lineage. And this one says that his father had him sent through the Hidden Ways to warn me that Sons have again been sent after my blood."

"And this father? Does he owe you such a blood-debt?" Minnie asked.

"No." Thorsen shook his head. "He may think he does, but if he and his did owe me and mine, the debt was long ago paid, and paid doubly." He looked from face to face. "But that does not obligate any of you."

"Stop talking nonsense," Minnie said. "Of course it does. I don't have to like it, but of course it does, as a matter of practicality, forgetting ethics for a moment."

Dave Oppegaard nodded. "And if it's impractical to abandon this . . . vestri to the authorities, then we don't need to concern ourselves with whether or not it's permissible."

It was strange for a Lutheran minister to prefer to dismiss something on practical, rather than moral, grounds, but that was the way Dave was.

He pulled the plastic tube back down from the Nutone

wall panel with one hand as he fumbled for his pipe with the other; he had sat in that battered leather chair often enough that he didn't have to look for the vacuum panel any more than he had to look for his pipe.

Doc Sherve snorted. "Well, I'm glad of that," he said. "Because I'd have an ethical problem with dumping one of my patients on a bunch of folks who wouldn't have the slightest idea what to do with him."

"Oh?" Oppegaard raised an eyebrow as he puffed his pipe back to life. The Nutone sucked the smoke silently away into the wall. "And you do?"

"Yeah." Sherve nodded. "You know of any other physician who has treated any nonhumans?"

"I do," Minnie Hansen said. "Dr. MacMurtry, over in Hatton."

"Minnie." Sherve looked at her over his glasses. "Minnie, he's a veterinarian."

Bob Aarsted laughed. "Yeah, not one of those narrow specialists."

"Valin is closer to human than anything Mac's treated, and he's my patient. Ever hear of the Hippocratic oath?"

"Yes, in fact, I have heard of it. But are you sure that applies to vestri?" Oppegaard puffed thoughtfully away for a moment, watching the smoke being sucked away down the tube, and away.

"Shit, Dave, it applies to dogs, in spirit."

"But not in letter." His eyes went vague for a moment. " 'Whatever I see or hear'—and here's the part I like—'in the life of men, which ought not to be spoken of abroad, I will not divulge, as reckoning that all such should be kept secret.' " Oppegaard nodded. "Father Olsen over in Hatton doesn't have anything on you, eh?"

"You left out a few words. But are you saying that we can and should throw that little man out into the cold just because he's not human?"

Oppegaard shook his head. "No, I'm saying nothing of the sort. What I am saying is that, as usual, we've got to figure out what it is that makes sense to do, and not just try to find some rule to apply to it." He sighed. "Because when you go looking for rules, there's always too damn many of them." He raised a palm. "And I don't particularly need to hear—again—how strange that is coming from a minister's mouth."

Jeff Bjerke nodded. That was the trouble with the rest of the world—it had long since gone rules-happy.

Jeff didn't have anything against rules, not in themselves. But he didn't sign on to this insanity everywhere else had gotten itself into, where the rules counted more than the substance.

That wasn't the way you did things, not in Hardwood. Taking care of your own wasn't something you had to do because it was written in a rule book somewhere; it was something you did because you just had to, and if the rules got in the way of that, well, then, the rules be damned.

That same Hippocratic oath would have prevented Doc from giving thirteen-year-old Lilly Norstedt an abortion, and the law would have required that he either get permission from her father—the man who had made her pregnant; her mother—the woman who had ignored what had been going on under her own roof; or find some judge who would more likely than not have made everything all public.

But you took care of your own. And if that meant pretending to believe that Mel Norstedt had actually lost his balance and fallen into the swine pen while feeding the pigs, well, then you did that, too, and told the busybodies for the State Police that if they wanted to do a full autopsy, they would have to start by slaughtering a dozen pigs, and besides, the deputy medical examiner had signed off on the death certificate anyway, and in case they didn't know, Doc Sherve was a living legend in these parts . . .

The clicking of Minnie Hansen's needles stopped, and all eyes in the room turned toward her.

Her lips curved in a rare smile, but she raised her coffee cup in answer to the silence, then took a sip.

"Thorian," she said, "we're not disposed to throw anybody to these wolves—or any wolves—and we're not going to. So," she said, setting down her coffee cup and picking up her knitting, "stop shuffling around like a second-grader that has to go to the potty, and sit down."

She punctuated that last with a particularly loud click of her needles. "I don't much like craning my neck."

Oppegaard turned to Jeff. "Well?"

Jeff shook his head. "Well, we've got two extra men on duty at the Hidden Way, just in case. That was the first thing I did. I spent the rest of the day driving and scouting around, trying to find some tracks. Scared up an eight-point buck, and I think I know a real good place for a tree stand that nobody's been using lately, but no sign of wolf at all."

"Is that good or bad?" Doc Sherve asked.

Jeff wasn't sure whether Doc meant it rhetorically. "I wish I knew." Of course, Sons could change into human form, but he hadn't seen any signs of barefoot humans, either. Nor much of anything.

Jeff would have shivered, but the Law wasn't supposed to look scared.

Minnie pursed her lips for a moment. "The last snow was four days ago. So it would either have to be before that, or he's not here yet."

"Or I missed it."

"Just what I was thinking," Doc Sherve said, with a too broad used-car-salesman's smile, "but I was too polite to mention it."

Jeff nodded. "I've considered that. Sven Hansen is bringing his snowmobile into town tonight; he'll be staying with us." He glanced at his watch. "In fact, Kathy should be feeding him supper right about now."

Aarsted chuckled. "Hope she roasted an extra chicken, and baked another pie." Sven's appetite was legendary. And then he nodded. "But that's a good idea."

Sven was probably the most accomplished hunter in Hardwood, and was one of the few who made a habit of tracking deer, rather than finding a good place for a stand and waiting for game to come by. That was a risky proposition for most people, but Jeff had never heard of Sven failing to get his deer.

"At sunrise, he's going to take the north side of town while I take the south side." There was no point in staggering around in the dark, even if there was no danger out there. And it was a particularly good idea not to be staggering around in the dark if there was danger out there.

"No. Not good enough." Ian Silverstein stood, unsteadily, in the doorway.

He was dressed in an old gray terry cloth robe, ragged at the hem, tied at the waist with a preposterously bright red sash. His left arm was concealed in the robe, and the opening at the chest showed that it had been bound to his side by some sort of stretch bandage.

Hosea, moving quickly, was at his side. "Ian, you should be resting."

Ian shook his head. "No, not now." His face was pale and wan. "You didn't hear Valin. I did."

Jeff nodded. "Yes, but—"

"He didn't say that the Sons were after Thorian. He said that they were after his blood."

So? It—

Shit. He should have seen it. "Torrie."

Thorian Thorsen had already picked up the wall phone, and was dialing a number.

It was a long time before he shook his head.

"No answer."

Shit. Thorsen turned to Ian and muttered something, then carefully clapped his hand to Ian's good shoulder before turning back toward the council.

Thorian Thorsen drew himself up straight. "By your leave," he said. His voice had a formal tone in it that Jeff had never heard before.

Double shit. Thorsen was just going to walk out and drive to Minneapolis. He could almost get away with doing that, too—Jeff wasn't sure exactly what the Thorsens kept in the emergency kits they had in their car, but between that and a credit card or two, Thorsen really could be ready to leave for an extended trip at a moment's notice, or without any notice at all.

But hell, Thorian Thorsen left the Hardwood area only very rarely and reluctantly, and he would be like a fish out of water in the big city.

"Just you wait a minute, Thorian Thorsen," Minnie Hansen said. "You're braver than you are smart. Which wouldn't be all that difficult."

"She's right, Thorian." Sherve nodded. "You're going to need some help."

Bob Aarsted looked over at Jeff and nodded. He'd worked it out, too.

"Yeah." Jeff rose from his chair. "It's going to have to be me."

Thorsen wouldn't obey posted speed limits, not in this situation, but Jeff's badge would get them out of any of that sort of problem—particularly if he was driving. Town cop didn't pay awfully well, but there were a few side benefits, and no speeding tickets was one of them.

And if they were going to try to track a Son through city streets, Thorsen would need not only some help but also somebody who could, at least possibly, get them out of at least minor trouble with the local authorities.

Thorsen couldn't stand a search; Jeff could. In practice, if not in theory, his badge and ID would work as a carry permit pretty much everywhere, but if Thorsen was caught carrying a gun, his North Dakota permit wouldn't keep him out of a Minnesota jail.

Thorsen nodded. "Very well. We leave in five minutes." He turned and left the room. His footsteps made no sound at all as he walked quickly out of sight.

Bob Aarsted held up his right hand. "I'll cover for you with your wife, son," he said, anticipating the question Jeff was about to ask.

"I'd appreciate it if you'd get her to move in with you and Ellen while I'm gone." He was going to have to worry enough about his own back; worrying about Kathy sitting alone in their house with wolves maybe prowling around town again, well, that didn't have any appeal at all.

"Done. And I can be spared from the store for a while—better deputize me."

That would do for the moment, at least. Jeff would have to get on the phone to the Staties, and get it made official, just in case Bob would have to do anything official.

But in the interim . . . he pulled his keys out of his pocket and tossed them to Aarsted. "There's a couple of spare badges in my top right-hand desk drawer."

He thought for a moment, took his holstered pistol down

from the bookshelf, and handed it, holster and all, to
Aarsted, then pulled a speedloader out of his pocket and
gave him that, too. Aarsted removed the pistol from the
holster, opened the cylinder to make sure it was loaded,
then closed it gently—not flicking it shut like they always
did on TV—before he slid it back into the holster.

Doc Sherve raised an eyebrow. "You don't think you'll
need a gun?"

Minnie Hansen sniffed. "Thorian Thorsen is probably
loading half of Smith & Wesson's catalog into a bag right
now."

"I'll call when I know something," Jeff said, and went
to get his coat.

CHAPTER FIVE

~~

Scent of a Son

The trouble with any sort of construction project, big or small, was that there was always more to it than appeared at first blush. Anybody except Uncle Hosea quickly learned to allow—at the very least—a full day for an easy half-day job, and God Forbid you should plan a Saturday project without leaving Sunday open and hoping and praying that you'd be done before Monday.

So while Torrie had guessed that they would be able to finish the disassembly last night, he wasn't really surprised to find himself flat on his back, a chisel in his hand, the next morning.

What the hell; he wasn't complaining. He always slept better after sex, and he slept better with Maggie than alone, as though the back of his mind was more willing to shut down and rest when he wasn't alone, and if there was a better way to wake up in the morning than with Maggie in his arms and the smell of hot coffee in his nose, well, it was probably illegal.

Stickley buffets were put together like jigsaw puzzles, pieces joined with interlocking grooves that required only the smallest amount of glue to hold them together, solidly, forever. They'd been built to last, not just to hold together until they'd been bumped into a couple of times.

Too bad that nobody had thought to build them with some miracle varnish that would repel three goddamn layers of goddamn paint applied by some goddamn drooling idiot during the goddamn '50s who thought that old dark mahogany would look so much goddamn better if only it was the color of some goddamn shade of yellow plastic.

What was it with the '50s, anyway? Those were supposed to be lighthearted times, like on *Happy Days*. Why couldn't anybody build anything right then? And it was worse than that—not only had those idiots not built anything worth building but in addition they had screwed up things that had been done right.

Torrie wasn't at all sure he believed that *If you don't have something nice to say, don't say anything at all*, but he was sure he believed in *If you can't make it better, don't fuck with it*. Something that the idiot who had painted over this clearly didn't.

What a pain in the ass. You had to scrape with exquisite care around the joints, because you didn't want to damage the wood any more than necessary, and you really didn't want to do anything to the wood that would show worse than a thin scratch that could easily be sanded out.

The idea was to restore the woodwork, not to rebuild it, after all. You couldn't get old-growth wood any more, and while there was a beauty to the new stuff, it looked different.

He was lying on his back, having squirmed his torso halfway into the built-in so he could get at a troublesome joint, when the dog started barking outside.

The landlord had a dog, a Welsh corgi with short little legs that made it look like it would be a normal dog if ever it stood up, but it was a reasonably quiet animal, and not all that yappy the way little dogs all too often were.

"Torrie?" Maggie had heard it, too.

"Yeah," he said. He had spent too long in the city; if he'd been home, he would have been on his feet, already checking it out.

"Give me a hand, eh?" he asked, accepting Maggie's

help out and up. She was, he had long since discovered, stronger than she looked.

He hooked his arms around her waist and pulled her to him, intending a quick kiss and grope—there should be time enough for that, after all. She didn't quite push him away, but she just gave him a quick pat. "Later. Let's go see what Eustis is yapping about."

He followed her into the kitchen and to the back door overlooking the porch. From there, he could see out into the backyard, although there wasn't much to see. The high wooden fence was probably pretty when it was all ivy-covered in summer, but now it just looked like it had loose string scattered all over it. And the flowerbeds and planters were covered with snow, as was the ground.

He could still hear the dog, but he couldn't see him, or her or it. But it wasn't happy.

Probably directly underneath.

"I'll go check it out," he said, and tapped a finger against the wall phone. "In case anything interesting happens, call 911."

"You don't want me to come with?" Her face was impassive, no trace of accusation on it. She was deferring to him, and she didn't usually do that.

"No," he said, deciding. "If there's a problem . . ."

"I call 911. And I shout out the window that I'm calling 911."

"Good."

There wasn't a stairway going down the back, just a chain-link fire ladder in a box bolted to the wall. But the back stairs led to a door that opened on the backyard.

Torrie closed the apartment's back door behind him and waited until he heard the dead bolt slide home. He dug his knife out of his pocket as he walked down the stairs and held it in his right hand.

It was probably paranoid, but what the heck, sometimes paranoids run into trouble, too. And besides, the knife concealed in his hand just fine, and while its spring-loaded blade was probably technically illegal—what were the local laws on automatic knives? Torrie had never bothered to find out—a hidden catch could disable the spring, permitting it to be opened conventionally, too.

But right now, all it would take would be a thumb press on the hidden release, and four inches of steel would spring out faster than the eye could follow. He snicked the blade open once, to test, then closed it.

And if that seemed paranoid, well, so be it. At least it didn't look as paranoid as carrying his sword would.

The door to the yard was still properly dead-bolted, although with the window right there in the middle of the door all it would take would be a quick rap of the butt of a flashlight to shatter the glass and let some burglar reach a hand in and open the dead bolt.

It was amazing how much you could find wrong with an apartment building's security when you didn't want your girlfriend living there.

He unbolted the door and turned the knob. It rattled, loose in its collar, then gave. But the door was stuck, frozen shut; it took his shoulder against the door, just inside the glass, to break it free.

It swung out easily, and Torrie came out with it, his feet sliding on the packed snow.

The calf-high dog ran up to him, its little feet sliding on the snowy ground, and then it dashed into the building, leaving behind nothing but skittering noises and wet footprints on the concrete basement floor. Torrie was alone in the garden.

He stepped out to where Maggie could see him, and waved.

Nothing.

Whatever had frightened Eustis—and it had clearly frightened the shit out of the little dog—was gone, leaving behind nothing.

Well, maybe not frightened the shit out of it—there was no fresh dog turd in the back, but the dog had pissed in its fear and flight; the doorpost of the gate leading out into the alley was steaming.

No, wait. That didn't make any sense.

Firstly, Torrie was pretty sure that the dog was female, and bitches didn't mark their territory with a lifted leg; and besides, they weren't built for it. And secondly, an animal fleeing in terror wouldn't stop to mark its domain at all. It would have had to—

Torrie sniffed the air. The smell was there again, this time stronger and more distinctive.

He squatted down in front of the gate, rubbed his finger on it, and sniffed it.

Holy shit.

He backed away from the gate, wishing that he had eyes in the back of his head, and turned, scanning the enclosed backyard.

No, he was alone. There was an old closet door leaning up against the north side of the fence, but nothing of any size could be hiding in there.

To the dog, it probably smelled like wolf urine, which would frighten any dog to all hell. But there was an extra acrid note, one that Torrie remembered all too well.

It wasn't a dog. It was a Son.

Holy shit.

He didn't remember when he had pressed the release on the knife, but it felt small and ineffectual in his hand as he walked backwards, toward the door, then closed and dead-bolted it behind him.

Holy shit.

He ran up the stairs and knocked on the door twice, then twice again; the bolt slid back instantly.

Her eyes went wide when she saw his expression and the open knife in his hand. "What's wrong? Are you okay?"

"We've got a problem," he said.

He set the knife down on the kitchen counter and turned on the water, scrubbing hard at his left index finger, where he had touched the urine, as though making the smell go away would make it all go away.

There was a Son of Fenris in town, and Torrie didn't believe for a moment that it was coincidence that had made it choose Maggie's backyard to piss in.

Damn it all.

The water was cold, but that wasn't why Torrie Thorsen found himself shivering.

CHAPTER SIX

Night Moves

The drugs coursing sluggishly through his muddy bloodstream had dragged blurry cobwebs across Ian Silverstein's mind, but he couldn't sleep any more. At least not real sleep. He just kept drifting . . .

. . . in and out, waking only occasionally to reach down to the floor next to his bed and feel for Giantkiller's hilt.

He lay back in a blank timelessness that distantly reminded him of the Hidden Ways.

Whatever it was that Doc had given him took more than the edge off the pain in his shoulder—if it wasn't for the way his arm was Ace-bandaged against his chest and into immobility, he probably would have tried to use it—but it also messed with his time sense. Each eyeblink could last only a second, or for several hours. How long had he been lying here, staring at the ceiling? And when had the blue Depression glass pitcher of water beside his bed been replaced by a plastic one?

Consciousness doubled back on itself. He was only vaguely aware that he was aware, and only dimly conscious of that. The sheets beneath his back had been damp and clammy from sweat for some time, and his mouth was dry and metal tasting.

It took more effort than he would have thought it would, but thirst drove him to sit up and sip at the plastic glass of cold water that had just a few slivers of ice in it. When he looked at the old Big Ben alarm clock near the head of his bed, it was just a little past four, and only a sliver of black peeked through the opening in the thick green drapes that covered the window.

Night came early this time of year.

Okay, so he had been sleeping most of the previous twenty or so hours, waking only to follow Doc's instruction to take any pill left on the nightstand. Presumably, Hosea or Karin was coming up every few hours to leave whatever Doc had prescribed.

But, shit, he had just wrenched his shoulder, not taken a bullet or anything, and he more than half-suspected that Doc Sherve had put him on a diet of narcotics more to keep him from moving around than anything else.

He ought to be doing more than just moving around. What he ought to be doing was grabbing Giantkiller and a pack, and then dropping down into the Hidden Way beneath the Thorsen house.

It stood to reason. If—and it was a big if—Thorsen and Jeff Bjerke could track down the Son or Sons who were stalking Torrie, that only stopped the problem for the moment.

You don't stop a snake, after all, by whittling away at the tail. And you don't stop the Sons of Fenris from sending some of their number after people you cared about without stopping it at the source.

The source was in Tir Na Nog. But it was too hard to think, what with the warm glow of Demerol, and Vistaril, and Percodan, and God-knew-what in his brain. It was much easier to lie back than it was to think, and it was even easier to drift off than it was to lie back.

The narcotics interfered with his sense of time, but his kidneys had their own schedule, with his bladder their own alarm clock—and it was tight as a drum, painfully so. Moving like he imagined a pregnant woman would, he levered himself out of bed and shivered for a moment in the cold air until he could slip the oversized terry cloth robe over his shoulders and right arm. He held it together like an old dowager clutching a mink stole as he more staggered than padded down the dimly lit hall toward where a band of bright light leaked out at the base of the bathroom door.

The door was closed, and there were sounds of rushing water inside.

Now, that was strange. The Thorsen parents each had their own bathroom off the master bedroom, and Hosea had his own downstairs. The only time any of them would need to use this one was when they wanted a bath instead of a shower, and it didn't take Sherlock Holmes to figure out that they were shower people and not bath people, because they would have had more than one bathtub in the house if they weren't. The hot tub in the backyard went largely unused, as such things usually did.

Stop worrying so much, he told himself. The notion that the Thorsens would have another visitor or guest using the john in the middle of the afternoon should hardly have his hand itching for Giantkiller's hilt.

The brass doorknob rattled loosely in its collar, then turned slowly, hesitantly, and eased silently open.

Valin stood in the doorway, his eyes probably no wider than Ian's own.

He looked like shit. His normally swarthy skin was pale as skim milk, and one thick but trembling hand clutched his robe to his belly, probably more to hold his guts in than to hold his robe shut. Steri-strips were spread in a fan across the right side of his face, holding a half-dozen wounds together, and drool had caked at the corners of his thick, fleshy lips. His eyes had trouble focusing, and he leaned against the doorframe for balance or support, or probably both.

But the amazing thing about the dancing bear is not how gracefully he dances but that he dances at all: it was a wonder that Valin was alive, and a miracle on the order of the parting of the Red Sea that he could stand.

"Ian Silver Stone," Valin said, dropping to his knees,

"this one prays that he has not disturbed thy rest."

"To thy feet, Son of Vestri," Ian said, as he took a step forward and grabbed hold of the dwarf's free hand with his uninjured hand. It was like squeezing a side of beef—the muscles under Valin's skin were thick and strong.

But the dwarf came quickly to his feet anyway, supporting himself as he did, not pulling even a little on Ian's arm.

Which was just as well; Ian slumped against the wall. He probably shouldn't have been trying to move so quickly, not with his head full of narcotics.

Running feet pounded on the floor below and then thudded quickly up the stairs.

"What do you think you are doing?" Martha Sherve said.

Ian started to make some comment about how if she'd actually been a nurse as long as she said she had been, she'd have seen a patient on the way to or from a bathroom before, but the thought shriveled and died in the cold heat of her glare.

"I was just helping him, Mrs. Sherve," he said. "I heard something—"

"There's an intercom box on the nightstand beside your bed. I take it you're going to claim you were too loopy to remember me telling you to use that if you needed anything."

Well, any port in a storm. That probably was what it was. "Sure," he said with a nod. "That's it."

"Then how come you remember that now?" She sniffed, then wrinkled her nose. "Back to bed with the both of you; I'll clean things up in here and be along with another shot for you."

Before Ian could say so much as a word, Martha Sherve had her left arm around Valin's waist and his thick right arm levered over her shoulders, and had him halfway down the hall toward the guest room that the Thorsens called the Sewing Room, to distinguish it from the guest room that they called the Guest Room.

Ian could have followed her to argue, but discretion was the better part of valor, after all, and hydraulic pressure reminded him that his bladder was getting no emptier standing here. He closed and locked the bathroom door behind him and flicked on the light switch. With a high-pitched tinkling of flickering fluorescents and a low whirrrr of a hidden motor, the lights and fan came on.

The bathroom was spotless, as though it hadn't been used, well, ever—at least not since its last cleaning. And the roll of toilet paper . . . ? The free end had been folded into an intricate shape, sort of like what Ian had seen in some hotel—the Hyatt, maybe? Except there it had just been folded into a triangle; this looked like a piece of origami.

It would feel like a minor but real sacrilege to disturb that; it was just as well that he only had to take a leak, he thought, suiting action to thought. And just as well that a stream of urine couldn't overflow a modern toilet.

Yes, *And I've told you a billion times not to exaggerate.*

There was a quiet knock on the door.

"Ian?" Karin Thorsen's voice was pitched carefully, as though she feared being overheard. Which was strange?

"Yes?" Ian rearranged his robe and tied it hurriedly, then opened the door.

Why was Karin Thorsen standing there in her pajamas and robe, her long hair tied back for sleep?

One fugitive strand caressed her cheek. Ian didn't blame it.

Ian took a halting step forward. "Is everything okay?" he asked.

She grinned crookedly.

"That is just what I was going to ask you," Karin said. "I don't normally get up in the middle of the night," she went on, "but I heard you and Martha Sherve talking, and I wanted to be sure that all was well."

Middle of the night? Ian's head spun. He had either been sleeping a lot longer, or a lot shorter, than he had thought.

"Shorter," she said with a smile, as though she could read his mind, something he sincerely hoped she couldn't.

In Ian's view, you weren't responsible for what you thought—only for what you said and did. Not the way he had been raised, of course; George Orwell could have taken lessons from Ben Silverstein on the subject of thought-crime. There might be something psychologically perverted about being hot for a friend's mother, but he could live with that. What he couldn't live with was letting her use that to manipulate him again. He had known what she was doing last time, but it hadn't mattered. It was like with Freya; except, of course, that he knew he could trust Freya, and he knew he couldn't trust Karin Thorsen. To her, he was expendable, particularly in comparison with her son and her husband.

He knew that she liked him, and he had the distinct sensation that the sexual attraction was mutual, although what she would see in a tall, skinny geek like him was one of those woman-things that he had to take on faith because it never did make any sense.

But like him or not, she would gladly slit his belly and dump his guts into a basin if her son's or her husband's feet needed warming.

Unless, of course, he concentrated and persuaded her otherwise, letting the heavy golden ring on his finger pulse an indictment of himself as a scumbag. It would be a particularly safe form of rape, and Karin would think she had consented, as in fact she would have . . .

But what you felt and what you thought was your own damn business, as long as you goddamn kept it to your goddamn self.

"Do you think you're going to go right back to sleep?" she asked.

"Yeah," he said, after a moment. Then he changed his mind and shook his head. "No, I'd better not. I'm feeling groggy from too much sleep as it is."

And probably from too much Percocet or Percodan or Percodammit, as well as whatever other drugs were coursing their way through his system. His shoulder ached, true enough, but he hardly needed to have been taking so much painkiller. It wasn't like he'd just had his belly opened, or something. He'd royally wrenched his shoulder, and there certainly was a sore spot where he had hit his head, but what he needed now was probably more food and exercise than sleep and drugs.

"Coffee?" She smiled perhaps a touch shyly.

"I . . . don't think so," he said. At four in the morning? he didn't say. Still, it was probably best to stay up, anyway, and try and get some semblance of a regular sleep rhythm going again.

"You are due another Percocet. You can wash it down with some coffee and a piece of coffee cake."

"I'll pass on the Percocet, but come to think of it, maybe I will take you up on that coffee." He forced a grin. "Better yet, I'll show you how we make coffee in the city." He frowned. "After I get dressed."

After we both get dressed, he thought. He was far too conscious of the fact that there were only two layers of cloth and sensible inhibitions between them. Not that he would do anything, but he would worry about doing something.

"Your clothes are on the old bureau," she said. "Except for the socks; you can take a pair of Torrie's."

He was a little surprised to find Hosea down in the kitchen, sitting at the table over a steaming cup of coffee and a plate piled high with bacon, toast, and four eggs, sunny-side up, that made the plate look like a pair of Siamese twins staring up at Ian. Although Ian didn't know why he should be; Hosea didn't need much sleep, and when the two of them had been on the road together, Hosea had been up before Ian almost all the time.

Hosea poured thick cream from the pink Depression glass creamer until, by accident or design, the coffee was exactly the same shade of brown as the hand holding the creamer. "Good morning, Ian Silver Stone," he said. "You slept long; I hope you slept well."

"I haven't checked the scoreboard," Ian said. "But I think my inner demons finally won in sudden death overtime."

For a moment, Hosea's dark face creased puzzlement, but then the wrinkles in his forehead smoothed, and his tight lips loosened into a smile that revealed teeth white as good ivory. "Ah. Very funny."

Then why is neither of us laughing? Ian sat down gingerly in the chair opposite and poured himself a cup of coffee from the carafe. It was hot and strong, just as he liked it, not the thin, weak stuff everybody in Hardwood seemed to drink by the quart. "You made coffee?"

"No," came Karin's voice from the archway that led to the dining room. "I did." She was in her usual sort of outfit of plaid shirt and jeans, a common way of dressing around here, particularly in the winter, for people of both sexes. But, Ian had long since noticed, most of the clothes were not cut to fit quite so tightly, with just enough give to make them look comfortable.

And, of course, he thought, half-trying not to watch as she stretched up to bring coffee cake down from the top of the fridge, few women in Hardwood or elsewhere would have filled out the jeans quite so interestingly.

And if you can get your mind off your friend's mom's admittedly terrific ass, maybe you can figure out how to get out of doing what you know damn well she's going to try to talk you into doing.

She cut two large pieces and one small one, barely more than a sliver, and set each down on a piece of Royal Copenhagen china—part of a much better set than the Flora Danica that Benjamin Silverstein had spent an improbably large amount of money on. She set a plate down at each of their places before sitting down herself. Ian and Karin and Hosea had each picked up a piece of coffee cake and taken a nibble before Ian started chuckling.

Karin raised an eyebrow. "Oh?"

He waved a hand, dismissing it. "Never mind."

"Is this something that the whole class can share?" she asked, insisting.

No point in arguing about it. "It's nothing much," he said. "It just struck me as funny that we're eating with our fingers off of fine china."

It took her a moment to get it, and then she laughed, a sound of distant silver bells that almost painfully reminded him of Marta. "I guess it's just a matter of what you're used to," she said. "I mean, I know of people in the city who have rooms in their house with fancy furniture covered in clear plastic, and nobody ever sits, much less lives."

Ian nodded. He'd had a girlfriend, once, whose parents had had a living room like that. He'd actually thought it was kind of sweet, if a bit strange.

"There's a lot of people in the city like that," he said. "In the city you find a lot of people who say what they don't mean. Out here, you find a lot of people who don't say what they do mean."

"Oh?"

"Oh, like, 'I could eat' doesn't just mean that whoever is saying it could eat; what it really does mean is anything from 'I'm kind of hungry' to 'Thank you for bringing that up; I was about to chew my own arm off.' "

All three of them laughed. "Or," he found himself saying, "when somebody says, 'Would you like coffee and coffee cake?' what she really means is 'How can I talk you into going to Tir Na Nog, again, to stop the Sons from killing my son?' "

The room was suddenly quiet. Both Hosea and Karin sat motionless, utterly still. Ian heard the long, low whistle of a train approaching a crossing off in the distance. Which meant that he didn't need to look at the clock to know that it was 5:35 and that the Soo Line twice-daily was just passing to the north of town. He held her eyes unblinking for what felt like an hour, although one corner of his mind kept counting pulse beats and only got to twenty-five.

She opened her mouth, swallowed hard, then swallowed hard again. "I don't have the right," she said, her voice barely above a whisper, "to take offense at that." She folded her fingers in front of her on the table, interlocking them until her knuckles were bone white, like the china. "I lost that right when I talked you out of taking my husband along with you, when Hosea needed to be brought to Tir Na Nog."

Hosea nodded, like a judge pounding a gavel in judgment. "And so you did, Karin," he said, his voice gentle as always. "But you do take offense, don't you?"

"No." She shook her head. "No."

"Well," Ian said, "you're right. It makes sense." He wanted to work his shoulder, to see how it was healing, but that would have been stupid, so he didn't. He tried to limit himself to doing one stupid thing at a time, and what he was about to say was precisely as stupid as walking through a mine field. Which is to say perhaps very stupid, perhaps not stupid at all. But not safe, regardless. "It makes sense."

"Ian." Hosea leaned forward. "She is telling the truth. She does not want you to go."

Yeah, sure. And I'm the fucking Queen of the May.

"No. Please listen to me, Ian. Please don't go. Not now. Not with Thorian away. He'll—" she caught herself and closed her eyes tightly for a moment. "He won't believe me," she said. "He'll think I talked you into it."

"Why would he think that?" Ian asked. "Just because you did just that not six months ago?" The trouble was, still, that her arguments had made sense. And they made more sense this time. "But never mind that. I can explain things to Thorian. He can't come with me, not where I'm going."

Hosea nodded sagely. "The Dominions, of course."

"The Fire Duke." Ian folded his hands in his lap. "I think I can call on him for the return of a favor," he said.

He fondled the heavy ring on his finger. It would not disturb Ian's sense of morality to use the ring to persuade His Warmth to help him out. Not one whit, considering that the present Fire Duke owed his position to Ian's having killed the imposter who had replaced and impersonated His Warmth's father. And the dukes of the Dominions were known to have solid working relationships with at least some of the Sons of Fenris.

It was hardly a detailed strategy, but it was, at least, the beginning of a plan.

Hosea nodded again. "You seem to have thought this through," he said, placing his palms on the table and making as though to rise.

"I'll manage."

"I suppose I had best get to packing."

"No." Ian gestured him back into his seat. "I can't take you for the same reason that I can't take Thorian. You've got too much history over there, the both of you."

In the Dominions, Thorian Thorsen was known as Thorian the Traitor. Yes, Ian might—might—be able to trade some official gratitude for unofficial pardon. But he wouldn't be able to trade away the anger and the resentment of the Duelist's Guild, the House of Steel, as they called it. And he most certainly couldn't count on the support of Thorian del Orvald, the Duelmaster, because Thorian del Orvald was Thorian Thorsen's father, and he could no more let familial affection stand in his way than any other ruler could, even though the territory the Duelmaster ruled was a corner of his society, not real estate.

But Ian wasn't arrogant enough to think he was ready to take on Tir Na Nog alone. He would have liked to have had Arnie Selmo with him, but Arnie Selmo wasn't available. Torrie would have been fine, but he wasn't available, either. He might even have settled for Maggie—she really wasn't all that good with a sword, not by Ian's standards—but people didn't expect a girl to be even as adequate as Maggie was.

But she wasn't available either.

For a moment, he played with the idea of seeing if he could enlist Marta's brother, but he realized that would only be an excuse to travel to Vandescard and see Marta. It wasn't just the hunger for the taste of her lips on his, for the warmth and supple strength of her body at night, but that was part of it.

And while the Thorsen men could afford to think with their dicks, that was a luxury that Ian had never been permitted.

There was only one more candidate . . . "So I'll take Valin," he said.

Karin Thorsen's eyes went wide. "Valin? He's just this side of death."

"No, not really." Hosea pursed his lips together thoughtfully. "He was," he said, "but dwarves heal rapidly. That which doesn't kill them won't keep them down for long." His right hand, as usual, lay limp in his lap, but somehow or other he managed to eat the coffee cake without dropping so much as a crumb on his lap or the table. Ian wished he knew how Hosea did that.

Hosea turned to him. "You'll take the Hidden Way from

the clearing," he said. "If you don't look for hidden turns, you'll likely emerge at the place where the Sons brought Thorian and his family, only a few days from the Southern Pass, even at a fairly slow pace."

Ian frowned. "I was hoping you knew a way that could bring us directly back to Falias." The Hidden Way from Falias emerged in the clearing; there should be some way to take it back to Falias.

"I'm sorry." Hosea shook his head, sadly. "I'm sure there is a way," he said, tapping a long forefinger against his temple. "But I couldn't tell you what it is." His jaw clenched for just a moment, and his cheek muscles stood out in sharp relief. "There was a time . . ." he shook his head slowly, sadly, in resignation. "Regrets," he said, "are not the most useful of emotions." His eyes stared sadly at something infinitely far away as he sipped at his coffee.

Ian smiled. "I could've told you that myself."

Hosea shook himself, a tremor running up and down his body for just a moment, and when it stopped, his warm smile was back in place, and his eyes rested gently on Ian's. "Well then," he said, "let's take a look at you."

"Eh?"

Hosea turned in his chair and fumbled with the buttons of Ian's shirt with his right hand, while his left hand dexterously eased inside, dry, gentle fingers probing in a strange rippling motion that didn't feel at all clinical but still somehow evaluative.

"Hmm . . . there is some tearing, but only of the muscle; that should heal." The fingers probed harder, deeper, but the only pain Ian felt was the mild discomfort he would have felt anyway, if anybody had poked that hard at even undamaged tissue. "It seems to me that there's some inflammation next to what an acupuncturist would call a chi point, and what Dr. Sherve would call a nerve cluster, I think."

He removed his hand and buttoned Ian's shirt, the buttons and buttonholes aligning themselves instantly, as though leaping into place. If he hadn't been watching closely, Ian would have sworn that the buttons started moving just before Hosea's fingers touched them, but . . .

But, no . . . it was just too easy to see magic everywhere, once you hung around with these people for a while. It wasn't magic; it was just remarkable dexterity.

Just . . .

"I don't like this," Karin said, her lips drawn into a thin line that, for just a moment, made her look old and tired. She stood, and picked up the receiver of the wall phone; her slim fingers punched a number faster than Ian's eyes could follow.

"Bob? It's Karin." She smiled. "I figured you would; I don't sleep that well alone either. No, she's fine—a bit put out, but I think that Martha was born put out . . . yes, yes. No, that's not it—no word, yet. I think we need a house call. Yes, yes—both of them. Hosea says that it's not all that bad, but—yes, I know." Her lips tightened. "And truth is that I need you to swear to Thorian that I didn't talk him into it long before . . . yes. Half an hour is fine."

She hung up the phone and turned back to Ian. "He'll be here in an hour. I'll pack for you, but you're not to even think about leaving until Bob Sherve gives you an okay."

Ian shrugged, then immediately regretted the motion. "I'll wait for him to look me over," he said. He clenched his right hand, the one that wore Harbard's ring. *I am not afraid. I am cautious, certainly, but I am not afraid.* He concentrated on the thought, and then, as the ring pulsed once, twice, three times against his finger, he shook his head and wondered why he'd bothered with the ring again. It worked on other people—at least the few times he had used it, it had—but it didn't seem to do anything for him.

It wasn't like he was scared or anything. Maybe he should be, but he wasn't.

"But that's all; the sooner this is done, the better," he found himself saying. There was a metaphor he had never had any use for, but he finally understood it: he did feel like a large weight had been lifted off of him.

But going back? Again? If he kept doing this, sooner or later his luck would run out, and it was more likely sooner than later. It had been a close thing in Vandescard, and a closer thing in Falias.

And this time . . .

Screw it. He wasn't scared, and it would be good to be in a place where he could wear Giantkiller openly, where he wasn't just Ian Silverstein, a college dropout, but Ian Silver Stone, Killer of Giants—well, one fire giant, at least.

And if that had been at least partly luck—and it had been—what of it?

"You've become a hard-headed man, haven't you?"

A long time ago, Karin. "Well, yes."

Hosea smiled. "He comes from a long line of them. Trust me on this."

For a moment, Ian didn't know how it would break.

But then Karin smiled and reached out and touched his hand, and at least for the moment they were all friends again.

CHAPTER SEVEN

Day Time

J eff Bjerke looked over the prints in the snow with undisguised irritation.

The trouble was, all they looked like was dog prints. A big dog, sure, but still just a dog. In the back of his mind there had been the idea—the crazy idea—that he might be able to enlist some local help. Maybe through an anonymous call to MPD. Get the locals looking for a wolf, and yes, that would cause some fuss and bother—but that would also get a lot more eyes looking for prints.

Thorian Thorsen knelt down beside the clearest of the prints, the one Torrie had covered with an inverted cookie tin. "Can you make a cast of this?" he asked, although it wasn't clear whether he was directing the question to Torrie or to Maggie.

Torrie shrugged uncertainly, but Maggie nodded. "There's a hobby shop just around the corner," she said. "I can get us modeling cement, no problem—"

Torrie raised an eyebrow. "Can I ask what for?" There was just the slightest dubious tone to his voice.

His father let it slide. "Of course. I want to be sure, the next time we find some Son prints, that it's from the same one."

"You think there might be more than one?"

"I don't know. But I'd like to. Would you not?"

Jeff let his smile show. He had been afraid that in the city, Thorian Thorsen would be totally out of his element, and would be more trouble—other than in a fight, of course—than he was worth.

It was sometimes good to be wrong. It hadn't even occurred to Jeff that there might be more than one Son, but of course there could be.

"So where do we go from here?" Torrie asked.

"Yes," Maggie said. "I'm missing a modern lit class right now, and—"

Torrie held up a gloved hand, fingers spread wide, cutting her off. "No."

"Daytime? On campus?"

Thorian Thorsen nodded. "Of course, Maggie; as you wish."

"But, Dad—"

"Hush. Do you think one guard will be enough, or shall it be two?"

Maggie frowned. "You're going to stand outside my classes, like you're the Secret Service or something?"

Thorian Thorsen's brow furrowed, but Torrie smiled. "You bet," he said. "At least one of us. Me, I'm just going to skip classes and take incompletes if I have to, but if you don't feel you can do the same, well, then, you can surely do it with Dad or me watching your back."

Thorian Thorsen shook his head. "It would be best to ask leave from your school. I think that attending classes would be unwise, but if you insist . . ." he spread his hands in surrender. "As you wish at it."

As she turned to glare at Torrie, the elder Thorsen let a smile show through his stony expression, just for a moment.

"Well . . ." Maggie said. "If that's my choice, I can take a few days off."

"If it was up to me," Jeff said, "you and Torrie would hop in the front of the car and take turns driving, while Thorian and I sleep in the back. If the Sons are going to come for you, I'd like them to do it by popping out of the hole where I've got four men stationed with rifles, ready to blow their asses away, rather than anywhere else.''

Shit, if he had his way, the whole Thorsen family plus a Christensen by the name of Maggie would be on the next plane to Honolulu. No, come to think of it, Jeff had a friend in Honolulu. Maybe Paris or Port Moresby or Nuku'alofa or something.

But he wasn't going to get his way, at least not on that. And there was something about the idea of these dogs driving one of his people out of town, out of the Midwest, that didn't go down easy, not even in his mind.

It was okay for a lot of the kids to move away from Hardwood. He'd given that some thought more than once, himself. Small-town life is not for everybody, not even for everybody who likes it, and certainly not for everybody who happens to be born and raised in a small town. But he just didn't like the idea of the Sons forcing the Thorsens to flee, even if it made sense, and he liked even less the idea of bringing trouble home unnecessarily, and if he didn't even like it, there was no way he could sell Minnie Hansen on it, or Bob Aarsted—although maybe Reverend Oppegaard could be persuaded of the wisdom. Give Dave that; he was flexible.

But, shit: if you couldn't even get a consensus between your two ears, it was a foregone conclusion that you couldn't persuade a room full of elders of it, so there was not much point in trying.

''First thing we've got to figure out is what to do about you and Maggie.'' And the second thing was for Jeff and Thorsen to get some sleep. Night came awfully early this time of year, and if they were going to be any use in the dark, Jeff needed at least four, five hours of looking at his eyelids from the inside before then.

''As in, whether we stay in town or not?'' Torrie asked.

There was no point in having an argument that you knew you weren't going to win, unless you needed practice. ''No, the question is where. Maggie have a roommate?''

''Yes. She's due back some time tonight.''

Thorian Thorsen shook his head. ''That wouldn't be wise. Is there some way she could be kept away for a time?''

Maggie thought about it for a moment. "How about trying the truth, or at least some of it? Torrie and you are here to help me refinish the built-in, which will save both of us some money, and what with the mess and all it would be easier on the lot of us if she stays over at her boyfriend's for a few days."

Torrie nodded. "And as a thank-you for her absentee hospitality, we treat her and whats-his-name—"

"Brian."

"—to dinner at, oh, Goodfellows or something."

She shook her head. "You can't solve every problem with money, Torrie. That'd just make her suspicious. We're doing *her* the favor, not the other way around." On the back porch stood a small red plastic bucket, holding paint brushes soaking in turpentine.

She stooped to pick up the glass bottle of turpentine next to the bucket. "I'll sprinkle a little bit of this around her room, and if she decides to show up, she'll get sick and go away."

Thorian Thorsen smiled like he had invented her. "Very good, Maggie." He slapped his gloved hands together. "We have an errand to run, have we not?"

It was getting cold standing around outside, and with Maggie dispatched to pick up some modeling cement, Thorian Thorsen in tow, Jeff followed Torrie up the stairs to Maggie's apartment. A pot of coffee was just finishing dripping down into the Melitta, and after most of a night of road coffee—Karin Thorsen surely would have packed them a thermos if Thorian hadn't insisted on rushing off— the smell was tantalizing beyond belief.

"Does Maggie get the paper?"

The question clearly caught Torrie by surprise. "You want her to advertise for a new roommate or something?"

"No." Jeff tried to keep his expression neutral as he met Torrie's gaze, and he held it that way until Torrie looked away.

Torrie was going to be a hard case. That was the trouble with growing up around the people you had to watch out for. The ones who were older could never quite get the image of you as a little kid out of their heads, and the ones who were your age, or even a few years younger like Torrie, weren't used to taking direction—even when it was needed—from a peer.

He'd probably have to get that clear sooner than later. But maybe it could wait until he looked at the newspaper that Torrie was unfolding on the spool table.

Well, the mayor's driver had tried to shoot out some poor fool's tire, and all of the sports teams remaining wanted some money in return for not moving away. There had been a shooting in Phillips, and the homeless shelters were all full, but . . .

"What are you looking for?" Torrie asked.

Jeff tapped at the paper. "This." He smiled. As a kid, like a lot of other kids, he'd wanted to be Sherlock Holmes. You didn't get a lot of chances to do that. The strange thing that the dog did during the night.

"The shooting in Phillips?"

"No, it's the story that's not there. The dead men that the Son killed. Or the stories from surrounding farms about animals being taken by a wolf." The Sons had stalked the Thorsens for at least a week before the Night of the Sons— and they'd killed a fair number of farm animals to feed on.

But that had drawn a lot of attention, and it would draw even more attention this far south, where wolves hadn't been spotted in, what? A hundred years? It wouldn't take many kills to have the public all up in arms. One would probably do it. Two, for sure.

Torrie nodded. "I've got it. So either he just got into town, or . . ."

"Or he's taking his time, and trying to keep a very low profile."

Torrie's brow furrowed. "But if he just came through a Hidden Way, how did he find Maggie's apartment? Do you think there's a Hidden Way out in her backyard?"

"No." That wouldn't make sense.

Or, at least, it didn't make sense.

Hosea said there were lots of them, but Jeff had the impression that meant maybe hundreds or thousands, but surely not enough that there would be one in every backyard. No matter how hard it was to make yourself notice a Hidden Way for the first time, somebody would have stumbled across it, or stumbled into it like Benjamin Bathurst probably had.

Occam's razor: "What I think—the only thing I can think of that makes sense—is that this is one of the group who captured your mother and Maggie, and who knows what all of you smell like."

Assuming he was right, and it wasn't a terribly difficult assumption to make, the Son was looking for the Thorsens, and probably would return, sooner than later, to check for another familiar smell. It was a matter of luck that the Son had found Maggie first—and was a matter of more luck that he hadn't followed her to Torrie.

Quiet footsteps sounded outside the apartment, in the hallway.

Jeff was out of his chair, with his hand on the butt of his pistol as the door creaked open. It was a silly thing, but he actually regularly practiced a fast draw, even though he'd never heard of a case where a small-town type like himself really needed to do anything of the sort, legends about Bill Jordan to the contrary.

But it was only Maggie and Thorian Thorsen, each of them carrying a brown paper bag.

Which was what he should have been expecting, anyway. The Sons wouldn't use a key, any more than they would knock and wait to be invited in.

There was just the hint of a smile at one corner of Thorian Thorsen's lips. "We've brought breakfast, as well as the cement." He set his bag down on the floor, and stripped off his gloves.

The heady smell of garlicky meat made Jeff's mouth water.

"Geerhos?" Torrie asked. It took Jeff a moment to realize that he wasn't talking in that Bersmål language that the Thorsens seemed to slip into and out of without knowing it but that he was talking about those Greek gyro sandwiches.

Maggie smiled. "It was only a little bit out of our way," she said. "And I know how you like them."

She probably knew how Torrie liked a lot of things.

Jeff sighed to himself. It was only four years, but it felt like four centuries, since he was that young. But, hell, marriage had a way of taking some of the piss and vinegar out of you, and that was just the way that was.

Not a bad deal, if you got to trade it in for Kathy. He didn't have any complaints.

"So," Torrie said, "we start with breakfast, but where do we go after that?"

Well, he didn't much feel like mixing plaster or concrete or cement or whatever the fuck it was, and he could probably spot a wolf print just as well as Torrie, if not quite as well as his father.

"I think I'll go for a walk," he said, "with one of you." It wouldn't take three of them to make a plaster-of-Paris cast. Here and now, as far as he was concerned, hunting rules applied, and Jeff had always been taught that you don't hunt alone, unless the choice is between that and hunting with somebody you don't trust.

Of the three of them, he was most worried about Torrie not following his lead in an emergency—the elder Thorsen would defer to him in this strange territory, and Maggie seemed a sensible type, by all accounts.

"Maggie?"

She turned toward him, jerkily.

"Feel like going for a walk?" he asked.

Torrie started to say something, but he stopped at a quick head shake from his father.

"Sure." She raised an eyebrow. "I don't even mind skipping breakfast."

"Well, I do," he said, reaching for the bag of gyros. "Breakfast is one of my four favorite meals of the day."

Once, when he was a kid, Jeff had found the perfect game trail. It was on the first day of deer season, and he was out with Dad, just the two of them. A long freeze had been topped by two, three inches of light, fluffy snow, which lay across fields and roads in the still air like a blanket just waiting to be disturbed.

It had been absolutely wonderful. He had spotted a big

set of tracks moving upwind, and the two of them had silently followed the big buck through fields and little stretches of woods, ever so often losing the tracks for just a moment in a thicket of brush, but picking up the trail momentarily. It was beautiful, and the feeling of the perfect trail hung bright and shining in his memory.

This was nothing like that. The snow had been driven over and blown around, and while he and Maggie were able to pick up occasional prints down the alley, leading away to 31st Street, they lost the trail at the 31st Street sidewalk and weren't able to pick it up again.

Four blocks down, Jeff finally gave up. They weren't going to find any more tracks, and there was no point in fooling themselves.

"Well," he said.

"That's a deep subject."

"What?"

"A well. It's a deep subject." She slapped her mittened hands together. "It's a joke. You know, a sort of funny thing that I say, and then we both laugh?"

"Oh." Except for the funny at the end part. Other than that, it surely was a joke.

It took him a moment to realize that at 36th and Emerson, they were only a few blocks away from the house where Billy Olson lived—as opposed to Billy Olson's House, which was across the street from where Jeff had grown up, just down the block from where he lived now, the house he bought for Kathy.

It wasn't just that the world was a small place: it was just that it was twisted in such a funny way. Billy's mom would want him to look in on Billy, and so would his dad, although Ernie would probably not admit to that under anything south of torture.

He had better look in on Billy, come to think of it—with a Son in town, he had damn well better. *Billy is what he is, but he's still one of us,* he thought.

"Let's head down this way," he said.

Jeff had always liked the East Calhoun neighborhood. Best place in the city. To the people of Hardwood, Minneapolis—even though it was almost five hours away and even a solid four hours if you didn't have to worry about speeding tickets—was always "the city."

If he ever was to give up Hardwood and move to the city, he would like to live here. The Dutch elm disease that had massacred trees over the entire Midwest had, for whatever reason, spared much of East Calhoun, and from spring to fall the streets were covered by a thick green canopy that in winter was reduced to a skeletal frame of branches that still held the occasional stubborn leaf, rattling in the wind.

If you had to have street names—and Jeff, reluctantly, conceded that a city had to have street names—it made sense to number them or alphabetize them. Beyond Emerson was Fremont, then Girard, then Hennepin, which didn't count as the H—Holmes, the next street, was the H; city folks could never keep to a simple set of rules—and then Irving, and finally James, where Billy Olson lived.

The house was one of those big, turn-of-the-century ones that nobody built anymore. It had probably come with its own servants—back when people had servants—but it had long ago been converted into apartments. A quick glance at the side of the house showed four electric meters, and Jeff's first impression was verified by the four doorbells next to the massive front door.

There were two hand-printed signs tacked up next to the door. The larger, laminated against the elements, read, "All Deliveries to Foyer inside Side Door," with a red curlicue arrow pointing around to the right side. The smaller one, tacked right next to the third of the four doorbells, read, "buzz once for Billy, and twice for William."

The other names on the buzzers were unfamiliar to Jeff, so he buzzed once on the third bell, and waited.

Nothing.

"Well," Maggie said, "I don't think it's getting any warmer standing out here. Do you want to leave your friend a note, maybe?"

"I don't have a pencil or a pen," he said, which wasn't quite true; in fact, it wasn't even vaguely true.

He made a mental note not to tell stupid lies to Maggie; she had already produced a pen, and was fumbling in the pocket of her parka, probably for a piece of paper.

Maybe it was time to try the truth, or something close to it.

"No," he said, "I'd . . . rather not leave a note, I can come back later, or something." He turned and walked quickly down the steps, carefully avoiding a couple of icy spots—and Maggie's eyes, for that matter.

He'd tried, and that was all that was required. With a bit of luck . . .

His luck, though, wasn't with him. The two of them were barely a dozen feet down the sidewalk when the door swung open behind him. He could practically feel the heat waft out, and the heady, homey aroma of freshly baking bread had his mouth watering.

"Jeff!" a familiar voice cried out. "Jeff Bjerke! I'd know the back of that bullet-shaped head anywhere."

Jeff turned. Billy Olson stood in the doorway beckoning to him.

The Olsons were thick-boned types, with square jaws and blunt fingers, but not Billy. He was as tall as his brothers— a full head taller than either his mother or his father—but delicate and angular, with long, thin fingers and a sharp chin, now covered by a scanty goatee.

Billy's smile was tentative and more than a little fearful, but he stepped out of the door and quickly walked down the steps and onto the sidewalk, with nothing more than jeans, a light, almost impossibly white puffy shirt, and a waiter's apron to protect him from the cold air.

"Please," Billy said, stopping before he quite got to hugging distance. At least there was no lisp in his voice, and his steps on the icy sidewalk weren't quite mincing. "It's been years."

"Really?" Maggie gave Jeff a knowing look. She turned her back on him and stuck out her right hand. "I'm Maggie Christensen."

"Ah." Billy smiled as he took her hand in both of his. Say what you would about Billy, his smile would warm anybody. "Still seeing Torrie?"

"Yes, how—"

He patted her hand, then released it. "I don't get back home much, but my dad writes me every week, and every once in a while my mom calls to talk—just for five minutes, she always says, just for five minutes—and we spend the rest of the afternoon on the phone." Billy shivered theatrically. Billy had always done everything theatrically. "It's far too cold to stand chatting out here; come in, please."

Jeff wouldn't have been surprised if he'd stamped his foot, but he didn't.

Quite.

With a sideways disparaging look at Jeff, Maggie took hold of Billy's arm, and Jeff had no real choice but to follow the two of them inside.

Billy's apartment was on the ground floor, in the back, and the mat on the tiled floor in front of his door read, in ornate letters, "Mi Casa Su Casa."

It might as well have had some sort of insignia, say, a limp wrist rampant on a field of pink flamingos.

The apartment was, as Jeff had expected, neat as a pin, down to the vacuum cleaner prints on the gray carpet that made it look as though Billy had just finished vacuuming. And while the air was filled with the warm, yeasty smell of freshly baked bread, there was not even a dusting of flour on the kitchen counter.

He patted them down into seats, then hurried off toward the kitchen. "Coffee, tea, or . . ." why did Billy have to put a pause in there? ". . . hot cocoa?"

"Cocoa," Maggie said. "Cocoa would be wonderful— we'll both have some." She unbuttoned her coat and took it off, glaring at Jeff to do the same.

The walls had been painted with one of those pattern-painting gimmicks that made them look all splotchy, and probably covered up stains on the wall as well as wallpaper would have. Track lighting on the ceiling splashed warm buttery light on the Broadway posters, but also on the wall behind the red leather love seat, where a lap desk lay.

"Are you a marshmallow person, a whipped cream person, or a purist, Maggie?'' floated out from the kitchen.

"Marshmallows, please,'' she said, sitting back and clearly enjoying Jeff's discomfort.

The truth was that Billy Olson had always made Jeff uneasy. Jeff had been more than happy when Billy had relocated temporarily to the city in high school, then permanently for and after college.

It wasn't that he had anything against queers, not really, but they made him uncomfortable. It wasn't a feeling he could speak out about very often—Doc Sherve and the rest of the elders were always ready to politely, carefully, explain to him that queers were no different than anybody else, but that just didn't matter, not to Jeff.

He was allowed his own feelings, as long as he behaved himself, wasn't he? And it felt strange being around homosexuals.

Yes, it felt strange being around black folks, but at least you knew going into it that they were black. You didn't have to take showers next to them in gym class for years and years before you knew they were black. And while you could expect that Jews were smarter than you, most of them were nice about it, and, shit, Ian Silverstein was really one hell of a guy, once you got to know him.

"You look familiar, Maggie,'' Billy called out, still clattering dishes in the kitchen. "I'm sure I've seen you before. Do you live in the neighborhood?''

"I was just thinking the same thing about you. I know I've seen you some place,'' she said. "And I'm not quite in the neighborhood—I'm over at Lake and Bryant.''

"But you haven't been there long?''

"No. Just this semester.''

"Then that's not it—although I used to practically live at the Bryant Lake Bowl, back when I was—last year. Probably somewhere in Uptown?''

"That would probably be it,'' she said. "I sometimes go over to Uptown for coffee.''

"Hmmm . . .'' There was more clatter of dishes and silverware, and a moment later Billy appeared, backing up through the swinging door to the kitchen, a silver tray heavily laden with plates, silverware, and three steaming mugs balanced easily on the flat of his hand.

"You're in luck," he said, "I just made up a batch of pâté last week," he said, scooping a small dollop out of a ramekin and spreading it on a piece of thin bread with a smooth, practiced motion. He set it on a plate, and set the plate in front of Maggie. "Taste."

"With hot cocoa?"

"Chef Louis's pâté goes with anything."

Jeff accepted another plate from Billy, and bit into the pâté. It was smooth and meaty and rich, and while there was a definite liver note in the medley of taste, it didn't predominate.

Billy was showing off.

As usual.

He was frowning, though, which wasn't usual. "But if you live around here," he said, "why haven't we met, then? I'd surely have recognized Torrie. I knew he was going to the U, but I didn't really expect to see him in this part of town." He made a moue. "Not really butch enough for him."

Maggie giggled. "Should I tell him you said that, or should I be sure not to tell him you said that?"

"Either way."

Billy echoed her giggle. The two of them were getting along just fine and dandy, like a pair of old girlfriends. Jeff felt like a stranger, and he didn't much like the feeling. Trust Billy Olson to find a new way to make him uncomfortable.

"So," Billy asked, "what are you in town for, Jeff?" He gave a sideways smile to Maggie, then held out his wrists. "If you are here for me, just slap those cuffs on me; I'll come quietly."

Maggie spurted a mouthful of hot chocolate back into her cup. "Don't do that when I'm drinking," she said. "I almost ruined your carpet."

"Just here on some . . . private business," Jeff said, ignoring the way Maggie tried to catch his eye. She was young and cute and bright, and anybody who Thorian Thorsen thought so highly of was worthy of respect, but . . .

. . . but, dammit, this was Billy.

Billy looked from her, then back to him. "Okay," he said, quietly. He set his mug down and sat back in his chair. "How can I help?" There was nothing mincing in his manner, not now. How much of it was Billy teasing him, and how much was just Billy being Billy?

Billy was always Billy, but . . .

There had been a time . . . Jeff remembered him and Billy running through the woods, a six-year-old Torrie Thorsen in their wake, carrying an increasingly heavy Davy Johansen for what felt like miles after Davy had fallen out of the tree they were building their fort in and cut his leg open from knee to hip. The other boys—shit, he couldn't even remember who they were, which was probably just as well—the others had frozen, but Billy had gripped Jeff's right wrist with his left hand, and his left wrist with his own right hand, and the two of them had carried Davy into town on the seat that the four hands and arms made.

Billy had had to be Billy all the way into town, and no matter how hard it had made him pant, he had kept up a stream of babble all the while they ran, but he hadn't flagged, and he hadn't for a moment taken his eyes from where the firm pressure of his blood-soaked bandana had turned a spurting of blood into only an oozing, and he hadn't slowed Jeff down, and it shamed Jeff to the bone that he hadn't even remembered that day in at least ten years.

Okay, Billy. "Yes," Jeff found himself saying, "there is something you can do. I think Thorian Thorsen and I could use a place to stay for a couple of days."

No, not Thorsen; what was he thinking of?

He knew damn well what he was thinking of. He was uncomfortable around Billy and would have preferred to have somebody else around with the two of them, but not somebody who would smell like a Thorsen to a Son—and Thorian Thorsen would smell like a Thorsen.

"No," he said, correcting himself, "not Thorsen. He'll be staying with Maggie; it would just be me. If that's not a problem."

"Not a problem, Jeff. You know that's not a problem at all," Billy said, with an entirely nontheatrical shrug. He sat back in his chair. "Mi casa, su casa, of course," he said, with a flick of his hand.

CHAPTER EIGHT

Chest Pains

oc Sherve let the big Suburban roll to a stop, the icy snow crunching pleasantly beneath the thick tires. It took too long before Chuck Halvorsen, rifle shouldered like he was on a march, stepped out of the shack. He stepped back at a quick wave of dismissal.

"It's nice to see that he's alert," Sherve said, sarcastically.

Ian shook his head. "Hey, he's not there to be watching out for cars."

"Good point." Ian reached for the door latch, but Sherve laid a hand on his arm, stopping him.

"You can finish your coffee, first," Sherve said, gesturing at the travel cup still steaming in the cupholder. "You're not in that much of a rush, are you?"

Ian ignored the question, but sipped at the coffee.

The truth was, he didn't know how much of a rush he was in. And that's what worried him. Ignorance wasn't bliss; it was fucking scary.

"Coffee seems to be more the local religion than Lutheranism in Hardwood," Ian said.

Sherve's teeth were surprisingly white when he smiled,

except for a brown stain that Ian assumed came from his cigars. "Absolutely. Go to church or not, that's your concern. But if you don't drink coffee, people will assume that you're some sort of weirdo."

"But I am some sort of weirdo," Ian said. "You get used to it after a while." He took another small swallow of the hot, black brew.

In the backseat, Valin finished his cup with a loud slurping, and then, when Doc Sherve silently passed the thermos back to the dwarf, he poured himself another cup. Well, you'd never know what you'd like until you tried it, and Valin had taken an instant fancy to black coffee, something that Ian had always thought was an acquired taste.

As a kid, before a trip, Ian would have been concerned not to drink too much of anything, for fear of having to go to the bathroom too soon. Being thirsty on the road was your own problem, and you could always drink later. Having to go to the bathroom too soon after leaving or too often during a trip was high on the list of Benjamin Silverstein's lengthy list of punishable sins. Then again, breathing was probably fairly high on the lengthy list of sins Benjamin Silverstein thought punishable.

It was kind of disgusting that such things still affected Ian, that he couldn't wipe every influence of that scumbag father of his from every corner of his mind, but that was the way it was.

Fuck.

And the worst of it was that he couldn't simply figure out what his father would have wanted him to do, and then simply do the opposite. A stopped clock is right twice a day, after all. You just never know quite when.

Ian hated that.

He ached for the feel of a foil's grip in his hand, for the shiny firmness of a fencing strip under his feet, for the vaguely metallic smell of the air inside his fencing mask. That was the one place he could trust his reflexes, the one place he didn't have to figure everything out, as though figuring things out was some sort of panacea.

But here it didn't matter. He would no more have to stop to take a piss in the Hidden Way than he would have to stop to rest or eat or sleep. And even beyond the Hidden Way, if you needed to relieve your bladder on the road, as long as you weren't being followed, it was just a matter of unbuttoning your trousers, as strange as it felt, at first, to relieve yourself out in the open.

So he swallowed his coffee, and one more time silently cursed at his father for making him have to figure every damn thing.

"I don't suppose it'll do any good, but I'd just as soon get it said, anyway," Doc said. "You can hold off on this for at least another few days, you know."

"You think so? Really?" Ian forced a smile. "And risk losing my nerve?"

Doc Sherve's lined face might have been able to express more skepticism, but if that right eyebrow had gone any higher, flesh would have torn. "You?" Sherve snorted, spurting a booger out of one nostril and onto his sleeve, something that would have embarrassed anybody else, but which Sherve merely wiped off with a Kleenex. "Yeah, sure."

He was silent for a long moment, then: "Just take care of yourself, okay?"

"What says the Honored One, Ian Silver Stone?" Valin's voice graveled from the back. "Does he speak of what a great privilege it is for him to have been permitted to convey thy person in his carriage-of-steel?"

"He, err, he hasn't quite gotten to that yet," Ian said, then realized that while Valin had spoken in Bersmål, Ian had answered him in English. "The Honored One has not, as of yet, found such an opportunity," Ian said in Bersmål.

Valin grunted skeptically. "There seems to have been ample."

Sherve's expression was a question. But Ian didn't feel like answering this one.

"See you, Doc. Thanks for the ride."

"Yeah."

Still careful of his sore shoulder, he opened the door, exited the Suburban, and had the back door open before Valin could manage it.

It was cold out, but he wouldn't need his parka shortly,

and he quickly stripped it off, replacing it with the fringed leather jacket that he had bought in a Grand Forks pawnshop. Arguably, it would break up his silhouette against almost any background—and that was a good thing—but mainly he wore it because it was comfortable, and he liked it.

He took Giantkiller's scabbard out of the pool cue case and slung it over his shoulder, following that with one broad strap of his rucksack. He stalked over to the hole and dropped the rucksack unceremoniously down into the darkness—Karin Thorsen had helped him pack his gear, and she knew what she was doing; nothing would break from a much harder impact—then hurried back to the car to get the other rucksacks and the long, telescoping walking stick.

The two other rucksacks and the walking stick followed the first rucksack down the hole.

And then it was Ian's turn. Doc Sherve and the Hansen boys had made one end of a two-inch-thick rope fast to the towing ball at the back of the Suburban. Careful of his bad shoulder, Ian gripped the rope with his good hand and stepped over the edge, carefully sliding down the rope to the bottom of the hole. He pitched each of the rucksacks down the tunnel, and by the time he turned back to pick up the walking stick, Valin was standing, albeit a bit shakily, beside him.

The dwarf looked almost comical in his jeans and oversized boots, and particularly in the parka—but Ian didn't even crack a smile. It would hurt Valin's feelings.

Ian extended the walking stick and tightened the locking rings into place.

"Ready?" His voice sounded steady, at least in his own ears.

Valin cocked his massive head to one side.

Ian gestured an apology and then switched to Bersmål: "Are thy spirits ready to return to Tir Na Nog?"

The dwarf gave a shy smile. "This one would ask the same thing of thee, Ian Silver Stone, if such a thing would not be an impertinence."

This constant bowing and scraping wasn't going to get any less tiresome. "Then, I ask of you," Ian said, watching the dwarf's eyes widen at Ian's deliberate use of informal mode, ''if you will do me the great favor of speaking informally with me, as an ancient curse causes formal language to make my piles bleed, and I would not have blood running down my leg and into my boots throughout our journey together.''

He turned away, without waiting for an answer, and walked down the tunnel—

—and into the Hidden Way.

The hurt was gone. At least for now. Ian felt, well, nothing. His shoulder would neither ache nor heal, and in the timeless walk down into the tunnel, through the gray light that neither brightened nor dimmed, he would feel nothing. There was, perhaps, a distant sense of foreboding at the back of his mind, but that was an intellectual artifact, only. He was not excited or scared—or calm or brave. He could, if he decided to, stand here forever in the gray nothingness, without any pain in his joints from a lack of shifting position, without hunger, without the pressure of a full bladder, without loneliness or boredom.

But not without time passing outside, though.

So he did what he had always intended to do: he stuck the walking stick through the straps of the rucksacks, and as Valin—now walking without the gingerness Ian had become accustomed to—lifted one end to his shoulder, Ian shouldered the other end.

The two of them set off walking, neither quickly nor slowly, but just placing one boot after the other, always surrounded by the directionless gray light, which faded off into the distance to a darker gray than Ian had ever seen before, that never quite made it to black.

Ian tried to count his steps, as he had every time before, but this time he gave up after only a little more than a thousand. At one point, he tried holding his breath as he walked, and he was able to do that for a long but timeless time without any pain in his chest, but he found after a while that he had started breathing again, and he couldn't even remember when, or how long.

It was easy to maintain the even pace; it was impossible for him to maintain any other resolve. He found that he couldn't even daydream, not even about anything sexual. He tried to remember the feel of Marta's lips on him, of the warmth and slightly acrid taste of her mouth . . .

. . . but nothing.

He didn't need to breathe, or piss, or think. While he could reach up and touch the end of the walking stick resting on his shoulder, and he was aware in an intellectual sense that it bore quite a few pounds of weight, it caused no pain, no stress, no nothing. Perhaps it should have been difficult for him and Valin to match paces so easily, but it slipped neither back nor forth on his shoulder.

And that was strange only in a vague and theoretical sense; it wasn't the sort of puzzlement that you worried over in your mind, like a tongue that couldn't help probing at a sore tooth.

It was just there, and if anything in the Hidden Way could be said to be difficult, it was difficult to keep thinking or caring about it.

It was just easier to simply be . . .

Ian Silverstein walked on.

Bob Sherve sat with the engine off, trying to ignore the distant pain in his chest. If it got worse, he would have to take another nitro tab, and he didn't like doing that.

Cold seemed to bring it on; warmth helped. If you huddled into your parka and didn't fidget, you could stay comfortable in the cold for a long time. Add a little heat source, and you could be toasty warm.

Well, it was as good an excuse as any. Sherve chuckled to himself as he reached into his pocket and pulled out his silver cigar case.

A single lonely cigar rattled inside. He took it out, and unwrapped it—a Romeo y Julietta Churchill. Seven inches of dark, rich satisfaction, and yet another occasion to tell all his patients to "Do as I say, not as I do."

Much of the time, they even did.

He sliced off the tip with his pocket knife, careless of where the sliced-off portion bounced, and flared his old, battered Zippo to life. People who smoked cigars for style would tell you to slice the end off with one of those little guillotine things that people were always giving him for Christmas and which he could never be bothered to carry, or to never light a cigar with a real lighter. You were supposed to use one of those butane things, or a match.

Bullshit.

Sherve liked the acrid smell of the lighter fluid, and it only lasted for a few moments, anyway. And puffing a fresh-lit cigar to life wasn't some sort of religious ritual, after all; it was habit and pleasure.

By the time he had the cigar going the way he liked, the car was filled with so much smoke that he couldn't see through the rear window. He cracked the windows on both sides, and let the breeze sweeping across the hood suck the smoke out of the car. In summertime, when he was out on one of his extended walks, sometimes people would tell him that they'd known he was coming for miles, just by the smell.

He had maybe a half dozen of the Churchills left, and only one box of the Punch Double Coronas. Time to send off to A.E. Lloyd & Son again, if he didn't want to have to start smoking legal cigars. They just didn't taste as good. Forbidden fruit, maybe?

Hard to say. Damn expensive, but nowhere among the frustrations of being a small-town doctor was low pay. Besides, what the hell else was he going to spend it on? His kids were grown and gone, back only for every other Christmas, and if either of them were going to have the decency to present him with a grandchild or two to spoil, they would have done it by now.

New toys for the clinic were always a possibility, but it made more sense to have the county pay for as much of that as they could, to help establish the precedent. Once Bob Sherve retired—and he would retire eventually, no matter what everybody believed—it would be hard enough for them to get high-paid MDs to staff the emergency room, and just this side of impossible to get another young buck, fresh out of medical school, to take over.

He'd had an idea that maybe Barbie Honistead could be steered into medical school, and maybe she still could be, but she had gotten involved with some boy from Florida in her first year at William and Mary, and was making noises about getting married.

The chances of luring some Florida type to Hardwood were close enough to zero, zip, and null to be not worth the trouble to think about.

If he had been smart, he would've realized how bright Karin Roelke was, twenty-odd years ago, and steered her into medicine, and maybe there was a chance with Thorian, although likely not. But, shit, when he went it was going to be bad for the town, and though he still had more than a little life in his body, he was far closer to the end than the beginning.

Enough wool-gathering.

Give an old man a cigar and a warm place to sit, and he could sit there all day, particularly since he'd had to start wearing those damn Depends diapers. As if old age didn't have enough indignities built into it.

Which it did.

The pain in his chest returned, and then was gone. Good.

He reached for the car phone and punched a number. "Hello," he said. "It's me. If he's going to do this, it's about time to get going. Ian's probably been gone long enough."

He sat back and considered the glowing end of his cigar.

It couldn't have been more than a couple of minutes before her brown Ford rolled quietly to stop next to Bob's Suburban. Karin Thorsen probably had had the car started, with her and Hosea sitting in it, the engine running.

Which meant she was nervous. Sherve didn't blame her.

He gestured at Karin to stay seated, then opened the back door to help with Hosea's gear. The air in the brown Ford puffed out at him, smelling of warmth and cinnamon and a distant hint of Karin's perfume. Something musky enough to make an old man remember he had been a young man, once, long ago.

"You sure this is a good idea?" Sherve asked Hosea.

"No, I'm sure about very little," Hosea said. "Certainty is for the young, and whatever I am it is a certainty that I'm not young."

"Then why?"

The tall man was silent for a long moment. "Because I might be useful. And these days, I'm not all that useful."

"You're just fine, Hosea."

Hosea shook his head sadly. "No. There was a time when I could have led Ian to that which he's going to be seeking, but that time is gone. That's a good thing, in many ways. It's good that I'm not the powerful being I once was, yes, but it's not a comfortable thing." He shrugged, or at least Bob Sherve thought he probably shrugged—his parka was far too large for his frame, and it hung loosely. "Besides, I have little choice in the matter. I promised Torrie's grandfather that I would always look out for Karin and Torrie, and . . ." He shook his head. "And I hardly see a way I can do that here, or in the city."

"And you always keep your promises."

Hosea nodded. "Always. Which is why it's perhaps for the best that I make promises so very rarely."

"I see." If anybody else had claimed that they always kept their promises, it would have been only politeness that would have kept Sherve from laughing out loud at them, and even politeness could only do so much.

But Bob Sherve didn't doubt him for a moment—Hosea's willingness to do things for other people was almost as much a legend in town as was his almost invariable refusal to promise anything. But there may well have been more to that. There was a spring in Hosea's step that Sherve hadn't seen before, that Sherve doubted had been there very often for centuries—how many centuries was anybody's guess; Sherve sometimes wondered if he could count that high—as Hosea shouldered his bag and walked quickly to the hole, neither looking back nor pausing for even a heartbeat before he dropped down into the hole and vanished from sight.

Sherve stood there, puffing on his cigar and wondering. Shit, he was half tempted to go chasing after Hosea himself, just on the off-chance that he might be able to find out what this was all about.

But, no, that wouldn't do at all. And it wasn't just that he wasn't a kid anymore, or because of the episodes of angina that had become more frequent of late.

He had work to do, and the truth was that he really liked his work.

Most of the time. It got harder every year, but you couldn't let old age catch up with you. The only way to keep it in line was to refuse to give in, to fight every inch of the way.

He puffed at the cigar for a moment, then walked to the driver's side of Karin Thorsen's car. Her window stuck for a moment before it rolled down.

"It'll be okay," he said.

Her smile came easily, but there was a trace of fear behind her eyes. "I worry about him—about them."

" 'Man is born to trouble, as the sparks fly upward,' " he said. "And which him was it—Torrie, or Thorian, or Hosea . . . or Ian?"

Her mouth worked silently, then: "All of them. I was thinking about Hosea, this time." Her mouth took a firm set. "I'm not worried about Thorian, or Torrie, not now. I don't think there's ever been a Son born that would stand a chance against my Thorian, and if those . . . things didn't disgust me so much, I'd feel sorry for it."

Bravado looks good on you, Karin, he thought.

The distant pain in his shoulder grew sharper, and he patted at the pocket where he kept his nitroglycerin tabs. "I'll see you later, Karin." He turned without another word and thumbed open the bottle without taking it out of his pocket. He'd had too much practice doing that of late. By the time he was seated back in his car, he had a tab under his tongue, and he sat quietly for a few moments while the bitter taste drove the pain from his chest.

That was better.

Bob Sherve puffed on his cigar, put the car into drive, and drove back into town.

Part Two

MINNEAPOLIS, MINNESOTA AND TIR NA NOG

CHAPTER NINE

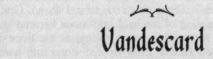

Vandescard

Last time, the transition had been instantaneous: in an eyeblink, the weight that Ian had been carrying had weighed heavily in his hands, and instead of walking on the rippled gray stone of the Hidden Ways, he had been in an underground tunnel, reinforced with beams and timbers.

It had been simple and painless from the start, and it had remained simple and painless for an eternity.

Ian had been walking forever through the gray tunnel, his steps effortless and uninteresting, his mind unfocused and incapable of focusing.

He had been, he thought, but, now, and for a long while, although physical sensations were still distant and devoid of meaning, each step had slowly become more difficult, more laborious, more strenuous although, strangely, hard as it was to take the next step, it wasn't tiring.

It felt like the very air around him was congealing into something transparent but gelatinous, so that he simply could not keep on drifting grayly as he walked but had to force his body into each step forward, each arm swing, each movement. But the resistance was only one way: he paused for a moment, and took an easy, effortless step back, unsurprised that Valin was matching his every motion.

It would be simple to go back, in a distant way that almost angered him. Making it easy was of no importance at all.

He pushed forward, and things began to change.

Slowly, the directionless gray light dimmed and became a splash of golden sunlight down the tunnel ahead. Gradually, the even rippling of the hard gray stone became less even, and if not softer, then more giving, as the floor of the tunnel changed slowly from rippled stone into hard-packed dirt. Senses didn't quite return, for they had never abandoned him, but they gained salience and relevance.

His left shoulder had been aching for a long time, but it had been sort of like what he remembered having a tooth drilled while breathing nitrous oxide was: there was pain there, but it was somebody else's pain, somebody he didn't particularly care about, one way or the other.

He realized, with a shock, that he was breathing heavily, and had been for a while, what with supporting his share of the weight of the gear.

"I . . . ," he said, his own voice strange and foreign in his ears, ". . . I need to rest."

"Then rest ye shall, Ian Silver Stone," Valin's deep basso graveled, and Ian turned to ease the walking stick to the ground.

The cave was like the inside of a roughed-out, flattened cylinder, the incline ahead sharp for about ten yards, but becoming suddenly shallow to the opening where golden daylight trickled in through a veil of cool greenery. Behind them, the cave was dark, but it seemed . . .

No.

Ian took three running steps back down the tunnel.

But it wasn't a tunnel any longer: it ended with a top-to-bottom narrowing that he knew he hadn't walked through. Above, the roof of the cave was a concavity of smooth stone, roughly square on three sides, but curved where it dropped to almost meet the floor.

He reached up a hand: it was smooth, but not perfectly smooth; long striations ran the length of the concavity, to where it vanished into the tunnel.

A sense of panic washed up from the pit of his stomach. His gut spasmed, and it was all he could do to keep from shitting his pants.

Sour vomit spewed from his mouth.

Valin, moving easily as though he had never been injured, was at his side. "Come ye with me, Ian Silver Stone," he said, leading Ian up the steep slope to the cusp, where it became shallow. "All ye need is fresh air and light."

Ian staggered out through the leaves and into the warm smell of rotting humus.

Strange that the odor of rot would ease his nausea, perhaps, but . . .

But it hadn't been the smell that had made him nauseated. It had been the realization that the cave he had been in was shaped like it had been made by the impression of some gigantic thumb, pressed so hard into rock and soil that it even left the striations of the thumbnail impressed on the roof of the cave.

As perhaps it had, but . . .

His hand found Giantkiller's grip, and he clung to it tightly. He thought, for just a moment, about flinging its scabbard aside, freeing the blade.

But no. He wasn't holding it for physical protection. It was a thing to center his universe, an anchor for his mind.

He almost giggled: at the moment, his sword was a security blanket. He might as well hold it to the side of his face and suck his thumb.

Three rucksacks draped across his neck and shoulders, Valin pushed through the brush covering the mouth of the cave. It was all Ian could do not to laugh. There was something about a dwarf in jeans and a workshirt that just wasn't right.

"Are ye well, Ian Silver Stone?"

Ian nodded out of reflex, then realized that he was telling the truth. He did feel good. There was a distant sour taste at the back of his mouth, but an Altoid from the tin in his shirt drove that away instantly. He worked his left shoulder, and found that while there still was some pain when he tried to move it, it was by no means disabling.

"Yes, Valin, I am most well." He rose and stretched. "Do you have any idea where we are?"

Valin sniffed the air judiciously. "Vandescard," he said, "I believe." He sniffed again. "Definitely Vandescard."

Ian was reminded of an old joke about a little old Jewish woman and a Long Island duckling, but it would've taken too long to explain, and besides, Valin probably wouldn't have gotten it anyway.

How many dwarves does it take to screw in a lightbulb? One to hold the bulb and the rest to turn the universe?

"How can you tell?" Ian asked.

"It . . . smells like Vandescard. There is an acrid note in the pine scent that you only get near the Gilfi—the river the Vandestish call the Tennes—but there's no hint of sun-baked snow, which there would be were we nearer to the Dominions." He sniffed again, and his thick face wrinkled into a coarse frown. "No. I must be wrong. I smell an old oak, and there's . . ." The dwarf spread his hands, helplessly. "This one is sorry, friend of the friend of the Father of Vestri. I don't know where we are."

Well, figuring that out was the first order of business.

Ian belted Giantkiller around his waist, and slung his rucksack over his right shoulder, book-bag style. Valin shrugged into one rucksack, then slung the other backwards, hanging down in front of his chest, which looked strange but probably made sense.

"I'm told," Ian said, "that vestri are great pathfinders—can you lead us to somewhere where we can figure out where we are?"

Valin bowed his head. "It would be this one's great honor."

CHAPTER TEN

Lake Calhoun

Jeff Bjerke leaned back under the hot water and scrubbed hard enough to hurt. There was a faint scent of patchouli in the bathroom, although, thankfully, it was only faint.

There was a knock on the door. "Your clothes are clean and dry, Jeff," Billy's voice came floating through the door. "They're on the chair just outside of the bathroom."

Jeff glanced down at his wrist. 11:23. He gave his watch a heavy scrubbing, then rubbed the plastic scrub pad hard against the bar of Dial, then harder against his chest.

At home, Jeff was an Ivory soap kind of guy—the way he saw it, deodorant was what you put on after a shower, not what you slathered yourself off with. In hunting season, of course, that wouldn't do—any soap smell shouted human—and he always did this same routine with Scentkiller.

But here in the city, a human who didn't smell at all might be suspicious. It would be best not to take any chances on that.

Waiting tables not only paid better in the city than it did at the Dine-a-mite in Hardwood but it apparently paid pretty well indeed—Billy had the fluffiest towels that Jeff had ever seen. He dried himself quickly, but thoroughly—

among the stupidest things you could do in winter was to go outside wet at all—then he wrapped the towel around his waist tightly before he unlocked and opened the door.

His clothes had been folded neatly on the chair—even the socks—and were still warm to the touch. He dressed quickly, enjoying the feel.

There was an uncharacteristically loud rattling of pots from the kitchen.

"There's a spare key at the bottom of the candy dish on the coffee table," Billy said. He emerged from the kitchen, wiping his hands on a dishtowel.

He had exchanged his white shirt for another one, and there was a shiny black stripe down the outer seam of the pants that probably would have broken perfectly if he had been wearing the shiny black shoes that stood under the coatrack next to the door. Billy's hair was slicked back and wet-looking and, as always, he looked freshly shaved.

"Thanks," Jeff said. He had left his gun and handcuffs in the liquor cabinet; he retrieved them and unlocked the cuffs from around the topstrap.

"Really, Jeff." Billy's laugh hadn't changed, still more of a snort than a real chuckle. "Is there some reason you snapped the cuffs on your, err, 'piece'?"

Jeff decided to give him the straight answer. "It's just basic handgun safety. If it's not under your control, you have to lock it up."

But Billy knew that. While Jeff didn't know whether or not the Olson family had kept a handgun or two around, Billy's father and his older brother were both hunters, and Gresh Olson had always been as much of a bear for gun safety as anybody else. Open the cylinder and snap a cuff over the topstrap, or behind the trigger, and what you had was a hunk of neutral metal, not a gun.

He thumbed the six cartridges into the cylinder, and pocketed the two spare speedloaders.

"Silvertips, eh?" Billy said.

"Sure," Jeff said, lying.

No, they weren't Winchester Silvertips. Winchester Silvertips were fine commercial loadings, and a good number of the hunters Jeff knew who didn't handload preferred them, but on the Night of the Sons, Jeff had seen more than once that a normal bullet, no matter how good, would do little more to a Son than slow it down.

These bullets were silver. Thorian Thorsen had cast them, and then loaded them into new brass on the Dillon 550 in his basement.

Wait a minute. "I thought you don't know anything about guns."

"Well . . ." Billy shrugged. "Oh, if you're not careful you pick up a little bit of everything, here and there." His grin was just this side of an insult. "Me, I'm careful—but I still pick up a little bit of everything."

"And you've always liked putting your friends on."

"My friends?" Billy's smile didn't even flicker. "I had to put everybody on. At least I used to. After a while, it becomes a habit," he said, his voice light and jovial, "and you forget you can turn it off." He glanced down at the Rolex on his wrist. How could Billy afford a Rolex? "But if I spend any more time chatting with you, pleasant as that is, there will be a hole in the air where the town's best waiter is supposed to be, and tables of people wondering out loud what ceviche could possibly be with nobody to tell them that it's scallops soaked in lime juice, with some finely diced bell pepper, scallions, Guajillos chiles from New Mehico, garlic, extra virgin olive oil, a hint of coriander and the veriest suggestion of cumin. But, of course, you knew that," he said, as he pulled a gray woolen coat down from the coatrack and put it on.

A quick pat at his pocket to jingle his keys, and he opened the door, then closed it, and turned back to Jeff.

"I . . . don't need to know anything more than you want to tell me," he said, all trace of lightness and joviality gone from his voice as he knelt to put on his shoes, "but if there's anything you ever want to tell me, or you need to tell me, well . . ." His smile returned. "You know where I live, don't you?"

He stepped out the door, and then he was gone.

Jeff wondered what that had been all about, but it was probably just Billy being Billy, and while many things in the world would and could change, Billy being Billy wasn't one of them.

He wondered why that didn't bother him as much as it used to, then he dismissed the thought. It didn't much matter, did it?

There was a phone on the end table next to the overstuffed sofa. He picked it up and punched a number.

Thorsen answered on the first ring. "Yes."

"It's me. I'll be outside the apartment in maybe fifteen minutes," Jeff said.

Thorsen was silent for a moment. "It should be me."

They had been over this for what felt like a thousand times, but probably was only ten. "And what are you doing in Minneapolis? If it smells you, it's going to be a lot more alert, and you know . . ."

"I understand." Thorsen was silent for a moment, and then hung up without saying goodbye.

Jeff shook his head. Thorsen knew as well as he did that even with surprise on their side, taking on a Son was by no means a sure thing. What were they going to do—call the MPD for backup?

No. A Thorsen was needed for bait, and Torrie was the right choice this time. Of course, since they were dealing with a Son, and they didn't know what the Son was really after except for Thorsen blood, leaving Maggie alone would be just asking for trouble. And Thorian Thorsen would be as useful there as anybody else.

Jeff Bjerke walked out into the night, his hands in his pocket, the right one holding the gun, with his finger very deliberately slipped inside the trigger guard, behind the trigger. That way, if he slipped on the ice and fell, there would be no way that it could go off by accident. That would be hard to explain.

It would, of course, be hard to explain him standing with a smoking pistol over what appeared to be a dead wolf, but his badge should be able to get him out of that without too much fuss.

And if not, it was unlikely that shooting a wild wolf within Minneapolis city limits was something that would be heavily punished. More likely, it would be something that would be hushed up. People panicked at the thought of wolves.

Jeff didn't particularly blame them.

Of course, something like half of the Sons were humans that could turn into wolves and half were wolves that could turn into humans, and that meant a fifty percent chance that this Son would, in death, turn into an incredibly inconvenient naked human corpse, but if Jeff didn't get caught, he wouldn't have to try to explain it to anybody.

He never liked nights in the city. Even where it was dark there was too much light pollution. You could see only the brightest stars, never any sign of the Milky Way, as a dark and distant creamy band across the sky. And the stars lost all their colors, and the redness of the hissing and spitting neon light over the pool hall across the street from Maggie's apartment was no substitute. Torrie walked quickly but tentatively down the steps of the fourplex, looking past Jeff as though he wasn't there. His overcoat was belted loosely around his waist, and if you didn't know to look you wouldn't see the bulge at the back of his neck where the hilt of his sword pushed out against the dark cloth.

At least, Jeff hoped nobody would notice. Particularly the MPD. He didn't know the details of Minnesota law about concealed weapons, but he bet that you weren't allowed to go walking down the street carrying a sword.

As they had planned, Torrie took a left on Lake Street and headed toward Uptown, Jeff following across the street, lagging behind.

It would have been convenient if some dark shape had detached itself from the shadows to follow Torrie, but if life had suddenly decided to arrange itself for somebody's convenience, it wasn't for Jeff Bjerke's.

Lake Street to Uptown, where yuppies chatted over noise and drinks at Figlios, or over coffees flavored any of a thousand strange ways, while bands of leather-clad punk types hung out on street corners and in the malls, pretending that it wasn't too cold to be hanging out on street corners or in malls in just leather jackets and ripped jeans, although maybe, through some strange process, piercing

your nose or eyebrow or tongue or God-knew-what kept
you warm.

Jeff was skeptical, although some of his Norski ancestors
had done stupider things.

Probably.

City people had a strange attitude about their tiny lakes;
they were always walking or running or jogging or bicy-
cling or skating around them.

Hell, if you put a leaky pail of water in a field in the
city, you'd probably get a dozen city people walking
around it before the water drained out.

Probably it was because they didn't get enough real
work. Even on a cold evening, you could see them, some
in street clothes, some in their exercise clothes—always
those plastic things; never a set of unfashionable sweats—
walking or running around their lakes.

Not that Jeff was complaining. After all, that was what
he was doing, at the moment.

Torrie picked up the pace as he crossed the Parkway and
joined the few dozen brave and foolish souls still out walking. Jeff swore quietly under his breath, but he forced himself not to break into a jog in order to keep up with Torrie.
If he looked like he was trying to keep up with Torrie, he
would be easy to spot.

Would the Son be looking for a trap?

Good question. Jeff didn't have an answer.

He had let Torrie get too far ahead, so he picked up the
pace carefully. As long as he kept narrowing the gap, it
should be all right, although the heaviness of his breathing
was beginning to remind him that Torrie spent a lot of time
working out in the gym that Jeff spent driving around in
his patrol car, sitting on his butt.

There had been a time when he could have walked almost anybody he knew into the ground, but, without some
effort, that time would be gone again.

By the time Torrie was halfway around the lake, Jeff had
halved the gap between them. He was sweating under his
coat, and the sweat was freezing. A hot shower was definitely in his future, as soon as he got back to Billy's. It
would have been sensible to leave his towel draped over

the radiator; the thought of a warm, dry, fluffy towel was almost erotic.

Nails clicked on the tarmac behind him.

Yes! His finger had almost frozen inside the trigger guard; it twinged as he pulled it out—

—and he spun around as a pretty blond girl in a jogging suit, not even having the decency to pant as she jogged after her German shepherd, ran by him, smiling a quick apology for the disturbance.

Her jogging suit was skintight, but her nicely rounded buttocks—the jogging suit made it clear that her buttocks were plural, not singular—barely jiggled.

There was such a thing as being too fit.

Jeff hurried along, closing the distance. You could keep moving along, even if it made your heart pound, if you had to. It was just like when you were ground-hunting, the way Jeff and his father always had. You couldn't outrun a deer, and it was stupid to so much as try, but if you were going to make trailing them work, you'd have to go as far as it took, not as far as you felt like. When it worked, it was wonderful. When it didn't, you envied those folks who picked a spot for a tree stand, then climbed up there and stood, freezing, until a deer wandered underneath, relying on the fact that deer didn't have any enemies—any other enemies, at least—that attacked them out of trees, and didn't have looking-up genes.

Of course, the one time that Jeff had ignored Dad's advice and decided to hunt from a tree stand, he'd stood there freezing and uncomfortable, wishing to God he was on the ground, trailing a deer, and while he did get his first fourteen-point buck that way, somehow the venison never did taste all that good.

It was, so Torrie had said, a measured 3.3 miles around Lake Calhoun, but it felt a lot longer. Still, it was about right. According to Jeff's watch, it took just a little over an hour for them to make the full circuit.

A cold and boring hour . . . but the trick was to keep alert, because what was boring could—and likely would— turn dangerous without any warning.

Torrie slacked the pace as they approached the intersection where they had entered the lakeside path, and Jeff caught up with him. Over the engine noise of the passing cars, Torrie muttered, "Anything?"

"No."

"Shit."

"Tell me about it."

Jeff followed Torrie back to Maggie's apartment, then walked a few blocks beyond before turning around and looping back to Billy's place.

He barely had closed the door behind him when the phone rang. His first thought was that the last thing he wanted to do was take a message from one of Billy's boyfriends—or, worse, be mistaken by Billy's boyfriends for another of Billy's boyfriends—but his second thought was that there was one of those Caller ID gimmicks on the kitchen phone, and it was on the fifth ring that he was able to read out Maggie's phone number, and answer the phone.

"Hello," he said.

"Did you get any hint of anything?" Thorsen asked. Thorian Thorsen wasn't much for preliminaries. Jeff hoped, for Karin's sake, that that didn't apply to their sex life.

"Nothing." No, that wasn't quite true. "A woman and a German shepherd ran by, and I practically jumped out of my skin. But nothing useful."

Thorsen actually laughed. "Perhaps you'd best get some sleep. I'll call you tomorrow, after we have taken an opportunity to look things over."

"Makes sense."

But first, a shower. The water pressure was high, and the hot water was hot and plentiful, and he stayed under it a long time; by the time that it started to go tepid, Jeff was as wrinkled as a prune.

He lay back on the firm mattress and pillowed his head on his hands. Every few minutes, the distant roar of an overhead jet would remind him that he wasn't home, as though the rattling of the ancient pipes and the city street sounds didn't. Didn't the city ever shut up?

A hot bath was supposed to make it easy to go to sleep; maybe he should have taken a bath instead of a shower.

Shit. Tying his robe around him, he padded barefoot into Billy's living room, and above the collection of more liqueurs than Jeff had ever heard of he found an unopened bottle of Four Roses on the top shelf in the liquor cabinet, apparently stuck as an afterthought between half an almost-empty fifth of sherry-colored Glendronach and a half-full liter of 18-year-old Macallan.

He broke the seal on the bottle and poured three fingers into an oversized shotglass, then drained it in one quick gulp. The harsh whiskey burned its way down to his stomach and set up a nice warm glow.

This was going to be bad.

CHAPTER ELEVEN

Marks

Sunlight glared harshly against the thick ice that covered Lake Calhoun.

Well, after all this cold, it had better be thick. Every winter some fool walked on the ice too soon, and went into the water, usually dying of hypothermia before he—and it always was a he; this wasn't the sort of stupidity that women were capable of—could be brought out and warmed up.

Well, it was worse up north. Every winter, one or more fools drove on a lake before it was fully frozen over, and went through the ice with all hands.

The lake was dotted with perhaps a dozen ice houses, and wisps of smoke from most of them announced that even on a cold weekday morning, some crazy people would find the time to sit over a hole in the ice, watching for a trip to signal that a fish had taken the bait.

Well, thankfully *something* was taking some bait; nothing had last night.

Torrie tried to avoid handling the snub-nosed pistol in his pocket. He had had to learn how to use a handgun to Dad's satisfaction—which didn't come easily—but he didn't much like it. A gun was an inert piece of metal, not

136

like a sword, which became an extension not just of your arm but of your mind.

And then there was the fact that while he was a decent rifle shot, he could barely knock a can off a fencepost at ten yards with a full-sized handgun and was absolutely hopeless with a snubby.

Still, what could he do? It was one thing to walk around with his sword strapped to his back at night, expecting the darkness to hide the bulge, but in the daytime it would have stood out as much as the gun felt like it did. It was silly, but he felt like everybody he passed could see that he had a gun in his pocket.

When a siren blared from behind him, it was all he could do to not jump out of his skin while the cop car shot by, lights flashing as it sped past the lake, heading toward some problem down toward St. Louis Park.

Maggie flashed him a knowing grin. "It's okay," she said. "I feel the same way."

It was silly, though. When was the last time anybody he knew had been stopped and frisked? Hell, even the time that that idiot salesgirl at Target had forgotten to demagnetize the magnetic gimmick on the Indigo Girls CD he had just bought, he had stepped through the theft detectors, the alarms had gone off all over the place, and the only thing that had happened was that the cop watching the exit just waved him through when he stopped and pulled his receipt out of his pocket.

Life was unfair. Maybe a black guy—no matter how law-abiding—would have to worry about such things, but a reasonably well-dressed, sober, vaguely working-to-middle-class-looking white guy just didn't get stopped and frisked, not unless he went out of his way to look guilty, and probably not even then.

So he concentrated on not looking guilty for a moment, then realized that that wouldn't work, and tried to distract himself, to just forget about the damn gun.

His left thumb stroked his knife where he held it in his pocket. He liked things with sharp edges. You could count on a blade, although Torrie wouldn't want to be close enough to a Son of Fenris to have to count on one.

But it was hard to worry on a bright, brisk day, with the sun shining down, a half dozen strips of Nueske's bacon and scrambled eggs warming in his belly, walking between Maggie and Dad. Tir Na Nog and the Sons seemed far away, and not capable of reaching out.

Maybe he had been mistaken. It was possible that it really was a wolf, and not a Son. When you hear hoofbeats, you should think horses, not zebras—not unless you're on the plains of Kenya. But the piss, it had smelled like a Son. Torrie remembered that smell; it gave him nightmares.

And then there was this dwarf that had popped, injured, out of the Hidden Way.

Where was the Son?

Dad's forehead wrinkled for a moment, and he broke into an easy jog that took him a hundred yards or so down the path.

Maggie's raised eyebrow was a question. Torrie shrugged.

"Should we? . . ."

"No." Torrie shook his head. It might draw attention.

They caught up with Dad just across from the pier near 36th, just beyond where a small sandspit stuck out into the frozen lake.

Dad's face held that calm expression that Torrie had always both loved and hated. "There's a print behind that rock," he said. "He was here last night."

"How can you be sure?" Maggie asked.

Thorsen led them to the rock.

It was hard to see, at first. The tracks weren't as clear as the one behind Maggie's apartment had been, and it could have been a large dog, he guessed.

He said as much. "The claw marks are deep, but there are dogs whose nails don't get trimmed often enough." There was no trace of that particular, acrid smell of wolf piss in the air, either.

"Too few tracks," Dad said. "A dog walks clumsily, feet going here and there, not caring. A wolf knows where he puts his feet, and puts the rear paw in the print of the front. He does nothing by accident."

Well, wolf-dog hybrids weren't unknown. It was a stupid

idea, and generally they made lousy pets—too eager to strike out, and prone to chase sheep and goats, not caring about such formalities as property lines and fences. One of the Thompson boys had picked up one somewhere, but Shep Rolvaag had shot it just outside his own barn after the fifth or sixth time it had gotten into his chicken coop.

And maybe hybrids walked like wolves. Torrie might have argued the point, but he had seen where the tracks led. A dog might walk like a wolf, either from breeding or accident, but the prints of a large dog didn't, in a quick set of three steps, turn into a bare human footprint.

Dad had already made sense of it. "Why change here into human form?" he asked. "As a wolf, the cold bothers him less, and he can better attack, or defend."

A heel print was the only answer.

The heel of a boot, perhaps, or a shoe.

Maggie's mouth was a thin line. "It's where he left his clothes." She looked up at him. "He was following you last night, but he was doing it in human form, not wolf."

Dad nodded. "Yes. He's been here long enough to settle in and . . . represent himself as someone local." He shook his head. "I don't have any idea of how to track him, not now. Do you?"

Torrie shook his head.

Shit.

CHAPTER TWELVE

Bóinn's Hill

The woods finally broke on a hilltop, and the valley of the Gilfi, the river that the Vandestish called the Tennes, spread out in front of them.

In the mountains, distances were deceptive. Harbard's Crossing was probably just behind a bend somewhere down there, but it could easily be more than a couple of days' march away, even if they could see it from here.

But it was pretty. What had been lush greenery was now a million shades of orange and red, painting the hills with a banquet for the eye. Rock outcroppings peeked through here and there, lending a look of solidity and permanence to an autumn display that could only feel transient.

Most of the ridges were fringed with bands of evergreens, a green beard for the brown and gray land of Tir Na Nog.

"You wouldn't happen to have a AAA Triptik in your rucksack, Valin, would you?" Ian asked.

"Excuse me?" The dwarf was a good straight man, but a lousy audience. "I beg thy pardon, Honored One?"

"What I was saying," Ian said, "is that I have some idea as to where we are." He pointed north and east. "If we make our way down to the Gilfi and follow the riverbank, we should be able to make our way to Harbard's Crossing.'' That would be nice. A chance to drop in on Arnie and Freya would be pleasant, and it was always possible that Arnie could be prevailed upon to come along to the Dominions.

Ian chuckled to himself. He doubted that anybody would buy the notion of the wielder of Mjolnir as Ian's manservant. Which would be fine with Ian. He had never really enjoyed having his landlord pretend to be his valet.

It would be a different sort of trip this time than the last, just as the last had been different than the time before. What was that about how you could never set foot twice in the same stream?

Valin's thick brow furrowed, as though he was working on a thought and found the exercise both difficult and unfamiliar. ''Yes, Honored One,'' he said. ''Of course we may do that. And if it is your wish, surely we shall travel that way.'' He held out a thick, short-fingered hand. ''But it would be better if I were to carry your gear, now that my strength has returned to me. May I?''

''No, you may not,'' Ian said. ''I can carry my pack, and I can carry my sword,'' he said. *And, among my many skills is my ability to wipe my very own nose—and my very own butt, for that matter.*

His shoulder was still sore, but not nearly as painful as it had been. It was as though there was something in the very air of Tir Na Nog that healed and refreshed him, or at least eased the inflammation around the strain. Whatever damage was left could be easily healed by Freya; her healing touch had cured much worse.

But he was not at all sure that Valin was being entirely candid about his own renewed health, and, besides, Ian could stand a short break.

''Let's take five,'' he said, and at the dwarf's look of puzzlement he resolved, once more, to stop speaking in English to Valin. ''Let us take a short rest,'' he said. Five minutes was about right. Enough that it counted; not so much that your muscles started to cool off. You could go a long way in a day with only a few short rests, and still have enough energy at the end of the day to make camp.

He eased his rucksack down to the ground, then seated himself on a flat rock, gesturing at Valin to do the same. "Let me see your wound," he said.

The dwarf had already lowered both of his rucksacks to the ground, had one open, and was reaching inside. He produced a curved silver flask and held it up with a thick hand and a broad smile. "Your chirurgeon sent this along for you," he said, bringing it over. "He said to tell you that it is for medicinal purposes, and you are to feel free to take some if you need such medicine."

That sounded like Doc. Ian accepted the flask. "I thank you, and him, and I still wish to see your wound."

Not that he was tempted. He didn't drink. The way he figured it, Benjamin Silverstein had done enough drinking— and beating, and shouting, and generally acting like an asshole—for the two of them, and Ian tried hard to bring the average down.

Nothing wrong with getting a little buzz on, mind. Ian had been known to take a toke of pot every now and then, among friends. But he had never seen a pothead beat the shit out of, well, anybody.

"But there is no need—"

"Then there will be no problem." Ian made a beckoning gesture. "Now, if you please."

"Yes, Ian Silver Stone," the dwarf said, his flat face impassive. He dropped sharply to the ground, like a toddler falling back on a diaper, and began to unlace his shoes with clumsy fingers. Why he thought he needed to take off the shoes in order to drop his jeans was something Ian didn't know, and couldn't think of a polite way to ask.

Shoes and socks off, finally, the dwarf rose, unbuckled his belt, and then dropped his jeans. He wasn't blushing, but he couldn't meet Ian's eyes. He probably wasn't used to being naked around humans.

Or maybe, among dwarf women, size did count, and Valin's short, albeit preposterously thick, penis was something to be ashamed of.

There wasn't exactly a polite way to ask.

But the wound had healed, well, miraculously. The stitches were still in place, but the flesh they held together

was pink and healing, no trace of scab or blood, no redness
from a spreading infection. Valin reached tentatively to
touch at it, then drew his hand back.

"It looks good, but I'm surprised Doc Sherve didn't put
a dressing on it."

"He did. I took it off." The dwarf looked down at his
toes. "It itched."

It itched. The dwarf had taken his bandage off because
it itched.

Ian would have made some sort of speech about how any
idiot knew that when a fucking doctor put a bandage on a
wound and told you to leave it on, you fucking left it on,
but . . .

But . . . but it was healing, faster than Ian would have
thought possible, and this was Tir Na Nog, and maybe he
should just leave well enough alone. "Very well; you might
as well get dressed."

He sat back on the rock, thumbed the flask open, and
tilted it back, just for a taste. Instead of the whiskey he had
expected—not that he could have told good whiskey from
bad—it was some sort of chocolate-orange liquor. Nice
tasting, but Ian didn't drink.

He flipped the top back on and tossed the flask to Valin,
who deftly picked it out of the air and put it back in the
rucksack.

"No, no," Ian said. "Try it."

"I?"

"No, the vestri standing next to you." Ian softened the
sarcastic reproof with a smile. "Yes, you. Is there a problem with that?"

"Yes." The dwarf looked skeptical. "It's . . . just not
done."

"Vestri don't drink?"

Valin's crooked smile revealed a missing tooth. "Some
vestri have been known to. But it's not proper to drink from
the vessel of an Honored One."

"You don't have to have any of this stuff if you don't
want to, but I don't see the harm." Ian gestured at the gray
Gilfi, far below and away. "When we get to the river I plan
to take a drink. Are you planning to go thirsty?"

"No. But that is different." The dwarf furtively eyed the flask, as though considering how different it was or wasn't, then pushed it deep inside the rucksack, putting the temptation out of his way.

"If you say so." Ian rose from the rock and stretched carefully. "Well, shall we be off?"

"Yes, Ian Silver Stone," the dwarf said. "In whatever direction you order."

That was the second time Valin had said something to that effect. "You don't think we should go that way?" Ian asked.

"It is not for this one to say," Valin said, not meeting Ian's eyes as he gathered the gear together. He had taken on a formal mode again, which probably meant something, although Ian wasn't sure what.

"And if I were to say it was for you to say?"

"Then this one would say that the route via Harbard's Crossing would add almost a day to the trip. If we head north, we can reach the Village of Mer's Woods in a day or so, even if we swing west, further into Vandescard, to avoid spending the night too close to Bóinn's Hill."

Ian's sense of direction spun for a moment. He had been near here before; he and the others had just used a path along a ridge that ran parallel to this one. He pointed. "Bóinn's Hill is that way, just over that ridge, maybe three, four hours away, if we hurry."

Valin's ruddy face went pale. "Yes, but surely you're not thinking of spending the night there?"

"Yes, I am." Ian grinned. Yes, the hill was haunted, but he was on good terms with the spirit haunting it. "I've done that before. Twice, in fact. Let's go."

The dwarf made no move. "I would not spend a night on Bóinn's Hill, Ian Silver Stone."

"All will be well, Valin. We're welcome." Well, at least he was explicitly welcome, and Bóinn wouldn't turn a companion of his away.

"I would not spend a night on Bóinn's Hill, Ian Silver Stone. Please do not tell me to. It's hagridden, and the very idea scares me so much that I can barely hold my water."

Ian could have argued the point, but the day wasn't getting any longer, and he was getting increasingly irritated with the way that the dwarf alternated between bowing and scraping on one hand, and nagging and insisting on the other. A little consistency would have been nice, for a change.

"Well, then, you can sleep in the woods nearby; I'll spend the night on the hill."

"As thou wishes it," the dwarf said, ducking his head in something halfway between a nod and a bow. His face could have been carved from stone.

They reached the base of Bóinn's Hill just at sunset. The trail swung wide to the west, as though it was every bit as much afraid of coming close to the hill as Valin was.

"Ian Silver Stone," the dwarf said, eyeing the slope nervously, "there is an ancient burrow but a short march ahead; we can spend the night comfortably sheltered from the wind and rain, surrounded by nothing but the good wishes of long-dead vestri."

Ian nodded. "That sounds like a good idea. I'll meet you there in the morning."

"But . . ."

"Can you mark the trail so that I won't walk by and miss you?"

The dwarf's expression was of fear mixed with something else that Ian couldn't quite figure out. But it wasn't necessary to figure out everything. That was a mistake that he should have outgrown. Get all your ducks in a row, and all you have is a row of ducks. Figure out everything, and all you get is knowledge. And there were many times when knowledge was a vastly overrated commodity.

"Of course, Ian Silver Stone. This one lives to serve and obey," the dwarf said. If there was any sarcasm in his mind, it didn't show in his voice or his face.

The climb up the hill was easier than it looked, which was the first time that Ian could recall a climb or a hike ever being easier than it looked. Usually, the grasses snatched at your ankles, pebbles slipped from beneath the soles of your shoes, and roots and vines hid waiting in the grass to snare and trip you, and if that was only what it felt like, well, that was what it felt like.

But this was different. It was almost as though the hill welcomed each step.

Which wasn't, all things considered, entirely impossible.

The top of the hill wasn't quite as he remembered it. The four ancient stone pillars were still there, but either they had been moved, or Ian misremembered them as having been in a rough line.

Now, they formed a shallow arc to the north of a huge, spreading oak that Ian had seen before, but only in a dream.

In a dream.

He dropped his rucksack to the soft, welcoming grasses and ran to the base of the old, gnarled tree, more than half-expecting that it would vanish at his touch. But the rough bark of the trunk was hard and real beneath his fingertips, and the golden leaves clinging to a low branch were crisp and cool.

"Bóinn?" he called out.

There was no answer. Only a whisper of wind rattling the leaves overhead.

Ian smiled. This was his tree. He had planted the acorn himself, and watered it with his own urine, but that had been only months ago.

Fear washed over him in a cold wave. It would have taken dozens of years for such a tree to have grown. Could that much time have passed in Tir Na Nog since he had last been here? Enough time for an acorn to grow into an oak?

But that would mean that Marta, and Ivar del Hival, and every person in Tir Na Nog that he knew would be long dead of old age, even Arnie. Freya would still be the same—which was good and reassuring, and so would Harbard, which wasn't—but . . .

Shit. Now he knew how Rip van Winkle felt. Or how Peter Pan ought to have felt.

The toe of his boot brushed against something. He looked down, and dropped to one knee.

It was a piece of plastic, poking up through the soft ground, thin brown plastic like the tube that the peanut butter in his rucksack came in. He stooped and pulled it out of the ground; it came easily. That was exactly what it was: an empty peanut butter tube—he could even read the black letters against the dark brown plastic.

They had buried their trash when they had last camped out here, but while plastic wasn't biodegradable, it wouldn't look so new after dozens of years.

And that was good. Ian hadn't realized that he had been holding his breath, but now it all came out in a heavy sigh. It was going to be okay: It hadn't been years. Marta wasn't a great-grandmother, and he was still Ian Silverstein, not Rip van Winkle, and not Peter Pan.

The sun had set while he was climbing the hill. It was time to get ready to settle in for the night.

The perversity of the universe, Ian had long ago decided, tends toward the maximum.

There were times when you just couldn't win: Ian had decided to spend the night on Bóinn's Hill because he was sure he would sleep well there, and now Ian couldn't sleep at all.

There was every reason that he should be able to. Bóinn's Hill felt safe and friendly. Insects chirped and clicked off in the night; it wasn't the too-quiet that would make the hairs on the back of his head twitch.

His blankets were warm without being too warm, and he had always slept best when he was warm but the room was cold. He had cut some of the long grasses that grew downslope and laid them under his groundpad, and the pad itself was good enough insulation to keep the ground from sucking the heat out of his body.

Even the ground beneath him seemed to support him without being too hard—like a good futon. He had eaten well—Karin Thorsen had filled the bottom of his rucksack with freeze-dried camping meals, and a little hot water added to a packet of peppery beef stew would have been a good meal back home, not to mention here.

Giantkiller was close to his hand, and the broad trunk of the old (new?) oak tree sheltered him from the discomfort of a cold gust of wind. The clothes he had been wearing hung from a branch, airing out overnight.

The night breeze brought him warm woodsy smells, leavened with a minty note of evergreens.

And he was tired. Walking through the Hidden Ways hadn't tired him, although in a strange way it had taken something out of him. But making his way through the forest and up the trail had left him bone-weary, the way a full day's march always had—and presumably always would—ever since his brief tenure as a Boy Scout.

But insomnia was something Ian had always thought of as a luxury. Sort of like indigestion. When you had to use every moment of the day for studying, practice, or work, you couldn't spend a lot of time eating, and while you had to rest, lying awake at night in bed was something that you just couldn't afford.

There was a full complement of drugs in his kit—Doc Sherve never had a problem writing a prescription for somebody's first aid kit, for he felt that when you needed, say, Demerol and Vistaril, what you should have was Demerol and Vistaril, and if you didn't understand the difference between great pain and recreation, Doc would be happy to explain it to you in excruciating detail, with short, Anglo-Saxon words.

So he could pop a Valium.

Right. And then he could wash it down with a few snorts of whatever that orange-chocolate booze was. And then maybe he could skip going to Falias to try to get the Sons off the trail of Thorsen blood and settle down, say, with Marta, have kids, and by the time she died perhaps he could get drunk every day and then slap the kids around some.

His father's footsteps were, after all, always available for the walking-in.

Maybe he was just being silly, he thought, as he lay back, pillowing the back of his head on his hands. Bending a little made sense. He didn't have to always be such a goddamn hardass.

"Sure." Ian laughed out loud. "Yeah, right."

Well, yes, he did always have to be such a hardass. If he couldn't sleep without drugging himself, then fuck it: he wouldn't sleep. His aching legs could drag him through another day's march if he had to, and then—

This time it would be better.

Ian lay back on the creaky old bed, pillowing his head on his hands. Dad and The New Girlfriend were due home from the party any time now. TNG would take her pills and go straight to bed—this one went through tranks the way Ian went through Tic-Tacs—but Dad would head for the liquor shelf for his nightcap.

This time, he would smile.

Ian had a surprise ready for him. It wasn't quite perfect— he thought he had earned an A in Biology, but Mr. Fusco hadn't seen it that way. Not enough class participation, he'd said, and then there was the occasional absence—fencing meets weren't scheduled during school hours, but Ian needed extra practice when an important tournament was coming up—and a few latenesses. Biology came right after gym on Tuesday and Thursday, and gym was Ian's time to shake a few things loose, whether it was faking Bobby Adajian out of his shorts in football, or going for a jump shot with great enthusiasm and absolutely no skill during the quarter that basketball was the gym teacher's sport of choice, because if he showed enough enthusiasm, and did at least passably well, Mr. Daniels would bring out his foils and masks and give Ian a quickie lesson while the rest of the class was taking their final laps. Mr. Daniels had, in his younger days, tried out for the Olympic team, and he had a deceptively defensive style that Ian was trying to pick up. Milking that lesson for every minute meant having to rush through a quick shower, and that usually meant being late, but that was no big deal. Or at least it shouldn't have been. Shit, Mr. Fusco usually spent the first ten minutes of every class flirting with the senior girls.

It was a good report card. Except for the one B+, it was straight As. Even in driver's ed, although that technically didn't count.

For once he had a report card to brag about, instead of one to try to hide.

He would, as usual, pretend to be asleep, and if he didn't

hear raised voices, he would pretend to be woken up by their coming home, and would stagger, sleepy-eyed up the stairs, from his basement bedroom after Dad had had a chance to notice. Oh, Dad would probably make some sort of comment about the one B+, but even he would have to admit that this was as near-perfect a report card as an imperfect person could be expected to have.

Ian heard the car door slam outside, and then the garage door go up—you'd think that somebody with a bad back like Dad would have bought one of those garage door openers—and then the muffled roar of the big V-8 engine pulling the Pontiac into the garage, and the dieseling *chk-chk-chk-chk* as it refused, for just a moment, to shut down, and then the thunk-*thunk* of the car doors, followed by the footsteps, the opening and closing of the door, and their footsteps and quiet voices out in the laundry room as they came into the house.

Ian let out a long breath. They were talking, and quietly. That was good. He didn't even have to pretend to be asleep, although from long habit he forced himself to breathe slowly and regularly when the door to his room was swung open.

"He's asleep," TNG's husky voice said. Her cigarette lighter hissed briefly.

"Good. Room doesn't look too bad, either. Bet you he didn't do the dishes, though."

I did so, Ian didn't say. Well, dish, really.

You didn't need more than a frying pan to make fried rice of the leftovers.

And if you didn't actually use a dish, then you couldn't have loaded it into the dishwasher incorrectly, and if you didn't load it into the dishwasher incorrectly, you weren't to blame if—make that when—the dishwasher wasn't loaded correctly.

The idea was to keep as low a profile as possible; what didn't show wasn't something you could get in trouble for. Ian had never understood that old question about the tree falling in the forest. If there was nobody around to see it, and if you had a good enough alibi, then it didn't matter.

If he just moved quickly enough, if he just hydroplaned

across the surface of Dad's life, then he wouldn't sink and drown.

He was congratulating himself, and just getting to stretch and get ready to go upstairs when he heard Dad's feet pounding on the stairs.

The door swung open quickly. Dad stood there, framed in the doorway, the light from the hall making him only a silhouette. Ian's dreams were ruthlessly honest, and he found himself wondering, once more, why it should be that a little man no taller than five foot seven could loom so large in a doorway.

But this time it would be okay.

"Nice try." That wasn't right. Dad's voice was calm and level, the way it was when he was so angry that he could barely restrain himself, and wasn't going to restrain himself much longer. It was the voice that he used when Ian had really screwed up, yet again, and the shit was about to hit the fan.

"But, Dad—"

" 'But Dad,' butdad, butdad, butdad," he said in that mocking tone that made it seem like Ian had sounded like Porky Pig, "haven't I told you a thousand times I hate butdads?"

"But, I mean, well," he said, panicking. "One B+? That's near perfect."

Dad snorted. "Yeah, it sure is. I bet you thought that when you folded the report card over and taped it to the cabinet, I wouldn't notice that you've got five absences and seven tardies this quarter. Been ditching school to go play with your little sword again, eh? That Robin Hood shit isn't any reason to skip school, and sneaking away to do it without asking me pisses me off more. Why didn't you ask me?"

There was no right answer to that. *Because if I asked, you would say no* was the truth, but telling Dad the truth about this, here and now, would be talking back.

"I don't know," he said.

"None of that shit. Tell me why, now!"

"Really, I don't know."

"You think if you keep saying 'butdad' and 'I don't

know' that'll make it okay? If you gave a good goddamn about me and about yourself, you'd put first things first and leave your little Robin Hood games for your free time. Pisses me *off* . . .''

He took a step forward, and—

"This should be a place for more gentle dreams, Ian Silver Stone,'' a familiar voice spoke out of the soft, warm darkness.

Ian rose quickly, his blankets tossed aside, Giantkiller naked in his hand.

"Oh, Ian Silver Stone, do not worry. Your instincts have, this time, served you well: you've chosen a fine place to sleep.''

The voice was high and clear, a flute rather than a clarinet.

He lowered the point of his sword, and the air in front of him gained light and substance, until Bóinn hovered about the grasses in front of him.

Her mouth was small and perfect, her chin dainty and pointed. She had one of those faces that had no apparent age; she could have been twenty or forty, although he knew she was much, much older. The left side of her face was lit brightly by the starlight that somehow left the right side of her face in such utter darkness that he couldn't make out even its coarsest features.

You couldn't see colors in this kind of darkness. It was a physical impossibility: there just wasn't enough light to power the cone cells. But Bóinn's hair was the red of fresh blood, curled tightly against her head, and when she smiled at him, her freckled cheeks were dimpled.

Her body was slim but decidedly curved, more covered than hidden with the woven clouds that constituted her shift; her right nipple, set high on her small breast, kept peeking through. She was a full head shorter than Ian, but her eyes were level with his: she floated en pointe, her perfect toes never quite touching the grasses above which she floated.

He had the strong impression that if one of her toes so

much as touched a blade of grass, she would vanish, she would pop like a soap bubble.

"But in a dream you can," she said. The movements of her mouth were slightly out of sync with her words, like a movie where one language had been dubbed in over another, but not well enough.

"Eh?"

"You can see colors in the dark in a dream. That's how you know my hair is red, the red of fresh blood." Her smile widened for just a moment. "You're not the first person to think that, you know."

"No, I didn't."

"Well, now you do." She rotated, slowly, until she was facing the oak, and her dark side was completely hidden from him. "Yes, this is but a dream. It's just about all I can do, these days, to take form and substance in a dream. Oh, perhaps I can whisper on the wind, or send a shiver up a spine during the daytime, but it tires me to try."

"You're looking well, for such an old woman, Bóinn," he said, realizing the moment the words were out of his mouth that that could have been taken the wrong way.

Her quiet laugh told him that he hadn't offended. "I thank you for the tree," she said. "It's been a comfort to me."

"It's huge," he said. It had only been a few months. It should be no more than a sprout, or a mini-sapling, or whatever you called a baby tree.

She laughed, silver bells in the wind. "There are reasons why people fear my hill, and leave it and me alone. Someone who slept here against my wishes would fall asleep as easily as you did, but might not sleep quite as well." Her lips parted, revealing bone-white teeth, and for a moment, her smile was skeletal and menacing. But the moment was quickly gone. "I didn't enter your dream until it turned on you—but you're welcome here, after all."

"I know. The dwarf I'm traveling with—he didn't want to sleep anywhere near here."

"A friend of yours is, of course, welcome on my hill." Her mouth twitched. "After all this time, I find my feelings can be hurt."

"You always were of a delicate temperament, Bóinn," came from behind Ian.

He spun about. Standing behind him, his skinny frame wrapped in a traveling cloak, Hosea stood leaning on his staff.

"There are some who would argue with that," Bóinn said, her voice casual, but perhaps concealing some heat.

"But none who know you quite as well as I do, perhaps," Hosea said. He turned to Ian. "It's good to see you, Ian. I hope you don't mind."

Ian chuckled. "Hey, you're welcome in any dream of mine, as long as you've brought some coffee. With all the rush, I forgot to pack some."

Hosea nodded, producing a thermos from his pack. "I wish you'd mentioned that in Hardwood. I would have brought more than just ten pounds, which I thought would find their way to Arnie Selmo, sooner or later." He unscrewed the top and poured Ian a steaming cup of coffee, which Ian accepted gratefully.

Why was dream coffee always hotter than real coffee could be without scalding?

"Because it is a dream, Ian," Bóinn said.

His left shoulder twitched with pain. Not nearly as bad as it had been, but he hoped it would be better than this when he woke. Good coffee was nice, but no pain would be nicer.

Bóinn was at his shoulder.

"Don't move," she said, her voice a whisper of cold breeze against his cheek, which somehow warmed him thoroughly. Her long, elegant fingers stroked the air around him, never quite touching his shoulder. But they were cold; he could feel them soaking the heat from his body.

"There's little I can do for you, Ian Silver Stone, but your heart and head have picked a good place to rest for the night." With a creaking of branches and a rustling of leaves, the old oak reached down and lifted him up, wrapping him tightly in its leafy embrace.

"You should remember to follow both your heart and your head. Not either, but both; together, they may well lead you well. Most of the time. For now, rest."

Ian started to voice a protest, but the warm darkness swallowed him up.

Ian Silver Stone woke in the early morning light, lying next to the oak tree. He rose and stretched, utterly unsurprised to see Hosea's form, wrapped in his brown cloak, sleeping just a few feet away.

Ian worked his left shoulder. No pain, no stiffness. If anything, he felt better than he had before. Sleeping under the tree had been, well, restful, the way sleep was always supposed to be and too often wasn't.

He was ravenously hungry, and while a quick Hershey's bar from the outer pocket of his rucksack eased the pangs, what he really wanted was hot food.

Last time he was in this part of Vandescard, he had had to keep a low profile. But now, perhaps not. He was, at least technically, engaged to the Margravine of the Eastern Hinterlands, although that probably didn't amount to much—unless he wanted to actually marry Marta and settle down to be a margrave.

Surely the fiancé of a margravine could light a fire to warm his breakfast. On the other hand, the nearest source of wood, other than the oak, was at the bottom of Bóinn's Hill, and while it had been a surprisingly easy climb up yesterday, Ian didn't fancy the idea of starting off a daylong march by playing the Noble Duke of York.

Hosea, though, was a thoughtful sort. Perhaps he had gathered some and stashed it in his rucksack as he had walked. The only problem with doing something about that was that he didn't really want to wake Hosea—if the old man was sleeping, he probably still needed his sleep—and you just didn't open somebody else's pack without permission. On the road, be it in the U.S. or in Tir Na Nog, your pack was your home, and what little privacy you had, you deserved.

No big deal. Cold sausage would make an adequate breakfast, and he could drain his canteen now, and refill it later. As long as you weren't in danger of going a long time without—and this close to the Gilfi, that wasn't a concern—the best place to carry water was inside you.

No hot meal, but hmmm . . . that was strange.

He hadn't noticed it yesterday, but one of the smaller low-hanging branches was dead, the leaves long gone brown. He thought he would have to use the coil saw in his pack, but it snapped off cleanly with just a tug.

In a few moments he had a small fire going, shielded from the wind by the smallest of the menhirs.

Hosea's eyelids flickered, and then opened, and the dark face split in a broad smile. "I brought some coffee," he said, as he sat up, leaning on one elbow. "You left it behind in Hardwood."

"I realized that," Ian said. *And if I'd wanted you to come along, I wouldn't have said no when you asked me if you could. And, then again, if my saying no meant a lot to you, you wouldn't have followed anyway.*

Relaxing to the inevitable never came easy to Ian, but to tell the truth, it felt good to have Hosea along. There was something about the old black man's smile that was reassuring, and he certainly knew more about, well, everything involving Tir Na Nog than Ian did.

"Let's have breakfast, and then hit the road. Valin should be camped out somewhere down there."

Hosea nodded. "I could track him, but it would seem much simpler simply to let him find us."

"Indeed."

Hosea raised an eyebrow. " 'Indeed?' Am I mocked?"

"You bet."

It took only a few minutes to roast the sausages over the small fire, a shorter time to wrap what they didn't eat for later consumption, and almost no time at all to put the fire out by the traditional method.

Ian buttoned his fly before he belted Giantkiller on; he hefted his rucksack to his shoulders.

Hosea was already ready, his pack slung, his cloak rolled and tied like a bedroll, below. "Shall we?"

Ian nodded. "Yes, let's." He felt like he was forgetting something. "You go on ahead; I'll meet you down the trail in a few minutes."

Hosea nodded and walked off.

Ian waited until he disappeared around a bend before he turned to the tree. "Thank you," he said. "It was nice of you to give me peace for the night, and fuel for my fire." He patted at the rough bark.

It felt silly, but there was nobody else to hear him, except maybe Bóinn, and she wouldn't tell on him. He couldn't feel a breeze, but the leaves above his head rustled quietly, as though in answer.

Ian smiled as he set off briskly down the hill, Giantkiller slapping gently against his leg as he walked. For somebody who had gone for some years without any kind of home, it felt good to have two.

CHAPTER THIRTEEN

~

Morning After

T he damn phone wouldn't stop ringing, and even
though it was right above Jeff's head it took
him a moment to wake up enough to think
about answering it. He shouldn't have had that second
drink; his head was pounding, and his gut was threatening
to rebel, and every rrrring-*ring* was a personal assault.

He reached up and pulled the receiver down, and croaked
out a "Hello."

"Hello yourself," the sweetest voice in the world answered. "Well, you sound even more chipper than usual
this morning."

"Hi, Kath." He rolled over and glanced at the clock.
The painfully red letters said 7:33. Too damn early, even
if his head hadn't been pounding, and taking a short drink
and heading back to bed—his usual cure for a rare hang-
over—wasn't going to be practical.

"Everything's fine," she said. "With me."

Wait. "How did you know to call me here?"

"You mean," she said, with some heat, "how could I
possibly know something when you didn't bother to tell me
anything at all?"

"Kath—"

"Or do you mean that since you never tell me anything, I shouldn't expect to know anything now?"

That was unfair. Along with the badge came the requirement for a certain amount—a certain large amount—of discretion and even secrecy. It was part of his job. And, yes, he could trust Kathy, but for Jeff, as it had been for old John Honistead, having a wife who was publicly irritated with him for not being open-mouthed was an asset. People were much more willing to talk to you if they knew it wouldn't go any further unless it had to, and you could avoid all sorts of problems if you could nip them in the bud, and the bud was, well, discretion.

And Kathy knew that. That was part of the deal, and he had thought that most of her protestation was for public consumption, not because she really was irritated with him.

But the one thing Jeff knew about women is that you never really knew about women.

"Look, honey . . ." he started.

She giggled.

His jaw dropped. He had seen Kathy smile, and he had occasionally heard a deep laugh. But a giggle? A chuckle? Never.

"Okay, who are you and what have you done with the real Kathy Aarsted Bjerke?" he asked.

She giggled again. "Oh, I'm still me. Really. Actually, I'm calling with a message for you."

"Oh?"

"Yes. Thorian Thorsen called Dad, and Dad said to tell you . . ."

Paper rustled in the background. Kathy had always figured that if you didn't write it down, it didn't count, and she always made it count because she always wrote it down. Shopping lists, directions, little notes in his lunch pail that said "I love you!" with the dot under the exclamation point a little heart—she wrote everything down.

Jeff didn't know why he found that so endearing, but he did. There were worse things in the world than to find your wife's habits charming.

"The first thing he says is to not call over there, and not

to come over there. He'll explain why later, when you meet him."

And where was Jeff going to meet him?

"The Ramsey County Humane Society, Beulah Lane, St. Paul," she said, answering him before he'd gotten the chance to ask.

St. Paul? Yuck.

Well, Thorian Thorsen undoubtedly had his reasons. But St. Paul?

She giggled again. "Yes, I know how you feel about St. Paul. 'It's a nice place to live, but you wouldn't want to visit there.'"

Cities, even if well laid out, were hard enough to find your way around in. St. Paul had clearly been laid out by a madman who thought it would be funny to have Sixth Street and Seventh Street intersect, and have that be an entirely different place than the intersection of Old Sixth and Seventh. And then there were the streets like Chatham, that started and stopped like the dotted line down a highway.

As far as Jeff was concerned, the only sensible way to find your way around St. Paul was to let a native guide drive you, and even then he wouldn't want to bet on it.

"Do you have a pencil?"

He had dropped his shirt and pants next to the bed before crashing out last night, and, as always, there was a notepad and pen in his shirt pocket.

"Go."

Billy was stretched out on the king-sized bed—Jeff had half-expected him to have a queen-sized one, and felt vaguely guilty at the thought—in his bedroom, wearing one of those black satin sleeping masks that looked like the Lone Ranger's mask, except without the eye-holes.

Sunlight splashed in through the venetian blinds, striping his hairless chest with bands of gold and dark.

Jeff knocked on the door frame.

Billy came awake instantly, as though he hadn't really been sleeping; he reached up and pulled off his sleeping mask and propped himself up on an elbow.

"Well," he said, his smile just a touch too wide to be unforced. "Good morning to you."

"Where's the nearest place I can rent a car?" Jeff asked. "Preferably cheap." He hadn't been able to find a phone book—either white or yellow pages—and, besides, he had never rented a car.

What was the cheapest choice? Hertz? Avis? He didn't need anything fancy. Just transportation.

"Oh, there's a Rent-a-Wreck downtown, but why rent when you can borrow from a friend?" Billy's fingers scrabbled on his nightstand and came up with a set of keys. "Bright red Saturn parked out front. There's a spare key in one of those little magnetic boxes under the left rear fender if you lock the keys in. And please do lock up? This is the city."

"Billy, I . . ."

"You're very grateful, and you just don't know how to thank me, because I've been so wonderful despite everything and gee, Billy, let's get together some time." Billy tossed the keys overhand into the air, and Jeff had to lunge forward to catch them. Billy never did have a good pitch; he always threw like a girl.

"Don't worry about getting the car back; I wasn't going to use it today, anyway. My plan is to sleep the morning away, then take the bus downtown for my class at the Y before work. It's cheaper, and it's just as quick, and it gives me an excuse to ask the new bartender for a ride home after work again, and he's very, very cute." He frowned as he fumbled for his mask. "But just be careful, okay?"

"I won't scratch your car."

"I'm not talking about the fucking car."

CHAPTER FOURTEEN

Branden del Branden

Ian was surprised, although not shocked: the Village of Mer's Woods wasn't exactly prepossessing, but either it had grown since Torrie had been there or Torrie had exaggerated its smallness, so to speak.

Torrie had talked about a few huts and shacks in a clearing at the edge of a hunting preserve owned by the Margrave Mer, but as the trail through Mer's Woods broke on the clearing, Ian could easily count a couple of dozen houses straddling the cobblestone street that was the only paved road in the village.

It was one of the last outposts of Vandescard before the mountains of the Middle Dominion, and while there was little commerce between the two—wars and rumors of wars tended to interfere with trade—it was the quickest way to get to the Cities from Eastern Vandescard . . .

As long as they didn't want you not to come. As an invasion route, it would be a problem. The mountain road rose up in the distance, twisting and turning up toward the clouds.

"Just as well we're friendly, eh?" Hosea said. "It's amazing how many deadfalls one can build when you've had a few centuries to build them."

"So why leave the road up at all?" Ian asked, instantly realizing that it was a stupid question the moment the words were out of his mouth.

"Because," Hosea said, his smile a gentle reproof, "the road goes down," he said, his hand making a downward arc, "as well as up." His hand arced up.

"This one is sorry for his stupidity, friend of the friend of the Father of Vestri, himself the father of the Folk," Valin said, his forehead wrinkled in confusion, "but he does not understand. All roads go in both directions. This road is not special in that respect."

Well, at least he had relaxed enough to only slip into formal mode now and then. The bowing and scraping never did sit well with Ian. Thank goodness he didn't know that Hosea was the Father of Vestri himself, or he never would have loosened up even this much.

"Truth to tell, young one," Hosea said, "most roads do. But not all."

"I . . . don't understand."

"Well, you know that some of the Hidden Ways only go in one direction, and they are roads of sorts. And time, much as it may speed by or slow down, does only speed by or slow down in one direction."

"But must that always be so?"

If it wasn't a silly question, then it was one that Valin wouldn't be able to understand the answer to. Nevertheless, Hosea was interminably patient with Valin's slowness—and Ian's, as well, come to think of it—and he didn't simply shrug it off the way Ian was tempted to. "No one can outrun time. Do you know the story of Asa-Thor and his visit to Utgarda-Loki?"

"Loki?" The dwarf's eyes went wide.

"No, no, not Brother Fox—Loki and Honir were travelling with Thor at the time. I speak of Utgarda-Loki; he was a giant, who entertained the three of them for an evening in his cave.

"Eating and drinking had become bragging and boasting—remember, we are talking about Asa-Thor, and he was always a loudmouth—enough to irritate their host.

"So he had a red-headed man challenge Loki to an eating contest; he challenged Asa-Thor to pick up his cat; and he had a lame old woman run a race against Honir. The three Aesir lost all the contests, for the red-headed man was Fire itself, and no one can eat more than fire; the cat was really the belly of Ourobouros, the Worm of the world, and not even Thor could raise the world; and the lame old woman was Time, and nobody, not even one as fleet of foot as Honir, can outrun time, or cause it to go back when it steps forward.''

Time passed more quickly and pleasantly, as usual, when Hosea was telling a story, and despite his age and his limp, talking while he walked never seemed to slow him down. Yesterday, the story of Honir's Run had taken them from breakfast to lunch, and his extended version of the tale of Bóinn and the Salmon of Knowledge had carried them to their campsite, and now the story of Thor's Visit to Utgarda-Loki took them down the trail and to the margrave's cottage that stood guard on the road into the village.

The closest thing to an inn the village had was the margrave's hunting lodge, a long, low, thatch-roofed cottage completely surrounded by a raised deck that wouldn't have looked out of place on the shores of Lake Bemidji—if it wasn't for the green vines that Ian knew were carved into the pillars rather than real because they were veined with gold leaf—but the high windows were shuttered and the entryway was boarded, the only sign of life a wisp of smoke from what Ian assumed was the simple wattle-and-daub building behind it.

That was too bad. If somebody from the margrave's court were in residence, they might have been able to spend the night, or trade on Ian's name for some horses. But even though the village was larger than its reputation, there would hardly be a stable full of horses awaiting some traveler's purchase or borrowing.

Too bad. It would be—

His thoughts were interrupted by the pounding of horses' hooves off in the distance, drawing closer. Valin dove for the brush on the side of the road. His rucksack's straps hung up in some brush, but he wriggled out of it and vanished, only a rustling of leaves and twigs marking his passing.

Hosea smiled forgivingly. "The Sons of Vestri have not always been the most courageous of creatures, but I'm fond of them nonetheless."

Ian grunted. "Valin managed enough courage to get to Hardwood with the warning, even badly injured."

"There is that." Hosea set his rucksack down on the dirt of the road and leaned against his staff.

Ian had already shrugged out of his rucksack and had loosened Giantkiller in its scabbard. Not that he would be able to do a lot of good against a troop of soldiers, but the Fire Duke had taught him that there were times when bravado was even better than cheap: it was free.

A troop of twenty horsemen in the orange-and-black livery of the House of Fire thundered around the bend in the road, blue pennants fluttering from the tips of the lancers' lances.

Blue?

"House of the Sky," Hosea answered the unasked question. "They're on an assignment on behalf of the Scion, of the Dominions as a whole, not just of the House of Fire."

"Is that usual?"

"No."

The horsemen slowed as they approached the wide spot in the road where Ian and Hosea stood waiting. None were armored cap-a-pie, but each of the lancers held a highly burnished shield on his free arm, while his lance arm was covered with a metal sleeve from the gauntlet to where it disappeared under a riding cloak.

All wore peaked helmets that covered the top, back, and sides of their heads, with what Ian thought of as a nosepiece, although it probably had a technical name, covering the face from brow to mouth.

The leader wore the three red and silver stripes of an ordinary of the House of Flame on his shield, which he deftly tossed to the horseman on his right side, then dismounted with an easy vault.

He removed his helmet, and handed it up to another of the horsemen. "Ian Silver Stone," he said, with a shallow smile that went no deeper than his teeth, ''I'm pleased to see you here.''

Branden del Branden still wore his moustache, but his sharp chin was clean-shaven; apparently beards were, at the moment, out of fashion in the House of Fire, and Branden del Branden was nothing if not stylish.

He was only a little shorter than Ian, and his build was a compromise between Ian's own lankiness and the thick muscularity of the Thorsens.

Except for his wrists: both were thick and muscular, like Ian's own. They were a swordsman's wrists. An ordinary of the House of Flame might not be the equal of a professional duelist, but he was, first and foremost, a swordsman, in both law and practice, and the wrist was the fulcrum around which the world of the sword balanced.

Ian hadn't known Branden del Branden long or well, but he had known him long enough to dislike him. It wasn't that Branden del Branden clearly had a thing for Maggie—Ian understood that, and Torrie could have taken him handily if he got out of line—but it was something about his self-assurance that grated on Ian's nerves. Branden del Branden, no more than thirty, had felt perfectly comfortable taking charge of Falias while the new Fire Duke was being sent for.

Maybe it was just jealousy. Branden del Branden not only had a solid place in his world but he had always had it, and always would. He was the oldest son of Branden del Branden the Elder, and while that made him heir to his father's responsibilities, it also had always made him heir to his father's place.

It was probably his move, so Ian stepped forward and offered his hand; Branden del Branden stepped forward and accepted it, gripping Ian's wrist as Ian gripped his. Branden del Branden's grip was, if anything, stronger than Ian's.

''It's good to see you, as well,'' Ian said.

''Oh, and why would that be?''

Because it was the polite thing to say? ''Why shouldn't it be?''

''I don't know why the man the Vandestish call the Promised Warrior would be happy to see an ordinary of the House of Flame,'' Branden del Branden said, his tone light, but with the definite undertone of menace that Ian had heard before.

Or, for that matter, why an ordinary of the House of Flame would be happy to see someone who had snatched the Brisingamen ruby almost literally from under his nose, and conveyed it to Freya for safekeeping.

''Then why did you say you were happy to see me?''

''I didn't say I was happy; I said I was pleased,'' Branden del Branden said, as though daring Ian to take offense. ''Vereden del Harold, whose troop waits for you at the northern pass, owes me a ram, and his troop owes my troop a feasting.'' He gestured at the men behind him, who sat eyeing Ian and Hosea with what Ian hoped was professional interest rather than the cold hostility that it felt like.

Gratitude apparently wasn't high on the list of attributes among the ruling class of the Dominions. Well, that didn't make them different from rulers in other times, other places, did it?

Shit.

''How did you know I was coming?'' Ian asked.

Branden del Branden barely glanced skyward before his eyes fastened back on Ian's. ''I couldn't say,'' he said.

Oh, Ian thought. *I think maybe I'd like to teach you how to play high-stakes poker, Branden del Branden. You've got a wicked tell.*

''A little bird told you—told him, eh?'' he said in English.

''I would imagine a large one,'' Hosea answered, also in English, from behind him.

That was the trouble with messing around with the gods. Once they took an interest in you, they kept an interest in you. Would it have been Freya or Odin who had sent Hugin or Munin to the Dominions, sending word that Ian was back in Tir Na Nog? And why?

If it was for his own good, somebody would have already told him about that. So it wasn't.

''So you're here to meet me?'' Ian nodded. ''For what purpose?''

Branden del Branden shrugged. ''To give you food and

horses, and convey you safely to the Dominions and to the House of the Sky.'' His expression grew inutterably bland. ''There's been word that there are Sons seeking the blood of your friends, and perhaps they might settle for yours.'' He turned to Hosea. ''If you'll see to getting the attention of that vestri servant of yours who seems to be emulating a gopher, perhaps we can serve you a quick repast, and then be on our way.'' He chuckled quietly to himself. ''I never thought I'd be ordered to convey the Promised Warrior safely into the Dominions at all, and much less into the presence of the klaffvarer to the Scion himself.''

Not this again. Damn. ''I'm not sure there will ever be a Promised Warrior, but even if there is, it's not me. I'm not the Promised Warrior,'' Ian said, tiredly. ''I'm just Ian Silverstein, from—from Hardwood, North Dakota, USA, and while I'm not the worst man with a sword that there's ever been, there's nothing legendary or magical about my abilities, and I not only couldn't lead the armies of Vandescard to conquer the Dominions, I wouldn't. Truly.'' He spread his hands. ''I'm not somebody you have to worry about.''

Harbard's ring felt heavy on his finger. It would be easy to use it to persuade Branden del Branden of that—but would it be wise? What would the others of the Dominions think if Branden del Branden was persuaded of something they all doubted? Particularly since he probably didn't have a reputation for being easily convinced.

And if he couldn't rely on the gratitude of the men of the Cities, perhaps a bit of fear would help.

Or perhaps not.

The road up to the Cities was long and twisting. If you were an ordinary of the House of Flame, and you thought you might be accompanying the man who had somehow been destined to conquer your otherwise unconquerable home, you might well want to see how many times he could bounce down the side of a mountain.

''There is nothing to worry about, you say?'' Branden del Branden nodded briskly, his smile broadening. ''Ah. I thank you for that reassurance.'' He took a step back and drew himself up straight. ''I choose to take offense at your insult, and accept your insult as a challenge.''

''Eh?''

''You've accused me of worry, of fear. That's not the worst insult a man has ever faced, but I've certainly fought over less. It is a matter of honor, after all.'' He swallowed, once, heavily. ''Will my first blood be sufficient to satisfy your honor, as yours shall satisfy mine?''

He's scared of me. So why is he picking a fight?

It didn't matter, not now. No, of course it mattered. Knowledge of your opponent's motivations could be as useful as a counter-riposte, on or off the fencing strip.

Hosea took a step forward. ''Of course first blood shall satisfy Ian, Branden del Branden, if it comes to that,'' he said, gently. ''But I say to you, as his second, that no insult was intended.''

Branden del Branden nodded sagely. ''I accept that, of course.''

The thickset man that held Branden del Branden's shield tossed the shield to another, then dropped heavily to the ground. His boots thudded hard as he stalked toward where Ian and Hosea stood facing Branden del Branden.

''As Branden del Branden's second,'' he said, ''I reject your assurance. Offense has been given; challenge has been given; acceptance has been given.''

If Branden del Branden had any objection to his second's intervention, it didn't show in his face, or in his silence.

It was starting to fall into place. The men from the Cities had tried something like this with Torrie, once. Their intent had been, at least in theory, simply to see how good he was.

It had gone horribly wrong. The idiot who had challenged Torrie had tried for the sort of wound that runs from the front of the chest to the back of it. Torrie had killed the idiot in self-defense, and while Branden del Branden had eventually agreed to accept that the death hadn't been deliberate, he had not agreed to believe it.

So, rather than have another of his men challenge Ian, he had done it himself. A quick testing duel to see how good Ian was with his sword was apparently the idea, and he had to admire Branden del Branden's courage, if not his good sense.

Shit, if all you wanted was to fence with me, that could have been arranged without all this. Try asking next time.

"When?" he asked.

Branden del Branden turned to his second. "Shall we eat first?"

"I think not." The heavyset man shook his head. "Not until honor has been settled," he said.

Branden del Branden raised his hands. "What can I say? Iwald del Dergen thinks we should proceed now."

"Very well." Ian nodded. "As you wish. I'll want a few moments to prepare, if that's not a problem. And if it is, I'll still want a few moments to prepare."

Branden del Branden made an openhanded gesture. "Of course," he said, smiling. "Take all the time you need, Ian Silver Stone."

Ian's mind raced as he sat on the dirt of the road, removing his heavy hiking boots while Hosea dug a pair of sneakers from his pack. The kind of boots that protected your feet when you were tromping up and down the sides of mountains didn't make for a light touch or quick movements in a duel. Yes, he would fight in them if he had to— shit, he'd fight buck naked, or wearing a grass skirt, if he had to; that's what *had to* meant—but Ian always believed in taking every advantage he could get.

And he had been walking all day; it wasn't like he was coming to this cold, so he didn't need to do his stretches.

Like hell he didn't.

You didn't use the same muscles and tendons in a hike, and even more than your equipment—and he had no worries about Giantkiller letting him down—you had to be able to count on your body to do what you told it to.

Yes, the wrist was the center around which a match or a duel orbited, but the legs were the force that drove the orbit, that powered the match. One stretched tendon, one charley horse, one momentary muscle spasm could anchor you in place on a fencing strip or in a dueling circle, and end it all—because in any universe, if your opponent could control either space or time, he controlled everything.

Hosea had his right sock off, and the way he was massaging Ian's smelly, sweaty foot dry felt obscenely good. "I know little about Branden del Branden's style," Hosea said. "Only what Thorian and Ivar del Hival have discussed, and that was largely the observations of Ivar del Hival, who is by no means the best duelist I've ever seen."

Ian had fenced with Ivar del Hival and could beat the older man easily. On the other hand, in hand-to-hand grappling, Ivar del Hival knew how to use his bulk and strength to good advantage, and while his wrist and arm were strong but slow, his eye was reasonably keen, although not in the same league as Thorian Thorsen's.

"And . . . ?" Ian launched himself into the first of his stretches, like he had done more times than he thought he could count. He stood flatfooted, and bent over far enough to grasp his calves, and then bent forward slowly, inexorably.

The tendons in his hamstrings and his butt felt like hot piano wires. So he stretched them more, not ignoring the pain, but insisting on it. The more it hurt, the better. Pain in his hamstrings wouldn't kill him, or even harm him; he couldn't stretch hard enough to hurt himself, not as long as he did it slowly and deliberately.

"He's strong," Hosea said, "and perhaps overly fond of the pris-de-fer, or perhaps insufficiently fond of fencing in the absence. He tends to fight Ingarian-style—"

Ian straightened, and worked his shoulders. "Fancy. Like he's fighting with a foil. Close in; high speed; up-and-down until you think you've caught the pattern, and then wham."

"Exactly."

Well, that could easily work to Ian's advantage, he thought, as his body brought him through the rest of his stretches, letting his mind float freely.

Ian had been exclusively a foil fencer, until recently. It had been a logical necessity; he had stayed with the foil for the same reasons that a plumber would stay with a plunger—not out of affection for it, but because it was a tool that put money in his pocket, and because the money in his pocket put food in his mouth.

The way you got beginning students to tutor was by winning matches—ideally, every fucking point in every damn match you entered. Almost all beginning students started with foil, some moving on to the so-called advanced weapons—épée and saber—as though there wasn't enough to learn about supposedly simple foil fencing to fill a hundred dozen lifetimes.

And if Ian was going to get through school—and he was—he couldn't do it working at McDonald's. The time that you could pull yourself up and through to the other side of college at anything near minimum wage was long gone, if it ever had existed, something Ian was skeptical of in the first place.

Other kids had parents to put them through. Or families. Or scholarships.

Ian had himself, and that was all. Until recently.

And that sucked.

He shook his head to clear it. Yes, it sucked. Yes, it was horribly unfair that he'd had an asshole of a drunk of a childbeater of a father who had kicked Ian out when Ian had decided he wasn't going to be a punching bag for his asshole of a drunk of a childbeater of a father, not any more.

All that was true.

But he had better leave the angst for another time. If he didn't concentrate on the duel instead of on what a shitty hand life had dealt him in the person of that shitty excuse for a father, Benjamin Silverstein, what he might get was a sword through his gizzard.

Wherever his gizzard was, he didn't need a sword stuck through it.

He let his head roll around on his neck, ignoring the occasional jeer and titter that came from the line of now-dismounted horsemen.

Go ahead, assholes. Laugh.

Branden del Branden had stripped himself down to what passed for informal dueling clothes in the Cities: light slippers over bare feet, tight white trousers covered by a loose white tunic that looked like a karate gi except for the lace embroidery at the hem, belted tightly at the waist.

White for purity? White because it was hard to clean, and the nobility of the Cities could never do things the easy way when the hard way would do? Or white because it would show blood, and a Cities duelist might well choose to claim that a touch never happened if he could get away with it?

Maybe it was for all those reasons. It undoubtedly wasn't poverty that had caused Branden del Branden to have several small rips inexpertly stitched across the right arm, with a larger one on the right thigh and left knee. Those were advertisements, presumably, of points lost, a matter of pride, perhaps, like a Heidelberg scar—except you couldn't take a Heidelberg scar off and throw it to a vestri servant to wash it for you at the end of the day.

And a Heidelberg scar, perhaps, wasn't a road map to how you lost points. Branden del Branden's fencing outfit said that he took most of his hits on his swordarm. Perhaps he was too eager to close, too eager to lunge, too eager to extend.

Too eager to win? It was entirely possible to be too eager to win.

But you could never tell with the men of the Cities. For them, honor and deviousness were woven together in a complex pattern—it was entirely possible that some of the rips were artificial, intended to mislead; and it was equally possible that to do that was as dishonorable as a Heidelberg fencer getting his schmiss by plastic surgery.

But it didn't matter.

Ian could take him. He felt it in his muscles, and he knew it in his bones with a certainty that frightened him: Branden del Branden could not beat him. Not here, not today, and probably not anywhere, not ever.

Ian smiled as he slipped out of his thick flannel shirt, and put on the Villanova T-shirt he had won in his first college fencing match—Ian had a lot of T-shirts from other schools. He had thought for a moment about skipping the shirt—no need to get it sweaty if he didn't have to, or bloody, for that matter, if it came to that—but wondered if the play of his muscles under his skin could give Branden del Branden a clue as to what his next move might be.

At the poker table or on the fencing strip, you never wanted to give away any information accidentally. You couldn't always win, but when you couldn't, you made the fuckers earn every pot. Every point. Every time.

You gave nothing away, not to the person on the other side of the poker table, and not to the person on the other end of the fencing strip, and not because you hated them—Ian saved his hate for those who had earned it—but because any pot you could win, any point you could take, was yours, and little enough in this world was yours.

Branden del Branden took up his sword and gave it a few tentative swings through the air.

It was, through no coincidence, similar in shape and size to Giantkiller: technically a saber—it was sharp enough on both edges well back from its needle point—but in practice used more like an épée. Branden del Branden's sword had the simple quillons that were common hereabouts; Giantkiller now sported a shiny half-bell guard that Hosea had fitted to it, to suit Ian's preference for more protection of the hand.

He took Giantkiller in his hand—and it felt almost embarrassingly good, as always, to wrap his fingers around his sword's grip—and raised the sword in a simple salute.

By Middle Dominion standards, that was an arrogant thing to do. Here, as at home, you could tell who somebody's teacher was by the salute, and here, unlike at home, to use a simple salute was to declare that you were sui generis, but that was fine with Ian. Branden del Branden's salute was a complex cloverleaf that Thorian Thorsen would probably have been able to read like a book—but he wasn't here, and Branden del Branden's point was.

Ian advanced tentatively, but Branden del Branden closed the distance with a bound.

Within moments of their first crossing swords, Ian knew how to take him. Branden del Branden was a show-off, and he could never use a simple attack when a complicated one would do.

Ian repressed a smile. It was like fencing with his younger self: Branden del Branden fought like a foil fencer out to show off every trick, every change of engagement that he had been taught. Parry and riposte, then counter-riposte, taking the blade from high to low or from low to high.

This was too easy. You beat complexity with simplicity at épée, or in a duel, or in life.

Dismiss the multiple compound attacks, the second intention, the attempt to force you to close and play his game. Don't let him take your blade, but draw an attack, and control the distance on retreat. Don't fence foil, don't try to match his complexity with yours, but wait for the opportunity to end it simply.

Patience was a virtue. A duel was a contest not of strengths but of weaknesses. You didn't have to win by being better than your opponent; you won most of the time by exploiting his mistakes, while not making one he could exploit.

So keep it simple, and remember that to touch, to cut, to win required extending the arm, but that extending the arm brought your arm into his reach for the touch, for the cut.

Ian's had greater reach; Branden del Branden's had strength and perhaps a touch of speed.

But none of it mattered. He could—

No. Ian exposed his wrist to draw a stop-hit, then disengaged and extended—

—and Branden del Branden dropped into a low-line lunge, bringing Ian's blade harmlessly over his shoulder, while his point slid past Ian's defenses to scratch a line of pain across Ian's thigh.

Ian beat Branden del Branden's blade aside as he retreated, hobbling. There was a moment where Branden del Branden would have been able to redouble his attack, and might have been able to make a second touch—

But no; that wasn't what he was trying to do, and Ian didn't even have to beat the blade away.

Branden del Branden's eyes were wide with surprise as he looked at the blood on his blade and at the dark stain spreading across the outside of Ian's jeans, but he brought himself to attention, and held the pose until Ian managed to straighten and salute him.

His eyes narrowed for a moment. He was wondering if it had been too easy.

"Perhaps I'll do better next time, Branden del Branden," Ian said. "But nicely done," he said, Harbard's ring pulsing hard on his finger, "and well scored."

It still made sense to never give up a point. But Branden del Branden hadn't been out to win a first-blood duel; he had been out to take Ian's measure. And giving him the wrong measure made it Ian's match, not his.

And if the warm blood trickling from the aching cut in his thigh made him wonder if he'd been as clever as he thought he had, Hosea's brief nod said that he'd gotten it right this time.

CHAPTER FIFTEEN

Sons of Fenris

It all depended on your point of view, Ian supposed: either clouds or fog were rolling in.

Did it matter? Well, maybe not, but it was nice to know the right names for things. He would have asked Hosea, or Valin, but—undoubtedly through no accident—Branden del Branden had put Hosea and his tired brown mare at the front of the party and Valin on his preposterously large but spiritlessly plodding black gelding in the back.

Ian turned to the soldier riding at his side. "Are those clouds or is that fog?" he asked.

The question, like all of Ian's questions, was bluntly ignored. Apparently, the Promised Warrior could take any information—like, say, when they were going to stop for lunch—and turn it into a plan for a Vandestish invasion of the Middle Dominion.

The familiar—if only vaguely familiar—outline of the House of Fire was, if he figured it right, going to be obscured behind him, and he would have been hard put to retrace the twisting trail even on the clearest of days.

Which this wasn't going to be.

Off in the distance, past the jagged horizon that con-

cealed Vandescard and the gray Gilfi below, an unseasonal
thunderhead rose like a white mountain. Every once in a
while, there was a flash of lightning that lit it up brightly
against the darkening sky, but it was far too far away for
him to hear any thunder.

Well, thank goodness for small favors: the cloud bank—
or fog bank; Ian refused to make a choice if the locals
weren't going to give him the full information—rolling in
looked like it might well be thick and dark and wet, but
there was no sign of lightning.

It covered them more suddenly than he thought it would.
One minute he was riding in bright sunshine, looking at the
fair hills, and the next he was surrounded by a milky whiteness, perhaps a ten-yard ring of visibility surrounding him,
eerily reminding him of the gray glow of the Hidden Ways.

He had never been in such a thick fog, and he was surprised to find that it didn't interfere with his hearing the
way it did with his vision. He could still hear the clopping
of the hooves of the horses out front and behind him; he
just couldn't see them.

He hadn't seen any woodland ahead, but maybe he had
missed something: he found that he had to duck under low-
hanging branches that seemed to sweep out of the mist
faster than the slow pace of the plodding horses.

For a moment, he idly considered leaping up into one of
the trees, just to see what would happen, but . . .

What would that do?

Branden del Branden called for a break at an ancient
stone piazza that stuck out from the side of the road, a disk
perhaps twenty yards across, rimmed by a low stone lip,
hanging out over damp white emptiness. They—or at least
somebody—had been expected: a wooden barrel held water
for the horses, and when two of the soldiers pulled up a
dozen yards of the rope that had been fastened to a brass
post, they pulled a chain of three bags out from the white
milkiness. The first contained oats; the second apples; and
the third the limpest, most dubious-looking carrots that Ian
had ever seen.

While the troopers saw to the animals—horses were so
much work to take care of that Ian would often have pre-

ferred traveling on foot, if it weren't so much slower—Ian took the opportunity to stretch his legs and empty his bladder, never having quite gotten the knack of standing in the stirrups and twisting to one side to relieve himself. It wasn't exactly something they covered in high school, or at the U, after all.

Branden del Branden walked over with a pair of meatrolls from the provisions bag, and he offered Ian a choice, politely taking a bite from his own immediately.

"How is your wound?" he asked.

"It stings," Ian said. What would the right attitude be if he really had been beaten? Forget right—what would be believed?

Resentment? Scorn? Anger? Harbard's ring had helped persuade Branden del Branden of something he had wanted to believe in any case, but that didn't mean he would stay persuaded.

Casual. Casual was the right approach. "Perhaps you'll do me the honor of a return bout at some point?" *Ideally, at some point where it isn't in my interest to hide the fact that I'm one hell of a lot better than you'll ever be.* "I might be able to give you a better contest when I'm not so tired from the road."

Branden del Branden smiled knowingly. An excuse was the sort of low-class thing he would expect from an unfamilied commoner. "I'm sure that is so. Perhaps we'll find the opportunity for a friendly contest while we're visiting the Old Keep."

"Your men have been quite . . . discreet," Ian said. "How soon do we get to the City?"

"In due course, in due course." Branden del Branden dismissed the question with a wave of his hand. "I couldn't say for sure."

Ian let his frown show.

"No," Branden del Branden said, "I don't mean I won't say; I mean I can't say. Can you find your way in this fog?"

"No. But—"

"But you assumed I can." He raised a finger. "Never assume, Promised Warrior." The corners of his mouth twitched. "Ride with me, and I'll show you just one of the problems you face when you lead your Vandestish troops up to rape and pillage."

"I'm not the Promised Warrior," Ian said. "But I don't mind riding up front."

If he had to be looking at a horse's ass, he'd just as soon it be riding next to him.

Ian didn't know how to explain the fog thickening while simultaneously becoming less cold and clammy, but it had done just that: he could barely see ten feet ahead on the road, and there were times when waves of billowing whiteness made even that impossible.

Branden del Branden gestured at the surrounding whiteness. "Do you see what I mean? Could you remember the turns we have made?"

"Turns? We've just followed the trail."

Branden del Branden gave the sort of knowing smile that Ian never liked to see on anybody's face, including his own. "Oh, there's been a few forks, here and there. It's just a matter of taking the one that isn't obscured by fog. I don't think an invading army would find such openings, and I'd much rather not find out for sure." He gave a quick loosening pump to the hilt of his sword. "Would you?"

They rode in silence through the milkiness for a long time, until with each step the fog seemed to thin, the radius of his vision widening.

"Ah." Branden del Branden kicked his horse into a faster walk. "Now I can tell you that we'll be at the City soon, quite soon."

The road ahead widened and lengthened, and the sun broke through the clouds so bright and golden that it dazzled Ian's eyes, bringing tears that clouded his vision even more effectively than the fog itself had.

And then they were through the clouds and into startlingly clear air, a billowy, cottony cloudscape obscuring everything below, the only solid thing visible from horizon to horizon the mountain road that crossed the saddle from the peak they were on and twisted up to the City high above.

A bell clanged somewhere above them, and on the high ramparts, the tips of spears or bows could be seen moving quickly into position.

The Old Keep—if it had any other name, that name had been lost in time as surely as an invader would have been lost in clouds—hadn't been built at the top of the mountain; it had been carved from the top of a mountain by a master artisan, who had made a keep out of what clearly had been a sharply pointed and jagged peak, the highest of the spires, a turret that looked more like a Moslem minaret than anything more familiar to Ian, and poked high into the blue sky, while six smaller spires barely rose half its length.

The ramparts and balustrades were similar to the ones Ian had seen in Falias, the City of the House of Fire, but the piazzas weren't roofs for lower levels the way they were in Falias, but rather they projected out from the side of what remained of the mountain, sticking out of the keep like ear mushrooms on a tree. There were probably stairs inside as well, but dozens of stairways twisted up the naked side of the dark stone, and while Ian could see no sign of railings, forms moving up and down them made it clear that they were in use, and not just decorative.

Patches of greenery filled slashes in the side of the mountain, rimmed in a way that made it clear that they had been left by design, not by accident.

Ian would have liked to have turned to Hosea and congratulated him on the job, but that would have been, at best, imprudent.

There was no gate that Ian could see: the wide road across the narrow saddle between the two peaks vanished into a dark, wide hole in the side of the mountain wall.

"Rather something, isn't it?" Hosea said as he came abreast of them, Branden del Branden's horsemen making no motion to bar his passage.

"I was thinking that myself," Ian said. He would have asked Hosea something to the effect of, *Are you looking for a pat on the back?*

But it wasn't wise to assume that nobody listening could speak English, not if he didn't have to.

As Branden del Branden had pointed out to him, assuming wasn't always a good idea.

As they crossed the saddle between peaks, Ian considered the steep slope on either side that vanished in the clouds below. It would be a long fall.

He shook his head. It was just as well he wasn't this Promised Warrior; it would take more than a prophecy—even if he believed in prophecy, something he would have said he didn't a year ago—to make him want to cross this road under opposition, even assuming that he could have found his way up through the clouds to the road.

The men of the Dominions were an awfully superstitious lot, if they were worried about an invasion through this route.

But, no, that wasn't it. Control the bottleneck, and nothing gets into the bottle without your permission. A tiny force could hold this road indefinitely against a huge invading army. It didn't matter if you outnumbered your enemy ten-to-one, not if you could only confront him one-to-one, with his reinforcements coming from nearby, while your supplies and reserves had to follow you up a long trail.

No, they weren't afraid of an invasion on this route. For all Ian knew—and presumably for all they knew—a Hidden Way leading from, say, the Seat in Vandescard to the Dominions popped up in the Scion's bathroom, and the Promised Warrior could at any moment and without the slightest of warnings lead a division of Vandestish swordsmen and archers up through His Altitude's—or whatever they called him—bathtub.

It was easy to make fun of that fear, at least within the confines of his own mind, but he understood how frightening an attack through a Hidden Way could be. There wasn't anybody who remembered the Night of the Sons who wouldn't empathize, and there wasn't anybody who had taken his turn on duty at the cairn who would fail to understand, how even the possibility of such a thing could keep you up nights.

As they rode into the cool darkness of the entrance tunnel, Ian glanced up, unsurprised to find that his eyes were still too dazzled from the outside brightness to make out the murder holes that were undoubtedly hidden there.

Not that he tried hard to look; paying too much attention to the defenses of the Cities was probably something that somebody suspected of being the Promised Warrior would probably find it healthier—and would certainly find it more pleasant—not to be caught doing. And the easiest way not to be caught doing it was not to do it, after all. Even in the Byzantine politics of Tir Na Nog, there was a place for simple sincerity.

A hundred yards or so inside, just past the first turn, a stone door blocked the way; a brass oblong, patinated with age, set chest-high in the middle of it. Branden del Branden dismounted momentarily and pounded a gloved fist against the brass.

Thrummmmmm. The deep bass note rang through the tunnel.

Ian nodded. Just like the knocking posts on the Thorsen house. Understandable, given that they'd been built by the same person.

The stone door sank silently into the floor of the tunnel with no creaking of hinges or whirr of machinery, until the top of the easily two-foot-thick stone door was flush with the floor of the tunnel. Hosea built things to last.

The tunnel, unsurprisingly, twisted and turned into the mountain, then doubled back on itself as it climbed steeply toward daylight, so steeply that Ian was afraid that one of the horses would slip and fall, sending the other people and animals behind it scattering like bowling pins. But somehow they kept their feet beneath them, and soon the slope became more shallow, and just when Ian's eyes had finally adjusted to the darkness, the tunnel dumped them out on a courtyard, too brightly lit by the sun.

The courtyard was about the size of a football field, except football fields were not typically surrounded by thirty-foot-high walls topped with bowmen in livery of sky blue—or any other color, for that matter.

The walls were smooth and polished, canted ever-so-vaguely inward, and the hole they had come through was, as far as Ian could tell, the only way into or out of the courtyard.

Okay, fine, he thought. You've brought us in through the high-security entrance, and I'm suitably impressed with your security.

Ian didn't believe for a moment that this was the only way in and out of the Old Keep. He had been shown the well-guarded front door, but that wasn't the only one. If this was the only way in, the City couldn't possibly survive.

Yes, there surely were gardens on the slopes and piazzas of the City, and he had no doubt that herbs and fruits and vegetables were among the produce of those gardens. But the Cities didn't feed themselves; they were fed by the peasant farmlands of the Middle Dominion, and he didn't think it was possible that tons of food would be hauled up into this killing ground daily, to be lifted up and into the City proper.

What was that old Yiddish word that Zayda Saul used to use for somebody who could get by on nothing, who seemed to be able to get his nourishment out of the air, like a human air fern?

Airman—luftman, no: luftmensch, that was it. Luftmensch.

Ian had seen some healthy-looking—and some downright fat—people in Falias. He doubted that the Old Keep was populated solely by luftmenschen.

Above his head, the sudden appearance of a skinny, almost skeletal-looking man made Ian doubt himself.

"I am Darien del Darien, hereditary klaffvarer to the Scion," he said, his voice echoing sharply off the polished walls. "I greet you on behalf of the Scion, Ian Silver Stone," he said. His skull was naked of any hair, thin skin stretched tightly over a sharp-edged cranium. Long, bony fingers gripped the rail of the balustrade as he leaned out over the edge, and the heavy golden chain and medallion draped around his neck jingled not unpleasantly with his movements. "Do you come in peace?"

No, a crippled old elf, a vestri, and a single swordsman are going to beat the shit out of an entire City, he thought, but he knew better than to actually say that. His sense of humor never had gone over well in Tir Na Nog.

Or much of anywhere else, for that matter.

"I do," he said. Might as well get the rhinoceros in the corner out in the open. "I've heard it said that some think I'm the Vandestish Promised Warrior, foretold to lead invading hordes from Vandescard into the Cities, brushing aside the Crimson and Ancient Cerulean companies like so many draughts off a draughts board.

"I swear to you that that is not so, that I am no such thing, and have no such intention." He patted at Giantkiller's hilt. In for a penny, in for a pound. "And I offer to anyone who doubts that the opportunity to prove it with his blood, or with mine."

Look, folks, he thought. *Taking me up on this would be the sucker bet of all time, from your point of view. If I am this Promised Warrior, you can't beat me; and since I'm not—since I'm just simple Ian Silver Stone, who just got beaten by Branden del Branden in a short, first-blood affair—there's no need to do it at all.*

"My brothers and companions of the Old Keep, hear me: I would think long and hard before challenging Ian Silver Stone." Branden del Branden's voice was louder and stronger than Ian had heard it before. "He could have easily beaten me in a small matter of honor, but he managed to lose while receiving a trivial wound, and still protecting himself from further injury. He may or may not be the Promised Warrior—this is something about which I say very little and know even less—but he is a fine swordsman, one trained by Thorian del Thorian the Elder himself. And he's such a persuasive man that if the Scion himself hadn't told me that he would likely do such a thing, I would have believed Ian Silver Stone's claim that I had won by strength and skill."

Ian didn't meet his eyes. Well, maybe he wasn't so clever after all. Well, so much for that deception.

Ian wasn't sure whether or not he was looking forward to meeting this Scion, but it was going to be interesting. As, perhaps, in the old Chinese curse, "May you live in interesting times."

Darien del Darien beckoned with one skeletal finger, and

a device that reminded Ian of an overly ornate window-washer's scaffold was quickly set up and then lowered. Ian took his place on the platform next to Branden del Branden, and gripped the overhead strap. Hosea did the same, looking curiously like some sort of skinny New York subway strap-hanging commuter, while Valin, too short to reach even the lowest of the straps, clung tightly to Ian's left arm.

"You haven't done this before?" Ian asked.

The dwarf's eyes were wide. "No." Valin must have been intimidated: that was all he said.

After days on the road, a hot bath was an almost obscenely pleasant luxury. In the Old Keep—or at least in the suite of rooms Ian and Hosea had been assigned—a tub was a concave circular depression in the bathroom floor, rimmed by a calf-high wall of polished marble, broad enough to sit on.

The tub was filled from a thigh-thick golden pipe that descended from the ceiling, which dispensed not-quite-scalding water at the pull of a chain, and it was, presumably, emptied through the drain in the bottom of the tub under the domed wood plug where Ian rested his feet.

The soap in the small stone pot resting on the bathtub rim smelled of licorice and honey. Ian rubbed a third helping of it into his hair, then washed it out with another pull of the chain, which brought the level of water in the tub to within an inch or so of the rim.

Hmm . . . it would probably take only another few moments to make it overflow, which would at home be something he would worry about doing—downstairs neighbors had a way of disliking being rained on—but he didn't think that would happen here.

So he pulled hard, again, and the water splashed down and slopped over the sides of the tub.

Ian ducked down for one final rinse, then vaulted to the rim and out of the tub. The tiled floor was wet, but not slippery, but there was no standing water anywhere.

Over in the corner of the bathroom, a wooden privy seat stood over a white porcelain thundermug that was probably clean enough to drink out of, although the idea didn't have a lot of appeal. What did was using it to scoop up a gallon or two of water and pour it on the floor.

It drained quickly into the spaces between the tiles, and when Ian repeated the experiment in other corners of the room, the same thing happened.

"No, it won't flood." Hosea's voice came from the arched doorway. His vaguely nappy hair was dry and clean and seemed to be freshly trimmed. He had exchanged his road clothes for an off-white tunic and leggings that made his thin legs look absurdly skinny, like a couple of matchsticks, the knees bony. "Given how many years the ladies of the Keep have spent knotting the carpets of these halls, they wouldn't thank you if it did."

"Well, I didn't think it would." Where did it go? Down the side of the mountain?

"That would be wasteful. There's a system of pipes and shunts, which divert it to any of several of the piazza gardens below, depending. Water isn't exactly scarce in the Old Keep, but it's not overly abundant, and the first inhabitants of it were frugal folk." He frowned. "So I'm told."

That was in case they were being overheard, presumably. Hosea knew well what the first inhabitants of the Cities, the Tuatha del Danaan, were like, as he had built the Cities for them.

How long ago was that? Ian's spread hands asked.

Hosea shrugged, dismissing the question with a helpless wave of his hands. "Would you like that in ages or eons?" he asked, the only answer Ian would get.

Hosea picked up the white shirt that lay on top of the pile of clothes that a vestri servant had brought in. "Time to get dressed; we've been summoned."

"By whom? The Scion?"

"I hardly think so. Darien del Darien has politely sent a squad of guards to bring us to him."

"Valin?"

"I'm told he's being interrogated," Hosea said. "I think that Darien del Darien meant that in an informal sense, but . . ." He shook his head.

But it's their ballpark, and their rules. "And whatever gratitude they may have for my having exposed the fire giant masquerading as the Duke of the House of Fire doesn't weigh very heavily against a suspicion that I'm this Promised Warrior.''

"Would it with you? Would gratitude for a past favor overwhelm your good judgment in the present?''

Ian smiled as he belted Giantkiller around his waist. "Probably.''

Hosea laughed. "I hope that is just a joke, Ian.''

"Me, too.''

Darien del Darien and party were waiting for them at the edge of one of the circular piazzas that hung out over the white cloudscape below.

It would have been, perhaps, a nice time to have a parachute. Leap to the railing and out into the mist, pulling the cord as he went, hoping that he would break free of the cloud bank well enough to steer before he smashed into the side of the mountain.

Then again, Ian had never gone skydiving—nor had he ever had any desire to, for that matter—and he didn't have a parachute.

But it was something to think about.

Of the four men waiting for them—and they were all men—only Branden del Branden was armed. Were there archers on one of the surrounding piazzas with arrows nocked, waiting for Ian to make a threatening move?

Or was this chief butler of the Scion so sure of himself that he knew that Ian wasn't stupid enough to draw his sword when all he could do with it was make more trouble for himself?

Maybe this is what the bull in a bullfight felt like—the guy facing him only had a cape, after all. Ian would have rather the men of the Old Keep had a squad of pikemen with them.

Ian recognized Branden del Branden and Darien del Darien. The third man, however, he only recognized for what it—he—was.

He was six feet tall, covered with salt-and-pepper hair from his toes to the top of his head, thick wiry hair that concealed neither his potbelly nor the fleshy red penis peeking out from the dark fur below. The Son wore only three items: an amber amulet on a golden chain around his thick neck and two rings that looked like wedding bands, both worn on his right little finger.

His fingernails were laterally curved more than they ought to be, but cut short, and he eyed Ian with unconcealed loathing that, Ian hoped, masked fear.

Ian's hand itched for Giantkiller's hilt. The sword could do in a Son, in human form or lupine.

"My name," the Son said, his voice a deep growl, "is Herolf. I'm leader of the Northern Pack of Packs, and it seems that you have been telling lies about me and mine."

Well, the Dominioners had brought the two of them together to confront each other, and that was fine with Ian.

"I've told no lies," he said, smiling broadly. For a wolf, a smile was the baring of teeth. "There've been some of your cubs and bitches sent after my friends before." He forced his grin to widen. "I even know where some of them are buried."

If he had been expecting the Son to leap at him—and he had been half-expecting it—he was surprised. Herolf tilted back his head and laughed. It wasn't a nice laugh, but, then again, Sons weren't known for their niceness.

"Well done," Herolf said, sniffing the air, "although I'd certainly expect courage from someone who smells like a Promised Warrior."

Branden del Branden's eyes darted from Herolf to Ian, but Darien del Darien merely raised a skeletal knuckle toward his lips. "Please, O honored guest," he asked, his voice low, "tell me—how would a Son of Fenris, loyal to the Scion as you are, have had the opportunity to know what the Promised Warrior smells like?"

"There are some things," Herolf said, his voice rumbling, "that you know from birth."

"The odor of the pack, perhaps," Hosea said, taking a step forward. "The scent of fresh blood, of course," he went on. "But the smell of a legend? I rather doubt that." He turned to Ian. "On the other hand, Ian, do remember who the father of Fenris was."

Ian was sure he wasn't the real audience, but he picked up the cue anyway: "Loki."

Hosea nodded. "Loki. He's been called the Father of Lies, but," he said, raising a palm at Herolf's growl, "I always thought that something of an overstatement, and that Brother Fox was far more complex than his reputation allowed, and more unfortunate.

"After all, all the Aesir were liars and deceivers—Loki and Odin were just better at it than most, which is perhaps why they were such blood brothers, at least at first. Thor tended to boast, and Tyr was a red-handed fool—and eventually a one-handed fool—but Loki was a teller of tales, and a good one, and while the Sons of Fenris seem to have inherited little of his skill in falsehood, they've surely inherited his inclination to plot, to scheme, to lead and mislead."

Ian turned to Darien del Darien. "There's no question that there's a Son of Fenris searching for Thorsen blood," he said. "One left his mark outside of the . . . the residence of a friend of mine."

"Footprints can be forged," Herolf said. "Or lied about."

"That is certainly true." Darien del Darien nodded. "And the purpose for that lie would be?"

Herolf growled. "The relationship between the Sons of Fenris and the Dominions has long been beneficial to both. If it can be harmed by a few lies, who benefits?" He shook his hairy head. "It would not be the Dominions, and neither would it be the Sons of Fenris."

"Yes," Darien del Darien said quietly, "but it's not as though Sons haven't gone after Thorian del Thorian before."

"At the command of the Fire Duke, we did!" Herolf pounded on his own chest. "We couldn't have done it if he hadn't shown us the way."

"Well, no," Branden del Branden said. "It was not at the command of His Warmth. You did it at the command, at the hire, of a fire giant impersonating His Warmth."

Ian was surprised to find any kind of support at all coming from that direction, but he didn't let it show. Keeping a poker face had been second nature to him for a long time.

Herolf was just launching into a heated—and likely true—explanation that the Sons had been as well fooled by the imposter as everybody else, when Darien del Darien held up a slim finger, interrupting him.

His unblinking eyes settled on Ian's. "I think our guest has something to say," he said.

"I'm not here to pick a fight," Ian said quietly. "I'm not even here to make accusations toward anyone. That's not why I came; it's not what I want."

"Then what do you want, Ian Silver Stone?" Darien del Darien asked.

"I want it all to stop," Ian said. "I want it all to be done. I want the Son who is chasing after my friends to be recalled, and I want there to be no more sent after their blood—or mine. I want my friends, the people of my home, to not have to stand guard on the Hidden Way, wondering when the next Sons of Fenris will pop up to murder their friends and family," he said. "That's what I want. And I think, perhaps, I've earned that much from you," he said, looking from Branden del Branden to Darien del Darien. "Or were you happy with the House of Fire under the rule of a fire giant? Do you think he took human form because he meant well for your Cities?"

Branden del Branden smiled. "A strange fire giant he would have been, were that the case."

Darien del Darien made a clicking sound, tongue against teeth. "But that is done, is it not?" He chewed idly on a knuckle. "The Cities, the Dominion, the Scion himself," he said, gesturing toward the tall spire that rose overhead, "are all duly grateful, of course . . ." he spread his hands.

" 'But what have you done for us lately?' "

"Nicely put," Darien del Darien said. "Yes, what have you done for us lately?"

"I've exposed these dogs as having another . . . agenda, haven't I?" Ian shook his head. "How many of these Sons do you think have been given a guide through the Hidden Ways? How many do you think can find their way through to Earth?"

"Earth?"

"Midgard," Hosea said. "The Old Lands."

"Yes, that is another good point. But it was the false Fire Duke who gave the Sons directions into the Hidden Ways, and to . . . Earth, was it not?"

"Yes, but . . ."

Darien del Darien nodded. "I think the Scion would want me to talk with this Valin of yours. The details as to who said what to him, and when—it's the details that will tell."

"Details, hah!" Herolf dismissed the thought with a growl. "These two, they could have told the vestri what to say. Vestri have always been weak of character, and easy to dominate. It's what makes them such good servants for all; it's why they serve us in our warrens, and you in your Cities." He shrugged. "Give me a moment with him, and I could have him saying what I want. It's no great trick."

"Yes, they could have coached him . . ."

Herolf's sharp teeth showed in his smile.

". . . and if, say, this vestri can tell me the details of just who told him to do what, and when, the Scion will have to decide for himself if it is more likely that he got those details from people who have been dwelling on Earth, or from actual knowledge."

He raised a finger in a beckoning gesture, and a soldier in the sky-blue livery of the Old Keep, of the House of the Sky, stepped out of the greenery on the piazza to one side and above them. "I think we should see this Valin right now, if you would be so kind, Hival del Derinald."

"But . . . klaffvarer, that was what I was coming to tell you. We can't."

The fucking bastards. They'd killed Valin while interrogating him. Vestri were tough, yes, but they weren't unkillable. It had been a close thing in Hardwood; if Thorian Thorsen and Ian had been just a little slower, the dwarf would have died without bringing his message to them.

And now, after all of this, for him to die here, under the noses of the Sons of Fenris?

It was murder. Ian's hand dropped to Giantkiller's hilt, and Herolf took a step back, his back arcing forward, his features already starting to stretch and melt, a musky odor surrounding him.

"Not now. *No.*" Darien del Darien's sharp command cut through the air like a whip. Herolf straightened immediately, his features flowing back toward human, his claws becoming hands, his chest flattening.

It took every bit of self-control Ian had to keep his hand from the hilt of his sword, but this wasn't a time to let himself go. Self-control is something he had had to learn a long time before, and while he knew his gut would spasm and his head would ache later, he would appear calm and controlled, and that would only be half a lie.

He could avenge Valin later, at his leisure. The dwarf had shown courage and loyalty, a credit to his Folk.

Darien del Darien's voice was quiet and even. "Why can you not bring him? I am sure I gave strict instructions on behalf of the Scion that he was not to be harmed."

"No, no, no. He wasn't harmed. I chained him in his cell myself, and he was fine." Hival del Derinald spread his hands. "He's disappeared. He's gone."

Escaped?

Ian kept the smile from his face, but it probably showed in his eyes.

CHAPTER SIXTEEN

The Wrist

"It's all a question of strategy," Thorian Thorsen had explained to Jeff, over the yips and barking of the dogs.

It had seemed to make sense at the time. "In Bersmål, the words 'dueling' and 'strategy' and 'fencing'—they are all the same word."

Thorsen reached forward to let the big black dog nuzzle at his hand through the wire fence. "Some parts are easier than others."

"Like meeting here."

Thorsen nodded as he took a tiny dog biscuit from the wicker basket to the side of the cages, then fed it on his open palm to the dog. Two workers in coveralls were working their way down the row of kennels, moving the animals out of their own cells to a holding cell long enough to clean them out. But the smell of Pine-Sol and bleach couldn't quite cover the reek of dog piss and dog shit.

"We can be sure there is no Son here, or the animals would let us know." Thorian Thorsen smiled thinly. "Even if it likely would be by pissing down their legs."

Jeff nodded. "So you want to buy one?"

Thorian Thorsen shook his head. "That would just delay

things.'' He pursed his lips. ''Imagine that this is a duel in
the mists of—in the mists. What's the most important thing
the mists hide?''

''Who the players are,'' Jeff said, slowly. ''What they
want. What they're doing.''

Thorian Thorsen nodded. ''He, or they—there may be
more than one, although I doubt it—is hidden from us. We
don't even know what he wants.''

''But—''

Thorian Thorsen shook his head. ''We know what the
vestri thought he wants. But he has been here long enough
not only to locate my son, but to . . . to fit in here, perhaps
as well as I have.'' He shrugged. ''If he had wanted my
son's blood, he would have had it by now. Thorian is as
fast as I was at that age, and much smarter, if not as de-
vious, but it doesn't matter how fast and smart you are, not
when a dark shape leaps out of an alleyway or a doorway
when you're not expecting it, to rend you flesh from flesh.''
He looked up. ''Do you fence at all? No? Nor play chess,
nor draughts? Pity. They're really much the same, complicated by the same contradiction: in order to strike, you must
move forward; but the moving forward exposes you to be
struck.

''With the sword, the wrist is the center of it all, the
fulcrum around which the fight swings. If you hit his wrist,
be it a first-blood affair or a duel to the death, you've won.
You have a saying about the fastest way to a man's heart;
the one I was taught is that the fastest way to the heart is
through the wrist. Disable his wrist, and you can cut out
his heart at your leisure.

''So from that truth there flows a classic move: you offer
your opponent your wrist, hoping that as he lunges for it,
he exposes himself to you for the riposte. Much of the time,
if you're good, it even works.'' Thorsen pulled back his
sleeve. His thick wrist was badly scarred, at least a half
dozen thick white lines speaking of old wounds. Blunt fingers rubbed at his scars. ''But not always, not always.''

Which is what they had been doing with Torrie, last
night. If the Son had gone for Torrie, he would have exposed himself to Jeff, just like a fencer dropping his guard

as he lunged. "So why didn't he go for it? He was watching."

"There's another classic move, and that's to, oh, turn a tactic into a strategy. Instead of trying to hit, you try to manipulate your opponent into being . . . off the ideal line. Take his balance, control his timing or the spacing, and you can win by indirection what you can't win directly."

"Which is what he's done here."

"Off-balance, aren't we? Out of place?"

"Not we. You."

Thorian Thorsen nodded. "Me. That's the only thing that makes sense. I'm both the wrist and the heart, here, the center of it. Ian was wrong; the Son is after me. The only reason he revealed himself to young Thorian was to force me to be out of line, off-balance, here where I don't have a feel for the space, where the time and the balance are his."

Jeff nodded. "Then what we need to do is get back home. There's been, oh, a death in their individual families, and both Torrie and Maggie need leaves of absences."

Thorian Thorsen shook his head. "Look another move ahead. What does he then do? Give up?"

"Maybe he comes at us again at home."

"Perhaps. Or he could try a much simpler move: he could start killing here. One kill, one mauling, just to let me know that he can continue. Then another and another." He reached through the bars and let the black dog lick his fingers. "How much blood would you have it take to draw me out, to bring me here?"

Jeff sucked air through his teeth. You can't protect the whole world, just your little piece of it, and sometimes not even that. Sure. They could go home, and wait until the Son started killing, and hope that it only killed people that he didn't care about; they could let the bloody bodies pile high until the weight of the corpses finally tipped the scales and tumbled them back here.

How high a pile of bodies would it take? "Okay," Jeff said. "So you're the wrist, and we offer him the wrist. We use you as the bait, and when he goes for you, I nail him. Just like we tried with Torrie."

"But not following so closely, eh? He's smelled you now, and he'll know you."

"You're saying I've been made?"

Thorian Thorsen shook his head. "Not really. But you will be—'made,' you say?—you'll be made, then, if you follow too close to me. He is several steps ahead of us, this one. He waited last night, and simply observed—in wolven form, where his senses are their sharpest, perhaps? He crouched there, sniffing the winter wind, and now can identify each of the people who were out walking around Torrie last night. If he finds the same smell again, he'll recognize it. Were he to find your smell close to mine, he'd know you."

And all he has to do is take me out, and then he's got a clear shot at Thorian.

He wouldn't even need to kill Jeff, not really, although he might as well. Just distract him for a moment, and it would all be done, as long as he could maintain the element of surprise against Thorsen.

Thorian Thorsen nodded. "So you have to keep your distance, far enough away that he can't even smell you, can't see you, doesn't know that it's you . . ."

"Unless," Jeff said, each word sour in his mouth, "you're not the wrist, but I am." The Son feared Thorian Thorsen—but more as a strategist than as a fighter. Thorsen wasn't exactly ancient, but he wasn't young anymore, his legs full of spring and his eye sharp as a hawk's—maybe the Son had figured out that the real threat would be whoever was watching Thorian's back, not Thorian himself.

You couldn't play chess with somebody who could see two moves beyond where you saw.

Well, you could, but you'd lose. Badly.

Thorsen didn't look at Jeff as he fed the dog another biscuit. "I was wondering if you'd say that."

Were you? Jeff thought. *Or were you really just wondering when?*

CHAPTER SEVENTEEN

The Scion

The bars of the cell, the last of six set into the side of the corridor, had been carved from the stone of the cities itself, a latticework of stone that reminded Ian of those crinkle-cut deep fried potato chips that he had always thought were innately too greasy.

It was lit by a frosty circle set into the outside wall, which looked like quartz. Wan light trickled in, overpowered by the twin lanterns set into the far wall.

It was still doubly locked, both by the brass padlock that Ian thought even he might be able to pick, and by the long, thin stone slab that slid across the base of the cell door, preventing the door from being removed.

A simple mechanism, if you even wanted to call it a mechanism. Assuming you couldn't break the stone—and the stone of the Cities was incredibly tough stuff—you'd have to lift and slide the slab, and that was anchored in place by a brass spike that went through a hole in the slab and into a corresponding hole in the wall. Reed Richards might be able to have enough reach to remove the spike while still in the cell; no human or Vestri could.

"You haven't opened the cell yet, have you?" Ian asked the guard.

Folivan del Folivan—the job of jailer was apparently hereditary—was a fat and ugly man, but well-tanned, despite his job. This suggested that he didn't spend a lot of time on duty, an impression that was substantiated by the thick dust on the floor and each of the combination bench and sleeping slab in the other five cells. So the job of jailer was probably a hereditary sinecure.

That made sense. There was a lot wrong with dueling to settle arguments, no matter what rituals you wrapped it in, but it did have the virtue of settling them, of leaving somebody injured or humiliated—or both—rather than jailed.

Folivan del Folivan gave Ian a who-the-hell-are-you-to-be-asking look, but at a subtle finger gesture from Darien del Darien he shook his head. "No," he said. "I have not opened it." *No,* he might as well have said, *I am not a blithering idiot.*

Ian had worked out that the klaffvarer—literally "key-bearer"; less formally, chief butler—had more authority in the Old Keep than the one in the House of Fire had had, but he put that aside for a moment.

Why was everybody looking at him, though?

It had started with Hosea looking at him . . .

. . . and that explained it. Hosea had looked to him, as though Ian was in charge, and Ian had, perhaps unconsciously, taken his cue from the Old One. Darien del Darien had found it convenient or expedient to play along, and even Branden del Branden and Herolf, both of whom seemed to want to play alpha male games, albeit probably for different reasons, had done so, as well.

Folivan del Folivan looked from face to face, and then back to Ian. "Do you wish me to open it?" he asked, his gaze carefully focussed on a spot halfway between Darien del Darien and Ian.

Darien del Darien eyed Ian levelly. "What do you think, Ian Silver Stone?" he asked.

I think that I'd like this to be your problem, and not mine. Valin had clearly escaped, and that was fine with Ian. The only question was how, although Ian was fairly certain he knew, in general outline.

If Ian was right, though, Valin should be long and safely

gone. And that made helping out the men of the City a line item under the category of Maintaining Friendly Relationships While In A Foreign Country, and not one under Stooling for the Guards.

"I think he's gone." *And I sure hope he is.* "Herolf," he said, "do you smell him?"

The Son growled. "Who are you to be asking me any questions, friend of Thorian the Traitor?"

"Why, he's nobody to be doing any such thing," Branden del Branden grinned. He seemed to have relaxed some since the announcement that Valin had escaped. The idea of torturing information out of a dwarf probably hadn't gone over well with him, either. "You're quite right, Herolf. Ian Silver Stone has no authority here, and his suggestion is offensive. Folivan del Folivan, unbar the door, and let us remove it. If—and I say if—the Vestri somehow remains in there, and uses the opportunity to escape, why, it's none of Herolf's concern, after all."

"Pfah." Herolf smiled, but there was no warmth or friendliness in the smile. A wolf's smile was the baring of teeth for threat or use.

Ian smiled back. *Go for it, Herolf. Any time is fine with me.*

The Son sniffed the air once, then again. "There's been vestri here, but I can't tell ... pfah. Not in this form. My thoughts are clearer, but it dulls the senses." He looked to Darien del Darien, and, at the klaffvarer's slight nod, Herolf bent forward, his back arching ...

And he changed.

Torrie had described it to Ian once, but it was different to see it happen in front of him.

The worst part of it was the sound. Ian had always assumed that the transformation was a flowing thing, a gentle quick morphing like the movie special effect.

But the change happened with the crackle of breaking bone and the ripping of flesh, with the smell of old sweat and a horrible, almost comic flatulence.

Vertebrae popping like firecrackers, the Son's back arched, then flattened as he fell forward to land on hands that were already mostly paws by the time they hit the ground. The two gold rings that had been on his fingers ting*ting*ed on the floor, and bounced off somewhere.

Ian didn't pay them any attention; he was watching and listening as, with an awful liquid ripping sound, the front of Herolf's face lengthened into a muzzle, and arms and legs thinned and became spindly wolf-legs, while his chest thickened, ribs snapping into barrel shape, each with the heavy slap of bone against flesh.

Already sharp teeth shattered and reformed in Herolf's jaw, but despite the obvious pain, the wolf had already lowered his muzzle to the floor and was snuffling around.

Herolf stuck his snout through the interlaced stone bars of the cell, sniffing heroically; in a few moments he withdrew it, and then slowly, stiff-leggedly stalked down the line of cells, growling the humans out of his way, sniffing at each cell in its turn.

He growled, then barked at Ian, baring his teeth and snarling when that got no reaction except for Ian's hand again dropping to the hilt of his sword, and Hosea's hand dropping to cover Ian's.

"Noise is only noise, Ian," Hosea said, quietly. He shook his head. "He says he didn't smell anything useful. He was there—Valin's sweat and piss reek of fear, he says—but he isn't in any of those cells now."

Well, good, although there went one theory. It was the sort of ploy that would have appealed to Ian, if he'd been in the cell. Conceal himself in the cell—perhaps under the bench, if he could improvise some sort of screen to mask his presence, or pressed up against the ceiling, at the blind spot at the juncture of the front and side walls.

Then wait until they unlocked it.

"There's a hidden passage," he said, echoing what all the others were thinking.

Not that it took much of a stretch. The Cities were known to be littered with such, some so well known and their entries obvious to the point of being used as regular corridors, others hidden.

Ian himself knew two hidden passages in Falias, the House of Fire—one of them led to the Hidden Way that had first brought the Sons to Hardwood, and later had been used as an escape route by the Thorsen parents and Maggie. He knew that there were others, as well.

The Builder of the Cities had been perhaps overly fond of hidden passages and hiding places, a fondness that hadn't abandoned him. Perhaps it had come from the knowledge that he used to have in his head.

Well, this was going from bad to worse. Here Ian was, suspected of being the Promised Warrior, with an unknown hidden passage having been identified as being in one of the prison cells, a passage that had gone undetected for centuries, suddenly opened and used in moments by Ian's vestri companion.

Shit. What other knowledge had Valin been hiding?

Darien del Darien had been thinking some of the same things Ian had been. "A curious situation," he said, quietly. "Here we have a talented swordsman who wants to appear to be less than he is, and who says that he is not the Vandestish Promised Warrior. While there's been no new hidden passage discovered, as far as I know, since my grandfather bore the Scion's cup, within the day of his arrival here we find evidence that not only is there one, but that one of his companions has used it to flee." He smiled thinly. "Shall I lock you in this cell to wait on the Scion's pleasure?"

"I'm not sure if you're going to believe this, but I'd rather you didn't." If the hidden passage had remained hidden in, of all places, a jail cell, it was unlikely that Ian would be able to figure it out within his lifetime.

"You're quite correct; I'm not sure if I do believe it." Darien del Darien stared at Ian for what felt like a full minute before he turned to Herolf. "I have a commission for you and your pack," he said. "Search the mountain. Find the Vestri; bring him back, alive, if at all possible."

The wolf growled and scampered out the door, nails clicking a rapid tattoo that slowly diminished in the distance.

Darien del Darien turned to Branden del Branden and bowed, stiffly, formally. "I thank you for your service to the Scion, and to the Sky, and on his behalf, I now dismiss you from that service. I'm sure you'll want to report what you've seen to His Warmth as soon as possible.''

Branden del Branden nodded. ''That may well be the case,'' he said, drawing himself up straight and returning the bow, accompanying it with a flourish of his hand that may have had meaning, or maybe just meant that Branden del Branden was the sort of fop who liked to make flourishes with his hand. ''I'll depart come morning, if it pleases you; or now, if you think that His Warmth will be impatient for my report.''

Even Ian could translate that last to mean *I'll get out of your hair tomorrow or right now; take your pick.*

What Darien del Darien probably wanted to do was have Branden del Branden, Ian, and Hosea killed quietly, quickly, but . . .

''But the cat is out of the bag,'' Ian said.

''Eh?''

''An expression from my homeland—no point in locking the barn if the horse has already been stolen.''

''Ah.'' Branden del Branden's lips may have turned ever-so-slightly up at the corners. ''Here it is: 'Do not smoke the meat when it has already turned green.' '' He nodded.

''So, your advice would be, Branden del Branden?'' The klaffvarer's voice held no hint of alarm; he could have been asking if Branden del Branden thought the Cubs were going to finish last, again.

''I think you'll want to have some ordinaries and majors of the Keep looking for that hidden passage. Knowing that it's there . . .'' He shrugged. ''Or you might want to lock Orfindel in there, under watch, and let him try, or find out for sure if he's lost forever the trick of breaking the stone of the Cities, but,'' he shook his head, ''I'd advise against it. I know of none who has profited from imprisoning Orfindel, and that's been tried more than once over the centuries.''

Promise him that you'll tell him all you know about this hidden passage, Ian was about to say, in English.

Shit. More than one man in the Middle Dominion knew English—there had been more movement between Tir Na

Nog and the Old Lands than was generally acknowledged.

That wouldn't have been a problem if Ian had spoken another language, ideally a rare and obscure one. Hosea had the gift of tongues, after all, and could even bestow languages, unknowingly. Maybe he had thought this out in advance and had given Ian the right tool for this occasion. It had happened with Bersmål, after all; Ian hadn't even suspected that he spoke it until he had first heard it spoken. Hell, he had never heard of Bersmål until he began speaking it. Maybe Ian spoke Vietnamese, say. Or Linear B. Or even if he remembered any of his high school French, or Hebrew school Hebrew.

How do you flex a muscle you don't know you have?

Just a few phrases stuck in his mind. *Ani lo midaber ivreet.* No good. *Parlez-vous francais?* wouldn't help; Ian didn't speak Hebrew, or French.

La plume de ma tante est sur la table. Yiskadal, v'yiskadash, sh'mai rabba. Voulez-vous coucher avec moi ce soir? Honi soit qui mal y pense. Non compos mentis. No, that was Latin, come to think of it—and he apparently didn't speak Latin, either. *Chad gad ya, chad gad ya. Shma, Yisroel . . . Alons enfants de la patrie, le jour de gloire est arrivé. Legion Etrangere. B'nai Brith. Baruch atah, ado—*

Yes.

"Make a *bris*," he said quickly in English, then switched to Bersmål. "Tell them all you know about this passage, please." Thank whatever for a mind that collected minutiae. Ian had seen a cartoon, a long time ago, of a white-bearded man in long flowing robes, holding a pair of tablets, with the caption: "You want us to cut off the tips of our *whats*?"

B'nai Brith had reminded Ian of bris, which was usually used to mean circumcision.

But that was only its usual meaning; literally, it meant "covenant." Make a covenant with them; promise them, Ian had said, that you'll help them find this passageway. It was possible that it led to a Hidden Way, but unlikely. When you hear hoofbeats, think horses . . .

And even if it did, then so what?

Ian, Hosea said, in a low-pitched sibilant language Ian

had never heard spoken before, *if I made promises lightly, or easily, I would be required to make them all the time.*

Darien del Darien looked sharply at them. "And what was that all about?"

"Brick it up," Hosea said. "I . . . might have been able to tell you once, long ago, how to access it. But I can't, not now." He tapped a long finger against his forehead. "Information that one doesn't have can't be given out to the wrong people, eh?" He tapped a fingernail against the stone. Tick, tick.

"That's an . . . interesting position." Darien del Darien pursed his lips. "I think that this should be left to the Scion, though." He nodded to himself. "We shall go see him now, Orfindel. You and I and Ian Silver Stone."

Ian had thought himself in good shape, but by the time they reached the top of the long staircase that twisted around the spire, he knew better. Perhaps it was the altitude, or perhaps he was just road-weary, but his lungs burned with every breath, with every step.

What *was* it with Hosea and Darien del Darien? Darien del Darien looked to be in his sixties, and Hosea was older than mountain ranges, but neither of them showed any real effort, save for a slightly faster rate of breathing on Darien del Darien's part and a light beading of sweat on his forehead, and perhaps as much as a touch of strain at the corners of Hosea's mouth.

Around and around and up the spire the staircase spiraled. There was a railing, a brass helix green with age, but hauling himself up with his sword arm would only tire that out, too, so Ian just kept plodding along.

The dark disk atop the spire grew closer and closer. Ian found himself looking for openings in it. There ought to be something. Surely the Scion couldn't have teams of vestri servants hauling supplies up and waste down all the time.

Or could he?

It was embarrassing that he was barely able to keep up with these two old men. Were their muscles made of some untiring rubber?

Or were they every bit as tired as he was, but just more stubborn?

More than two could play at that game. "Does he ever come down from here?" Ian asked, forcing his voice to be as level and normal as he could.

"Rarely," Darien del Darien said. "And more rarely, of recent years. That's largely traditional, though. The Scion is, oh, special, not like the rulers of the other Cities. He can't afford to be . . . as involved as His Solidity or His Warmth typically chooses to be, not in everyday affairs."

If speaking while climbing caused Darien del Darien the slightest physical distress, it didn't show in his face or in his voice.

"That's where you come in, I take it."

"Come in? Ah." Darien del Darien nodded. "Yes." His thin lips pursed, then split in a smile. "I see. You were under the impression that the klaffvarer in the Old Keep is like the klaffvarers of the other Cities?" He shook his head and turned to Hosea. "Is there some reason you didn't tell him otherwise, Orfindel?"

Hosea didn't answer for a moment. "I did, but I'm not sure that Ian took the point."

Great. So now I'm stupid.

"No," Hosea said, responding to the unvoiced thought, "it's not stupidity. It's lack of, oh, orientation. Things are different here, and they don't quite fit into the same molds that you're used to."

"Everything's different everywhere," Ian said.

"Ah. My point precisely," Hosea said. "Although," he said, idly, "it's not always been the custom that the Scion remain so much above it all as this one appears to."

"He feels," Darien del Darien said, "that the less he interferes in everyday matters, the more puissance his presence has when he does choose to involve himself."

Well, maybe that was the pravda, and maybe it was even true. But a theoretical ruler, kept isolated from actual rule, wasn't unknown.

For something like a thousand years, the emperor of Japan and his court were virtual prisoners of whatever clan or family was actually running the country, trotted out only rarely to show the other nobles who really ran things. The Shogunate had ended sometime in the nineteenth century—Ian wasn't clear on the details—during the something-or-other Restoration. Meiji, that was it: the Meiji Restoration.

But the Japanese had slipped into a sort of civilian-military Shogunate again, and that had brought them into and through World War II . . .

. . . only to be ended at Hiroshima and Nagasaki.

Was Darien del Darien afraid that the rule of the Scion's klaffvarer would end with the Promised Warrior? If there was a polite way to ask, Ian couldn't figure out what it might be—he'd ask Hosea later.

With every turn around the spire, the disk above grew closer, and Ian could—finally—make out the dark hatchway that stood as the only entrance.

If the Scion wanted to keep himself aloof and away from it all, this certainly did it. The circular stairway terminated on a landing, where a preposterously ordinary-looking wooden ladder stood as the only way up and into the darkness above.

"If you'll be kind enough to wait for a moment, I'll see if the Scion will receive us." Climbing with infuriating ease, Darien del Darien disappeared up into the darkness.

Ian leaned against the cold stone and took a deep breath. "Well, we know who has gone soft lately."

"There are different kinds of toughness, Ian," Hosea said. "And Darien del Darien and I do have less muscle to haul around than, well, some other people do."

Darien del Darien's face appeared in the hole above. "Come up, if you please."

Ian hadn't quite known what to expect—that was always a problem in Tir Na Nog; you got used to it after a while, maybe too used to it—but he had expected something comfortable and luxurious. This was, after all, where the Scion lived, and given the luxury that went with even guest chambers in the Cities, Ian had expected at least another few levels of higher opulence and comfort.

But the round room was spare and almost monastic. A

series of quartz windows, curved like the wall they were set into, let in light, if not a view. The floor was a mosaic of small pieces of wood, seeming randomly cut, carefully fit together so that only the contrasting grain revealed the joint.

A small, curved dining table was set into the far wall, supporting a crystal pitcher of water and some glasses—Ian had seen more elegant-looking glasses in the Thorsen kitchen—and a small pot of tea on a cast-iron stand, warming over an alcohol flame. The smell of the burning alcohol cut through a musty smell of rot and mold, like that of a damp basement.

There were only two chairs in the room, both deep and low, each with a small table next to it. One table was piled high with papers, some loose, some bound together; the other was clean, save for a pen and inkwell set, and a small, rather ordinary-looking knife that Ian would have wanted to call a hunting knife, although he doubted that there was a lot of hunting going on up here.

A long black curtain, suspended from a brass bar set high into the walls, cut a chord across the back curve of the room. If there was any real luxury to be had up here, it was concealed behind there.

Well, Scion, why don't you leave your dancing girls for a moment, and come out and chat?

"Good day to you," a quiet voice said from behind the curtain. "I thank you for coming to see me." It was hard to guess the age of the speaker. Male, certainly, and not young, but not with any quaver of age in the voice.

"You are welcome, of course," Hosea said. "I'm curious, though. Do you mind me asking a question?"

"That would, I suppose, depend on the question. Chance it and see."

"Why are you sitting behind the curtain?" Hosea gestured at it, not that the Scion could see it. "This isn't the first time I've visited the Old Keep, and—"

"That is certainly true. You built it, after all, Orfindel."

"Well," Hosea said, "there's legends that it was built by an Old One who was called Arvindel, and Orfindel, and undoubtedly many other things less savory—but that hardly makes me one and the same Orfindel, does it?''

"No." There was a thin chuckle. "That isn't what makes you the same one. But let that pass, for now."

"I was saying," Hosea went on, "that I've been here before, but I haven't known the Scion to be quite this, well . . .''

"Private," the Scion said. "The word you're looking for is, I think, 'private.' "

Or reclusive, Ian thought. Was that the Scion's choice, or his supposed majordomo's?

And why the curtain?

Right about now it would have been nice to have a little dog handy to pull the curtain back. You couldn't blame a dog for doing that, after all. He wasn't at all sure what the dog would find—other than it wouldn't be Frank Morgan. The Scion's voice sounded a lot more like Wallace Beery.

Then again, I'm no Judy Garland. Although the temptation to click his heels and say, *There's no place like home, there's no place like home, there's no place like home* would have been irresistible, if Ian had thought it might even do some good.

"No, Orfindel, you haven't. I am of . . . of a quiet temperament, these days, and I have arranged to be seen by very few people."

"The Heir and the klaffvarer are the only ones, I hear," Hosea said.

"You hear too well, perhaps. Solitude and distance suit me."

"Okay, fine," Ian said. "And if solitude and distance suit you, why go digging up trouble by sending your dogs after the Thorsens? Sounds to me like you're buying yourself a lot of trouble."

Darien del Darien's jaw dropped, and Hosea took a step back.

Apparently, it just wasn't done to speak bluntly to the Scion.

"An . . . interesting question, Ian del Benjamin," the Scion said.

Ian wasn't sure what the point of that naming was—so

what if the Scion knew about Ian's shithead of a father? If there was a threat there, it didn't bother Ian.

Hey, Scion, go ahead and send your dogs after Daddy Dearest, eh? I won't give a shit.

Well, that wasn't true. He shouldn't care, but he would. That was the way of it. Another addition to the list of unfairnesses in life; in the back of his head, a little voice would always be saying to Ian that if only he had said and done the right things, if only he'd cleaned his room better or had better grades or listened better or had better friends or hobbies or knew when to talk and when to shut up better . . . if only he'd done better, his dad would have loved him.

And while he could remember nights lying in bed when Dad was out, hoping against hope that this time he would have managed to wrap his car around a tree and killed himself, every time that goddamn garage door wheezed its way into life, sending Ian turning toward the wall, hoping that this time he could feign sleep well enough that Dad would just stagger off to his own room and pass out . . .

Each goddamn time there was a hint of something vaguely like relief in his gut.

"I prefer to be called Ian Silverstein," Ian said, "or Ian Silver Stone. That's what *she* calls me," he said. There could be no harm in reminding the Scion that Ian had some powerful friends.

"You mean Freya? The *she* who is better known as Frida the Ferryman's Wife?" the Scion said. "*She* is rather well-preserved for her age, isn't she? You know, Orfindel, I've always envied you Old Ones your long lives, but I guess you're used to that envy."

Hosea didn't answer.

"Arnie Selmo, though," Ian went on, "the fellow who wields Mjolnir?—you've seen his lightning to the south— he just calls me Ian."

"You think they'd avenge any harm done you?" The tone was casual, as though the Scion was asking the time of day, just for the sake of conversation.

"I certainly hope so," Ian said. "More to the point, I hope *you* think they'd avenge any harm done me."

"Very well. Do I misunderstand that they're friendly to

the Thorian del Thorians, both the older and the younger?''

"Well, yes." Arnie? On the Night of the Sons, Arnie had charged out into the night to face a pack of the Sons in their wolf form, armed with nothing but a shotgun, a shotgun that could do little more than annoy a Son.

"Then why, you fool, do you think that I'd go to great difficulty to make myself such powerful enemies? And for what? Am I insane, that I'd earn their enmity—and yours, if you're the Promised Warrior of legend—just for some cheap retribution against a former subject, over a matter that Orfindel himself has rendered moot?

"No." The Scion's voice lost all hint of lightness and gentleness. It curled and rasped like a sandpaper snake. "It's never been me. It's never been the Cities. It wasn't the Dominions that sent the Sons hunting through the Hidden Ways for Thorian del Thorian; it was an Old One, a fire giant, masquerading as the Fire Duke, and he did it not for the Dominions, but for himself, to lure Orfindel out of hiding and into his hands."

Because, at least then, Hosea knew where the Brisinga-men jewels were, and although he had resisted torture before, although his body had been tormented for years, badly enough to stir the conscience of even a Cities duelist, he had bound himself by his word to protect Torrie and Karin, and if that meant giving up the jewels, the fire giant had thought he would.

Was he right?

Yes, he was. Hosea didn't give his word easily not because he *disliked* breaking it, but because he *couldn't,* because his oath bound him absolutely, inescapably. He had returned to Tir Na Nog at least twice to protect Torrie and Karin, not just because he cared for them—although he obviously did—but because he had promised Karin's father that he would, a promise given knowing that Old Man Roelke would turn him and Thorian del Thorian away at a time when he couldn't afford to face that possibility.

"So it wasn't you," Ian said. "Okay, I'll accept that."

"How very generous of you," the Scion said, his voice low and icy.

"But then who did it?"

"I don't know," the Scion said, his voice noticeably weaker after the outburst. He coughed, and the coughing became a coughing fit.

Darien del Darien rose from his chair. "The Scion is very busy," he said, "and he needs his rest."

"No, klaffvarer, I need to—"

"No." Darien del Darien's manner had none of the servant in it. "You need your rest, Scion. You must save your energies for, for other things."

Only iron self-control kept Ian from nodding in self-congratulation. He had had it right, after all. The Scion was the vassal of his supposed butler, and it was Darien del Darien that ruled the Dominions.

Was it Darien del Darien who had sent the Sons out again? Certainly Herolf had responded obediently to him. If so, why? And what could Ian do about it?

"But, no, Darien," the Scion said. "I have enough energy, enough—"

"If I'm to serve you properly, I must be the judge of that, Scion." Darien del Darien drew himself up straight, no trace of a servant in his manner. Not servant, not vassal . . . but what was he? "I have promised to serve you faithfully—not with blind obedience, Scion, but with utter faith—as long as I breathe, and if I can no longer keep that promise, I'll no longer draw a breath."

There was a hollow chuckle from behind the curtain. "Are you threatening me, old friend?"

"No; I make no threats against you, Scion. But if you'll not listen to me, perhaps after my body lies broken and bleeding at the base of your spire, perhaps then you'll listen to my son and heir—he can't serve you with my experience, but he has no lack of loyalty in him."

Darien del Darien walked to the ladder, removing the heavy gold chain and medallion from his neck as he did. He dropped it to the floor with a clanking of chain that echoed loudly in the confines of the small room. "Shall he assume his duties this day? I warn you—no, Scion, I threaten you—he will keep faith with you with every bit as much loyalty as I always have, and if you won't heed his counsel on matters of your own well-being, you'll find yourself with nobody but my twelve-year-old grandson to wait upon your needs.''

There was a thin laugh. "I understand that Darien del Darien the Youngest is a bright boy, and a good companion to my Heir.''

Darien del Darien apparently took that as surrender; he stooped to pick up his chain of office from the floor, and then slowly straightened, draping it again about his neck.

How many times, Ian wondered, had the two of them played this scene? It had the reek of familiar routine to it, but if it was for show they were better actors than he thought; it felt sincere. Darien del Darien really would have killed himself if the Scion hadn't relented.

Darien del Darien stroked the black curtain with an outstretched hand, a motion familiar and affectionate. "Rest now," he said, quietly. "I'll be back later with some broth, perhaps, and a bit of bread. Yes, I know you have little appetite, but you must eat.'' He made a brushing-away gesture toward Ian and Hosea. "I'll deal with these two, you may trust me on that.''

"Trust you? I have always trusted you, my old friend.''

CHAPTER EIGHTEEN

A Cry in the Night

Torrie finished buckling Jeff into the vest, covering the high white collar with a plaid scarf, its frayed edges showing that it had seen better days.

"Pull the straps tight, Torrie," Jeff said, then let his breath out with a whoosh so that Torrie could tighten them, which he did.

It didn't look like much, but Torrie had tried his knife on a spot near the hem. Even the covering had been difficult to cut, and he had not been able to get his knife to penetrate the core, much less cut through.

Kevlar? Dad didn't know, he said. "I'm fond of the brand name, though."

" 'Second Chance.' " Jeff Bjerke grinned. "It's supposed to be able to stop a hot .44 Magnum. With any luck it'll at least slow a Son down." He chewed his lower lip for a moment. "If he goes for me first."

Dad shrugged. "If he goes for me first, he has to expose himself to you, if you stay close enough. So he has to. Just some broken timing, one quick beat, and we should be able to bring him down."

With luck. Torrie helped the two of them dress and arm themselves, then walk out the door.

Their footsteps pounded on the stairs, and then they were gone.

"Your father can handle himself," Maggie said, taking his hand. Her hand was warm and dry. "And Jeff impresses me as pretty sharp, pretty fast, too."

Torrie nodded. There was something about the relationship between Maggie and his father that he had never quite liked, as though . . .

Well, no. He looked down at Maggie's face. Was there more than a hint of fear in the eyes?

"If you're scared," he said, "that means that you understand the situation."

She didn't answer; she just turned away and stalked off to the kitchen, busying herself straightening out something that clattered, although what there was to straighten out or clean in that spotless kitchen was something that Torrie couldn't figure out.

It felt wrong to be here, but somebody had to be with Maggie. Yes, she could take care of herself under most circumstances—and would resent being taken care of even when it was necessary—but this wasn't most circumstances.

Shit.

He glanced down at his watch. 10:51. Three whole minutes since they had left.

He tried to read the newspaper, but he couldn't focus. Maggie didn't believe in TV, so he couldn't zone out in front of it. He considered taking out the Arkansas stone to touch up the edge of his sword, but the edge of his sword was sharp already. The snubnose revolver was in his pocket, and he was tempted to take it out and check it again, but it was a gun, and you just didn't handle guns out of nervousness.

So he picked up the newspaper again.

10:57.

Okay. If you couldn't do anything useful in a given situation, it made sense to do something else, even if that something was only entertaining yourself. If you were needed, you'd be more useful well-rested than you would with nails bitten down to your wrists.

An idle thought crossed his mind. After all, if the two of them really needed to relax . . .

No. Not a good idea. He and Maggie were here to watch out for each other, and that wouldn't count as watching out. Besides, there was something vaguely obscene about the idea.

And, more to the point, Maggie would say no.

More clatter from the kitchen.

He found he had been reading the same line in a story about the Vikings over and over again, and couldn't even keep it in his head long enough to consider what it meant. And who cared, anyway? A bunch of bull-necked millionaires in tight pants fighting over a football.

Shit. He leaned back and closed his eyes tightly.

Torrie was trying to relax his neck muscles when the phone on the coffee table next to him rang, and he thought he was going to jump out of his skin.

"Don't pick it up!" Maggie shouted from the kitchen. "I'll get it."

"I wasn't going to," Torrie shot back, irritated. It was Maggie's phone, after all, and if she was afraid that her parents would call, find some guy answering the phone, and draw all the right conclusions, well, so be it.

On the other hand, the two of them shouting at each other was not okay; it looked like Torrie wasn't the only one on edge.

He rose and walked to the kitchen, to apologize.

". . . oh, no, Daddy—everything's fine. It's just been a long day—tests and stuff . . ."

Sorry I snapped at you, Torrie mouthed. *I'm just a little on edge.*

A little? That was like saying that if you slam a hammer on your thumb, it's going to sting a touch.

She kept talking into the phone as she raised her hand, and smiled and nodded, mouthing *"It's okay"* during a pause in her side of the conversation. Torrie backed out of the kitchen, closing the usually open swinging door behind him to give her at least the illusion of some privacy while she talked to her father.

That was nicely done, if I do say so myself, he thought. Yes, she had snapped at him first, and she hadn't apologized, and probably wouldn't. But that was part of getting along with Maggie, and he could live with that. All you had to do was be willing to let her be right even when she was in the wrong, and while she wouldn't come out and admit that she was equally or more at fault—not directly— she knew that she had been.

It was one of the reasons he had never worried about Ian and Maggie, not even when he had first started seeing her. There had been a bit of a temptation to be uneasy—Maggie had just started fencing then, and Ian was always better with a foil than Torrie was—but Torrie had quickly realized that not only was Ian focused on other matters, but that his stiff-neckedness was definitely a turnoff for Maggie.

It wasn't a problem for Torrie; doing right had always been a lot more important to him than being right, and one of the things you learned early living in a small town was that you couldn't afford the luxury of always being right, not only because you weren't, but because it was much more important to get along with your neighbors, because neither you nor they were going anywhere, taking bad blood with you.

Shit, Torrie had learned that one so early that he hadn't even realized it until he'd started college and found himself among a bunch of city folk, a lot of who figured that it didn't much matter if you didn't get along with the guy down the hall or down the stairs, because neither of you was going to be around the other long.

It seemed to get worse, the bigger the city was. New York was—

Bzzzzt. He spun around at the sound of the doorbell, his right hand dropping to where the hilt of his sword should have been.

Who the hell was dropping by? A Son, perhaps, hoping to find them defenseless?

He swung back through the kitchen door.

Could you get that? she mouthed

"Everything okay?" he whispered.

She frowned disapprovingly at his having talked. "Hang on a second, Daddy—I've got to turn down a pot on the stove." She held the receiver against her chest. "It's just some family stuff," she said, quietly. "Can you get the door?"

"Yes," he said, just as quietly, "and I'll do that just as soon as I see a gun in your hand."

It's not paranoid to be concerned when you've got Sons seeking your blood. Ringing the doorbell in front, then running around the back and crashing in that way might not be the most subtle of deceptions, but if it worked . . .

She frowned and reached behind her back, coming out with a small automatic, which she held properly, her finger outside the trigger guard. "Happy?" She turned her back on him and brought the phone back to her ear.

Torrie bounded for the front door and the stairs, pausing only to grab his coat and use it to cover the snubnose. Answering the door with a sword in his hand was the sort of thing that was liable to get you talked about.

The man out in the cold looked familiar, but it took Torrie a moment to place him. He was wearing a black leather trench coat with the belt tied around the waist, not buckled, and a hat that looked like it was something that Sam Spade would have worn pulled down low over the eyes, either for effect or to protect against the wind.

But then Billy Olson raised his head and smiled, and Torrie relaxed and reached for the doorknob.

The cold wind accompanied Billy inside.

"Billy," Torrie said, "I'm sorry. For a moment, I didn't recognize you."

"If you'll invite me in and feed me some hot cocoa, I'll be happy to change into dungarees and a T-shirt, if that'll make you feel better." Billy pulled the front door closed behind him, waiting for the click before he turned back. "Honestly, Torrie, I thought I was going to freeze to death out there, waiting for you to answer the door."

"I said I was sorry, and I am, honest. Come on up," Torrie said, adjusting the jacket around the pistol. This wasn't a great time for a visit, but there was no way to say that, and he wasn't about to leave Billy out in the cold.

"If you're on your way out, I'm glad I caught you," Billy said. "It's fucking cold out there; you'll need more than a light jacket."

Torrie patted at the jacket. "Nah. It's not that." *Then what is it? Quickly, quickly.* "A friend of Maggie's was going to be dropping by with some tools, and I figured I'd help him carry them in."

"Some things never change," Billy said.

"Eh?"

"Never mind."

Torrie had always liked Billy Olson, but Billy had never quite gotten over the image of Torrie as the little kid that used to tag along with him and Jeff and Davy, and if Billy was talking about things that had never changed, being irritating hadn't changed, either.

"It's good to see you," Torrie said, which was only the polite thing to say, after all. But then he realized that it was true.

"I was just thinking that myself," Billy said with a quirked smile.

Torrie led Billy inside the apartment, and while Billy had his back turned, removing his coat, Torrie stuck the pistol in his right pants pocket and pulled his shirt out of his pants to cover the butt of the gun.

That was the trouble with these damn things. You had to worry about hiding them, because in the city, at least, if anybody saw somebody with a gun, they'd piss all over themselves in panic, as though it was some sort of metallic demon that would leap up and bite them without warning.

Which was exactly backwards. A good sword, even a good practice épée, had a kind of soul, a spirit to it. It came alive in your hand, leaping and moving swiftly and surely, as though of its own volition, its forte and foible coming to your defense, its tip probing for weakness, like an extension of your finger.

But a gun was just a piece of dead metal. Point it, pull the trigger, and there was a loud sound and a hole somewhere. If you'd pointed it right, maybe the hole was even in what you were pointing at.

Maggie came through the swinging kitchen door, her right hand behind her back for just a moment.

"Billy!" she almost squealed, as though they were long-lost friends.

"Hello, Maggie," Billy said. "I was in the neighborhood, and I figured I'd drop by and say hi for just a moment. If that isn't a problem—if the two of you aren't on your way out somewhere, or . . . busy with something?"

She laughed at Torrie's obvious discomfort. "No, we're spending a quiet evening in," she said, gesturing at the pieces of the Stickley buffet, neatly laid out on spread newspaper. "Working on some refinishing."

Pleasantries exchanged, hot cocoa for Billy and coffee for Torrie and Maggie poured and tasted, Billy sat back on the couch, next to Maggie, and looked from Torrie to Maggie, and then back again.

"I guess I could have called," Billy said, "but I couldn't find a number for you, Maggie."

"It's under my roommate's name," she said, as she sipped at her coffee. "But you're welcome to have it—do you have a memory like Torrie's, or should I write it down?"

"Paper, please."

They all sat quietly while she found a small notebook and a Bic pen in the scattering of newspapers and magazines on the coffee table, opened the notebook, and wrote down the number.

"I think this is one of those awkward silences," Billy said, his smile too light, too easy.

"Shit, Billy . . ."

"Such language, Torrie." *I could ask you why you haven't called or stopped by in the past three years,* Billy's expression said. "No," he said, lifting a palm, "I'm not here to give you a hard time, although there is a temptation. I guess it's partly because I enjoyed tweaking Jeff a little bit with Maggie . . ."

Maggie snickered. "You should have seen him, Torrie. He looked like he was going to jump out of his skin."

"You have a mean streak, Maggie," Billy said. "I like that."

Torrie felt disloyal sitting and listening to the two of them making fun of Jeff, while Jeff was out using himself like a worm on a hook, hoping that the Son would bite at the right wriggle.

Torrie glared at Maggie, who ignored him.

"That's not fair," Torrie said. "And you know it. Both of you know it." So much for getting along, and not insisting on being right.

But it was unfair.

"Life is unfair," Billy said. "I don't mind the city. In fact, I like it. There's a lot here that I . . . didn't know about." He lifted a finger. "And I'm not just talking about men, either." He shrugged and sighed. "I just wish I felt like I could go home, every now and then."

Oh, dammit, Billy. You always have to be so—"You can come home any time you want to," Torrie said. "If your folks don't have the room—"

"They do. And you know Mom and Dad. They might find it awkward to have me around. People will talk."

Torrie didn't know the details around Billy's leaving. It had something to do, he was fairly sure, with something that had happened with one of the Quist twins. He knew that Billy and Nathan had gotten caught by somebody *doing something,* and didn't really want to know anything more. Both Billy and Nathan had gone off to the city to finish high school, and Torrie hadn't seen Billy since.

Everybody knew, of course. But you didn't rub people's noses in it.

"You're always welcome in my home," Torrie said. "And you know that. But I can't make you feel comfortable . . ."

Billy bit his lip; he closed his eyes and held up his hand. "Please don't tell me about being comfortable or uncomfortable until you've . . . minced about in my shoes." Billy was angry, but he was still Billy. "That's not really what I'm here about, although if you want to meet for coffee sometime and talk—about that, or about anything else— it'll be good to see you."

"If not that, then what?"

"What do you think? Jeff Bjerke shows up on my front

door, and needs a place to stay but can't—or won't—talk about what he's doing in town. Obviously there's some problem, and a serious one, or he wouldn't even be here, much less taking a shower in a bathroom where he's afraid to drop the soap.''

Maggie nodded. ''I see.''

Torrie didn't. ''It's nothing that I can talk about; I'm sorry.''

''Yes, yes, yes, we never talk about Private Family Secrets, whether it's a couple of strangers who move to town, one of whom doesn't even speak the language—or Bob Aarsted all of a sudden having a teenaged daughter that nobody's ever seen before, from a first marriage that nobody ever heard of before; or that queer Olson boy who disappears because there really is no place for queers in a little town, is there?'' When Billy got this angry, his voice had a hint of the old Norski accent that his mom and dad still had, even though neither of them actually spoke any Norwegian.

''But I know,'' Billy went on. ''We don't discuss any of it. We keep our secrets. And I'm not asking for any secrets, Torrie.'' Was that a tear in the corner of Billy's right eye?

''I'm not asking you to tell me anything,'' Billy said. ''I don't need to know anything. I didn't come over here to pry any of your precious secrets out of you—or to share any of mine, for that matter. I didn't walk here in the freezing cold for gossip, although I'll tell you that I really, really miss gossip from home. I'm just asking,'' Billy said, his words shaming Torrie with every syllable, ''I'm just asking if there's anything I can do to help. I—''

He was interrupted by a loud, liquid scream from outside, high and terrified.

Torrie was on his feet in an instant, Maggie barely a fraction of a second behind.

Again, somebody screamed outside.

Billy had gone city; he was already reaching for the phone, punching 911. It was a city thing, but not a bad idea.

"Yes," he said, "the alley behind Bryant, just south of Lake. Somebody outside just screamed, I mean really screamed. No, I don't know . . ."

Billy's eyes widened as he saw Torrie and Maggie, both with guns in their hands.

Torrie shut off the lights in the kitchen and moved to the back door, unbolted it.

The damn hallway window frosted over immediately. Shit, shit, shit.

Maggie lived in a quiet neighborhood, for the city, but this was a city, after all.

Again, the scream came, high and shrill.

Shit. Back home, there would be people all over the place by now, but this wasn't home.

And the timing of this was very suspicious.

"No, no, it's not in here, it's outside," Billy's voice was shrill and penetrating. He was scared, but he was functioning, and Torrie was distantly ashamed of himself for the vague sense of surprise at that.

"To the south, in the alley, I think. I don't know—no, I won't stay on the line; I'm going to go see what's happening and see if somebody needs help. Just get the police here, and quickly."

"Torrie?" Maggie was framed in the doorway of her bedroom. "I can't see anything out there. The windows are too frosted."

Fuck, fuck, fuck, fuck. "Billy," he said, still rubbing his hand against the window, "get in here, and bring my cue case."

He had expected some argument, some discussion—it was Billy, after all—but Billy was there, with Torrie's cue case in hand. Torrie handed him the snubnose and took the cue case in hand. "Okay, both of you. Stay together, and watch where you point those things."

He had his sword in his hand, and while there wasn't much in the universe you could count on, you could count on being able to follow the point of your sword out into the night.

You had to.

He took the stairs two at a time, then forced himself to

slow down. This wasn't a time to be tripping down the stairs and breaking a leg.

The bolt on the outside door was intact, and the landlord's damn dog was nowhere to be seen. Not that Torrie blamed it. He would rather have been somewhere else. Almost anywhere else.

He didn't wait for Billy and Maggie—he wanted them behind him, not ahead of him—as he pushed on the door. Damn thing had frozen shut; he hit it hard with his shoulder once, twice, then took a step back and kicked at it, flat-footed, right under the lock.

Wood splintered and ice cracked as it gave. He had expected the door to fly open when it gave, but it stuck, again, only a few inches open, probably on some hunk of ice or snow, so he kicked it again, harder.

As he lunged out into the backyard behind the point of his sword, bright lights came on overhead, dazzling his eyes. The asshole of a landlord had put motion-sensor lights not just on the apartment building itself but also on a post of the backyard fence, although Torrie couldn't imagine why anybody would want to.

The gate to the fence hung open, which was not the way it had been left before dark—Dad had made sure it was latched—and he dashed through, counting on Maggie and Billy to deal with anything that he had left behind him. There were times to go slowly and carefully, and there were times when you just had to launch yourself headfirst into things.

With any luck, this was one of those times.

He slid on ice that lined the wheel ruts of the alley, barely keeping his balance, riding in and out of the ruts like a skier on a set of moguls, his feet solidly underneath him. He hadn't questioned why Dad had had them spar outside sometimes during the winter, but he hadn't thought much about why, either.

Thanks, Dad.

Dark, backlit faces peered over the edge of the fence across the alley, and somewhere off in the distance a car alarm was hooting. He held his sword down and out, the flat of the blade pointing skyward. With no light flashing off it at them, it was unlikely that the bystanders would even notice that he had a sword.

But where had the scream come from? He had thought that the sound had come from down the alley, and he wasn't doing any good standing here freezing in the cold, so he broke into a quick trot down the alley.

Nothing here, and no sound, other than shouts in the distance, and the pounding of Maggie's and Billy's feet behind him. He turned. Maggie looked ghastly pale in the harsh green mercury light, or maybe it wasn't just the light.

"There," she said, pointing with her free hand, her pistol down at her side, hidden behind her right thigh the way Dad had taught her.

"There's something there," she said again, pointing to a pool of shadow in front of the next apartment's garage door. The only thing that Torrie could see there was the outline of the large, blocky plastic garbage cans that the city provided.

Billy was jingling his keys for some reason, but then a flash of light, strong and actinic, came from his direction, illuminating the shadowed region under the eaves.

It was silly, but the first thing that registered on Torrie's eyes was the plastic bag of garbage that had been broken open on the snow-packed ground, widely scattering egg-shells and Melitta filters filled with coffee grounds and bits of crumpled paper and discarded food.

It was only when Maggie gasped that the gray lump lying on the ground next to the garage door resolved itself into the shape of a woman, dressed only in the sort of shapeless gray sweats that nobody seemed to wear in the city, crumpled and smashed like a broken doll.

There was a dark spot beyond her, beyond the edge of the garage that could be hiding something, somebody, anything, but when he lunged past her and into it, yet another one of the motion-sensor lights came on, cutting through the darkness.

Nothing.

Torrie dropped painfully to his knees on the ice, the woman's still-warm blood warming his knees and legs. His probing fingers found not only blood but also flesh, but when he reached through the long hair for the neck, he must have pulled at her somehow, and she tumbled over onto her back, thick yellow worms of intestine spewing out and onto the dirty ice, the horrible shit-stink almost physically pushing him back, gagging.

He only noticed the blue and red lights flashing off the ice and snow and the garage wall when a loud voice barked, *"Police. Don't move.* Partner, he's got a knife."

"Fuck the knife. The other two have guns."

Torrie Thorsen was still rubbing at the red marks on his wrists as he waited at the battered, aged front-desk counter, resolving to add a handcuff key to his keyring and sew another one inside the seam on the back of his belt.

He really hadn't liked being handcuffed.

No, that was the polite, Hardwood way to put it—the truth was that he hated it, that it made him feel helpless and furious and it was all he could do to control himself, even now. It wouldn't have taken a Son to kill him, not with his hands locked behind his back, leaving him open and vulnerable from toes to nose.

Anybody could have walked up and stuck anything in him.

But it wasn't just the danger right then and there. He resented that portable cage-for-the-arms, that turned him from Torrie Thorsen into something helpless and dependent on the goodwill of people he didn't know and didn't much like.

No, this hadn't been the time to break free, not caring what the consequences were. But maybe next time would be. He'd be ready then.

"Hey, shit happens, er . . ." he looked down, ". . . Thorian. Sorry about the cuffs, but, you know . . ."

"Yeah, Stan, I'm sure shit does happen."

Sergeant Donaldson, badge number 615, a white-haired, thick-set, fiftyish man who reminded Torrie vaguely of Charles Bronson, wrinkled his forehead as he looked down from his place behind the counter. "Stan?"

"Your name isn't Stan?"

"No. It's Bob. You can call me Sergeant Donaldson, if you don't mind."

"And you can call me Mr. Thorsen, Sergeant Donaldson. If you don't mind."

After a moment's hesitation, Donaldson's broad face split in a not-entirely-friendly grin. "Okay; I get the point. It's just procedure, you know, Mr. Thorsen."

"Right, sure."

Yes, Torrie knew what it was. Standard procedure. Standard city police procedure.

In the city, everybody was always suspected of anything, and if you saw somebody who was only trying to help standing over a body, you assumed he was a vicious murderer, and you pointed guns at him and threatened to shoot him, and you slammed him up against the side of a building and handcuffed him.

Then you threw him in the back of a cop car, and you made him call you sir while you first-named him, and the combination of that and the fact that you've got the guy goddamn handcuffed and in the back of a police car, sitting behind a wire grating, gives you some sort of psychological edge in wringing information—preferably a confession—out of a guy.

And if he actually did what you think he did, so much the better, right? It was the old Ed Meese "If they weren't guilty, they wouldn't be suspects" thing.

It also came far closer than Torrie liked to taking away his dignity for good. Asking permission to go to the bathroom didn't sit well with him, and from the moment the cops had put the cuffs on his wrists, the thing he had wanted to do most of all, silly as it sounded, was to take a leak.

And maybe, even, if you didn't get him to confess to whatever it was that you suspected him of, maybe he had something else to hide, something that he'd blurt out in exchange for a Coke, or a trip to the bathroom, or just a kind word and a pat on the head.

And maybe Torrie had come too damn close to talking for his own comfort.

Maybe. Maybe the only thing that had stopped him was that he knew he wouldn't be believed.

"Relax," the cop said. "There's no charges, no yellow sheet, and hey, once this all shakes out, I'm sure the chief is going to write you a nice attaboy for all your help." He shrugged. "Not that I think that running out into the night to chase down a scream makes a lot of sense for civilians, but it's brave enough."

He tore open the yellow envelope and dumped the contents on the counter. "One watch, Winton's Triple Calendar—which means it isn't likely to be fake; who fakes a Winton's?—stainless, expensive. Very nice." He looked up. "Don't see a lot of mechanical watches these days. One knife, handmade, also very nice, and we're not going to look closely and see if it's an automatic, you being a hero and all, Mr. Thorsen, rather than a scumbag. Fifty-three dollars and forty-six, no, forty-seven cents in cash, a ring of assorted keys, one wallet, complete with credit cards, see separate inventory, attached, and why they bothered to grab that I don't know unless it's because they like making work for me like the damn separate inventory, attached. Two condoms." He reached behind the counter and came up with a long brown paper package, wrapped in string. "One antique sword, wrapped up nice so that you don't get hassled on your way home, open it and check it if you want to."

He spun the clipboard on the counter and slapped it to a stop with a practiced motion. "Sign *here,* Mr. Thorsen, unless you want to claim you're missing something, in which case you sign *here,* and list the missing property *here,* Mr. Thorsen." He handed the clipboard to Torrie and was silent until Torrie signed with a quick scribble. "And yeah, I'll say for the record that you and your friends were a bunch of idiots to stick your dicks out like that, but shit, boy, you got guts. Not a lot of sense, but a lot of guts."

Torrie couldn't help smiling. "I'll tell Maggie you said that," he said.

"You do that, Mr. Thorsen. The girl's got balls, too." He took out a business card and scribbled something quickly on the back of it. "This isn't exactly a get-out-of-jail free card, Mr. Thorsen, but if you ever run into just a little problem in this city, you give this to the officer and ask him to call me, and I'll see if maybe, just maybe, the MPD can cut you a little slack." He slid the card across the counter, and then waited until Torrie tucked it in his shirt pocket before he stuck out a thick hand. "We okay, Torrie?" he asked, his head cocked ever-so-slightly to one side.

"Sure, Bob," Torrie said. The cop's handshake was firm, but he wasn't a squeezer. "You bet."

"Well, then, you take care." Donaldson picked up his pen and used it to point without looking toward the Exit sign behind and to his right. "Your friends are waiting out there. For some reason or other, they didn't want to go through the metal detector. Have a nice night."

Well, Torrie thought, he'd still get the handcuff keys. But for a fact, the desk sergeant could easily have been more of an asshole.

Dad and Maggie were waiting for him out in the lobby. At—he glanced down at his watch—a quarter after two in the morning, it was empty, and their steps echoed off the old marble.

"Well, they said they let you go," Torrie said.

Maggie kissed him quickly. "We weren't the ones with blood all over us." She slipped an arm around his waist. "We even got our guns back, with a little lecture about how civilians should leave handling murders to the professionals."

Dad snorted.

"Billy and Jeff are out in the car," Maggie said. "You okay?"

Torrie shrugged. "Yeah." Shit.. At least he was in better shape than that poor woman.

He looked at Dad, about to ask the obvious question, but Dad shook his head, forestalling him. "We'll talk later," he said. "After you've had some food and a hot shower. I think your friend Billy has a few things he'd like to know about, too.''

"But . . .''

"Yes.'' Dad's voice sounded almost inutterably tired. "Yes; it was him. It was the Son.''

CHAPTER NINETEEN

The Heir

There was less of a chill in the air as Ian and Hosea were conducted down the broad halls by a quartet of soldiers.

The Old Keep may have originally been built by the Tuatha, but humans had inhabited it for long enough to make it entirely homey. The broad corridors were thickly carpeted down the middle, and the cold, ornately carved walls were covered by tapestries in places, which at least gave the illusion of warmth.

And they were pretty. Ian's favorite, lit only by a pair of lanterns and reflectors set high in a niche in the opposite wall, showed a half dozen almost preposterously cute little children playing in a flower garden, caught in mid-throw of a surprisingly mundane-looking ball, while a trio of tall, ethereally slim women watched over them with a smiling benevolence that was almost tangible.

That would be the first tapestry Ian would have looked behind, if he was looking for hidden passages, just because it looked too pretty to risk disturbing.

The endlessly complex patterns carved into the walls probably hadn't come from some affection for a sort of monotone paisley. They covered a whole bunch of hidden passageways, if the Old Keep was anything like Falias, or the Thorsen house, for that matter.

They crossed a high open walkway between two towers, Ian clutching at Giantkiller's hilt for reassurance, because if none of the guards were going to grip the ancient stone railings, neither would he. Then they took a long, spiraling staircase down to where distant music and laughing voices grew nearer.

At their approach, a pair of doors swung open, into a room filled with light and sound, with the clinking of glasses and, off in the distance, what was unmistakably a drinking song almost guttural enough to be German.

There were perhaps a hundred or so well-dressed men and women scattered in little clumps around the ballroom, although it still would have been roomy with several times that many. One group sat and stood on an island of carpet in front of a man-high fireplace that must have been a good fifteen feet wide, while over at the other end of the room sixteen couples formed four squares of two couples each, dancing through the intricate steps of what Ian would have been tempted to call a minuet, if the music didn't sound more Japanese than anything else.

Perhaps a dozen vestri servants in sky-blue livery passed among the speakers and dancers, refilling tankards and glasses, none carrying serving trays. Food was served on a long table near what, if Ian had his bearings right, was the southern wall.

As they entered the room, raised voices near the fireplace resolved themselves into two men dropping their capes to one side and walking, side by side, into the center of the room, where a golden circle perhaps twenty feet across was inlaid into the white marble floor.

Ian was so involved with watching them square off that he didn't notice Branden del Branden walk up behind him until he had cleared his throat, quietly, not enough to startle Ian.

Branden del Branden was dressed much as Ian himself was: a white tunic over dark trousers, except that Branden del Branden's tunic was filigreed with black and gold in an ornate design, while Ian's was plain and unadorned. Most of the men had blue designs on their tunics, although Ian spotted one brown and a couple of grays.

"Good evening, Ian Silver Stone," Branden del Branden said. "I've been asked to assist as your host for the evening." He gestured toward another small island of carpet and chairs in front of one of the smaller fireplaces set up against the west wall.

By the time Ian and Hosea had passed the dancers, the fight was over, and the loser was hobbling back toward the large fireplace, hopping on one foot, mostly supported by the winner.

The two swordsmen had exchanged salutes, touched swords, and then begun fighting, the motion too fast for the casual eye to follow. Ian would have bet that the taller man would have won, but the shorter fellow performed some sort of complex maneuver and ended the fight almost instantly with a quick toe-stick, which brought a yelp of surprise and pain from his larger opponent and then brought out two vestri, each with a tray of bandages and ointments, who met the pair and began work on the tall man's foot, while the conversation picked up among the group of men and women, as though nothing untoward or unusual had gone on.

Darien del Darien was waiting for them in the larger of the chairs; he waved Ian to one chair opposite him, and Hosea to another.

The fourth chair was occupied by a boy that Ian would have guessed to be about twelve, maybe thirteen, redheaded enough to be Irish, and freckled across the nose and cheeks. He was dressed formally, like an adult, but the hilt of his sword was plain and unadorned, unlike the engraved and jeweled hilts that were so common.

"Good evening to you, Ian Silver Stone," Darien del Darien said. "I've promised the Scion that we will show you proper Dominion hospitality this evening, and I've asked the Heir to bear witness to him that I've done so."

The boy inclined his head, briefly. "It's not that my father doesn't trust the klaffvarer," he said, his face perhaps too serious. "But it would be bragging on his part to speak of how well he treats you, but not on mine. Do you dance?

There are more than several ladies of the court who would be happy to partner you.''

Ian shook his head. ''I'm sorry; I don't know any of your dances, and I'm none too comfortable on my feet.''

The Heir—if he had another name, Ian clearly wasn't going to get it from their introduction—brightened immediately. ''Oh, then, I'll tell the musicians to schedule a round, and we'll teach you.'' His grin was reassuring. ''There's nothing to it, Ian Silver Stone.'' He looked to Darien del Darien. ''May I? Please?''

The klaffvarer nodded indulgently. ''Yes, my Heir,'' he said. ''But don't interrupt us; the Silver Stone and I need to discuss some matters.'' The boy rose, bowed politely in all directions, and quickly walked away, Darien del Darien's smile dropping at his departure.

''I've had men out searching for this Valin—with orders to bring him back unharmed, to let him escape if there's no way to capture him. There's been no sign,'' Darien del Darien said.

''I can't say I'm sorry,'' Ian said. Well, he could, but it would have been a clumsy lie.

''Well, you should be sorry that he's escaped. If he's who he says he is, he should be able to lead us to whatever this pack is that has supposedly sent Sons after your friends.''

''This is something that you have grave worries over?'' Hosea asked.

''Worries? Worries, no.'' Darien del Darien shook his head. ''Concerns, yes. Knowing who is behind this would be, at the very least, trade goods, and while I'm no woman to be caught up in matters of trade and commerce, I very much wish to have something to trade with you. The head of your enemy, perhaps?'' He shrugged. ''But without knowing who it is, there's little I can do, directly.''

''And indirectly?''

''Indirectly, I've already taken some actions,'' said Darien del Darien. ''We can discuss those if we can reach an understanding on another matter.''

''You want something from me.'' *Fencing lessons, perhaps? I'm really quite good at teaching foil.*

He also wasn't all that bad at dueling, although his reputation had apparently overtaken his abilities. The Cities settled most of their internal political struggles by duel. Not the best way to settle things, perhaps—well, scratch that "perhaps"—but the important thing about many problems was that they be settled, one way or the other.

"Very much," Darien del Darien said. "I'm willing to do whatever I can for you and your friends. And, while my word is not, perhaps, as unbreakable as some, you'll find that it's been respected and respectable before, and it shall be again. I can promise you gold—surely you can always use gold—and I can promise you what aid I can muster, either of mine own or of the Dominions. I can arrange for your swift conduct between the Old Keep and Falias, and through the Hidden Ways back to your home; now or at some later time. And I can promise you my . . . my great gratitude."

Ian cocked his head to one side. "And for all this promising, what is it that you want from me?"

"Well, that is the heart of the matter, isn't it?" Darien del Darien nodded. "I need from you just one thing. I need to have you bring to me, here, for one day, and one day only, a jewel of the Brisingamen."

Ian thought he hadn't heard him correctly for a moment. Was that all? Was that what this was all about? Was that why Darien del Darien had sent Sons to Hardwood, to scare Ian into coming to look for the source so that he could make this offer?

Try just asking next time, he thought. "I . . . I must be missing something. Is that all?"

Darien del Darien snorted. "Yes," he said, his lips white against his skeletal face. "That is all."

Hosea shook his head. "That is much, as well you know. Ian Silver Stone doesn't have any of the jewels, and—"

"Yes, yes, yes, and you've carefully cut the knowledge of where you hid the rest from your living brain," Darien del Darien said, his voice low and angry. "As best I can tell, three of them remain hidden."

Three? But—

"Three?" Hosea cocked his head to one side.

"Three," Darien del Darien said. "I . . . I think—that the Vandestish have the emerald."

Hosea turned to Ian. "He is certain," he said, in that sibilant language he had used before, that Ian somehow recognized as Old Harvish. "His spies in—in the country in which you were asked to undergo the Pain say that they do."

It took Ian a moment to realize that Vandescard would still have been "Vandescard" in Old Harvish, and that Hosea had to circumlocute if he wanted to keep what he was saying secret from Darien del Darien.

"And you know this? . . ."

"As surely as it is possible to know anything. He thinks that this will be common knowledge shortly, or he would not have mentioned it. He seeks to ingratiate himself with you through honesty."

"I shall—" Ian choked on the words that he started to say, then said, "That's fine with me," in English. In Old Harvish, the closest he could have come to that figure of speech would have been *I'll not eat his children, then rape his women before his eyes, in my vengeance.* Whoever the Old Harvish were or had been, Ian hoped there weren't many left around.

"There's a rumor," Darien del Darien went on, "that the sapphire was found in Finvarrasland recently."

Ian looked to Hosea, who nodded.

"Ian Silver Stone has found two—the diamond and the ruby." The klaffvarer looked over the Hosea. "Ages go by with all seven hidden. The Aesir and the Vanir and the Sidhe and others of the Old Ones fade away, and all seven remain hidden. The Tuatha have the Cities carved from impermeable rock; they grow too old to live in cities, and vanish, one by one, like soap bubbles popping—and all seven remain hidden. The Tuarin—and races and people I've never heard of come and go—and the Brisingamen jewels remain hidden.

"And then, within less than two years, two of them appear—and then another two? Do I smell the Fimbulwinter coming, perhaps?" He raised his hand. "I know, I know:

if that is so, then none of this matters, for nothing matters. If it's going to be the end of it all, then—" he waved it away. "Then what we do is of no import. I have to believe otherwise. If it is to be otherwise, I must serve the Scion, and in order to do that I need the use, the possession of, for one day, one of your Brisingamen jewels."

Well, actually, Torrie had found the ruby, and Arnie had found the diamond. But Ian had had them conveyed to Freya, and she had safely hidden them away somewhere.

But this was the first Ian had heard that another two gems had been located. He and Torrie had been talking about going in search of the Brisingamen gems once Torrie graduated, if only as a reason to spend time in Tir Na Nog.

"And through some coincidence," Ian asked, "I have— we have—come here accompanying a dwarf who has conveniently—for you, perhaps?—disappeared just as you wanted to see me to ask me this favor."

Darien del Darien spread his hands in surrender. "I understand your suspicions; were I you, I would suspect much worse, perhaps. But if I had tried to bring you here, don't you think I would have found a way less cumbersome? Less hostile?" He leaned forward. "Yes, I could send Sons through the Hidden Way that His Warmth controls, and they could go to your home village just as easily as could I.

"But they wouldn't know any more about your world, about your country, than I would. This city where Sons seek Thorsen blood is far away from your village—is there some trail that they could follow, that would tell them where to seek Thorian del Thorian the Younger?" Darien del Darien sat back in his chair. "Doesn't that seem impossible to you?"

Impossible? No. Darien del Darien was being too much the advocate. Ivar del Hival had spent some time in Hardwood. But giving out the sort of information that would have enabled Sons to travel hundreds of miles from Hardwood to the city? Any questions that would have elicited that would have awakened his suspicions.

Sure, Ivar del Hival could have led a Son or some Sons to Minneapolis. But he wouldn't have, not to go after Torrie. You can't go through life trusting everybody, Ian had long learned, but you couldn't go through it trusting nobody, either. It would be nice if Ivar del Hival was here. Yes, he was fealty-bound to the Fire and to the Sky, but he was a friendly, familiar face, and somebody Ian had trusted, and could trust.

"Very well," Darien del Darien said, "perhaps not impossible, but does it not seem unlikely?"

But if the Dominions hadn't sent Sons after the Thorsens again, who had, and why? Was Valin lying?

It would be nice to know. And he was, perhaps conveniently, absent. But if Darien del Darien hadn't released Valin—if the dwarf hadn't been given the secret to the jail cell—where was he?

That was the center of it all, and Ian's mind was spinning around the center of it all.

It wasn't just that none of it made any sense. Ian had grown up in a home where nothing made sense, where the hands and voice that were supposed to support and comfort you beat and abused you.

What bothered him was the feeling that this all did make sense, that if only he looked at it from the right perspective, it would all fall into place and he would know what to do.

But that was just an artifact of his childhood.

He ached for the feel of the fencing strip beneath his feet, where there was only one opponent, that opponent was identified and in front of you, and while it was important to beat him every time, if you lost a point, all you lost was a point.

Unbidden, Harbard's ring pulsed hard against his finger. "I have to think about this," he said, "but I have to know: if I choose to, if I can, bring a Brisingamen jewel here, can you swear that it will be safely returned?"

Darien del Darien started to nod, then shook his head. "No," he said. "I wish that I could, but I cannot."

Well, that was honest of him, at least.

"I can promise that the Scion and I will do all we can to see that it is returned, but anything more than that would be a lie. I can tell you that I believe it would be, and that I'd agree to any conditions you would set, that . . . please, just think on it, please, Ian Silver Stone." He looked up and beckoned to somebody apparently far across the room, and then he rose. In a moment, his manner had changed from that of the ruler that he clearly was—in practice, if not in theory—to that of a butler, perhaps, or a host.

"In the interim," Darien del Darien said, "if you would, let us show you that the hospitality of the Old Keep has no superior at Falias, or anybody else. The Heir informs me that the Magnificent Lady Diandra has asked the pleasure of your company at the dance."

Hosea had long been asleep when Ian staggered into their rooms, tired in a remarkably pleasant way, for once.

There had been worse evenings in his life, and that was a fact. It turned out that there was a reason that the small corridors off the ballroom were dark, with small but remarkably comfortable rooms off of them. And the Magnificent Diandra had been fun to dance with, and incredibly funny as well as easy on the eye, and it turned out that there were fringe benefits to this becoming a legend thing . . .

. . . And there was a dark shape in the chair next to Hosea's bed.

Ian snatched at Giantkiller's hilt. "Hosea!" Panic washed over him in a quick cold wave that scrubbed every trace of that luxurious languor from his nerves and veins.

Hosea sat up instantly, only his eyes visible in a band of the dim light that streamed in through the translucence of the windows.

"There is no need to panic, Ian Silver Stone," the Scion's harsh voice said. "I won't harm either of you." He chuckled thinly. "Not that, even on a much better day, I'd have been much of a match for the Promised Warrior, or even a green ordinary of the House of Wind. But keep your sword out and at the ready, if it pleases you."

"How did you get in here?" Ian asked, realizing that it was a stupid question the moment the words were out of his mouth. The guards at the door wouldn't have hesitated to open it for their ruler, after all.

"An astute question," the Scion said. "I congratulate you on your presence of mind."

"You'll find Ian has more of that than you'd want to bet against, Scion," Hosea said.

Ian could barely make out Hosea reaching for something; the Scion gestured him into motionlessness. "Please."

"As you wish, of course," Hosea said. "I can see—"

"Yes, yes, of course you can see in the dark, you can see the past and the future, you can see anything and everything, but leave some things unspoken for now; I promise you that you'll have the chance to speak of them later." He shifted in his chair. "If . . . you were to go into your sleeping room, Ian Silver Stone, and stand on the headpiece of your bed, reaching up as high as you can, you'd feel a row of studs at the juncture of wall and ceiling, each with a small bit of give. Press the third, fifth, and sixth stud only, then quickly leap off the bed before your weight atop the headpiece resets the mechanism, and a portion of your wall will swing inward, giving you ingress into what appears to be a hidden closet of sorts."

"But it is not a closet," Hosea said.

"Oh, yes, it is. You'll find some old armor stacked there, and a rolled tapestry or two, as well as a few other odds and ends."

"It's not just a closet," Ian said. "If you know where to open another hidden door, you'll find that it's an entrance to one of the hidden passages that run through the Cities."

"That could, perhaps, be the case. I really couldn't say."

"And you know that passage."

"That passage?" The Scion laughed. "That one? Why, Ian Silver Stone, I know them all."

How, Ian Silver Stone (the Scion had said), do you think a ruler maintains his rule? What is it, finally, that makes people who certainly often have other notions do what he tells them to?

Oh, there are plenty of things, you'd no doubt say. There's a sense of legitimacy that comes with tradition and authority; there is, perhaps, the acknowledgment that somebody must decide, and if not this ruler, then whom?

And all that would be true.

But, truly, the final essence is force. You do what the ruler says because if you don't, you'll face the consequences. Men will come to your village and haul you away, or strap you to the whipping rack and lay your back open with a lash made of braided bull hide. You'll dance on the end of a rope or over a bed of coals.

Don't you like the picture? Well, since when does what you like have much to do with the way of the world?

You may think of us in the Cities as decadent, as long past our prime as a race, as a people, and I will not argue the point, because it is true. There was a time when the Crimson and Ancient Cerulean companies bought with their blood and bone not only peace for us of the Dominions but also comfort, and life in the Cities has long been comfortable. Our walls are solid; the fields and villages that feed us are lush and productive, and even the ordinaries of the Houses spend as much time in their City quarters as they can.

To do that, though, brings them under the hand of their rulers. It's a common pattern throughout—one way a ruler has of enforcing his will is by forcing his nobles to place themselves and their families, from time to time, under his roof, where their necks are exposed to his blade.

And if life under his roof is more comfortable—more interesting, more exciting, more lavish where lavish is good and more spare where spare is pleasant—then all the better, no?

But by doing that, by keeping your people close to your hand, you keep them close to your throat. What would you do, say, if a dozen nobles or a dozen dozen were to surprise you, and announce that they—or perhaps they and your klaffvarer, say—were now the rulers of the Cities?

In another place, at another time, a ruler might surround himself with trusted men, men whose brutality earned the enmity of all, so that it was only through the survival of himself and his line that they, too, would survive. But they would have to oppress the rest, wouldn't they? They would have to keep them in fear.

And that sort of fear breeds conspiracy, which breeds

instability. A ruler needs, then, an army to keep the nobles in line.

And, of course, there is a danger there. Keep too large an army, be too dependent on it, and its leaders will decide that they can better rule than these foppish nobles. Perhaps the general will overthrow the ruler and take his crown himself? Or perhaps not.

In the long run, it matters little. Forces will sway forward and back; factions and movements and conspiracies will move about like a square of squares on the dance floor, save that nobody will ever know what the pattern of the next round is to be.

Unless . . .

"Unless," Ian said, "there is one man, and one man only, who can reach out and touch anybody, anywhere."

Such a thing couldn't be in most places. A ruler couldn't be his own hatchetman, not for long.

But the Cities were different. They held their secret passages, as the universe itself was honeycombed with the Hidden Ways. And one man who knew all those passages could, if he was the only one who knew them all, reach out and strike anywhere, at any time.

And if his residence was the highest spire, unapproachable without warning—

"There's some sort of passage down the center of the spire," Ian said.

"That is, of course, possible. If so, the Scion would know," the Scion said, "for what do you think 'Scion' means if not descendant, if not inheritor, if not Heir?"

Ian sat back, trying to line up all the ducks in a row, as though that might do some good.

And it might, for once.

The Scion maintained his rule because he was the only one who knew all the hidden passages and abditories in the Cities—not just the Old Keep, but all the Cities—and because that let him reach out, either in person or through a trusted servant, to touch, or grab, or, if necessary, kill anybody in the Cities who was a threat.

Of course, he'd want to do most of the reaching out

himself, but it was like with any other sort of classified information. There would be the passages that were widely known, and those that were known to only a few, and then there would be as many as possible that the Scion would keep to himself.

Hell, the hidden closet in Ian's sleeping room here wasn't all that useful, not unless he could find a way from there into a passage, and given the proclivities of the designer of the Cities, it was likely that there were plenty of false entrances into the passages.

Or even, perhaps, routes that led to traps?

Possibly.

"Then what the Heir inherits is," Ian said, letting himself think out loud, "the secrets. Not all of them—if he has all of them, then he becomes too vulnerable, too much of a prize, and too powerful. He might be tempted to take over."

"There is no temptation; once he reaches his majority, my Heir can become the Scion the moment he wishes it. I would not stand in his way when he thinks himself ready, just as my father did not stand in mine."

"But he has enough so that he can pry the rest out himself, and pass them down to his Heir, when he becomes Scion."

"Now? Not quite yet."

"Shared key cryptography," Ian said.

"Eh?"

He had, of course, spoken in English. "He has enough, and your klaffvarer has enough, and probably one or two other people have enough of the information to put together . . ." (What? The complete map of the Cities' secret? No, that didn't seem right.) ". . . to figure out where the complete map of the Cities is hidden."

The dark shape nodded. "Yes," he said. "You will, I hope, understand if I don't choose to discuss all the details of how that would work."

"All? I'd rather I didn't know *any* of them."

The Scion chuckled thinly.

"So it was you who let Valin out?" Ian asked.

"No. It was Valin who let Valin out—that exit only

opens from the inside, not the outside. It was I who followed his tracks through the dust of the passageways and assured myself that the vestri . . . took a route to the outside that he would be hard put to return by, and it was I who dragged myself here.''

The Scion shook his head. ''No, I don't know who sent your vestri any more than you do, nor do I know who put Sons on your friends' scents. But I do know one thing,'' he said. He made a sudden motion with his hands, and yellow light flared, suddenly bright, in the table lantern.

He had been a handsome man, once, and that still showed in the left side of his face, in the strong jaw and firm cheekbones.

The right side of his face was a horror. The flesh looked, it looked . . . *melted* was the only word that came to Ian's mind. Open lesions had eaten into skin, revealing the muscle and sinew beneath. The right ear was gone, and the hair and most of the skin were gone from the skull on that side, white bone showing through in spots.

Amazingly, except for the juncture of the lips, the lips were still intact, and a thin layer of muscle covered the cheek. Soon, if this rot progressed, that would be gone, and with it the Scion's ability to speak.

A bandage covered where the flesh of his neck was red and raw and open; the cloth hung, soggy and limp, soaked with some sort of yellow fluid speckled with spots of red—like bloody lemonade.

''I know that if you do not help me, I do not have much longer. My flesh rots more daily, and it is all that my chirurgeon and the Old Vistarii woman who prepares my medicines can do to keep the maggots at bay.'' Moving slowly, perhaps so as not to give any reason for alarm, he reached into the front of his tunic and pulled out a folded square of white linen, which he quickly unfolded and pressed up against his cheek.

''And when I am gone—and it shall not be long, not at this rate—will this curse affect my son, my Heir, as well?

''Is this a curse laid on me, or on the Scion?

''Darien del Darien and I do what we can for you, and yours,'' he said. ''And, even if you cannot help me, even if it's too late, I swear that I shall bind him and his to your aid, forever, if you will protect my son from this."

His voice was full more with fear than with pain as he pulled the cloth away from his cheek. It came away with clotted bits of blood and pus; the Scion quickly folded the cloth and put it away.

Hosea was at the Scion's side. Here the old man slept naked, and there would have been something comical about his bony flanks—at another time. "Be still; I'll not hurt you more, nor harm you at all." He felt at the cheek, his fingers moving down the neck.

"You wash it frequently with clean water? Good; that should slow the progress down. I'm sure your chirurgeon is applying a poultice, but if you have him add one part goldenseal for every four of comfrey and five of calendula, it should be more effective. Boiled oats—they must be boiled past edibility, mind—allowed to cool should soothe it some, and if you add some eyebright, nettles, goldenrod, goldenseal, licorice root, red clover, burdock, and hypericum to your broth, it'll increase your appetite, which would be all to the good."

"What is it?" Ian asked.

"It's called by many names." Hosea's eyes closed, wearily. "The Wasting Disease. Elf-shot." His eyes met Ian's. "Or Odin's Curse."

A dome of stars hung over a milky plain of clouds, and when Ian looked down below, where music and laughter still rang out from the grand hall, it felt like they were on an island in an otherwise empty sea, and the music and laughter seemed more hollow and frightened than jolly.

Or maybe it was Ian who was more hollow and frightened than jolly.

Next to him, Hosea—no, here he was Orfindel—leaned his elbows on the balustrade. "So," he said. "It seems we have a problem."

"What do you mean 'we,' white man?"

"Eh?"

"Never mind." Ian shook his head. "Old joke, and not a very good one."

"But yes, we have a problem." Hosea touched a knuckle to his mouth. "Are you going to do as the Scion asks?"

That was a strange way to put it. "Won't it work? Is there some other way?"

"One question at a time, Ian, one question at a time. Which one do you want answered first?"

"Okay, first: will it work?"

"Is using one of the Brisingamen jewels to disrupt a curse possible? That's perhaps like asking if one might be able to damage a stick of soft butter with a chain saw. Together, the seven Brisingamen jewels hold—con-ceal? . . ." Hosea shrugged. "Together they contain enough hidden matter to start the universe all over again. The Scion has some natural resistance to the curse; simply keeping one of the jewels near him would magnify that."

"Is there some other way?"

"I see none." Hosea shook his head. "Oh, perhaps, if it were anyone else. There are some of the Old Vistarii still around, here and there, and perhaps one or two of them, together, might be able to do something. And, of course, Odin himself could lift the curse, no matter who cast it—"

"If we knew where he was." It would take more than that, of course. Bending the will of an Aesir was not the easiest of tasks, and were Harbard's ring capable of it, Odin would never have let it out of his hands. He wouldn't have given Ian a weapon that could be used against him, after all.

"No. He wouldn't help me out, would he?"

"That would seem unlikely." Hosea's lips made a thin line. "I doubt that Freya will actually be willing to let one of the stones go, but that does seem to be the thing to try, if you feel you have to, or ought to, try something."

Surely he was wrong about that. She wouldn't have either of them if it wasn't for Ian. And—

"Yes, Ian, she is quite fond of you," Hosea said, smil-ing. "Very fond. But she's been fond of mortals before, and she's only capable of getting involved so much about people, and no further. It would be difficult for her to invest much emotion in you, for your life comes and goes so quickly that you can't even watch a mountain crumble.

"You look at her like you look at Karin Thorsen, and you see a young woman—older, certainly, than you, but still a young woman.

"But she's not a young woman, Ian. She's not a human; she's an Old One, and an Aesir. She thinks differently than you do—and differently than I do, for that matter, since I'm neither a woman nor an Aesir. You couldn't have trusted the two Brisingamen gems into safer hands, but that's merely," he said, his smile reassurance, not reproof, "because there are no safe hands."

Well, there was that. Tossing the diamond into the hands of the Vandestish would have been even worse than putting the ruby in the hands of the rulers of the Dominion. And trying to keep either would have been suicidal.

Who better than Freya to hold on to the gems until the time came for the end of time?

"She wants to keep them for herself?" If Hosea were to say it was so, Ian would try to believe it, but . . .

"No. As I keep telling you, she's old; you seem to be unable to understand the implications of that. Remaking the entire universe in your own image is an urge that affects the young and the crazy, not the old and tired. Perhaps that idea would have appealed to her in her youth, and to the rest of the Aesir and the Vanir, to the Tuatha and Vistarii and Tuarin and all the rest.

"But they're gone. Like Bóinn, some have become tired and become hill spirits, or forest spirits like Morrigan—stay out of her woods, Ian!—and Damona. If they had enough vitality to sustain themselves, Ian, they would be what they were, and not what they are.

"Or so I think."

There was another way to look at it. Forget all the complexities, ignore the schemes within schemes and whatever subtle games the Old Ones played, and leave it as a simple matter. Two men—the Scion and his klaffvarer—had promised their help in return for his, swearing that they were not the source of the Thorsens' problems, and while that could be a lie, it felt true, and while he had willed them to believe that their only hope to persuade him was to tell the truth, that wasn't why he would have to go to Freya and ask for the loan of a Brisingamen gem.

"I'm going to give it a try," Ian said.

"Yes, you are." Hosea nodded. "I thought as much," he said. He stood silently for a long while, his eyes closed, as though in prayer, his body swaying almost imperceptibly from side to side. "If this was planned," he said, "whoever planned it—be it the Scion, or Harbard, or somebody else— couldn't have planned it one whit better to play to your weakness." His eyes opened. "I don't think that's a coincidence."

Weakness? Ian bristled.

"Yes, Ian, a weakness. Because, in the final essence, the plea that the Scion made was not for himself but for his son, for the Heir. It wasn't really that you save his life, but that you protect his son's future. Think on it, Ian Silver Stone—aren't you jealous of the Heir for that paternal affection? Don't you hate him, just a little?"

You have to be able to speak ugly truths to your friends. If you keep them inside, they'll eat your guts out, just as surely as Odin's Curse was eating away at the Scion's face.

"No, not a little," Ian said. "Much more than that." It was small and mean and petty to resent yet another son who had a caring father, but Ian couldn't control what he felt. Yes, he could look on a father's love with a cold envy that felt more like hatred than anything else . . .

But you weren't responsible for what you felt. You were responsible for what you did.

If Ian had been chosen as somebody's stooge, he had been chosen well and played perfectly.

So be it.

CHAPTER TWENTY

Valin

Branden del Branden himself checked the belly
straps on Ian's saddle, and only smiled thinly
when Ian checked them again.

"No offense meant," Ian said, pulling hard on the tight
weave. He waited until the horse let out a breath, then
pulled it again.

"It would be rather, well, awkward for me to take offense at the moment, Ian Silver Stone, even if you were to
unbutton your fly and void yourself on my boots, wouldn't
it?"

"Well, there is that," Ian said. "But let's not test that,
eh?"

"As you will," Branden del Branden said with a grin.

Ian slung Giantkiller's scabbard over the left saddle pommel, then stuck a foot in the stirrup and lifted himself up
and on to the saddle. Horses. Ian didn't hate horses, but he
wasn't overly fond of them, either.

Branden del Branden tied the end of the pack horse's
lead to the right-hand pommel of Ian's horse, then exchanged a brief handshake with Ian.

High above, on the ramparts surrounding the killing
ground, the blue-clad soldiers seemed less eager to start

shooting arrows and throwing spears than they had the day before. Which was fine.

"Are you sure you don't want me to send at least a demi-troop with you?"

Ian shook his head. "I think the idea of a troop of soldiers riding toward Harbard's Crossing would send the wrong message. Don't you?"

"We could dispatch riders to the appropriate margraves, bearing sworn oaths that we mean no harm, and merely see to the welfare of the intended of the Margravine of the Eastern Hinterlands, but . . ." Branden del Branden frowned and raised his hands in surrender at Ian's head-shake. "But you don't care for that."

"I think it's too risky." In more ways than one. There were ample reasons Ian would prefer not to have a bunch of Dominion soldiers as his putative bodyguard. If he was successful, he'd have to watch his back for the entire return trip. Some soldier, too clever by half, might figure to betray the Scion, or take it into his head to protect the realm by removing the jewel from the untrustworthy hands of this possible Promised Warrior.

"As you wish," Branden del Branden said. He was enough of a politician to know when further argument held no promise.

"Again," Ian said, "Hosea remains here of his own will, to help that Vistarii woman with her herb preparations. When he is ready to leave, he is to be—"

"Yes, yes, yes, he is to be escorted where, and as, he wishes. You have the Scion's word on that, Ian Silver Stone, and his klaffvarer's. You hardly need mine. But you have it, as well."

Ian nodded, and kicked his ankles against the black mare's meaty sides. Obediently, she clopped into a slow walk, the small pack pony following along behind, starting even before the braided rope fully took up the slack.

Why was it that the twisting path out through the tunnels was longer than the one coming in?

Ian shook his head. Maybe it was just his imagination, or maybe a horse really walked downhill slower than uphill, or maybe there was some sleight involved, but it felt like an eternity until the mouth of the tunnel opened ahead . . .

. . . above a sea of fog, where a long, narrow road in front of him vanished off in the mist.

Well, there had been only one road up, and there was only one road down. Ian made a *tsktsktsk* sound with his teeth, and the horse picked up the pace.

The fog still surrounded him, but the distance he could see down the trail had lengthened to perhaps twenty yards when he heard the expected coarse whisper from the fog.

"Ian Silver Stone."

He reined the horse to a stop, and waited, and in a few moments, a dark shape walked out of the fog.

Ian had seen Valin look worse, but mainly he had seen the dwarf look better. His thick, meaty cheeks seemed sunken, and his thin muslin tunic was damp. Vestri could live off the land better than humans, by and large, but living off fog was another matter.

"Greetings, Valin. You look miserable." Ian dropped easily to the ground and retrieved a blanket and a leather bag of meatrolls from the pack horse. With a little reshuffling of gear from the gray pony to Ian's mare, the pack animal could carry Valin, as well.

The men of the Cities knew much that Ian didn't, but they had their blind spots, as well. Once Valin had escaped the Old Keep, he was, at least in their minds, gone—even the Scion had only worried about the possibility of him sneaking back in, after all.

But if he was unknown to those in the Old Keep—and apparently he was—then it only followed that he was unlikely to be familiar with the environs around the keep. So what would he do? Stagger about in the fog blind, hoping that even though he was walking the trails of the Old Keep without the permission and blessing of its occupants, it would part properly to guide him?

Or would he simply wait for the next party leaving, and follow it?

Ian wrapped the blanket about the dwarf's shoulders and started to untie the gear. "Eat some of those meatrolls,

Valin, and get warm. I think we've a few things to talk about,'' Ian said.

Or more than just a few.

"Yes, Ian Silver Stone," Valin said. "Whatever you wish."

CHAPTER TWENTY-ONE

Reckoning

T horian del Thorian looked over the yellow crime scene tape at the dirty, bloody, snowy ground.

Your message has been received, he thought. *Whoever you are and whatever your intentions.*

The body had long since been hauled away by men in white coats and loaded into an ambulance—something that surprised Thorian del Thorian; wasn't an ambulance supposed to carry injured people to a place of treatment?—and an amazing number of men and women had spent all night and much of the day going over the ground first under the portable lights that they themselves had brought, and then under the lights of the unpronounceable television stations.

Maggie's landlord had already repaired the back door, and Thorian had already paid him for the costs and the labor.

Thorian del Thorian shook his head. There was an element of even minimal pride lacking in these city people. His son had kicked down that door attempting to rescue one of their own, and instead of honoring him for that, they had chained, imprisoned, and now fined him.

Well, at least they hadn't chained and imprisoned him

for long, and certainly the size of the fine was not a problem for Thorian del Thorian.

Karin would have argued over the price, but she was a woman, and matters of finance were properly her concern. Thorian del Thorian had simply reached into his inner jacket pocket and then removed by touch three of the ten-bill packets of twenties, as she had taught him to do. He was pleased that he had remembered to peel off five of the bills and put them back; that didn't come naturally to him.

The landlord had accepted the money with a grumble and a smile. He had actually *smiled* as he had taken the money! Had these city people no pride?

No. That was not fair. They had pride. It was just a different, inferior kind of pride to that which Thorian del Thorian had learned at the feet of his father.

As Thorian stood looking over the tape, one of the city's blue-suited proctors, visibly shivering in the cold, emerged from his still-running automobile, slammed the door hard behind him, and walked quickly over to Thorian.

"Is there something I can help you with, sir?" He was half Thorian's age, and the hair of the brown moustache under his lip was too thin. But he used the honorific "sir" and offered Thorian aid in that strangely impertinent way that neither showed respect nor offered assistance.

In the Cities, someone with that sort of arrogance had best be good with a blade and fond of pain—and quick of learning that arrogance had best be kept from display. For there was usually a better swordsman, and in any case there were always more swordsmen.

But Thorian del Thorian had not lived in the Cities for, now, more than half his life, and perhaps it was time that he accommodated himself to this cheap and common sort of rudeness. He didn't, after all, have to leave the environs of Hardwood often.

Or hadn't had to, until recent times. Amazing how one could get used to such a strange little place.

"Sir?" The proctor's voice was far too loud, and his manner gradually more aggressive.

"Assistance? No." Thorian del Thorian smiled as he

shook his head. "I thank you for the offer, but no. I am . . . fine."

He would have liked to look more closely at the bloody ground. But if he had decided to do it, crossing the tape was something that he would have had to wait another time for; still, he was sure that he knew what he would find, and since the Son had not attacked in wolf form, even if there were Son prints on the snow—and there were—the authorities would not understand their meaning.

"Then you're just looking?" the policeman asked.

"It's a sad thing," Thorian said. "A young woman killed so horribly, for no purpose."

"Yeah." The young man visibly relaxed as he nodded. "Yeah. It is sad, all right. We're, well, we're trying to keep this area clear, if that's okay."

Thorsen looked at the tape and thought about asking why, if they needed a larger charmed circle, they hadn't encircled a larger area, but the young policeman wouldn't know. The only thing he knew was that the big man with the scar looking at the area he was supposed to be guarding made him nervous for reasons he couldn't quite figure out, and that he would be more comfortable when Thorian del Thorian moved on.

So Thorian del Thorian would move on.

"I'm sorry to have bothered you," Thorian said, forcing himself not to make a stiff but slight bow-of-minor-reproof before he walked away. The customs in this land didn't allow for such things, and he wouldn't want to stand out as different in the young policeman's mind.

He walked evenly away at a marching pace—it was not a day for rushing, after all.

The Greek restaurant was on the corner diagonally across the street, and while the outer compartment was cold and unappetizing, when the inner door swung open, the scents of garlic and roasting meat washed over him in a pleasant wave.

There were two large—ovens? No, that wasn't correct. Ro-something . . . rotunda, that was it—there were two large metal rotundas, and what appeared to be a thigh-roast from some huge beast rotated on a metal spit on each, cooking and browning as it turned slowly past the red-hot metal coils, and every few moments one of the white-clad, swarthy men who looked like Southerners would take a long-bladed knife and a long-handled fork, cut off a few slices, conveying each with a practiced flip to a platter.

It was a popular restaurant, which meant, by Thorian del Thorian's standards, that it was too crowded. He enjoyed meeting strangers—a too-rare luxury at home that he had long since acquired as a taste in Hardwood—but only one or two at a time, not in rooms filled with raucous people seeking their privacy in noisy anonymity.

A too-skinny, horsy-faced young serving-woman with hair that was, preposterously, dyed a funny purple color, walked up to him with menus clutched against her chest, as though they were precious items she feared he might take.

"How many?" she asked.

It took him a moment to understand that. "I am . . . meeting friends."

She was pretty when she smiled. "Oh, I bet you're with that foursome. They said they were waiting for another, and they only ordered some saganaki."

She led him past the two rotundas and down to a room off the side.

The outer room had been busy, but the back room, equally large, was filled with tables but empty of people except for the four seated at the far table. Thorian took the remaining chair, up against the wall.

All four of them were grim and glum, even young Thorian. He knew that all of them, except perhaps Billy Olson, had seen death before, and now they had seen it again.

"The last of the television crews is gone," he said. "It was the one from Wicko."

He had never quite gotten the hang of that, why they would choose for themselves such names as Kubus or Nubuk or Abuk; Wicko or Kimstup.

"Double-u cee cee oh," young Thorian said to a puzzled Maggie. He was good at spelling and at reading, and always had been. Perhaps he was a little too accomplished at mat-

ters of arithmetic and money, but that was the only effeminate thing about him.

Unlike some people. Billy Olson extended his little finger
as he brought his cup of hot chocolate up to take an overly
cautious sip.

Jeff Bjerke was trying hard not to glare at him, and
looked uncomfortable.

Well, Thorian Thorsen understood that. But Billy Olson
had conducted himself with honor and competence, according to Maggie—and Maggie was Thorian's svertbror, let
no man make any mistake about that!—so it was the least
that Thorian Thorsen could do to ignore his disability.

"Torrie's been—" Billy Olson cut himself off as the
waitress, a fiftyish Southern woman with a bristly moustache that would have looked better on the young city proctor, arrived with a crackling hot pan on a tray balanced on
one hand, a small steel cup and cheap plastic lighter in the
other.

Billy set his mug down—his little finger hadn't been
extended, not this time—and watched.

She poured clear liquid into the hot pan, and with a tired
"Opa!" lit the flat yellow pancake in the pan, extinguished
it with a squeeze of fresh lemon, and set it down on the
table, along with a plate of soft flat bread wedges.

After all the drama, the pancake turned out to be cheese
baked in some sort of thin dough. Tasty enough, he
thought, and the tangy bite of the fresh lemon juice went
well with the hot cheese. Thorian del Thorian had eaten
worse things in his life; this was quite pleasant, actually.

Thorian del Thorian would have to—no. He would not
have to remember to try it again next time.

"They have lamb, Dad," young Thorian said. "I ordered
you some lamb chops, extra garlic, very rare."

"I like lamb." He nodded. "But what is that animal
cooking on the rotundas in the front?"

"You can't—"

"Rotundas?" Maggie arched an eyebrow.

"Rotisseries, Dad. And the meat is a mixture of things—
it's compressed-together beef, mainly, with some lamb and
spices. Called 'gee-ros' or 'hee-ros,' but it's spelled like

'gyro'—most people call the big blocks 'gyrobeast.' "

Thorian del Thorian sighed. He shouldn't have asked. Once again, the truth was less interesting than his imagination would have had it, as was true for so much in this world. "Lamb will be fine."

Billy Olson set his mug of hot chocolate down. This time, he hadn't been holding it in that strange and effeminate way. This time, Jeff Bjerke hadn't been looking at him.

Thorian del Thorian wondered what that was all about, but there was no polite way to ask. But it would have been nice to know.

"I was saying," Billy Olson said, "that I've been hearing some things that I wouldn't quite have believed if Jeff had ever had a reputation for telling tall tales."

How much of the private matters had they told this outcast? Thorian del Thorian started to say something, but he stopped himself. Family matters would henceforth be the problem of young Thorian, and he had always chosen his friends and companions well, better than his father tended to give him credit for. Ian Silver Stone and Maggie del Albert were special.

So he just nodded. "Yes, there have been strange things happening, of late."

"I mean, I knew you came from far away, but I'd figured you were, like, an illegal German immigrant, maybe, or a Dane or something, not . . . ," he looked around, ". . . from Oz or whatever you call it."

"We call it Tir Na Nog," Thorian del Thorian said, "for that is its name." He shrugged. "Although I always thought of myself as from the House of Steel, if I thought of myself as from anything."

"Eh?"

Thorian del Thorian could have shrugged it off, but there was no reason to. "When somebody asks you where you're from, do you tell them that you're an Earthling?"

"Well, no." Billy raised the mug and drank, his nod and frown a gesture of concession that would have been precisely the same in the Cities.

Thorian del Thorian had missed the Cities, more than he had known.

But he would not have traded a thousand years of life in Falias for a day with Karin. *Min alskling,* he thought, *I hope it is not too long before another man warms your bed.*

"Okay," young Thorian said, "so what's our next move? We have to do—"

"No. There is no 'we.'" Thorian del Thorian shook his head. "We do not have a next move. The next move is mine, and the one after that is his, and if after that I have another move left, why, that will be the last one for this game."

Jeff Bjerke shook his head. "I don't like the way this is going."

"You don't?" Thorian del Thorian helped himself to another piece of the lemony cheese. "I'm none too fond of it myself. But didn't you understand the message we were sent last night?" He put two fingers on the table and walked them away from his plate. "You and I set a second trap, offering you as a lure, to draw him out, hoping that I, the real target, would be able to protect you, my supposed protector, when he made his thrust at you.

"But no. He ignored that. He struck instead at an innocent, at one nearby so we would make no mistake that it was him, so that Thorian and Maggie would rush out to find that he can strike wherever he pleases.

"As he can."

What did this Son look like? Most were hirsute enough to look strange in human form, but in winter, with everybody wrapped up so, it would take little more than a wool cap and a scarf to hide the facial hair. And while it might make him a silly-looking wolf when he transformed, he could shave, if he wanted to, after all—and if he didn't bare his teeth or show you the stubble on the palms of his hands, how would you know?

"And who shall it be next? Maggie, your roommate is due back tomorrow—perhaps it shall be her? Billy Olson has exposed himself as being one of us; shall we wait until he's the victim? As I said to Jeff, we can't afford to toy with this one, for we have weaknesses aplenty that he can strike at, to lure me out.

"Because, for whatever reason, it's me that he wants."

And why? Thorian del Thorian doubted that it had any-thing to do with the Duelmaster, or the House of Steel, even though he was, technically, a traitor; that matter had been decided by champion, and Thorian del Orvald could easily let it lie.

Young Thorian's face was grim, but he nodded, slowly. "So you think he's making a threat—"

"No, not a threat. Think of it as an offer. He's being as gentle as his kind is capable of. His actions make it clear what he offers: if I face him, if I come out and fight him, one on one, he'll leave the rest of you alone, which is what he really wants to do." He shrugged. "It could have been worse, much worse. He could have taken you, Thorian, and made me the same offer for the life of your mother, per-haps. Or he could have taken Maggie . . ."

She clutched his hand tightly, her strength surprising. But she had always been strong, and strength, even physical strength, didn't always show itself in bulging muscles.

". . . he could have taken Maggie," Thorian del Thorian said, "and then made a thrust at you, letting me know that he was just missing—as he did last night, when he killed that woman."

"How?" Young Thorian was angry. "There were three of us, and I had my sword, and—"

"You dashed out into the night, trusting on two others to watch your back, and they had none to watch theirs. It's an old trick, Thorian—don't drop the foremost of your en-emies, but the rearmost, and then work your way forward." He smiled. "I once won a bet with a captain in an Ancient Cerulean company, using just such a method." He smiled again. "So we have few choices. We can let him kill and kill again, until either he runs panting from the killing, or we can give him what he wants now, or we can give him what he wants later." He raised a cautionary finger. "I'm not as old and feeble as you seem to believe. I've a chance, I think—"

"Dad, if he kills you, I'll avenge—"

"You'll do nothing of the sort!" Thorian del Thorian spread his hands. "Hasn't it occurred to you that moving you to vengeance might be what he's truly after?" He shook his head. "We deal with Old Ones in this, Thorian. And they are difficult to read. They are very subtle and very patient.

"You know the story of Honir's Run. You and I would not think to plant a small seed of a tree, and then nurture and direct its growth, carefully snipping here and wiring there, and cutting somewhere else to create a bough, just so you might, that you could, should need arise, someday lead a company of pursuing horsemen beneath that bough, that tree, and know that you could climb that tree, your feet going instantly to small lower branches, and carry yourself up into that bough, and with a knife cut free the sword you had planted just beneath the bark—but I know that long-legged Honir did just that, once."

He stopped himself. "No, he did that *at least* once; probably more.

"The only thing I can be sure of is that the one thing he does not want is for you to simply stay here, to simply proceed as you and Ian had spoken of, to finish your time at your school and then go off seeking the Brisingamen stones in your wanderjahr, because all he would have had to make that happen is, well, nothing.

"So that, Thorian del Thorian the Younger, is precisely—and I mean precisely—what you are going to do to avenge me. You—" He stopped himself. The waitress had brought a huge tray, heavily laden with things that looked good and smelled wonderful.

The first plate she set down was in front of him, and on it were a half dozen little chops of the lamb, each seared black on the outside, and to his probing knife, they were red, almost raw and bloody, at the center.

The lamb tasted of flesh, and garlic, and that surprising note of lemon that he had so enjoyed before, as well as a mixture of other spices that he could enjoy if not identify. He took his time with his first bite. There were things that needed to be said, and there was little time to say them, but there was no reason at all to hurry his final meal.

This wouldn't have been his first choice, or his fiftieth, if only because he had never heard of this restaurant before. He would have preferred that his last meal be a Thanksgiving dinner, for that had always been his favorite meal at home—no, in Hardwood.

No; he had been right the first time: at home. It had always been his favorite meal at home.

He swallowed heavily. "You, young Thorian," he said, "will do as you had planned, with your eyes and mind open, and remembering who and what you are. You are Thorian del Thorian, son of Thorian del Thorian and Karin Roelke Thorsen, and you will conduct yourself accordingly."

Young Thorian bowed his head, just a touch more than a bow-of-reproof: a bow that indicated reluctant concession, but concession nonetheless.

"And now, my friends," Thorian del Thorian said, as he turned from Billy Olson to Jeff Bjerke, and finally, affectionately, to his svertbror, his comrade-in-arms, Maggie del Albert, "let us enjoy our meal."

The others picked at their food—and in young Thorian's case, he could easily see why; a simple patty of ground beef, topped with a pale and awful-looking green cheese, would have been enough to make anyone lose his appetite, even if it hadn't had such an ugly name.

Thorian del Thorian took another bite of his lamb chop.

It was wonderful.

CHAPTER TWENTY-TWO

Harbard's Crossing

The bird had probably spotted them the day before, but it was only when they broke camp in the morning and emerged from the stand of pines and onto the trail that Ian spotted it overhead.

At first, he mistook it for an eagle—there were a fair number of eagles up in the mountains, making their homes below the cloud level. But, no; the shape of the head was wrong, and the sweep of the wings was wrong, and it was, he quickly decided, either Hugin or Munin.

He hoped that meant that the two of them were back at Harbard's Crossing, and not a sign that Harbard, or Odin, or whatever he was calling himself these days, was nearby. Ian had a high opinion of his own abilities, but he and Giantkiller would not be more than a moment's work for Odin, even without his spear, Gungnir, and with Gungnir Odin could shatter armies, at least.

But there was no point in worrying about it, any more than there had been a point, as a kid, in worrying about what to do if the Russians—no, the Soviets; they were still the Soviets—launched their missiles.

Somehow, that thought wasn't as reassuring as he had wanted it to be.

"Is there something I can do for you, Ian Silver Stone?" Valin asked from the back of the pony, as though there might be something he could do from the back of the pony. This increasingly groveling servility had quickly, all too quickly, gotten very old, and there wasn't much that Ian could do about it. If he gave Valin something to do, Valin would leap to it—like that sleeping mat that he had woven incredibly quickly, out of pine needles—and then ask for more. If he said no, Valin assumed that, after another minute or two had passed, perhaps *now* there was something that Ian Silver Stone required, but that Ian Silver Stone had somehow, for some reason, neglected to mention it.

It was only just this side of maddening because Ian refused to be maddened.

High above, the bird circled lower.

Yes, Hugin, or Munin, it's me, again, he thought.

The bird circled twice more, then flew off to the south.

They reached the cottage late in the afternoon; Ian had gone on ahead on foot, while he had had Valin lead the horses up the slope, taking his time. It was a good enough compromise: the horses needed some rest, and it gave Valin something useful to do, even though Ian's mare, usually docile, would only allow herself to be led by the vestri under whinnying protest.

Which was fine with Ian. Let Valin have to deal with the nagging for awhile. Valin and the mare would get along fine, the dwarf constantly asking her if there was something he could do for her, and her constantly whinnying at him to let go of the reins.

Maybe they could settle down, get married, and raise funny-looking children.

Ian picked up the pace.

The only reason that Ian recognized Arnie Selmo from so far away was that he was expecting to see him.

There had been changes, but not the changes that Ian had expected. Arnie was still skinny, although in Ian's mind, he had filled out some. But, sure, that made sense; Arnie was too old to be putting on muscle.

While Arnie's bald spot had, if anything, grown, so had

the length of his formerly short gray hair, and it hung down
now in a tight braid behind his head, flicking from side to
side as he walked. Arnie had always tended toward a pasty
complexion—that came from years under the hissing flu-
orescent lights when he'd been running Selmo's Drugs—
but his face and neck were now darkly tanned, and his
bearing was straight as he rose from his chair on the cottage's front porch and stalked down the path.

There was a bounce in his step that Ian hadn't seen before, but the easy smile was in place as he broke from a
walk into a run.

"Ian Silverstein," he called out. "I was told it, but I
didn't believe it."

"Told what?"

"That you were back in Tir Na Nog, and that the first
thing you didn't do was come looking for me." His face
fell. "Everything's okay, isn't it?"

"I'm not sure." Ian shook his head. "No, I am sure:
we've got some problems."

"Anything we can do to help?"

We, eh? Ian found himself unaccountably, painfully jealous of that "we."

But he shouldn't have been surprised. Freya was, after
all, a fertility goddess, and in her younger days she'd been
known to, well, get around. It was even said that she had
slept with seven vestri in return for giving her the Brisingamen necklace, back before it was broken, the jewels scattered.

"A lot," Ian said. "Rather a lot." He gestured toward
the cottage. "Is she at home?"

"No, not at the moment." Arnie shook his head. "She
left this morning, looking for some meat." He smacked his
lips. "Spit-roasted deer tenderloin, with hot applesauce . . .
wonderful stuff. She's picky—I wouldn't be surprised if
she's back tonight, but I wouldn't be worried if it's a few
days." He shook his head. "She's not accustomed to answering for her comings and goings, to me or anybody
else."

"That bother you?"

"Nah. It's different than—it just takes some getting used

to, that's all." Arnie clapped a hand to Ian's shoulder. "Come on into the cottage. I've got a pot of stew on, and it's really pretty good." He raised an eyebrow. "You wouldn't happen to have any coffee with you?"

Ian smiled. "Oh, just a couple of pounds—present from Hosea. You have a coffee grinder?"

"Sure. Fully electric, and all—sure." Arnie laughed. "They don't exactly stock those here. But, shit, boy, I was a pharmacist before you were born, and I do have a mortar and pestle, and a strong arm. I—" his head jerked to one side, and he took a step away from Ian while his right hand reached out; in instant response a gray blur streaked from the door to *whap!* itself firmly into his palm, and Arnie had Mjolnir in his grasp.

Ian already had Giantkiller out, turning his back on Arnie, his eyes scanning the tree line, and then the sky. "What—where?"

But there was nothing resembling a threat, unless you counted Valin, who at Arnie's motion had dropped to the ground, scurrying on his belly toward the brush by the side of the trail.

"Stand easy, boy," Arnie said. "It's okay. I'm just a bit jumpy, I guess. Glad I remembered to leave Mjolnir in the doorway—wouldn't want to have to fix a hole in the front wall again." You wouldn't think that Arnie's skinny arm could even lift that heavy warhammer, much less gesture idly with it, as Arnie pointed down the trail.

Ian turned.

"It's just Munin."

At the mention of his name, the bird swooped up from behind the tree line, wings pounding the air, something small and wriggling in its talons.

"Your friend seems to be a bit skittery," Arnie said, smiling.

Valin had courage when it counted, but he was perfectly willing to abandon it when it didn't, and Ian didn't blame him one little bit. Munin banked steeply, circling over the patch of brush, searching for Valin.

"Just leave him be," Ian called out. "He'll come out when he's ready."

"Your friend skulks and twists and squirms through the brush," the raven said, taking one last cartwheel through the sky before flapping down for a landing. "I just wanted to ask of him, 'what is the rush?' "

By the time the huge raven landed in front of him, the wriggling had stopped, and what turned out to be a rat the size of a small puppy was no longer wriggling. Munin ate it in two quick bites, then waddled forward, and it was all that Ian could do to force himself to sheath Giantkiller.

Munin gave him the fucking willies.

Yes, it was a magnificent creature in its way, its feathers glossy as though freshly oiled, its beak black as the night and its eyes penetrating and unblinking. But as the raven ruffled its wing feathers and pecked at something beneath, a tiny pink worm of rat entrails hung down from the side of its beak, and that made Ian's stomach twist even more than the way the raven looked at him did.

"What is the problem, I hesitate to ask," the bird said, cocking its head to one side, as it stared at Ian out of a cold, unblinking eye. "For you know that I'm helpful, no matter the task."

"Good," Arnie said with a nod. "Then go find her and tell her that we have company, while I settle that company in. We've much to talk about, it seems," he said.

"If you could flap your arms as much as you talk, you could take to the sky and would never need walk," Munin said as it ruffled its feathers. Then, with a loud beating of wings that drove so much dust and grit into the air that Ian had to cover his eyes with his hand, the raven leaped into the air and flapped away, climbing high into the sky before it headed off.

Arnie watched the bird until it was out of sight.

He turned to Ian. "Let's see about making some of that coffee, eh?"

"Sounds good to me."

Arnie sniffed the air.

"Winter's coming," he said.

CHAPTER TWENTY-THREE

Arnie and Freya

There had been some changes in the cottage, as well as in Arnie. The sleeping frame in the corner had been replaced by a rough-hewn bed with a massive headboard that showed the markings and divots of somebody roughing out a carving, even though the headboard was in use: it held a ticked mattress supported by woven leather straps. The rich, glossy furs were gone, replaced by a stack of fluffy comforters that would have looked like something out of an LL Bean catalog if the stitching hadn't been a little crude and the color hadn't been a blotchy off-white.

Over in the cooking area next to the cast-iron stove, what appeared to be a simple iron-handled pump hung out from the side of the wall, over the water barrel.

"I bet Valin's going to bring up some river water, anyway," Ian said.

"If he wants to, I don't mind. Carrying water up from the river never seemed to bother her, either—I just got tired of watching her balancing a huge barrel on either hand and walking up the road."

On the wall, where the trio of brass hands had supported Gungnir, a long wooden bow hung—probably Arnie's; the hooks that had held Freya's bow and quiver were empty.

The biggest change was in what was missing. Of the dozen or more wooden footlockers that had crowded the small cottage, only three were left.

The walls were surprisingly bare: the shelves that had stuck out from every free square foot of wall space were almost all gone, along with their collection of strange little mementos that had reminded Ian of his Zayda Sol's collection of crystal carvings and little brass bells. It had never looked much like Ephie Selmo's living room, but now it looked even less so.

The walls had been plastered, and only the irregularity of the rippling indicated that they were made of logs, interlocked like a giant set of Lincoln Logs.

The oval mirror remained, set high on the wall, angled slightly down. Just slightly, though.

Arnie frowned at the way the cast-iron pot was boiling too hard on the stove, and he used a thick leather glove to move it to the burn-scorched counter. He tasted it with a long-handled wooden spoon. "Hmmm . . . a bit bland, still. You mind chopping some onions for me, Ian?" he asked, gesturing at the wicker basket mounted to the wall.

"No problem."

"About two cups' worth, more or less?"

"Sure."

The cutting board was a slice of tree-trunk, two feet across, held fast by a quartet of wooden pegs, their tops flattened by the pounding of something. And the kitchen knife would have looked unremarkable in a kitchen back home, save for the fact that it was a little thicker and heavier than Ian was used to.

"How fine you want them chopped?"

"Fine as you feel like."

The onions were small and pale, barely more than bulbous scallions, and when Ian had finished trimming them to size and lined them up and began to chop in earnest, they quickly set his nose running, and brought tears to his eyes, and then to Arnie's, and after Arnie swept the onions from the cutting board to a wooden bowl and then dumped them into the pot, the two of them, laughing and crying at the same time, fled from the cottage, out into the fresh air.

"Damn, boy, but you didn't have to chop them that fine," Arnie said, as he removed the wooden lid from the water barrel on the porch, then dippered out a quick splash first for Ian's face, and then for his own.

"Point made," Ian said. He shook his head to clear the water from his eyes—rubbing onion-tearing eyes with the hands you'd been using to handle the onions was like putting out a fire with gasoline—then blinked, hard.

Well, that was a little better. "Then again," Ian said, "you might mention that the wild onions hereabouts are as sharp and biting as a good knife."

Arnie took another drenching from the water barrel, then lowered himself carefully into one of the pair of rough-hewn wooden chairs, gesturing at Ian to take the other. "Where's that dwarf of yours?"

"He's not mine," Ian said. "He's from a farming village near the south border. His family got word that Sons had been sent after the Thorsens—"

"How?"

Ian shrugged. "Who knows? Sons have vestri servants in their warrens, and you know that the vestri listen more than they talk. But the word was passed, until it reached his village that the blood of the Friend of the Father of Vestri was being sought, and somebody there knew of one of those hidden entrances into Falias . . ."

Arnie nodded. "And the vestri there have known of the Hidden Way that leads to Hardwood since at least the Night of the Sons, eh?"

"At least. They smuggled him in, he says." Ian nodded. "He got caught and half-killed by a guard slipping into the passage, but vestri are stubborn, and he managed to make it down the passage and into the Hidden Way before he quite passed out. Next thing he knows, he's waking up on an operating table, with Doc Sherve trying to patch him together . . ."

Arnie frowned. "You don't know who originally sent the dogs?" His mouth was tight, and the years showed in his face. Arnie had taken a bad mauling on the Night of the Sons, trying to keep them from dragging Maggie and

Karin off into the night. And he and Ole had nailed the three who had chased the Thorsens and Maggie back to Hardwood.

He didn't like the dogs any more than Ian did.

Ian shook his head. "Not these. Herolf says that it's not the Northern Pack—"

"And Sons never lie."

"Well, of course they do. But the Scion says that he's had no word of this—"

"And rulers never lie."

"Arnie . . ." Ian wanted to swear. That wasn't the fucking point. Finding out who was responsible was important, but it could wait. You had to take first things first, and the first thing right here and now was to get the Scion committed to protecting the Thorsens—and among other things, that meant keeping the Scion alive. If the Sons had been sent by the House of Fire again, the Scion could deal with it far better than Ian could.

And if it turned out, later on, that the Scion or his klaffvarer had, indeed, been behind this, that could be dealt with, later on.

If it turned out, later on, that the Scion had played on Ian's envy of the affection a good father had for his son, well . . . that, too, would be dealt with.

Ian said as much. "So I've got to assume that the Thorsens can handle this Son, but . . ."

"But there could be others." Arnie shook his head. "No, if Thorsen blood is really what they're after, there *will* be others. Maybe this Scion's influence can persuade whoever it is to, well . . . ," he brightened, for just a moment, "call off the dogs."

"Okay," Arnie said, after a long time, "but what if this is just a ploy? What if this whole thing is just the Sons and the Dominions scheming to get their hands on one of the Brisingamen jewels? I mean, even if this curse is real, even if they had nothing to do with sending the Sons after the Thorsens—once you've brought the jewel to the Old Keep, why would they want to let go of it? Just because they promised?" He made a face. "This is Tir Na Nog, Ian, not

Hardwood. You never heard of a politician breaking his word?"

"Not to me," Ian said. "Not here. Not now."

"What makes you so damn special?" Arnie asked. "Here and now?"

"I've got a friend," Ian said, "who could, if he got angry enough, shatter the walls of the Old Keep, and bring it down around their necks like a house of cards," he said.

Arnie smiled. "You've got something else," he said.

"Oh?"

"You've got a point, Ian." He clapped a hand to Ian's shoulder. "Go down to the river and drag that dwarf of yours back up here. Supper's ready, and for once I've got an appetite."

Dinner was over. The stew had been surprisingly good, and the apples from the applecellar under the cottage had been, as Ian had expected, remarkable—the skin crunchy, the slightly yellow flesh beneath sweet and tart and crisp.

Ian's boots were airing out on the porch outside. It was nice to have had a chance to take those heavy things off and wash his feet, and the sneakers were an almost suspiciously sensual luxury at the end of a long day on the road.

Food, rest, dry feet . . . and coffee.

Arnie had improvised a way to make coffee. He'd ground the beans with a mortar and pestle—and a grin at Ian's comment about how he probably hadn't used a mortar and pestle since pharmacy school. He'd dumped the grounds in a cast-iron pot he had let warm on the stove, and had poured boiling water over the grounds, had let them steep for a few minutes, and then had filtered the grounds through a double fold of white linen that Valin had scurried out the door to wash down at the river.

Arnie took his first sip, and broke out in a smile that dropped a dozen years off his face. "Damn, but that's good," he said. "It's—"

There was a thumping outside. Three, then two. "It's her," Arnie said, as he set down his cup of coffee and rose to his feet.

Ian followed him outside and closed the door gently behind them.

The only light in the cottage had been a trio of lanterns and the flames in the hearth, and Ian had thought of it as dark by the standard he always used—it was too dark to read—but the night outside was black as pitch, black in the quiet, out-in-the-country, middle-of-the-night sort of way that had frightened Ian the first time he had encountered it, and still gave him a chill that had nothing to do with the cold breeze blowing from the west.

This kind of blackness made you understand why men had always feared the night, why they thought of it as a black beast to be chased away with fire and defended from by a huddling together, and for just a moment, it was all Ian could do to stop himself from running back into the light and the warmth.

Light flared, harsh and bright, as Arnie, now well away from the porch and its flammable roof, lit a torch—how, Ian didn't see.

The flame of the torch flickered and crackled, and Freya stepped out of the darkness and into its light, the limp form of a small deer balanced easily with one hand over her shoulders. "Hello, my Silver Stone," she said, her voice still holding that curious lilt that sounded vaguely Scandinavian. "I was wondering who brought the coffee."

She brushed away Ian's gestured offer to help with the deer, and hung it by the bound-together hind legs from a peg at the corner of the porch. She had field-dressed it, but perhaps hadn't let it fully bleed out before she had shouldered it for the walk home; her left shoulder and side gleamed with blood, glossy and black in the dark.

Freya was solidly muscled, but not in any way masculine in that, her legs long and strong and well-defined, but not bulging as though swollen—Rachel McLish, not a female Arnie Schwarzenegger.

Looking at her still made it hard to breathe, although now there were laugh lines around the corners of her eyes and the edges of her smile, and perhaps her chin was not as firm as it had been, and her waist, while still slim, had thickened some, and while she had nothing that resembled a potbelly, it was no longer flat like a bodybuilder's, but gently rounded.

She could no longer have passed for a girl in her teens or early twenties, but Ian found that, if anything, more erotic. It seemed more honest, somehow, even though he was sure that the only reason she had taken on a more mature appearance was to make Arnie feel more comfortable, rather than because she had to.

"I'd best wash myself before I come into the cottage," she said, unbuckling her heavy belt. She dropped the belt onto the porch, then reached into the deer's body cavity and retrieved the hunting knife she had presumably used to field-dress it. Presumably, she didn't want to put it back in its sheath until it was cleaned.

Her fingers toyed for a moment with the hem of her shift, as though preparing to pull it up and over her head.

And then she dashed off into the dark, making it clear with a smile tossed over her shoulder that the hem of the shift hadn't been the only thing she had been toying with.

Arnie was already looking over the deer in the light of the torch. "Nice little doe," he said. "A few steaks will go well on the road, eh? We can do a quick butchering in the morning, assuming she can retrieve the gem tonight and we can leave then." He looked up. "That okay with you?"

"Hey, it's not like I'm in charge or anything." Ian tapped Harbard's ring against Giantkiller's hilt. "I'm a guy with ring and a sword; you're the fellow with Mjolnir."

"Which only means I can pound things real hard, and that's all, Ian. If you're not in charge, I don't know who is. I'm just hired muscle." His grin was wolfish in the flickering light. "Shit, boy, I was once one of Harry Truman's hired killers, but I haven't been hired muscle ever before," he said, "and it kind of grows on you. You can look to me for advice, but I'm just along for the ride."

"I'll remember that."

"You'd better," Arnie said, his voice sharp, cracked around the edges. "I'm too damned old to be running anything, Ian." The smile dropped, and the years hung heavily on his rounded shoulders. "You keep telling me how good

I look, but don't make too much of that. Freya's been good to me,'' he said, quietly, ''and she's been good for me. But she's not my Ephie. I'd trade it all and everything else I've ever had for another good hour with *her,* and know I'd gotten the better of the deal. There isn't a day goes by . . .'' he shook his head. ''Some things you never get over, eh?''

''Tell me about it.''

''Yeah.'' His voice caught. ''Give me half a second, eh?''

''Sure.''

When Arnie spoke again, his voice was calm and easy, no trace of the restrained tears of just a few moments before. ''You probably should hang on to this for a minute,'' he said, as he handed the torch to Ian, ''while I go inside and get Freya some clothes.'' He clucked his tongue as he walked away, shaking his head and chuckling. ''They never do outgrow being cockteasers, do they?''

Her water-darkened hair hanging stringy down her neck and shoulders, Freya bent to adjust one of the balks in the fire, sending sparks flying up the chimney. An ancient cast-iron poker stood propped against the wall next to the hearth, but she didn't use it. It would take more heat than a wood fire could generate to hurt her, just as it would have taken more cold than that of even the bone-chilling waters of the Gilfi to make her uncomfortable.

She must have liked the warmth; she tucked her legs underneath her and sat back on the thick gray rug that lay in front of the fire.

''Where is this vestri of yours?'' she asked. ''I'd like to talk to him for a while, if you've no objection.''

''It's fine with me.'' Ian didn't argue the point of ownership. ''He's down at the stable, settling my horses in for the night.''

Silvertop had made no protest, which was just as well—for the mare and the gelding pony. Ian wouldn't have considered putting a stallion in with him, but, Silvertop aside, Ian wouldn't ever have considered riding an uncut male horse. Silvertop's father was Sleipnir, which made him one-quarter Aesir, and tougher than nails.

"Well, that's just as well." She looked up at Ian. "I understand what you want and why." She shook her head. "But I'm sorry, the answer is going to have to be no."

CHAPTER TWENTY-FOUR

A Farewell

Thorian Thorsen looked from one face to another. "I have your word, then, each of you. That you'll make no attempt to follow me?" He met young Thorian's gaze unblinkingly. He would be the key.

"You have my word, Father," he said. "I . . . if I thought there was another way . . ."

"You would argue it out with me here and now, and not give me your word and then break it." His lips grew tight. "I've broken my solemn oath, once. It's not something you want to live with."

Well, that was a lie, but it was a lie that would be believed. Breaking his oath of loyalty to the House of Steel had bothered him on a daily basis for years, until one sunny morning he had woken up next to Karin and fully realized that there were things that were not only more important to him than honor but far more important.

If that made him inferior to his father and his father's fathers, well, then, so be it.

You preserved what of your honor you could, but you had to decide where honor ended and more important things began. Orfindel had not deserved what was being done to him, but Thorian del Thorian had freed him in what he had thought of as a moment of weakness, and with his oath and honor broken, stealing His Warmth's gold was merely, what was that phrase? Frosting on—no: icing on the cake. Yes, it was but icing on the cake, as was the rest of it.

Young Thorian nodded. "Yes. I would argue it with you, or I would not swear. I will stay here."

Jeff Bjerke was twiddling with his moustache. "I don't like it, but I don't see any alternative. You've got my word, Thorian." Jeff clasped hands briefly with him, then dropped down to the couch, avoiding looking at him.

"Not me; I'm not going after you." Billy Olson shrugged. "Pinky swear," he said, raising his little finger. "I'm a waiter, not an idiot, or a hero," he said. "Not that there's a lot of difference," he went on in a low mutter.

"No." Maggie's eyes were wet. "I'm not going to promise, not—"

"Maggie." Thorian del Thorian took her in his arms and held her tightly.

It was a pity; it would be wonderful to bounce her and young Thorian's child on his knee. A boy, another Thorian, would have been wonderful, but somehow he knew he would have been equally happy for it to be a girl. "Watch out for him," he said, quietly, then bent his head close. "Do not wait too long before you let him ask to marry you," he whispered. "Life is too short, my svertbror; grasp for the sweetness when you can, and grip it hard."

She clutched him more tightly and didn't answer him for a moment, but then she pushed him away and nodded. "I promise," she said, her quirked smile making it clear that she was agreeing to both of his requests.

She looked first to one side, then the other, then turned back to Thorian. *I'll watch out for her, too,* she mouthed, and made that strange X sign over her left breast, as though she was promising to cut it off if she broke her word.

Thorian del Thorian nodded. "Perhaps I shall see you all later," he said.

He turned and walked out the door, down the stairs, and out into the night.

CHAPTER TWENTY-FIVE

~~~

The Flesh of Ymir

The answer is going to be *what?*

Ian hadn't thought that his fingers were trembling as he set his coffee cup down, but it rattled on the floorboards until he let it go.

The firelight cast her face in unsteady light and dark shadows as she looked up at him from where she sat on the rug. She looked vulnerable, somehow, which just didn't make sense considering what she was saying.

"I'm sorry, Ian, but it's not a good idea. It's too dangerous."

Dangerous? The Scion was going to die otherwise—and horribly, at that—leaving his son fatherless. And without the Scion and the Dominions running interference with the Sons, sooner or later one would manage to get to the Thorsens. "If you want to talk about dangerous, look at the situation that Torrie is in. Or the Scion."

"Ian . . ." Arnie held up a hand. "Hear her out," he said. *Getting hysterical and angry won't help you any,* his headshake and frown said.

"Ian," she said, with a smile, "my Silver Stone . . ." She shook her head. "You should know what you're asking, but you don't. This isn't just something valuable, or even unique—like, oh—''

"Like Mjolnir," Arnie said.

"Like Mjolnir," she nodded her head. "Or Gungnir, or the Dagda's Kettle, or Morrigan's Shield, or . . ." she gestured to where Giantkiller's scabbard hung on a peg, ". . . other items forged of myth and legend, as well as matter and magic and energy."

"Trivial little things," Ian said.

"Now, now, my Silver Stone, don't fuss so. Gungnir and Mjolnir can break mountains, and your Giantkiller can kill the unkillable. That isn't unimportant—unless you put it in the context of the necklace." Her hand went to the base of her throat, fingers spread. Her nails weren't long, but they weren't bitten off at the quick, either. "I wore it once, here," she said. This time, there was nobody here to remind her of how she had gotten it. "Imagine that, Ian. Seven gems, and in them, squeezed off in a direction that makes them manageable, enough matter and energy to remake the universe, to begin it again, all fresh and untouched, sweet and new." She licked her lips, once. "But the time wasn't right for that, then. Do you think it is now?

"No, of course you don't." She shook her head. "But there will be a time. Creation and destruction are just two sides of the same coin. Ymir the Giant, the first of all, nurses on the milk of the cow Audumla, who licks salty stones into the form of man: Buri. Buri's grandsons murder Ymir, and create farmland from his stinking flesh, crimson seas from his blood, mountains from his bones and the vault of heaven itself from his skull. One of his eyelashes survives, to be forged into Gungnir; a fingernail is preserved, as Tyr's Shield; his wrinkled brain becomes the clouds. All for this." It seemed as if she thumped her hand only lightly on the floor, but crockery rattled in the cupboard, and Ian's mug danced on the floor. "All for everything you—and I, Ian, and I!—have ever seen, ever known.

"That is fine with me, every time I sniff the sweet morning air, or fasten my legs about a lover's waist." She cocked her head to one side. "But how do you think Ymir felt about it?"

Ian didn't have an answer, and besides, it was a rhetorical question. Of course this giant didn't want to—

"I think," Arnie said, into the silence, "at least I hope, that he was ready, that he had grown tired of being Ymir, and that he was ready for it all to start again, ready for flesh to become land, blood seas, and everything he thought and felt and knew just ashes in the wind." The flickering flames made his wrinkles tiny black canyons, twisting across the landscape of his face.

"As do I, Arnold," she said. "For the other choice was that he was robbed of what he was, what he could have been, what he was supposed to be.

"Shiva the Destroyer is Brahma the Creator, Ian," she said, turning back to him. "They're one and the same, or both of them are cruel imposters, destroying that which is not ready for the end to create that which is not ready to be.

"You chose well, when you put two of the gems in my hand, because of what I am."

"And what are you, then?"

"Oh," she smiled, "I'm many things. I'm Freya, an old fertility goddess, in retirement. Or you can think of me as Vishnu, wreathed in wilting flowers, the Brisingamen emerald the Kaustubha that he wears on his chest, next to the shrivatsa mark—or any of his other forms: Matsya, Kurma, Varaha, Narasimha, Vamana, Parashurama, Rama, Krishna, Buddha—but not Kalkin, for Kalkin has yet to come." There was suddenly a tight black curl of chest hair over her left breast; she touched it, and it was gone. "Or perhaps I *am* Kalkin, my time come at last, and Arnold here is Lord Rama, lowering himself to be servant and charioteer to you as Arjuna.

"Or maybe I'm Ishtar and Inanna and Astarte, and always a woman because women have to understand creation and preservation and destruction and renewal, because we prepare to do that in our own bodies monthly, and have to hold that which we are and we create within, instead of sticking it out into the world, like the point of a sword or . . . other things. You blush charmingly, my Ian, but I see that you take my meaning."

"But what does that have to do with—"

"No." She held up a hand, and her manner was no longer warm and charming, but cold and imperious. "I'll not allow you to pretend not to know, not in my presence. Two of the gems are safe right now, hidden by me, protected by me, and by the strong arm of my companion," she said, reaching up and taking Arnie's hand in hers. She pressed it briefly to her lips, then let it go. "For me to let one of them out of my hands—"

"But it's only one. You'd have the other. And without the other . . ."

"Without the other what? Without the other, the universe can't be destroyed and reborn?" Her voice rasped. "Are you so very sure? Could not six of them be enough? Or five? Or three? What is the critical mass that is necessary to build a monobloc? Ian, tell me, and tell me how you know that the diamond and ruby each hold but a seventh of it."

It was too much for Ian. How did you develop a sense of proportion that allowed you to let a kid's father die when just your word could save at least one life and maybe more? There was that old Talmudic saying that Zayda Sol used to quote, about he who saves the life of one it is as though he saved the whole world, but wasn't the opposite true, too? If you murdered somebody, if you let somebody die when he could live, wasn't that the same as if you murdered the whole universe?

Snatching Giantkiller from the peg where it hung, Ian fled from the cottage and out into the night. Arnie called out to him, but he ignored him.

"Let him go, Arnie," she said.

CHAPTER TWENTY-SIX

Harbard's Ring

If you waited long enough, if you gave yourself enough
time, enough patience, the inky darkness of night
would lift, if only a trifle.

But a little was enough to navigate by, at least down the
road.

By starlight, Ian made his way through the night down
to the path to the dock, where a long cable, thick as a strong
man's wrist, dripping with spray, reached out over the black
Gilfi. A windlass—powered by Silvertop, perhaps, although
Freya was easily strong enough to turn it—would pull the
flat ferry barge across to the other side, where a quick road
could take him up and north and into the Dominions.

Finding the Old Keep would not be a problem; there
would be watchers on all the roads.

And what would he say?

Hey, I'm sorry.

She said no.

She said that you and your son weren't important enough
to her, to risk one of the Brisingamen jewels that I put into
her hands. She has to take the long view. After all, we all
die, sooner or later. If we don't die young, we all become
orphans, sooner or later, and your turn to die and the Heir's

turn to be orphaned have merely come sooner than later, so why the fuss, why the problem?

Go gently, and if your son goes gently, too, why, all is eventually dust and ashes, reborn only in the rebirth of the universe itself, so why cling to life?

Let it go, Scion; it's of no importance.

And neither, of course, is the life of my friends. Why, in another hundred years, they'll all be dead and forgotten, so why should you or I worry if there are Sons out to drink their blood. It's not like their lives matter or anything. Whatever you've done, whatever you're going to do to save their lives, why, don't bother.

None of it matters, if you can look at things from a properly distant perspective.

Shit.

"Ian Silver Stone," the vestri's voice was quiet behind him.

"Yes, Valin?" *Is there anything I can do?' If I hear him ask that one more time . . .*

"Is there anything that I might do, to help you? Your animals have been fed and watered, and bedded down for the night; your clothes have been fully washed, as has her shift that she rinsed only briefly in the gray river. I can prepare food, or—"

"Or maybe you can just shut your fucking mouth and stop bothering me for a fucking minute." He'd said that in English, but the dwarf took the meaning from his tone of voice, anyway. Valin, tears in his eyes, backed away, and then turned and ran back toward the cave that served as stable.

Oversensitive little shit, wasn't he? Ian shrugged. *Not my problem.* It was just hurt feelings—and if lives were trivial, to be disposed of easily, what were the feelings of a dwarf?

Fuck. "Hey, Valin . . ." He ran after the dwarf. "Shit, man, I'm sorry. I mean," he called out in Bersmål, "this one regrets his currish behavior, as it reflects badly on his father," who deserves worse, "his sept, clan, and Folk."

And everybody who knows me, really, Valin, knows that I'm not really such a fucking asshole. I'm an entirely different sort of asshole, honest.

The dwarf ran faster than Ian could have, but Ian followed his thudding footsteps along the riverbank, past the outcropping where he stumbled and almost fell, barely getting his left leg underneath him, scraping his right ankle hard in the process.

Shit, shit, shit. It was his own goddamn fault, too. If he hadn't run out into the night, like a little kid having a tantrum, he wouldn't have been down by the river in the first place, and insulted the—

It was his fault, again. Couldn't he do anything right?

He had struck out with Freya, and then he had hurt the pitiful little dwarf's feelings, cut his own ankle open on a piece of rock, failed the Scion—*let's see if there's anything else I can fuck up tonight.*

He more hopped than limped toward the cave.

A brass lantern hung in a niche at the entrance to the cavern, and just inside, dozens of round bundles of hay were stacked atop a rough pallet high enough to rub against the ceiling. A long hooked pole had been stuck in one of the hay bales; he slung Giantkiller's belt over his shoulder, and used the pole as a staff and crutch. He was afraid to look down at his ankle—his foot was already warmly wet, and it hurt like a sonofabitch.

Leaning heavily on the staff, Ian hobbled down into the cavern, following the sounds of sobbing past the first turn, past the wooden stalls where the mare and the pony stood, munching on hay and looking bored, past a final turn to where the dwarf was busily engaged in trying to squeeze himself into the juncture between cave wall and floor, and where Silvertop stood snorting, one large, liquid eye watching Ian with unconcealed irritation.

Silvertop was a huge horse, easily the size of a Percheron or a Clydesdale, although built along more slender lines— still, his legs seemed thicker and his untrimmed hooves larger than they should have been.

Save for the white blaze across its forehead and its long, ragged mane, he was black like the raven, but there the similarity ended: Silvertop's black was not glossy or oily or shiny, it was the black of night, the black of coal, the black of hell.

Silvertop snorted heavily, whipping straw and dust and dried manure up and into the air hard enough that Ian had to momentarily cover his eyes with his forearm to protect them. One massive hoof pawed at the stone, striking sparks that set the straw smoldering—although the blacksmith's hammer and iron shoes had never touched Silvertop.

It was unlikely that Silvertop was very angry—he had not bitten off Ian's head, after all.

That was always a good sign.

It was something the horse was physically capable of—those thick teeth could bite through a small tree; Ian had seen it do just that.

"I am sorry," Ian said, to both of them. "I would say that I meant no offense, no harm, but that would not be true, Valin—I meant to strike out, to wound, to hurt your feelings, simply because I am hurt and confused. I was wrong, and I'm sorry."

It was important that both of them believe him, at least it was important to him. Ian had thought he had earned the Aesir horse's respect, although its affection was beyond him—and Ian was, still, grateful to Valin for having brought the warning, and he did respect his courage.

It was important . . .

Harbard's ring pulsed against his finger, painfully hard once, twice, three times.

Valin straightened, wiping with the back of his hand against the puzzled expression that had his face all wrinkled. Silvertop stopped glaring and snorting, clopped over to a stone bin filled with some grain that Ian didn't recognize, and began to chomp at it, idly.

Ian's ankle had been hurting all along, but he had forced himself to try to ignore it. Now, grunting in pain, Ian sagged back against a wooden bin, and then eased himself down to the cold stone floor. He bent forward and pulled up the hem of his trousers.

He hadn't cut himself as deeply as he had feared, but it was deep enough, and the red flow of blood had already soaked his sock and sneaker.

The sock wasn't that big a deal, but the sneaker couldn't be replaced, not here. Maybe it would wash out. Or maybe it would rot and make the sneaker unusable.

Valin, ever-faithful Valin, was immediately at his side, the first aid kit from one of the rucksacks in his thick hands. "Please, Honored One," he said, "friend of the friend of the Father, himself the father of Vestri, Father to the Folk— please instruct this clumsy one as to what to use of this to ease your pain."

There was a selection of syringes in the kit, filled and labeled, their tips covered with some sort of green high-tech plastic that was supposed to keep them sterile until it was removed.

Fuck. The last thing he wanted to do now was ask Freya for help healing himself, but shit . . . it hurt, and knocking himself out with Demerol and Vistaril, while tempting, just wouldn't do, not now.

He shuffled through the syringes—what was atropine, anyway?—until he found one labeled "Lidocaine—use to numb injured region for stitching of minor wounds. Sterilize everything!!! RLSMD" and pulled the gunk off the tip of the needle, then sprayed a little of the clear liquid into his open wound before sticking it several times into the flesh around the wound—it stung hard enough to draw tears from his eyes, but you can't wet a river—until he couldn't push the plunger in any further.

He wasn't sure how long it was supposed to take until the lidocaine kicked in, but by Murphy's Law, if he tried to use Harbard's ring to persuade himself that it didn't hurt, it would either not work on himself, as usual, or it would start working about by the time he concentrated—

The ring pulsed, hard, once.

His ankle went numb.

It was like somebody had thrown a switch on the pain.

What the fuck?

Carefully, gingerly, he touched a fingertip to the wound. He could feel it, but the pain was gone. Ian wasn't sure how long the lidocaine was supposed to take, but it had to be a matter of at least a couple of minutes.

It wasn't supposed to happen that fast.

The ring? Well, that was possible, but . . . no. He could
never seem to get it to work on him, although he had tried,
and tried hard, but usually by the time he was done concentrating, whateverthefuck he was using it for was—

Holy shit.

Ian's trembling hands opened the black plastic bottle of
hydrogen peroxide. ''Please use this to wash out the wound,
and then please dry it with those gauze pads. We'll disinfect
it, and then dry it, and then close the wound with a few of
those Steri-Strips—there, yes, those.''

He should have tried it before. And he should have
thought it out. Freya wasn't W. C. Fields—''Keep all your
eggs in one basket, then watch the basket''—any more than
Hosea had been, when he had originally hidden the Brisingamen jewels.

Put them in one place? But what if somebody found that
place? And if you stayed to watch over them, what if somebody found you?

No. That wasn't what either of them had done, because
neither of them was a fool.

Freya had hidden one gem far away.

No, not just one: she had hidden the first one, the ruby,
far away. She had still been living with Odin at the time,
and she had promised not to give it to him, or to anybody
else. And then, when Ian had given her the second gem,
the diamond, she had kept it near her. Perhaps it was in the
caverns somewhere, or beneath the floorboards of the cottage. Or maybe she had buried it deep in the ground at
some spot she would remember. With her strength, that
might have made sense.

But, in any case, it was near enough to magnify the
power of Harbard's ring.

Had it made the ring powerful enough to persuade an
Aesir that she had to let him have the diamond, if only for
a few days?

Ian's jaw clenched.

It was time to find out.

CHAPTER TWENTY-SEVEN

Acton's Legacy

T he door had been left open about a foot, but Ian knocked on the doorpost anyway.

It swung open so quickly that he wondered if she had heard him hobble up the walk and was waiting for him.

"Ian, I'm so—" she glanced down. "You're hurt," she said, slipping an arm around his waist before he could object.

He had never doubted that she was strong, but still he was surprised at how she lifted him off his feet without any apparent effort, bracing his hip against hers. It would have been embarrassing, but Ian had never had any illusions about their comparative strength.

Arnie was up and out of his chair, then down on his knees in front of him. "Do you think you broke it?"

Ian shook his head. "No. Just cut it some."

Arnie took a familiar-looking first aid kit down from one of the few remaining shelves. "You wash it out?"

"Valin did. Hydrogen peroxide, a few Steri-Strips to hold the edges of the wound together. I'll be fine."

"Yeah, right. I'll take a look at it anyway." He broke

the seal on a pair of slant-nosed scissors and propped Ian's ankle on his lap.

Freya rested a hand on his shoulder. "Perhaps I might? If we're still speaking, my Silver Stone? Even if we're not, might we possibly call a truce between us for long enough for me to help you?"

"We're still speaking," Ian said. "But it doesn't hurt all that badly."

In fact, it didn't hurt at all. The ankle didn't want to move as quickly as Ian wanted it to, and if it hadn't been for the Ace bandage that had helped him hobble up the path, he might have fallen; he probably should have taken the hay crook to use as a crutch.

He had no objection to Freya healing him, though.

Shit, she owed him. Besides . . .

"We're talking, but we're not done talking," he said.

"Of course, my Silver Stone. I'll always give you a fair hearing."

A quick glance down at his ankle made Ian queasy; he looked away as Arnie cut away the bandages for her ministrations. Between the hydrogen peroxide and the Bacitracin, he was probably safe from any real risk of infection— when was his last tetanus booster?

"Well, I've seen worse," Arnie said. He looked up at Freya. "I think I should debride it before you do anything, though. I wouldn't want to count on a vestri having washed all the grit out of the wound."

She held up a finger to warn Ian to silence. "That would be very nice, Arnold; thank you," she said, the grin she shot over her shoulder and Arnie's head as she walked toward the water barrel making it abundantly clear to Ian that she was going to some trouble to make Arnie feel useful, and that she would be pleased if Ian would have the decency to go along with the charade.

Maybe it wasn't even a charade. Maybe rinsing the wound would actually help a little. Still, Freya had been healing much worse than this without a retired pharmacist to prep for her since the world was young. But true healing wasn't just a matter of curing physical damage; part of being a healer was in not hurting people unnecessarily in the first place, and there was a gentleness in the way she was handling Arnie, manipulative though it was.

"Ian?" Arnie raised his head. "When was your last tetanus shot?"

"I was just trying to remember. Six years ago, I think—I took a broken point in the thigh during a bout."

"Mmmm. Doc Sherve should have made sure you were up to date." The corner of his mouth twisted. "Maybe taken out your appendix, too, for that matter?"

"That occurred to me, too. Too late, but it occurred to me, too."

"Not your job, though. It's Doc's." Arnie made a tsking sound between his teeth. "He wouldn't have let either of those slip by, ten, twenty years ago. Doc's getting on in years. Not going to have him around forever, eh? Thank you, dear," Arnie said, as he accepted a bucket of water from Freya. She held a basin, which appeared to have been made by slicing the top third off a barrel, under Ian's ankle, while Arnie poured fresh, cold water over Ian's wound. There was just a twinge of icy pain, but it definitely hurt. Spraying Lidocaine into the wound had probably been just a waste of the stuff.

Damn.

"I'm not sure, though, that you'll be able to do anything with this," Ian said, looking at Freya, who was watching Arnie's cleaning of the wound as though she had never seen anything quite so miraculous in all her centuries. Arnie didn't seem to be looking at her, but his chest puffed out just a trifle, and he nodded sagely to himself as though this was some sort of big deal.

"Why would that be, my Silver Stone?" she asked.

"I don't know," he said quietly, intensely, willing her to believe him, "but I just don't think you can." The ring pulsed against his finger, painfully hard, so much so that he was surprised that the finger didn't start to swell from the lack of circulation.

"I think he's right," Arnie said. "It just looks too, I don't know, too something—too substantial, maybe?—to heal so quickly." He tore open a sterile sponge and dried off the wound, ignoring the small amount of suppuration. "But I guess it's worth a try."

She seemed puzzled, but then nodded. "Let me see." Her hands were soft and warm against his ankle. Gently, slowly, she cupped one hand over the wound, and the other under the other side of his ankle.

You can't do it, he thought. *It won't work. There is something wrong, and you can't heal me now. Maybe you're getting old, maybe my body is just rejecting your help, or maybe it's something else entirely, but you can't heal me, not now. It's hopeless.*

Harbard's ring was tight against his finger, at least in his mind, although he wouldn't have been able to tell by looking at it, and when he forced his hand to clench, it closed without difficulty.

The pulsations came faster and faster, the interval between them shorter and shorter, until they merged into an ongoing painful tightness that only relaxed when Freya shook her head, released his ankle, and with a puzzled shake of the head, sat back.

"That was frustrating," she said. She looked at his ankle again, and again at her hands. A streak of wet red blood and pieces of dark clotting lay spread across her right palm. She rubbed her two hands together at first gently and then harder and harder, until smoke began to rise from them, accompanied by an awful charring smell.

Arnie laid a hand on her shoulder. "It's okay," he said, softly, gently, patiently.

She rinsed her hands in the basin, the water steaming and sizzling for just a moment at her touch. When she looked up at him, she looked older and sadder. "I'm so sorry, my Silver Stone. I guess your Doctor Sherve isn't the only one who is getting old these days."

Now it was easy. All he had to do was bring up the subject of the jewel, and of the Scion, yet again. He had good reasons, and she would melt beneath the heat of the jewel in the ring, like butter on a hot summer day.

"Freya, I . . ."

She looked up at him and smiled. "Why, my Silver Stone, I don't think you've ever called me by my name, save for that first time, when you realized that I wasn't just a simple ferryman's wife. Please don't stop. Now, you were saying?..."

He couldn't. He couldn't look down into a trusting face, and bend her will, overrule her judgment by the force of his will, amplified by the ring and jewel. She was wrong, and he was right, and a loving father would suffer before the eyes of his beloved son if she didn't change her mind, but molding a friend's mind was to treat her like an object, a thing, to be controlled.

That wasn't right.

He slipped the ring from his finger, and tucked it into his pocket. "Freya," he said, "I need the diamond. Just for a few days. But I do need it for those two days. I don't know what I can say to persuade you—I can swear that if I ever find another one of the jewels, I'll not give it to you if you don't do this for me now; I can promise that I will bring it back. But it's important.

"Look, when I get back with the diamond, I'll go out on the road, again, in search of a third jewel. And I swear that I'll bring it to you, when I find it. But for now, I have to ask you to trust me, as I have trusted you."

"Ian, please." She took his hand in both of hers. It was strange that hands so strong and powerful could be so soft and warm. "I'm so very sorry, Ian. I hope you will still be my Silver Stone, as I shall always be your Freya, but I can't be swayed by your appeal, as it hasn't changed anything. Swear, if you will, to never give me another jewel—but what of that? You are not likely to find another, not again. But should you find one, who would you give it to? Harbard the Wanderer? Or to your father-in-law to be? You'd hardly pick either Odin or the margrave.

"But even if you would, my reasoning still applies. Even if you promise to go out and search for the other jewels, and bring them to me, one by one as you find them. I can't let even one..." her brow wrinkled for a moment, then she shook her head as though to clear it, "...I can't let even one of the jewels be risked on the chance that if it comes back, you might someday find another." She rose to her feet and looked down at him, still holding her. "I don't think you can accept that, but so be it.''

"No." He returned her gaze, steadily. "I don't like it, but I do accept it. I hope you'll believe that, both of you."

She nodded. "I do," she said. She squeezed his hand, once, gently, and released it.

Arnie had finished bandaging Ian's ankle, and it was hurting again. "Me, too." He looked up and smiled. "Then again, Ian, I'm always easy to persuade, eh?"

"Yeah, a real softie."

Arnie laughed.

So be it. *Scion, I'm sorry. Although, in truth, I'm sorrier for your son* . . .

"I'll leave in the morning. I promised I'd return." Hosea wasn't exactly a hostage, but he wasn't exactly not a hostage, either. What was the Scion's word worth, if you couldn't deliver?

There was no way of knowing. Would the Scion still work to take the Sons off the Thorsens' trail?

What if I tell him I tried, really hard? Would that work?

No. Why should the Scion care if he tried? The world paid off results, not effort.

Ian had screwed up, again, and all it would take to fix that would be to remove the ring from his pocket and persuade Freya to let him borrow the diamond.

Borrow? Shit, he could even keep the Brisingamen diamond; he could persuade Freya that it would be best off in his hands—and that might even be true; it certainly was true that he could talk anybody out of taking it away from him.

With Harbard's ring and a Brisingamen stone in his hand, he could make anybody believe anything.

He could even knock on a door of a particular condominium in Bloomington and make the twisted old man who lived there care about him the way a father should care about a son, the way Ian had always had the right to be cared about—the way every kid does, the way you never stop needing because, deep inside, there's a way in which you never stop being a little kid.

And he would rather have snapped Giantkiller across his

knee and used the jagged edge of the shard to cut his own throat than to do anything of the kind.

Arnie nodded. "No—*we* leave in the morning. You're going to need somebody to watch your back, and I've got a special qualification or two, squire," he said, touching his forelock with a finger.

"Nobody will believe that."

Arnie shrugged. "I ever tell you the joke about the pope and his driver?"

"Only a couple of dozen times."

"I think you may have told it to me before," Freya said with a smile. "But could you tell it to me again? I'm not sure if I remember it."

"Well, okay. The pope is out for a spin in the countryside, when his driver turns pale, and pulls over. 'Your Holiness,' he says, 'I am most unwell.'

"Well, the pope gets into the front seat . . .'"

CHAPTER TWENTY-EIGHT

The Son

The wind blew, dry and chill, across what, at other times of the year, was a lake; Thorian del Thorian quickened his pace along the lakeside path. Days of subzero cold and feet of hundreds, perhaps thousands, of dedicated if more than slightly odd circle-walkers had left the path clean, save for a few icy spots.

Of course, there was the biggest icy spot of them all: Lake Calhoun. A rough oval, a mile across the long axis, about three-quarters of that across the short, it was frozen over deep and hard enough to drive a truck on, although Thorian hadn't seen any vehicles on any of the city lakes. A canoe rack stood, lonely and coated with ice, at the north-west corner; over on the west side, a pier projected out over the ice, a wooden tongue sticking out, daring someone to use it as a diving board and break their fool neck.

Somebody had probably done that, at some point. There was nothing so stupid that nobody would ever do it.

At the north end of the lake, and at the south, the ice had been polished into large, vaguely circular skating areas, but the rest of the lake was covered with ice and icy snow and tracks of skiers who used it for their exercise, if only to avoid the crowds of locals too foolish to come in from

the cold, too esoteric in their largely strange and effete oc-
cupations to work with their hands and backs and legs.

And then there were the ice houses. A strange sort of
sport, indeed, sitting out in the cold, trying to pull fish out
of a hole in the ice.

He would have glanced down at his watch, but there was
no need to know the time. He could pace out the time with
his own paces, count his own heartbeats. If only he could
count down his own heartbeats. It would be interesting to
know how many he had left.

He wasn't totally helpless. Young Thorian had insisted
that he take his gimmicky little knife, and Thorian del Thorian had that in an outside pocket, although if he had the
opportunity to draw that, he surely would be able to draw
the larger dagger slung underneath his left armpit, or the
medium-sized one strapped to his right arm. His own, very
plain, folding knife he held in his right hand—it wasn't
much, but its blade had been made by Orfindel, and Thorian
del Thorian had carried the knife with him every day for
fifteen years.

If he had time, he would draw the revolver from his left-
hand coat pocket—but he could not do that until he was
sure of his target, and it was unlikely that he would be sure
of his target until the Son was upon him. Guns had no
loyalty to you, no essence to them—and if bullets had an
attitude toward their targets, it had always been a desire to
avoid them.

It would be worth a try.

But the Son would hardly have gone to this much trouble
only to be shot down just out of reach of its prey.

Lights flickered in the windows of the houses on the hill
that cupped the east side of the lake, and off in the distance
there was that strange deep booming sound—thumpa
thumpa thumpa, thumpa thumpa *thumpa*—that Maggie had
identified as a ''boom car,'' whatever that might be. She
had said it was annoying but not actually dangerous, and
as long as it was this far off the sound was actually some-
what pleasant, in much the same way that the distant smell
of skunk on a summer night was pleasant, as long as it kept
its distance. He quickened his pace to keep time with the

thumpa of the boom car, but forced himself to slow down. If his own breathing was loud enough for him to hear, and it was, then how could he possibly get warning of the Son?

He likely had only his sense of sight to rely upon, although if the Son was more of a fool than Thorian thought, there might be a moment of sound, right before the Son leaped. If he heard the clicking of nails against the icy tarmac, he might even have time enough to draw the pistol.

The smells and sounds of the city gave no clue. At home—and even back in the Dominions—the sounds at night of insects and birds and animals gave you a dim map, and silences gave you a loud warning that somebody, perhaps even you, was being loud and clumsy. You could tell that the Thompsons were having a pot roast for dinner, or that Inga Svenson's old Ford Pinto was burning oil, or that a new tomcat, at least half feral, had marked your back fence as one of the boundaries of his territory. In the fall, you could find deer scrapings by the musky smell as quickly as you could by the rub marks. In the Dominions, the acrid smell of its piss would have announced that there was a Son in the area.

Perhaps, given a few years, he could have sorted out all the strange and exotic smells of the city, but right now it was all he could do to tell from the wood smoke on the wind that somebody was foolishly burning pine that was far too green, far too heavy with creosote, and that same foolish somebody would surely find themselves with a chimney fire sooner than later. It was wasteful to burn green wood; much of the heat of the fire would spend itself on drying the wood—and didn't their apothecaries have any use for creosote?

Any advance warning from the sounds was impossible. Every few moments there was a roar overhead, as one of the lights lined up in the sky passed: airplanes, seeking the airport. Perhaps that was the strange gasoline-like smell in the air? And then there was the rush of cars on the roadways, and every so often the plaintive wail of a siren— how could these people ever sleep?

Well, you could get used to anything, eventually, perhaps.

If he had had it to do all over again, he would have thought it through better. If young Thorian was to go to school in this city—and he was—then Thorian should have spent enough time here to make it familiar, just as he had always made it a point to acquaint himself with the arena in which a duel would take place before any duel. A loose tile in the floor was only a problem if you didn't know about it, and an advantage if you did and your opponent didn't.

Or if you did, and he did, but he didn't know that you did. He had won a memorable point off the Duelmaster himself with just such a tangled advantage.

He had completed a circuit of the lake, and there was no Son, no sign of such. There had been opportunities for somebody or something to spring out at him—at least six opportunities, by his count, assuming that the Son wanted to do this privately, discreetly.

Could it be that this was a diversion? That the real attack was to come against young Thorian and Maggie?

No, that didn't make sense.

Then what was it?

One lone jogger was circling the lake, but other than that, they were alone. Even the ice fishermen had closed up their ice houses for the night. As a recreation, ice fishing in the cold was silly enough, for what little such a small lake could provide—but even the city people were not so strange as to do it in the dark, as well.

Am I supposed to walk around in the dark until I freeze to death?

That would take some time. His cheeks were cold, but the warming band kept his ears just this side of numb, and he had automatically unzipped his parka to let some heat and moisture out when the exertion threatened to make him sweat.

It was on his third circuit of the lake, well past midnight, when he noticed the chalk diagram on the tarmac. It hadn't been there on his first turn around the lake—he had been watching the ground, memorizing the icy spot on the path—but it could have been there on his second.

It was a rough outline of a pistol, with a large X through it.

Had it calculated that he would have a pistol? Or could it smell it? There were probably gun oils that had no distinctive odor, but he had always used Hoppes oil, just as Mr. Roelke had taught him.

He shook his head. No guns.

Did it know? Or was it just guessing? Would it believe him if he spread his hands and proclaimed that he had nothing of the sort, that it had not occurred to him to bring a pistol to this affair?

But if that was so, why had he noticed the drawing? Why was he standing here looking at it?

He had been outmaneuvered yet again.

Very well: no gun.

He could take the cartridges out and just fling the pistol away, but that idea bothered him. What would happen if some child found it? An empty gun wasn't dangerous, in and of itself, but it just seemed wrong to go to his death with such an irresponsible gesture.

He could smash the gun to pieces—but how was he going to destroy a piece of metal while walking around the lake? If it was summer, he might have been able to find a piece of rock to use as a hammer, to try to bash it out of shape. Or, for that matter, all it would take would be a screwdriver to disassemble it. Throw the springs one way, the cylinder another, and then he could pitch the rest into the lake.

Pity he couldn't throw it in the lake . . .

. . . but, of course, he could, and he would.

"Perhaps then you'll face me?" he asked, quietly.

The only answer was the sound of a car, off in the distance, whining its refusal to start in the cold. Chka-chka-chka-chka-chka. Chka-chka-chka-chka-chka-chka-chka-chka-chka-chka.

He made his way down the shallow embankment and onto the rough ice. It really wasn't as slippery as it looked. Hard-driven snow and days of cold had made the surface rough enough that it really wasn't much different than walking on snow would have been. He hadn't expected that, but, then again, walking out on a frozen lake was something that it had never occurred to him to do before.

He had learned to skate because Karin enjoyed skating, but that was done at the hockey rink down at the high school, which was made every winter simply by spraying water on the football field after the ground was fully frozen. That was slippery ice, although it was most slippery not on the coldest days but on the warmest.

His thoughts and steps had taken him to the nearest of the holes in the ice, now covered with a square of plywood.

Somebody with more optimism than sense had cut a hole big enough to step into, and probably somebody else—somebody with more sense—had covered it over so that blowing snow wouldn't turn it into a trap for the unwary and unlucky.

Ice had formed in the hole, but it broke easily with the heel of his boot. He slowly drew the pistol out of his jacket, and held it by the barrel over his head, then carefully, deliberately, dropped it into the dark water with a solid *plunk.*

He wouldn't have been surprised if a dark form had leaped out of the shadows of one of the nearby ice houses and run across the ice toward him, but there was no movement, save for that of the lights of the cars on Lake Street, at the far end of the lake.

Well? I'm waiting.

He started to walk back to the shore, but stopped himself. That was the obvious thing to do, and perhaps the Son was expecting the obvious—why make it easy on him?

He turned and headed toward the shiny skating area just off the south shore.

It seemed that the Son wanted a fair fight: Thorian heard the growl as it stalked out of the shadows under the pier. It walked, stiff-legged, out onto the ice for a few paces, then broke into a deceptively easy lope that would quickly eat up the space between them.

He turned to run and yanked at his zipper as he did so, pulling the sheathed knife from under his armpit. A flick of his gloved thumb released the leather tie across the sheath, and a snap of his wrist sent the sheath tumbling end-over-end away in the dark.

The three pillars supporting the tripod of strategy were balance, timing, and space. Under most circumstances, two legs couldn't balance as well as four, but if he could reach the patch of slick ice, that might not be so.

He would have one chance, although it wasn't much of a chance: the Son would get to within springing range, and then it would leap. If he could ruin its timing, control the space between them so that they met at the top of its leap, he just might be able to strike at it, at least once. It was even possible that the Son wouldn't see the knife's blade— he had coated it with lampblack.

Thorian del Thorian ran with short, choppy strides, his legs pumping hard. Too long a stretch, and he ran the risk of falling, and then it would be all over in a second.

Which probably would be best, all in all, but that wasn't the way Thorian del Thorian had been raised, and that wasn't the way he was going to die.

You fought every duel, every affair for real, using all your strength, all your capabilities. Duelists would fortify themselves with herbs and prayers, asking that the justice of their cause aid your arm, your legs, your balance, and your eyes in support of their right. You were supposed to hope that if you were in the wrong, the other duelist would prevail, but Thorian del Thorian had never been able to feel that in his heart: no matter what the justice, he always wanted to win.

Knife held reversed, blade parallel to his forearm, Thorian del Thorian pumped his arms and ran ahead of the thudding footsteps behind him. He wanted to look over his shoulder, to gauge the distance, but with the rough ground ahead of him, that was too risky.

Too risky? He had to force himself not to laugh out loud. Too risky? He was about to be killed by the *kirdamled* Son of Fenris—what more risk was there for him here?

He reached the outer rim of the shiny ice of the skating area and leaped the last few feet onto it, sliding like a skater until he could break into a half-skating sort of running that he had tried once with Karin, the inner edge of his soles biting hard enough to send him leaping onto the other foot, then kicking himself along with the other foot.

It wouldn't have worked with good skating ice, but for reasons he had never quite understood, when it got this cold the surface wasn't quite as slick as it was when it was warmer.

He knew his running looked as clumsy as it felt, but when he heard the skittering sounds of the Son's claws against the hard ice start to recede behind him, he thought he might actually be able to reach the shoreline before the wolf was upon him, and that would give every advantage back to his enemy. He was considering how to fake a fall and recovery when the skittering became a fast, rhythmic click-clicking.

Not only was there going to be no need for that but it wouldn't work. He finally risked throwing a quick glance over his shoulder to see the Son loping toward him, devouring distance between them with every bound.

His timing was, he decided, just this side of perfect. Assuming it maintained this speed on the smooth ice—and assuming he could keep up his pace—the Son should catch up with him at about the middle of the skating area, at the point where his boots gave him the maximum advantage in control over its clawed paws.

The ice was scored with the scratches of skates, most heavily in the large circle he had already crossed, but there were lines and divots everywhere.

He spun himself around, sliding backwards, then kicked hard, once, against the ice with the edge of his foot, digging in as hard as he could. Which was hard enough: it jerked him to a stop so quickly that his teeth chattered.

He had seen larger Sons, but not often: this one would have stood chest-high, and probably outweighed him by twenty or more pounds.

Even in the dim green light of the distant streetlights, it was a magnificent beast in its way: head broad and handsome, although the skull underneath it was thick, while the limbs were more slender than he would have thought they should be.

Its chest was deep but surprisingly narrow, and its eyes seemed to pick up a distant red glow.

It reared back as it slipped into a skid, front paws stretched out in front of it as though to push the ice away; Thorian del Thorian turned to the side and launched himself into a kick-started leap.

If he could get on its back and slip the knife between its ribs, one twist and he could try to keep it away with his feet until it died.

But the wolf was as fast as he was, if not faster: instead of trying to regain its balance, it simply flopped over on its side, so that instead of leaping onto its back, Thorsen came belly-to-belly with it.

One front paw batted his knife arm aside, while the jaws snapped shut, just missing his left arm; he was barely able to rip his parka away.

The two rear legs curled up and slashed out; hard nails raked fire down his chest and belly, and its warm, fetid breath was nauseatingly foul in his nostrils for just a moment, until its body spasmed, once, flipping him away to land hard on the ice.

Reflexes and decades of practice saved him from having his breath knocked out; he broke his fall with a slap of his left arm against the ice, then somehow got his legs underneath him and rose to his feet in a crouch just as the Son did.

His parka was ripped down the front; cold agony had scratched itself down his belly to the beltline. If the Son's claws hadn't caught on his thick belt, unintentionally helping him to escape for the moment as it pushed him away, it would have emasculated him with its hind legs.

There was a low growling in his ears, and he realized that it was coming from his own throat, so he stopped it.

But the growling didn't stop, the roar didn't diminish—if anything, it got louder.

What—

Oh. It was the sound of a plane flying low overhead, coming in for a landing at the airport. Young Thorian would have been able to identify it by the sound.

His right arm was almost numb, so he held it, the knife

still clutched in it, out in front of him, holding the wolf's gaze with his own while his left hand fumbled for the knife that young Thorian had lent him.

"Come get me, dog," he said in Bersmål, in which the word was an insult that carried enough weight to turn a first-blood affair into a death duel. "I'm waiting for you." His words were slurred and clumsy in his ears, and he realized he had bitten his tongue badly enough to fill his mouth with warm, thick blood.

A wolf wasn't the only thing that could die with blood in its mouth, eh?

Snarling, hunched down, it approached him slowly, circling off to the left, just as his trembling fingers found young Thorian's knife.

Yes, to the left, he thought. *Circle off to my weak side, and avoid the knife that's out in front of you, and I'll let you grab hold of my right arm.* If he could push its head up for even a moment with his arm to expose the neck, he could slash into it. Open the jugular vein, and then let the Son drain its lifeblood out on the ice.

He took a step forward as it settled its haunches in for the spring, but instead of leaping into the air, it took an almost comically small hop to close the distance, then came *up* at him from the ice, knocking him back, sending his fighting knife flying off somewhere into the dark.

He forced his right arm between the teeth, his long knife falling from his fingers, and then reached his hand back, back into the wolf's mouth, trying to get his bare fingers to close around the slippery tongue.

But his fingers went limp and useless as the jaws clamped down on his wrist, the absence of pain from his fingers more frightening than the pain itself had been. He flicked the knife in his left hand open, and stabbed for the nearest eye, but a paw batted it aside.

The wolf shuddered against him as a shock rocked his body, and then another.

It was only then that he barely heard the distant twin cracks over the roar of the jet, and it was only then that the jaws started to loosen, and the acrid smell of the Son's piss filled his nostrils while his right leg grew wet and warm.

His knees buckled under him, and his right hand was useless, but he still had a knife in his left hand, and an enemy's throat in front of him. Thorian del Thorian slashed hard, twice, across the Son's throat, and then twice again, until warm blood flowed down his arm and onto the ice.

A dark shape was making its way across the ice with more grace than Thorian had had, and in a moment Billy Olson was at his side, helping him to his feet. He had a small plastic case of some sort in his hand—no, it was one of those small cell phones.

"Hurry up," he said. "I'll get your dad out of here, but, shit, you're on your own for the cleanup, and if I haven't heard from you by the time I've got *him* cleaned up, we're out of here." He snapped the phone shut and dropped it carefully into an inner pocket of his coat, then got an arm under Thorsen and helped him to his feet. "Come on, Mr. Thorsen—we need to get out of here, and quickly. My car's this way."

Thorian del Thorian spat warm blood out of his mouth. "You promised." He felt cheated, somehow, although he couldn't quite say why. This had been his fight, not this boy's.

"I lied. I spent a lot of years lying to myself and other people," he said, not slowing for a moment in their movement despite the chatter. "I'm very, very good at it," he said, brightly. "I didn't think the wolf hung around long enough to get a whiff of me the other night, but I didn't want to argue the point, what with you being so ready to go get yourself killed."

"But how—"

"Nice Starlight scope you have there. Even us sissy boys learn how to shoot when we grow up, and while I wouldn't want to trust your sighting-in for a two-hundred-meter shot, for thirty yards or so it worked just fine. I wish you had given me another moment or two, or I could have shot him before he got to you, but . . . never mind that; we'll have plenty of time to talk about all that later; if Torrie and

Maggie get caught, Jeff and I are going to have to take you home by ourselves.''

An unfamiliar car stood running, with only its parking lights on, by the side of the road. The twin headlights of a car were approaching, and Billy pushed him up, his back against a tree, while it passed.

''But where?''

''Sitting, freezing my cold but very cute little ass off, in an ice-fishing house,'' Billy answered.

''But you lied.''

''Absolutely,'' he said, as he nodded toward the car, and they resumed their progress while the rear door opened. ''I don't give a shit about promises, Mr. Thorsen. I don't care a fig about keeping my word, or telling the truth, or any of that shit. You may feel free to despise me, if you like. On the other hand, you are not free to leave town without at least taking my recipe for popovers to your lovely wife,'' he said, the stream of chatter never ceasing for a moment as he helped Thorsen into the darkened interior of the car.

''Where to?'' Jeff Bjerke's voice rasped.

''I'll drive,'' he said. ''You get into the backseat and patch him up,'' Billy said. ''Blood makes my knees weak, and needles make me faint.''

''Billy . . .''

''Well, they do teach you how to do at least some first aid in Boys with Badges school, don't they? I mean, every once in a while you simply have to run into a situation that can't be solved with handcuffs, even if they aren't lined with anything interesting. That steel is so plain. I mean, can't you even put a few appliqués on them? Or maybe get them in different colors, or . . .''

''Billy.''

''Oh. You mean, 'where are we going?' '' Billy Olson shifted gears and pulled away from the curb. ''I would have thought that was obvious. Mr. Thorsen is injured. We could just drop him off at a hospital, but there would be awkward questions asked, and we really don't want awkward questions asked, even if Torrie and Maggie do manage to get the Son's body off of the ice, then into the Bronco and out of town without anybody noticing. If you think Mr. Thorsen is going to die without treatment right away, well, then we put up with the awkward questions, and to hell with it, but—''

''I'm . . . fine,'' Thorian del Thorian said.

''Oh, of course you are, Mr. Thorsen,'' Billy said, bubbling like a soda fountain. ''Just a little walk in the park for the lot of you, but I'm one of those effete mincing queens, sir, and you'll forgive me if all this shit isn't something I take for granted, the way you—''

''*Billy.*''

''Okay, okay, Jeff, if I have to spell it out for you, I will: we are going home.'' He shifted gears and sped up. ''We'll need to gas up in a couple of hundred miles, and either you or me will have to be cleaned up enough so that the guy in the booth doesn't stain his bloomers and call the cops, but—''

''Don't drive too fast,'' Jeff said.

''Nag, nag, nag, all you straights ever do is nag.''

Jeff chuckled.

Thorian del Thorian leaned back and closed his eyes. Home.

Yes, they were going home.

CHAPTER TWENTY-NINE

The Sons

Ian Silver Stone came awake at a touch, reaching for Giantkiller, his hand closing on the familiar grip even before he could make out the dim form of Arnie Selmo leaning over him.

"There's something outside," Arnie said, his rough voice barely above a whisper.

Ian sat up and listened. All he could hear was what was left of the fire crackling in the hearth and the heavy snoring from where Valin lay sleeping over in the corner.

Arnie already had Ian's boots out, and he squatted down to help Ian ease his savaged right ankle into the right one, then tied it painfully tight. That was fine—support was more important right now than comfort.

Besides . . . Ian fumbled in his pants for Harbard's ring, and slipped it onto his finger. It would be very handy if it didn't—

Better. He forced himself not to flex the ankle. No need to tear the wound open through motion until he absolutely had to.

Maybe it would be—no. It would not be a good idea if he was unable to feel pain. Pain was a valuable warning, not to be dismissed with a wave of his hand. It would be wonderful, though, if pain couldn't blind, couldn't disable him, but was merely a warning that he could keep in mind. That would be absolutely—

Fine.

Ian accepted Arnie's help to his feet and into his shirt. His fringed leather jacket hung, limp, from a peg on the wall; he switched Giantkiller from hand to hand in order to put it on.

She stepped out from the shadows, her body tightly covered by finely scaled silvery armor from foot to throat. It clung tightly to her, as though it had been intended to emphasize the swell of her breasts and hip, and the firm scallops of muscle on her flat belly.

Her face, even in the firelight, now showed no trace of sag or age: it was smooth and ageless, and frightening in its inhuman perfection.

Her warhelm was a cap with silvery wings over her ears, cupping the top of her head, beneath which her golden hair flowed, almost dreamlike in its languor, over her scaled shoulders.

Her movements like something out of a dance, she walked over to an empty peg on the wall, reached up, and pulled down a black cloak.

Yes, the peg had been empty.

"It's called the Tarn-kappë, Ian," she said, her voice a whisper of silvery bells. "The cloak of, well, Vestri, originally, although he did give it to one of his lesser sons." She shook his head. "I told him better," she said. "Alberich was always a vile little shit, although a finer hand with hammer and chisel I never did see.

"But Vestri never did listen to me; a problem that others have had, before and since," she said with a smile as she held up the cloak. "I think you'd best borrow it for now." She shook her head. "In the daytime, it's not nearly as effective, but at night, the only thing you need worry about is sound and smell, and the Sons will likely let you escape rather than try to pursue sounds and smells through the night."

She threw it to him; he caught it, reflexively. It looked substantial, and the black cloth was coarse and thick in his fingers, but it weighed almost nothing, as light as though it had been woven of cobwebs and whispers.

Well, what the hell, eh? He slid the single plain bone button through the buttonhole, and settled the Tarn-kappë across his shoulders. Ian worked his arm experimentally, dropping into a tentative lunge, and then into a full lunge and recovery, with no difficulty—the cloak was compact enough, light enough that the edge floated out of his way when his arm moved.

Freya buckled a swordbelt about her hips, then pulled a silvery buckler out of one of the wooden footlockers. It had no straps that Ian could see, but when she touched it to her forearm, it hung there as though welded. She flexed her fingers, and for the first time he noticed that her fingernails were all silvered, like a mirror.

Her right hand free, she drew her sword from its heavy sheath. It was short and broad as his hand, its handle heavily jeweled, the blade black as night, black as Silvertop, and as she took a few quick practice swings, it whistled invisibly through the air.

What did Ian have to do to make the Tarn-kappë work? Was there some sort of switch? "Freya, I—"

"Shh." She turned at a low sound outside the cottage. "They're waiting for . . . something." Her brow furrowed. "Ian?" She was no longer looking straight at him.

"I'm here," he said, then walked around further to her side. Apparently he didn't have to do anything to turn it on. Which was handy, all things considered. It would have been awkward not to be able to see his own body.

As to Giantkiller? That wouldn't have been a problem; he had no more trouble knowing where Giantkiller's tip was than he would have knowing where the tip of his index finger was.

"Make for Silvertop," she said, as she addressed the air in front of her, "and ask him to carry you. The Son hasn't been whelped that can outrun him."

My pleasure, Freya. Don't mind if I do. Valin and I will be out of here so fast it'll make your ancient eyes spin— and who the fuck am I kidding?

"Nah," he said. "Arnie needs somebody to watch his

back.'' Which was true enough. Arnie was able to wield Mjolnir as though he was an Aesir, but he wasn't an Aesir; his human flesh was no tougher than Ian's own.

"I would have thought that to be my responsibility," she said. "But have it as you will."

"Would one of you please give me a hand with this?" Arnie was struggling with the unfamiliar straps and buckles of his leather armor.

"Sure, but I ca—"

Before Ian could so much as complete the word, Freya had sheathed her sword faster than the eye could follow and blurred to Arnie's side.

"Honored One? Lady Frida?" Valin rubbed his sleepy eyes. "Where is Ian Silver Stone? Is he unwell? Is there some sort of problem?"

Ian had grown to like the little dwarf, and he certainly admired his courage, but his impression of Valin's intelligence would have dropped if it had had anywhere lower to go.

"I'm right here," Ian said. "There isn't a back door to this place, is there?"

"Yes, there is," Arnie said, rising, "but it will be watched, as well." Arnie was now buckled tightly into a long leather cuirass and greaves, a metal gauntlet on his left hand, his right hand bare. He reached out his right hand, and Mjolnir leaped into the air from where Arnie had it leaning next to the fireplace, and it slapped into his waiting hand with a meaty *thunk*.

"How shall we do this?" he asked, his voice deeper and harsher than Ian was used to. "I'm not familiar with this sort of thing."

Freya laughed as she knelt back down in front of him, strapping another piece of leather armor Ian didn't know the name of on his right thigh, then his left. "This from a corporal of Dog Troop, Seventh Regiment, First Cavalry? How many men have you left to rot in the sun, buzzards pecking at their eyes?"

"None recently; the Iron Triangle was long ago and far away. I never stopped to count the bodies or the buzzards, anyway." He growled, deep in his throat. "Besides, the

one time I went up against Sons, I didn't acquit myself all
that well. So I ask again: how do we do this?''

"We walk out on the front porch, and we tell them to
go away,'' she said with a smile as she accepted his hand
and rose to her feet, a full head taller than Arnie. "Then,
O Thunderer, when they don't go fleeing into the night,
running like the dogs they are, we kill them all."

She took half a dozen torches from the bin by the door,
lit one by sticking it momentarily into the coals of the
hearth, then opened the door and stepped out into the night,
Arnie stalking after her.

It would have been nice to have had some idea as to
what was going on, but there wasn't anything to do but
follow.

He had never seen so many glowing eyes before.

Easily a hundred Sons were gathered in a ring around
the cottage, and even as Ian walked quietly onto the porch,
six more trotted up the path, and, one by one, snarled and
batted for a place in the circle.

There was apparently some sort of precedence involved;
the larger and noisier ones seemed clustered around the
front of the cottage.

Freya planted torches in a rough arc in front of the cottage by the simple expedient of throwing them like spears
into the ground; she then lit them one by one. She seemed
even taller now, although as she stepped off the porch and
onto the grass it was hard to measure her against anything
else.

Arnie gave Mjolnir a trial swing, and then he, too,
stepped off the porch. Ian felt incredibly naked and vulnerable, but he felt even more lonely on the porch, so he
followed them, moving off to the side. Even if he wanted
to leave—and the idea of running away suddenly looked a
whole lot better than it had before—there was no way he
could have: the Sons completely encircled the cottage, two
and three deep in places, and he would have had to go
through or past several of them at the very least.

Even with a running leap, like a beginner trying a flèche,
it was unlikely he could clear the circle without coming to

contact with one or more of them, and he had no illusions
that he could fight them off in two or three or four directions at once, not for long.

Freya drew her sword, her strange, wide-bladed short
sword, which was almost invisible in the dark, and pointed
with it. "Which of you speaks for the lot of you? Which
one of you cares to explain why you dare to interrupt my
rest?"

As if in answer, the largest of the Sons, a broad-
shouldered beast with one ragged ear, tilted back his muzzle
and howled, loud enough to hurt Ian's ears. It wasn't just
a simple cry, but a complex set of cries and howls, with a
four-note theme that was repeated several times, with variations. Another Son picked up the original theme, and then
repeated it with his own variations, and then another and
another until the entire pack was howling.

"*No,*" she said.

The pack fell silent.

"No." Freya shook her head. "You may not take my
guests, my friends. One of you: take human form, and we
will discuss what form your apology to me for this inex-
cusable intrusion shall take. That is the only matter to discuss."

The silence was unnatural and oppressive. Ian moved
around to the side of the cottage—if Arnie couldn't see
him, he might end up throwing Mjolnir right through Ian
by accident. It would have been nice to have had a chance
to discuss how to handle that, but it wasn't the first time
Ian noticed that old people often were as impatient with the
idea of discussing things with young people as vice versa.

Freya seemed confident, and certainly she was powerful,
but if she could easily handle dozens and dozens of Sons
by herself, she probably would have mentioned that by
now.

"Then if you do not care to talk," she said, her voice
strong but still melodic, "then leave, and take my ill will
with you—and a heavy burden may you find it."

"Last chance," Arnie murmured.

Whether that was the trigger, or whether one of the Sons
gave a signal that Ian didn't catch—it wasn't the big one;

Ian was watching that one at the moment—Ian wasn't quite sure, but without a warning, at least a dozen Sons leaped toward Freya while another dozen or more bounded toward where Arnie stood.

Lightning flashed and thunder crashed deafeningly once, twice, three times, and Arnie Selmo swept Mjolnir through a Son's head, shattering it like a pumpkin hitting the sidewalk. Another wolf leaped for the porch side rail, but Ian had anticipated that one would try to sneak around behind Arnie that way, and he met it with a quick thrust-twist-and-sidestep that left the animal tumbling noisily to the wood, blood and gasps bubbling out of a slash in its throat.

That went unnoticed by the other Sons in all the confusion, and Ian was able to slip his blade between the ribs of one, and then another, and then another before a hairy mass knocked him off his feet and bounced him hard off the cabin wall, slamming his head into it so hard that lights danced behind his tearing eyes.

Things were a bit vague for a few minutes after that. Ian remembered slashing out with Giantkiller over and over again, once having to kick a body off his blade when it jammed up against the hilt. And all the while, lightning flashed and thunderclaps crashed, and the sounds of his own grunts of effort and pain mixed with the howls and screams of the injured and dying Sons.

As he fought his way toward the front of the cottage, Freya was a silvery blur at the periphery of his vision, a metal-limbed tornado spinning through the pack of Sons, tossing bodies and parts of bodies aside as she slashed and cut and stabbed and smashed and kicked.

But even as the three of them cut down Son after Son, and even as the shit stink of their death spasms filled Ian's nostrils while the crashing of thunder and cries of the wounded filled his ears, more and more Sons ran up the path, and up the side of the hill, joining the fight.

Perhaps even Freya could be buried under such a swarm.

And what for? What was the point of it all? Sons chasing after the Thorsens, after Freya and Arnie—why?

Through all the noise, he heard a very human groan from somewhere to his left, and Ian kicked and cut and smashed his way through to the porch, and then onto the porch, where Arnie had been forced back against the wall, surrounded by four huge beasts who snapped at him, ducking back when he swung Mjolnir.

Arnie's left arm, the armor now torn from it, hung bloody and useless at his side, and it was all he could do to ward the Sons away. If he threw Mjolnir again, at least one of them would be upon him instantly.

Ian kicked the nearest Son aside, then thrust Giantkiller through the neck of the next. Spasming and howling in pain, the Son reared back, almost twisting the sword out of Ian's hand. He recovered quickly enough, barely, to keep his grip, but another of the wolves had leaped upon Arnie, and while one swipe from Mjolnir smashed its chest into gore and bone, there was another and another . . .

"Get away from him!" Ian shouted. Harbard's ring clamped down, painfully hard, against his finger.

The Sons stopped, and backed away, tails between legs, whimpering in pain and fear.

Ian unbuttoned the Tarn-kappë, and wrapped it around Arnie's shoulders. With the tiniest of shimmers, Arnie vanished.

"Sorry, kid," came a faint whisper from the air. "I told you I wasn't much good."

It didn't matter.

"Hear me," Ian said, letting his voice ring out. "Fear me." Harbard's ring gripped his finger like a vice as the growling and snarling first faded, then died.

"I am Ian Silver Stone," he said, "friend of Freya and of the Thunderer. Fear me, Sons of Fenris."

The Sons whimpered, and the pack surrounding Freya fell away. She was surrounded by pieces of wolves, and covered with blood, but her helm had been torn away, as had portions of her armor. One of the scaled leggings had been torn open from hip to ankle, and shreds of the armor hung freely from her hip, leaving her bloodied leg bare.

All eyes were on him, and he held them by force of will as he sheathed Giantkiller and raised his hands.

"Fear me," he said, again, as he stalked into the pack. It seemed like the right thing to say.

They parted like the Red Sea, some wolves walking awkwardly, almost comically backwards through the sea of bodies and body parts. Ian had forgotten that half of the Sons were werewolves, and the other half werehumans, and that the werehumans reverted to their human form when their abilities to maintain another shape failed in death, regardless of what form they were in when they died.

It reminded him of something out of Hieronymus Bosch: in the unsteady light of the spitting, flickering torches, bodies and pieces of wolves and humans lay scattered across the hilltop, fragments of white bones projecting out from the mess of foul flesh like broken shells on a beach of meat.

One head lay intact near his feet, that of a woman with long, dark hair, and a face that reminded him of Veronica Lake, dead, dirty, eyes staring upwards into his. Half of the Sons were humans in death; it would have been easier to look at if they'd all been wolves.

The largest Son, the one with the torn ear, stood alone in his path, whimpering, its long teeth bared. "Fear me," Ian said.

It did; it pissed down its own leg in fright—but it held its ground, snarling and panting.

"I am Ian Silverstein," he said, "slayer of Sons. The Son that so much as comes near me dies," he said, his voice low. "You, dog, you are dying right now. You can't draw breath—"

The panting stopped, as did the snarling.

"—and your legs have turned to water—"

It slumped to the ground, and Ian circled to the left to reach Freya's side.

The Son again lifted his head, its teeth bared. It was trying to snarl, but it believed Ian when he told it that it couldn't breathe, and all it could do was try to snap at him.

"—and your heart refuses to—"

"No." Valin's voice cut through the whimpering. "Enough, please, enough." Valin stood on the porch, one hand raised. He shook his head. "You have won; you've killed many Sons and you've frightened the rest away. Let him live, please. There's no point in it, not any more." The dwarf walked down from the porch, tongue clicking against his teeth as he did so. "Please, Ian."

Ian felt Freya by his side. "If you wish, my Silver Stone; I can see no harm in it." She was leaning on him, hard. "Not now."

Ian looked down at the Son. "You can breathe, and your legs will work—but only while you run from me. So run away—all of you—run away, while you can. *Run.*"

Unhurt Sons scattered and ran, the injured ones limping after.

Valin nodded. "Thank you, Ian."

It finally hit Ian: he wasn't talking in Dwarvish or Bersmål, but in English, and all the obsequiousness had vanished from his manner.

"Very cleverly done, Brother Fox," Freya said. "I had no idea."

Valin chuckled. "You must have had *some* idea. I was so hoping that you would lend one of the jewels to Ian, here. He means so well, after all." His mouth twitched into a smile. "You do have them—or perhaps just one?— around here, of course. I had thought that you'd seize it for power or for safekeeping if the situation presented itself correctly." He shook his head. "I'd look around for it, but I don't think that would be entirely safe, would it?"

"Of course it would be," she said, her smile cold and thin. "Go right ahead and look. Perhaps you'll find it. I don't think that we could stop you. *No,* Arnie, don't. I don't know what will happen if you throw Mjolnir at him, but he's thought that through."

"Alternately," Valin said, "it's possible that I'm bluffing, and could no more deflect Mjolnir than I could grow wings and fly." He stooped to *tsk* over the body of one dead Son.

"But you could grow wings and fly," she said. "Of all the Aesir, you've always been the best shapeshifter."

Valin—Loki—snorted. "Best? Most talented, certainly. Most adept, yes. But best? When did it ever do me any good, eh?"

"Keep your distance," Arnie Selmo said, as he folded

the Tarn-kappë over Ian's left arm and turned to face Loki. His right arm still held Mjolnir out to one side. He waved the heavy warhammer easily, as though it weighed no more than a druggist's pestle or pen.

Freya held up her free hand. Moving for the first time like an old woman, she sheathed her sword, slowly. "There's no fight here, Arnold," she said. "It's all over— for now." She nodded in admiration at Loki. "Very nicely done—it was all you?"

"You liked it?" Loki had already started to change, and as he reached her side, he was now a large, barrel-chested man in a black suit with a filigreed vest that looked as if it had been precisely tailored for his massive belly, although the cut and style were unfamiliar to Ian; it looked like something vaguely Western. The shirt was brilliantly white and ruffled, like a tuxedo shirt.

"I should have suspected it was you."

"Please," he said with a frown that vanished almost as instantly as it appeared. "After I've gone to such very great pains for so very many years to stay out of trouble?" He shot his cuffs and adjusted his cuff links—they appeared to be the skull of some small animal, although Ian wasn't even able to guess which—then crooked his arm. "If I may?" he said, offering her his arm, which she accepted, ignoring Arnie's glare.

"Slowly, now," Loki said, as she hobbled toward the cottage, supported by Ian on one side and Loki on the other. "There's no need to rush."

His face was large and round, his hair and the wreath of black beard framing his round face black shot with just a hint of gray. With a large nose and vaguely olive skin, he seemed a lot more Mediterranean than Nordic. He was pleasantly homely as he smiled, and his voice was a booming baritone.

"But yes, I thought it worth a try. It seemed to offer several possibilities." He shook his head. "I probably should have kept with it longer—that's always been my failing: I'm patient up to a point, and then . . . Enh."

All of it? Odin's Curse on the Scion? The Sons, here and those sent after Torrie in Minneapolis?

Loki smiled at Ian. "Yes, O Honored One," he said. "Just as you'll find that Orfindel can always count on affection from the vestri, you'll find that the Sons of Fenris are, by and large, willing to give their faith and obedience to the Father of Fenris."

Ian's lips pressed together. "Then Herolf was lying."

"Pfui," Loki said. "Why would you think that? He's loyal to the Dominions—you must remember that Sons are pack animals, and while they can and will joust for standing in the pack, they're loyal as, well, a good dog." He shook his head. "No. I gathered my help from the Southern Packs, not the Northern." He sighed as he toed a severed arm out of the way to make some space on the front step for his own foot. "Poor little things," he said. "Have you ever seen them as cubs?" His smile was gentle, but definitely lupine. "They are very, very cute—in both their forms, although the bitches do have to keep them separate for the first while, or the two-legged ones tend to get hurt." He cocked his head to one side. "Would you like to come with me and meet some? You'd be well-received. If there's anything the Sons respect more than their Father's father, it's somebody who can frighten a whole pack of them away."

Ian's jaw clenched. "You want me to join you?"

"Well," Loki said, "I've been carrying your gear up and down hills for a while now. Don't you want to return the favor?" What was surprising about his grin was the utter absence of menace in it. "Besides, I think there's a fair chance I'll get to, to a sufficient number of the Brisingamen jewels soon enough, and well, once that happens, you'd probably want to have a friend in the next Cycle—and who better than the God of the next Cycle, eh?" He looked around and nodded. "I think I'll bring this back, though. It's a nice enough place."

Freya shook her head. "I don't think so, Brother Fox. I think you're doomed to fail."

"Doom? Fate? What is that, eh?" Loki shrugged. "I know the Norns, and I've fucked the Fates and the Furies, and while they're all nice old girls, once I have—once I have a sufficient number of the jewels in my hands, well, we'll just see what I decide fate is and doom might be—

and step easy, now, old girl; you don't want to hurt yourself any more than you already have." He smiled at Ian, and it seemed genuine. "Seriously, boy, leave these old fascists, and throw in your lot with me. I can promise you a lot more fun than this old bag ever even teased you with."

"Really," Freya laughed. "Oh, Loki . . ."

"Seriously," Loki said. "I'm a fun date, boy." He gently detached Freya from his arm and stood to face Ian. "I know the noisiest bars in Paris, the best place to get a suit tailored in Hong Kong, and the most scenic hiking trails in the Dominions and camping sites in Mongolia—hell, I've got a house account at the finest brothel in Finavarra's Hell. Throw in with me, and we'll have a sweet trip, whether or not we end up snatching the jewels."

"No."

"Please, O Honored One," Loki said, in Valin's voice, "I'll even keep making your bed for you." He tugged at his forelock with an extra left hand.

Ian's hand never left Giantkiller's hilt. "What part of no didn't you understand?"

"You'll never make much of a businessman, kid. Always be sure you know what the other fellow's best offer is before you say no . . ." He took a step forward and gently touched a hand to Ian's forehead.

This time it would be better. Really.

Ian lay back on the creaky old bed, pillowing his head on his hands. Dad and The New Girlfriend were due home from the party any time now. TNG would nuke a mug of milk with butter and honey in the microwave, and go straight to bed—she said it helped her sleep—but Dad would head for the liquor shelf for his nightcap.

Which was only fair enough. One drink at the end of the day was a habit, not a vice.

Ian had a surprise ready for him. It wasn't quite perfect—he thought he had earned an A in Biology, but Mr. Fusco hadn't seen it that way. Not enough class participation, he'd said, and then there were the few latenesses. Biology came right after gym on Tuesday and Thursday, and gym was Ian's time to shake a few things loose, whether it was fak-

ing Bobby Adajian out of his shorts in football, or going
for a jump shot with great enthusiasm and absolutely no
skill during the quarter that basketball was the gym
teacher's sport of choice, because if he showed enough enthusiasm, and did at least passably well, Mr. Daniels would
bring out his foils and masks and give Ian a quickie lesson
while the rest of the class was taking their final laps. Mr.
Daniels had, in his younger days, tried out for the Olympic
team, and he had a deceptively defensive style that Ian was
trying to pick up. Milking that lesson for every minute
meant having to rush through a quick shower, and that usually meant being late, but that was no big deal. Or at least
it shouldn't have been. Shit, Mr. Fusco usually spent the
first ten minutes of every class flirting with the senior girls.

It was a good report card. Except for the one B+, it was
straight As. Even in driver's ed, although that technically
didn't count.

For once he had a report card to brag about, not try to
hide.

He would, as usual, pretend to be asleep, and if he didn't
hear raised voices, he would pretend to be woken up by
their coming home, and would stagger, sleepy-eyed up the
stairs, from his basement bedroom after Dad had had a
chance to notice. Oh, Dad would probably make some sort
of comment about the one B+, but even he, with his high
standards, would have to admit that this was as near-perfect
a report card as an imperfect person could be expected to
have.

Ian heard the car door slam outside, and then the garage
door whirr up and then the muffled roar of the big V-8
engine pulling the Pontiac into the garage, and the dieseling
chk-chk-chk-chk as it refused, for just a moment, to shut
down, and then the thunk-*thunk* of the car doors, followed
by the footsteps, the opening and closing of the door, and
their footsteps and quiet voices out in the laundry room as
they came into the house.

"He's asleep," TNG's husky voice said. Her cigarette
lighter hissed briefly.

"Mmmm. Room doesn't look too bad, either. Bet you
he hasn't done the dishes, though."

"So?"

"So, he is going to have to do that in the morning. That's the deal—I cooked supper, he does the dishes." They walked up the stairs.

Ian was just getting ready to get out of bed and put on his robe to go upstairs when he heard Dad's footsteps on the stairs.

There was a knock on his door. "Come in," he said.

The door swung open slowly. Dad stood there, framed in the doorway, the light from the hall making him only a silhouette. Ian found himself wondering, once more, why it should be that a little man no taller than five foot seven could loom so large in a doorway.

But this time it would be okay.

"Nice try." That wasn't right. Dad's voice was calm and level, like he was trying to restrain himself.

"But, I mean, well," Ian said, not understanding. "One B+? That's near perfect."

Dad snorted. "Yeah, it sure is. I bet you thought that you could fold the report card over and I wouldn't notice that you've got five absences and seven tardies this quarter. I wish you'd told me—I don't like you skipping school to go fencing. I can live with it, but I don't like it—I'm proud of how well you do on the fencing strip, but school is more important. But hey, as long as you can keep your average this high, I guess I don't have a complaint. Just tell me next time. But, hey, nice job, son." His face seemed ready to split in a smile.

He took a step forward and—

Ian backed away, staggering as he pulled Freya off-balance, and found himself supporting more of her weight. Ian's hand clenched painfully tight on Giantkiller's hilt.

"Oh, well." Loki shrugged. "Never hurts to ask, eh?"

"You bastard," Ian said. Iron self-control kept the sword in its sheath. If it had been wrong to attack Loki before, it was still wrong to attack Loki now. There was a deep growling in Ian's ears, and he realized it was coming from his own throat, so he stopped it.

"What is it, Ian?" Arnie asked, his eyes on Loki, never

leaving Loki. He gave Mjolnir a trial swing or two. "All I saw was him touching you on the forehead, but only for a second or two."

Freya's face was ashen. "I felt what he did," she said. "It's cruel, Brother Fox."

"Not at all, old woman. It's a fair offer." Loki spread his hands as he turned back to Ian. "If you'd prefer, I'd be happy to take you to your choice of mountaintop and show you the kingdoms of heaven and earth, but I thought something more, well, intimate and personal would have more appeal to you. You can have that on the next Cycle, or more.

"Just sign on with me. I can bind myself to keep my word, and why wouldn't I want to keep my word? You can have everything you ever wanted; the most you can imagine wanting wouldn't be a drop in the sea to me."

Yes, the most Ian could imagine wanting. Loki had been devilishly clever. He could have offered Ian much more, but he had played to Ian's weakness. The father in the dream wasn't a stranger; it was just Dad, as a decent father. Completely recognizable—save for him not treating Ian like shit.

Find the secret source of somebody's pain, and you could control them, if they were weak enough. Ian wasn't weak enough, but he would carry that dream around inside him like a sharp knife for the rest of his life.

He could kill Loki for that without the slightest misgiving, and then hang the body on a tree for the crows. Ian drew Giantkiller, just about six inches—

"It's your call, Ian," Arnie said softly. "Just let me know."

"No, Ian," Freya said. "Not here and now."

—then slammed his sword back into its scabbard with a solid *thunk*.

No. Not here and now.

But there would be another day, he thought. Somebody who would exploit that sort of weakness had to be kept away from the jewels. Let that miserable excuse for a god think that Ian couldn't control himself; let him underrate

Ian. That was fine. It was best to have an enemy that dangerous think you were less than you were.

But there would come a day when he would be able to plunge Giantkiller first into Loki's wrist to make him drop his weapon, and then, once more, blade held parallel to the ground, between the ribs.

He turned his back on Loki, and he and Arnie helped Freya hobble into the cottage.

CHAPTER THIRTY

The Crimson Sky

The morning sun shone down brightly, cheerfully, on what had been a scene of carnage just hours before. Of all the gore and bodies, the only thing that remained were dark stains on the grass and a foul smell of wolf-shit that was already starting to fade.

Where had Loki put the bodies and the parts of bodies? There were probably some things that were best not to know.

Ian sat back in the rough-hewn chair. With the Tarn-kappë as a cushion, it was quite comfortable, and with a steaming cup of coffee next to him, he was in no rush to get up. Let Freya sleep.

"You want me to check on her?"

Arnie Selmo smiled from where he sat in the wooden chair next to Ian, Mjolnir crosswise on his lap, as though he needed to touch it, every now and then, to be sure that it was there.

"Sure, Ian. She's fine, but go ahead."

Ian tucked the Tarn-kappë under his arm and walked into the cottage, taking down a lantern from the wall rather than waiting for his eyes to adjust to the dim light further in.

Stretched out like a corpse on a slab, Freya lay motionless under a thin sheet on the bed she shared with Arnie, her chest rising and falling with an almost impossible sluggishness. If it wasn't for the way that the white feather, which somebody—Arnie, presumably—had hung on an invisible thread from the rafter above, twisted and swung every few moments, Ian would have wanted to put a mirror under her nose to check.

The sheet clung tightly to her perfect body, but it was entirely unerotic.

Was he over her?

Nah. Maybe you never do get over your first fertility goddess.

But she looked so still and lifeless that to be aroused by the sight would have felt like some particularly perverted form of necrophilia.

The claw slashes on the side of her neck and face were already just old, healing wounds. Within a day or so, they would be just fading scars; within a week, just memories. She had a lot of memories.

Arnie was right; she was fine.

Ian blew the lantern out, hung it by the door, and returned to the porch, blinking at the daylight for just a moment. High overhead, Munin circled, on watch, presumably for more Sons, although Ian was sure that the Sons would give this hill a wide berth for quite some time.

. . . unless, of course, Loki sent them back for the diamond.

Well, if he wasn't going to take the gem from her, that meant he would have to leave it, and if he left it, then it was her problem.

Or everybody's.

"Shit," he said.

Arnie raised an eyebrow. "Is that a general comment, or you got something specific in mind?"

"General."

"Then yeah: shit." Arnie gestured with the flask. "He did clean it all up, like he said he would."

Loki had cleaned up the yard, but that was all. The Scion was still dying of the curse that Loki had put on him, and Ian and Arnie and Freya had still been badly cut up. Give

it a couple of days, and she'd be back on her feet as if
nothing had happened.

"Not what I expected," Arnie said. "I always thought
he'd be a lot more like, well, the devil, and less like a glad-
handing politician." He winced, and took another drink
from Ian's silver flask. "Kind of charming, really, didn't
you think?"

"Charming?"

"Sure." Arnie nodded. "Charming is what you seem;
it's not what you are. He seemed a nice enough guy, all in
all." But then he shook his head. "But when the sky turns
red as blood, and then goes all dark, you think it ought to
be Loki who sits in the darkness, grinning to himself, saying, 'Let there be light'?"

"No."

"Me, neither." He turned to look at Ian. "You willing
to hang around for another couple of days?"

"Sure. Why?"

"I think," Arnie said, eyeing the flask, "that I want to
get real, stinking, falling-down drunk, and while this isn't
enough to do it, she's got a few bottles of some fairly remarkable stuff in those wooden footlockers of hers, and I
think I'm going to drink a fair amount of it. I'm not a mean
drunk, but I'm kind of a stupid one—can you put up with
that?"

"Sure."

He looked Ian straight in the eye. "No, seriously—can
you?" His lips pressed into a narrow line. "I can wait until
she's up and around, and I know she wouldn't mind. Just
rather to have it out of my system before she wakes up,
you know?"

"It's okay, Arnie."

It would be nice to take a couple of days to figure out
what to do next, and Ian was in no condition to travel. By
the time he was, Arnie would be ready, too. They would
return to the Old Keep, certainly, and share the bad news
with the Scion, and then get Hosea home safely.

And then what?

He knew damn well then what. There was no point in
beating himself up about the past, but giving any more

gems to Freya held little appeal. But what had even less appeal was leaving the Brisingamen stones out for the likes of Loki to snatch up.

How well were the emerald and the sapphire guarded? Probably very well. But could Loki get at them?

No. That wasn't the question—the question wasn't *whether;* it was *how.*

It was something to think about.

Ian leaned back and closed his eyes. Perhaps a bit of sleep first, and some healing later. It would be nice if he could fall into a dreamless sleep on demand, a warm and comforting one, and wake later, rested and refreshed . . .

Harbard's ring pulsed once, lightly, against his finger.

CHAPTER THIRTY-ONE

Sons

The coffee was hot and the sandwiches were remarkable, even in the cold. Part of it was the fresh-baked bread, sure, and lettuce and black olives, but what was that note of salty fishiness that held it all together? Jeff took another bite. Not sardines. Anchovy?

Not that it was all that cold, not this week. You got used to that bitter cold; your body and your mind adjusted. And after a week of temperatures in the negative teens, twenty-three degrees Fahrenheit seemed absolutely balmy, to the point where you almost wanted to go out in shirtsleeves.

Almost. But both Jeff and his partner on watch had their parkas unzipped, their gloves off.

"Pan Bagne," Jeff's watch-partner said, pronouncing it 'pan ban-yay.' "Literally, bathed bread. Good, solid peasant food; I thought it was appropriate."

"It's good," Jeff said, leaning back against the wall of the warming shack, never taking his eyes off the hole, except for an occasional sideways glance at where Billy stood, leaning against the open door. He took another bite. "It's very good."

"Well, you did say that sandwiches were the traditional

fare for this sort of thing, and you know what an utter slave
to tradition I am.''

Jeff had to smile. Everybody else on duty at the cairn
wore parkas this time of year, sometimes accompanied by
earflap caps that may have looked silly to some—well, to
all—but which kept your ears and head warm.

Billy was in a solid one-piece suit, made out of some
shimmering blue fabric that had probably never even been
near a natural fiber, with what looked like gold racing
stripes down the sides. He looked absolutely preposterous
leaning against a wall of the warming hut with a Mossberg
500 shotgun cradled in his arms, like a duck hunter waiting
for game.

His ears were covered by a ski band of the same material
as his . . . snow suit, except a few shades darker. The only
concession Billy made to convention was the pair of battered old snow-pack boots and ragged gaiters that Jeff recognized as Billy's dad's.

That was enough, for Jeff, at least. He glanced down at
his wrist. 12:35, and that meant just under three hours until
he was off, and after a quick spin around town—and probably a trip out to the Hansen place to check on David Peterson—it was home to shower and change. It was
Wednesday, and that meant supper at the Aarsteds'.

''You got dinner plans, Billy?''

''First of all, yes, I do.'' Billy smiled. ''I'm cooking
dinner at the Olson home this evening. Second of all, you
don't have to try so hard.'' He sobered. ''You check on
Mr. Thorsen today?''

Jeff shook his head. ''Tomorrow, probably. He was fine
on Monday, though. Back on his feet and hobbling around,
but he's spending more and more time down in the basement, putting Torrie and Maggie through their paces when
he isn't doing his own rehab exercises.''

Doc Sherve thought he ought to heal some more before
trying to get back into shape, but you didn't get to be Doc's
age without knowing that there were some battles that you
just couldn't win.

Jeff knew that, too. Putting Billy on watch had been the
right thing to do—and it wasn't like he wasn't trustworthy,

or anything. But Jeff just didn't want to know who he could and couldn't put Billy on watch with, so until somebody came forward and volunteered, Jeff would take his watches with Billy.

"Well, good. I should stop by and see him tomorrow, on my way out."

"Way out?" But—

"Hey, I've got an apartment, and a job—at least I did, as of yesterday; Chef Louis understands about personal emergencies—and it's been nice to come back for awhile, but you know what they say: you can never go home again."

Jeff didn't know how to answer that. He hadn't really thought about Billy's plans—but he was home again.

"Nah," Billy said, as though he'd read Jeff's mind. "Not anymore. I like the city—and it's not just because I've got one hell of a lot more chances there than I would have here to meet Mr. Right, or even just Mr. Right Now— and hey, Jeff, if that makes you twice as uncomfortable as you look, that's got to be your problem, not mine."

"That's just what I was going to say."

"Still," Billy said, as he nodded with some satisfaction, "it is good to be able to visit, though." He shrugged. "I know: I always could have, right?"

Jeff kicked at the snow with the toe of his boot. "Yes," he finally said. "Yes, you always could have."

"Sure. Well, forget about the past." Billy eyed him levelly. "You tell me: would my old best friend still be happy to see me the next time I come to visit?"

Count on Billy to make Jeff feel like shit. "Of course I will."

Billy's smile spoke volumes. "Well, then," he said with a nod. "It's—fuck!" Billy racked the shotgun, hard, sending the already chambered shell flying into the air.

A white rag, on the end of a stick projecting out of the hole, was waving madly.

Jeff had his Garand up and shouldered, the safety firmly shoved off.

"I would very much appreciate not being shot, or even shot at," a familiar basso voice boomed, accompanied by an even more manic flag-waving. "It's only Ivar del Hival and two companions, seeking some shelter from the cold, a crust of bread, a bowl of water, and a warm corner in which to sleep."

Billy glanced at Jeff. "You know who this guy is?"

He nodded. "A friend of Thorian Thorsen. A good friend." Good. It would be nice to see Ivar del Hival again. Apparently, Ian and Hosea had picked him up on their way back.

But you could never be too safe. "Let's just take this one step at a time, okay?"

"Your play, officer; I'll just point my weapon in a safe direction and chatter brightly, and if you insist, I can even keep the chattering brightly to a minimum."

"That would be nice, and a change," Jeff said, without ever once turning his head to look at Billy. He brought the Garand up to his shoulder and took down the new rope ladder from its hook in the shack. He didn't know quite how he was supposed to anchor it, but he could always bring the car in and loop the top rung over his trailer ball.

It was Ivar del Hival at the bottom of the hole, a big, fat man in orange and black, his smile a white island in a sea of black beard. His hands were raised, fingers spread, as were those of the two bearded strangers, who stood next to him, shivering in their thin gray tunics and leggings. There was something strange about the both of them—their beards were too thick and—shit.

"Yes, yes, yes," Ivar del Hival said. "there is hair on their palms, and it's not from playing with themselves. I'd like to introduce my friends Hrolf and Luphen to you. They've been sent with me, on orders from the Scion himself, to help you with the Son problem we've heard about, and they really don't want to get shot any more than I do. Truthfully."

"Billy—"

"I'm on it." Billy, never turning his back toward the hole, took the brand-new cell phone down from its shelf in the warming hut. "What's the number?"

"Thorsen's?"

"Unless you've got a better idea."

"Just push Recall, and then 3."

"Done. Then I just hit the spend button."

"You mean the send button? Yeah."

"You've never had a cell phone, have you?—Oh, hi, Mr. Thorsen. I'm sorry to bother you, but if it isn't too much trouble, well, Jeff and I are on shift out at the Hidden Way, and we could use you and Torrie here? No, no, everything's just fine—at least I think it is?—but an old friend of yours—Ivan something? Ivar whatever, yes, that's him—we'll, he's just shown up and he's brought a couple of friends with him. I think it's okay, but, well—no, the problem is that they're Sons."

Billy listened for a moment, and then smiled that old Billy smile again.

"He hung up. I think that means that he'll be right here, don't you?"

The Norn

Spring was coming; she could smell it in the air. The buds on the trees had turned green overnight, and soon, seemingly without any intermediate stage, they would become full-fledged leaves. Further north it would be even more explosive.

She had heard, once, a long time ago, although she could not remember when, that the most explosive spring was in Siberia. That you could look at the branches of a tree and, if you were patient enough, actually see the buds slowly open. That would have been nice to see, but she was getting far too old for traveling.

It was all just a matter of time.

She was of hardy stock, though; Minnie was a Hansen on her mother's side by birth, as well as by marriage.

There would be no cancer to eat out her vitals, no arthritis to devour her joints; nothing progressive and debilitating. She would just get a little more feeble every day; each trip up the stairs more difficult, and every trip down the stairs more frightening; each meal just a tad less appetizing, until one day she would go to sleep in her own bed, and it would all give out at once. Just like Mr. Holmes's One-Hoss Shay.

She shook her head. They didn't teach that poem anymore. Too much to explain. Pity.

> What do you think the parson found,
> When he got up and stared around?
> The poor old chaise in a heap or mound,
> As if it had been to the mill and ground!
> You see, of course, if you're not a dunce,
> How it went to pieces all at once,—
> All at once, and nothing first,—
> Just as bubbles do when they burst.

Hansens were like the old One-Hoss Shay. There were worse ways to be.

Until the bubble burst, she might as well dress herself warmly this morning, step out the back door into the cold, leaving the storm door propped open and the wooden door not quite clicked shut behind her, take the old wooden yoke and the two disturbingly bright orange plastic buckets from the back porch, and haul them and her ancient bones down the back steps, and down the well-beaten path into the woods.

She walked with exaggerated care, practicing for the return trip. There were patches of snow here and there, and the ground was still frozen beneath the patches of black mud. It would be easy to slip and fall and break a hip.

The path twisted through the woods to her favorite stand of birches. They had been seedlings the year she had first started teaching school; now they were a giant's bony white fingers reaching up toward the sky.

An even dozen plastic buckets, colored like a box of crayons, hung from spiles stuck into the trees, catching the slow drips.

She set the yoke and the carrying buckets down. One by one, she took down the plastic buckets, poured the thin, watery sap into a carrying bucket, and then hung it back on its spile. There was no more than a quart in any of the drip buckets. She would only make one trip today. Tomorrow, she would stick the Makita drill in her coat pocket and drill new holes for the spiles.

She bent, half at the back and half at the knee—sharing the pain between back and legs was the best compromise— to pick up the yoke and settle it on her shoulders.

"Could you use some help, Mrs. Hansen?"

She looked up. Ian Silverstein stood in front of her, a cloak folded across one arm, his free hand hanging his rucksack over the stub of a branch. The insteps of his boots and the knees of his jeans were filthy with a reddish soil that wasn't from the Dakotas, and a clumsily stitched wound flared red and swollen on his right cheek. His sword was belted around his waist, and he made no move to unbuckle the belt.

She would have asked how long he had been home, but the only time she liked asking questions when she already knew the answer was in class, or when it was otherwise instructive.

"Of course you can help," she said. "You don't think I like carrying two heavy buckets, do you?"

"I rather thought you did." He smiled as he lifted the yoke from her shoulders with the annoying ease that the young always displayed when they did something physical. "I'm not much of a woodsman," he said, as they walked back up the path toward the house, "but those look a lot more like birches than maples to me."

She grunted. "Anybody who boils his own maple syrup when they can buy better at the Rainbow in Grand Forks, cheap, deserves to go to all the trouble. Birch syrup, though . . . well, if you have a taste for it, you make it yourself, or you do without."

"And Hansen women have all always had a taste for it, eh?"

"I'll make you some French toast for breakfast. You look like you could use a breakfast." She glanced sharply up at him. "Does anybody else know you're back?"

"Hosea. The Thorsens. That's all."

She raised an eyebrow. "Really. You managed to slip by whoever is on duty at the hole?"

His smile was thin. "I have my ways. I didn't want to get involved in a lot of discussion—I don't think I'll be back long; I've some business to take care of."

"Really?" She raised the other eyebrow. "With all this business, you came to see me? I'm flattered."

He nodded. "I came to see you, yes," he said, as he mounted the stairs.

"Go ahead and just push on the door," she said. "I left it unlatched."

She had him pour the sap into the double boiler that sat on her ancient stove, while she lit the burner with a practiced flick of the sparker, then adjusted the gas flame down to where its blue tongues barely licked at the blackened base of the double boiler. A quick poke of her index finger revealed that the water level was adequate, but she took an old, chipped china coffee cup down from the shelf over the sink and added another cup, just to top it off.

"Water still shut off at Arnie's?" she asked.

He thought about it for a moment, then nodded. "I guess so. I haven't been there."

She pointed toward the linen closet, and the bathroom down the hall. "There's clean towels and an old robe of my husband's that ought to fit you. There is a bathtub there in the bathroom, and a shower stall down in the basement, next to the washer and dryer. Take your pick."

"I'm . . ."

"Yes, yes, young people are always in a rush. But you've got time enough for breakfast, and a shower and a quick clothes-washing won't endanger you, unless you're bleeding freely?"

His smile was hesitant, like a scared little boy's. "A hot shower would be nice, and that's a fact."

"So go ahead. It'll give me time to make some French toast and put together a proper breakfast for the two of us."

By the time he staggered back up the stairs, his swordbelt slung over his shoulder so that he could use both hands to rub at his too-long hair with one of the old patterned towels that she really should have reclassified as rag stock, she had the French toast soaked and settled, the coffee ready, and the little Jones Farm sausages not only defrosted but also nicely browned as they hissed and spit on the old black cast-iron griddle.

"How do you like your eggs?" she asked.

"Cooked?" This time his smile was easier. "Scrambled would be fine; over easy would be better." He hung the sword on the back of his chair and sat down heavily.

It had been a long time since she had cooked for a youngster, but she was pleased to see that they were still made with real appetites: despite his skinny form, Ian managed to put away four sausages, three eggs, two pieces of toast, and a tall glass of orange juice before she set the French toast in front of him.

She scooped a teaspoonful of butter on top, then poured the birch syrup.

"Please, Mrs. Hansen, I'm full—"

"You asked about the syrup," she said, gesturing toward the stack. "Taste."

His face etched in skepticism, he cut a small piece and took a tentative bite. His eyebrows shot straight up. "That's . . . nice. Different."

"I do hope you mean that in a good way, young man," she said.

"I do," he said, taking another bite. "Remarkable. It's sort of like what root beer syrup would be, except that wouldn't taste good, and this does."

He hadn't noticed that she hadn't made a plate for herself. She was hungry, but it would have been embarrassing to eat in front of him, to have him see how little she ate these days.

But she poured herself a cup of coffee and sat down across the table from him, and waited for him to speak.

"I've got something to ask you," he said, finally.

She nodded, and raised an eyebrow.

"I'd like you to watch over something for me."

"For a long time?" She shook her head at his nod. "I'm not sure you should count on me having a long time."

His smile broadened. "I've worked that part of it out."

"Tell me about it," she said.

"Now, easy with her, easy I said," Ian's voice came from below, as Jeff Bjerke checked the improvised harness one last time before starting to lower her into the hole.

The rope grew tight under her arms, but she was able to support most of her own weight with her gloved hands wrapped around the rope, and it was only a matter of moments until she was at the bottom of the pit.

Ian Silverstein tugged for a moment at the knots and then, in the impatience of youth, produced a small, sharp knife and cut her free.

"This way," he said, as he walked into the darkness of the tunnel, his swordbelt and rucksack strap slung over his left shoulder so that he could pick up the plain folding metal chair with his free arm.

She followed him into the darkness and into—

—the dull gray light and silence.

If she could have, she would have marvelled at the way that all of the body aches that she had grown used to were suddenly gone, leaving behind not a feeling of health and strength, but no feeling at all.

It was like being a visitor behind your own eyes.

Ian set up the chair as close as he could to the curving wall of the tunnel, and she set her knitting bag down next to it, and sat. It was a plain metal chair from the church basement, but it wasn't uncomfortable to sit on. Discomfort just didn't seem to belong in this place.

"I wait here how long?" she asked.

He shook his head. "I don't know," he said. "But you will, Mrs. Hansen."

"Jeff Bjerke or somebody will come by, every few months, just to check on me," she said. It had sounded strange when Ian had spoken of it, but now she understood how she could sit here, patiently, as long as it took. "I suppose I can ask him to bring me more yarn."

"I suppose so," Ian Silverstein said.

He took a leather pouch from his jacket, and placed it in her lap. "You'll know," he said, as he removed a thick ring from his finger and slipped it on her left thumb.

It fit perfectly. She hefted the leather pouch, and toyed with the thong that held it shut.

"You can open it, if you like," he said. "Just don't give it to anybody until you know that it's right. And if somebody were to come by and want to take that away from you, you just tell him that he needs to move along, and he'll believe you.'' His smile was forced, as though he thought he should smile, but couldn't feel it, not in the empty quiet of the Hidden Way. ''With the ring that close to one of the gems, you can persuade anybody of anything.''

''You are sure of that?''

He nodded. ''That's how I got this one,'' he said. He belted his sword about his waist, and then knelt to remove his cloak from where it was, rolled and tied, bound to a pair of D-rings on his rucksack. A quick tug at its thongs, and he shook it out, holding it first with one hand and then another while he donned his rucksack.

''I'll be seeing you,'' he said, as he slipped the cloak over his shoulders.

And then he was gone, only the sound of his footsteps echoing dully in the distance until they were gone.

She opened the pouch for just a moment, to look at the green fire inside, then tied the thong carefully and put the pouch back on her lap. She bent over and picked up her knitting.

However long it would take, Minnie Hansen could wait.

Discover the secret ways built into the
structure of existence in

Keepers of the Hidden Ways

by Joel Rosenberg

"Combines a firm, practiced grip on reality with
an effective blend of Irish and Norse mythologies
in a taut, gripping narrative."

Kirkus Reviews

The Fire Duke: Book One
72207-0/$5.99 US/$7.99 Can

The Silver Stone: Book Two
72208-9/$5.99 US/$7.99 Can

The Crimson Sky: Book Three
78932-9/$5.99 US/$7.99 Can